It was more than flesh and blood could bear and certainly too much for Poppy's. She uncurled her fists and reached down and took Chloe by the arm, just at the soft part by the row of half a dozen gold slave bangles she was wearing above her elbow, and pulled hard. Chloe yelled and tried to pull away, but failed and was hauled ignominiously to her feet to stand glaring up at Poppy with tears of fury and pain forming in her eyes as she rubbed her arm.

'You've bruised me!' she cried shrilly. 'You hateful, horrid – you've bruised me – '

'High time someone did, madam, if you ask me.' The heavy voice came from behind Poppy and she turned to stare, shaking a little with reaction to her own behaviour.

To have handled anyone cruelly like that, and particularly this child for whom she was responsible; it was dreadful, quite dreadful, and she hated herself for it. But beneath the self-hatred was an even stronger loathing for Chloe, who had driven her to react so.

'If you ask me, madam, the trouble with this young lady is that no one never makes it clear to her what's right behaviour and what's wrong,' the police sergeant said heavily. 'If I might make so bold.'

Also by Claire Rayner in Sphere:

CLAIRE RAYNER

FLAPPER

THE POPPY CHRONICLES III

SPHERE BOOKS LIMITED

A SPHERE Book

First published in Great Britain in 1989 by
George Weidenfeld & Nicholson Ltd
This edition published in 1990 by Sphere Books Ltd

Copyright © 1989 by Claire Rayner

Printed and bound in Great Britain by
BPCC Hazell Books
Aylesbury, Bucks, England
Member of BPCC Ltd.

Typeset in Times by Fleet Graphics, Enfield, Middlesex

ISBN 0 7474 0265 5

Sphere Books Ltd
A Division of
Macdonald & Co (Publishers) Ltd
Orbit House
1 New Fetter Lane
London EC4A 1AR

A member of Maxwell Macmillan Pergamon Publishing Corporation

To Ramon and Shirley Green
in appreciation of two devoted readers

ACKNOWLEDGEMENTS

The author is grateful for the assistance given with research by: the London Library; the London Museum; the Victoria and Albert Museum; the General Post Office Archives; the Public Records Office; the Archivist, British Rail; the Meteorological Records Office; the Archive Department of *The Times*; Marylebone Public Libraries; the Trade Union Congress Archives and other sources too numerous to mention.

BOOK THREE

1

Chloe couldn't remember when she'd last had so much fun. Life had been getting quite dismally boring lately, one way and another, what with the fuss over her car and all that silliness when she'd toddled off for the weekend with Mary and not told them at home. As if it mattered tuppence where she was! It wasn't as though when she did spend weekends in Norland Square she was actually with them. The mere idea was enough to make one shudder – a weekend in the Bosom of the Family? Heaven forbid! But they'd fussed amazingly and even Uncle George had been tedious and taken horrid Poppy's side, which was unusual to say the least. So the last few weeks had been unutterably dull.

But not now. Now she was embarked on this wonderful adventure with these two totally divine boys and could almost have hugged herself with glee. Not that she did, of course; it was all right for a girl to be vivacious and sparkling, positively essential in fact, but she must never be naive and look as though she was excited just because something was new and different. That would never do. *Soignée* as well as vivacious and sparkling, that was the way to be. So Chloe sat head up and peering delightedly out at the world from beneath the eyebrow level brim of her very new yellow cloche hat, her yellow silk tussore coat making no attempt to cover her really very pretty silk-clad knees, and sparkled in the most *soignée* manner possible.

Spread out below her perch, which was high on the driving seat of a massive Carter Patterson's furniture pantechnicon, was Oxford Street, dear old familiar Oxford Street, but it didn't look a bit familiar this morning, the first day of the General Strike. The shops were the same of course, with the front of Selfridges brave with window boxes full of daffodils and hyacinths, and the roadway as solidly traffic-jammed as usual, with motor vans arguing with horses which reared and whinnied and stamped, and cursing drivers of both kinds of vehicle clearly hating each other cordially. But these were not the usual drivers, though they cursed as colourfully; these were mostly young men as totally divine as the two boys on the vehicle Chloe herself was occupying, and many of them were marvellously dressed in straw boaters and vivid striped blazers just as though they were out for a day's sport on the river at Henley on this bright May morning, rather than driving buses and vans in Oxford Street.

And the pavements were different too; as full as ever of people but many of them bearing placards and waving at the drivers of the vehicles in the roadway. Some placards merely had destination names on them, like Notting Hill Gate, or Hammersmith, and these were borne by would-be passengers who looked just like ordinary people, the usual denizens of London's pavements; but other placards were very large and carried high by groups of very un-London looking men in tattered old suits and knotted white neck-scarves and ugly flat caps who shouted in loud rough voices as they walked, and what they shouted were the same words that were written, often somewhat unevenly, on the placards, 'Not a penny off the pay, not a minute on the day!' Clearly, Chloe decided, these were the real and actual article, striking miners from South Wales, and she almost shivered with the excitement of it all.

'Put a sock in it!' bawled the boy on Chloe's right as one of the flat-capped groups moved through the crowded pavement to come alongside them, and 'Get you back to work, you lazy lump, look you!' shouted the boy on Chloe's other side, in a loud and recognizable if not very accurate imitation of a Welsh accent. And Chloe whooped delightedly as the men below glared up at them and joined in with the first thing that came into her head.

'Taffy was a Welshman,' she carrolled shrilly. 'Taffy was a thief! Taffy came to London Town to steal a leg of beef!'

The boys who sandwiched her adored that and one of them slapped her on the back and cried, 'That's it, Chloe, you tell the lazy devils!' And the other pulled off his hat and hurled it in the air and caught it again skilfully, while still holding the pair of great dray horses in front of him with a hard pull on the reins, as he shouted his approval too. It was all too much for Chloe who threw her attempts to be *soignée* to the four winds, and let excitement take over.

She jumped to her feet to stand there very precariously and pulled off her own hat to let her bobbed blonde curls fly loose, and swung it round and round her head, shrieking over and over again, 'Taffy was a Welshman, Taffy was a thief!' at the top of her far from inconsiderable voice. It had a high piercing quality that made it clearly audible even above the hubbub that was all around them.

At last a gap appeared in the traffic ahead which had been holding them back and the boy with the reins let out a shout of his own and whipped up the horses, which lunged forwards with a jerk that sent Chloe back into her seat with a bump and she caught her breath and laughed as the boy on her left threw an arm across her shoulders and hugged her close. Oh, she was having such a marvellous time, really she was!

11

'Oy,' shouted the boy with the reins to a couple of people on the pavement below who were bearing a placard reading 'Ealing'. 'We're heading that way! Climb aboard – watch out for the backboard, it's broken!' And he pulled up and the pair at once went scrambling round the back of the van to be hauled on by the many other people already there. 'Hold very tight please, plenty of room outside,' shrieked Chloe and the two boys roared with laughter as once again the horses were whipped up to move on their way.

But they didn't get very far; the flat-capped men below them had not fallen behind as the van moved on, but had made an effort to keep up and two of them were now running alongside towards the horses' heads, and the boy with the reins peered down, guessed what was about to happen and leapt to his feet and began to wield the whip to serious purpose. The lash snaked down and stung the horses' straining flanks so swiftly it could hardly be seen and the great animals twitched and one of them tried to rear and was only held back by the shafts and the straining leather traces; but then they put their heads down and began a lumbering gallop along what was a blessedly empty space in front of them. The huge van went swaying heavily towards Marble Arch as the people inside held on like grim death to each other and shrieked at the tops of their voices for all the world as though they were on a fairground helterskelter, as the boy with the whip went on berating the sweating animals mightily.

The van reached Marble Arch and the horses slackened their speed; but as they were built for long hard pulls rather than for speed, their unaccustomed efforts made them sweat and they were foam-flecked and steaming and the smell of them mixed with the odours of the flowering window boxes and the petrol fumes from the motor vans to create a heady brew and Chloe, who had been frightened for just long enough to have her excitement and delight topped up to even greater heights, whooped again with sheer joy. It was all too wonderful for words.

'Hey, Joe – Joe, watch out!' cried the boy on her left suddenly and pointed. Ahead of them, on the far side of the tall white arch, a group of marchers were coming towards them, bearing their placards high and shouting their slogan more loudly than it had been shouted by anyone so far. The words came to them in muffled waves of sound. 'Not a *penny* off the *pay*, not a *minute* on the *day* – ' And Chloe and the boys who flanked her began to shout their own slogan, and their passengers joined in reedily, so that they made a fair amount of noise. '*Taffy* was *a Welshman, Taffy* was a *thief* – ' and now people on the pavements began to realize what was happening and started to take sides, joining in one side or the other, and the din rose to a crescendo.

'I'm going after 'em!' shouted the driver of the pantechnicon and once again began to work hard with his whip to push the horses forward.

'You can't!' his friend bawled at him, holding on to Chloe with one protective arm while trying to hang on himself at the other side of the long driving bench. 'It's one way going round here – '

'No it isn't,' shouted the other, and sent the whip whistling at the horses' gleaming wet flanks again. 'That's at Hyde Park Corner. I'm going straight over. View Halloo – ' And he did, as the horses plunged and heaved and their massive hooves made the ground seem to shake beneath them.

Not that Chloe could identify quite what was happening now. The little *frisson* of fear she had so much enjoyed earlier had now thickened into something a great deal closer to terror as the van swayed sickeningly so that the people inside were hurled from one side to the other to make it even more unstable, and there were moments

13

when she thought it would not right itself but would go completely over; and then she saw in the blur ahead of her that one of the men from the marching group they had been jeering at had somehow managed to catch up with them, and was running alongside the horses' heads and reaching for their bridles. It was quite obvious to everyone what was happening; the now quite crazed and oblivious young driver was doing all he could to run down the marching group ahead of him, and the man now reaching for the horses' heads was equally determined to stop him.

The runner managed to get his hand on the bridle and the boy with the reins saw him and cursing at the top of his voice deliberately pulled hard on the rein on the right side to bring the horses' heads round; he intended to run this man down before he reached his target, it was clear, and now Chloe shut her eyes tightly and held on to the boy on her left, so hard that her hands seemed to tingle. She was more frightened than she could ever remember being and it wasn't at all an agreeable feeling.

Quite what happened then Chloe could never be quite certain. She opened her eyes just in time to see the man at the horses' heads sent spinning sideways as one of the shafts caught him in the ribs, and he lay sprawled in the road as the group of marchers ahead saw what had happened and broke into a run to come thundering towards them and the group of marchers they had left behind also ran and caught up and joined in.

There was, quite simply, all hell let loose. Several of the marchers leapt for the horses' heads and the shafts and held on grimly even as the boy with the whip, still bawling loudly and whooping, tried to force the sweating animals to more effort. They became bewildered, held in front so firmly as they were, yet still stung on the flanks by the insistent whip behind, and began to kick backwards and their ponderous heels and massive hooves did

14

shrewd damage to the fabric of the van which at last stopped swaying and came to a standstill, but at a drunken angle, for the axle of the back wheels seemed to have snapped in the *mêlée*.

The passengers who had been inside immediately scrambled down and melted away into the crowd as more people came running up, among them a couple of men bearing arm flashes with the now familiar 'Special Constable' label that had flowered all over the capital during the four days the General Strike had so far lasted. No one, of course, paid them the least attention. No one ever did. The marchers pushed them aside and began to swarm over the horses and the van, making for the trio on the driver's bench, and now Chloe's companions turned to each side and began to fight back.

The boy with the whip used it to keep off the infuriated men who were trying to rock him, and the one on Chloe's left had pulled a piece of broken wood from the side of the van and was using that to defend himself. Chloe, cowering in the middle of them, wanted to jump off and run, but there was no way out; and then, suddenly, courage came back to her as a stone, thrown by one of the men clustering round the van and being shouted at by the otherwise helpless special constables, hit her a sharp little blow on the cheek. The stinging pain shook her out of her fear and into action, and she began to hit out with her small handbag at the men now climbing over the horses' backs towards her, and then pulled off one of her shoes, little pumps with wickedly sharp little heels on them, and used that, and caught one man's hand so shrewd a blow that he swore and let go and dropped down to the road again.

The whole scene was now like a battlefield. Around the van marchers were fighting with some of the men in the crowd who had taken exception to what they were doing and fists were flying noisily as the special constables, now with their own tempers well and truly on fire, began to hit out at the marchers themselves, using their truncheons.

How much longer it could have gone on and what damage might have been done it was impossible to say. All Chloe knew then was that a police car with a loudly howling klaxon had arrived and with it a number of real policemen, the genuine articles with their helmets set four-square and firm on their heads and the heavy physique and strong presence that made even the most infuriated of marchers drop back a little.

It took only minutes to bring back order. The crowd began to crumble away as the bobbies pushed them firmly but not urgently back onto the pavements, and the marchers regrouped and put themselves to rights as an ambulance came clanging through the crowd to collect the man who had been injured by the shafts of the pantechnicon, together with a few others who were standing around looking dazed with bloodied heads and slowly blackening eyes.

'Right now.' The tallest and heaviest of the policemen, a man of at least eighteen stone, with a massive chest behind his silver-buttoned blue serge and a set of pre-war whiskers that stuck out on each side of his helmet, reached up and pulled first the young men down from the driver's bench and then reached up for Chloe, who had no choice but to be fetched down. 'We'll hear what all this was about, shall we? I want facts, now, and none of your shouting or carrying on.' And he frowned heavily at the boy who had been driving, who now looked a great deal less brave than he had, and indeed seemed suddenly very tired and not a little chastened. And since the horses had been exceedingly heavy to handle that was not surprising.

'You first,' the sergeant commanded, pointing at the driver. 'You in charge of this 'ere vehicle?'

'We both are,' the boy said sulkily, after throwing a

sharp glance at the large face under the brim of the helmet and clearly deciding that cooperation with this formidable person was much to be recommended. 'We've worked every day together ever since the Strike started.'

'I see,' the policeman said with heavy sarcasm. 'Pillars of society, are we, dedicated to putting an end to civil unrest, is that it?'

'Well, yes,' the boy said after a moment, unsure whether he was being mocked or not. 'I mean, we can't have these lazy devils holding the country to ransom, can we?'

'Oh, no, that would never do,' the sergeant said, more heavily sarcastic than ever. 'Why, only working underground sixty hours a week or more to get their three quid of a Saturday night, they'll be wanting jam on it next, won't they?'

'You sound like one of these damned Bolshies yourself,' muttered the other boy and the sergeant turned a look on him that made him shuffle a little and look down at his feet.

'We'll have none of that name-calling, sir,' the sergeant said magisterially. 'I'm here to ascertain facts, that's all, no more and no less. We'll set aside anything else in the matter of opinion, if you please,' after which barefaced piece of effrontery he pulled from his pocket a notebook and an indelible pencil which he licked and said, 'First of all, the owner of this 'ere van. 'Oo's is it?'

'Carter Patterson's, I suppose,' the driver said and looked back over his shoulder at the now very dilapidated vehicle and managed a grin. 'They won't be best pleased when they see it, I imagine. Still, fortunes of war and all that –'

'You have permission to use it the way you did, I take it? As a passenger vehicle?'

'We were running a much needed bus service,' the other boy said with all the dignity he could. 'We've done

17

it every day, and managed very well. We – er – got – borrowed the van and the horses from the yard near my father's office, down in Wapping, and we've taken good care of the horses, made sure they were fed and watered and so forth – '

'Big of you,' said the sergeant with a return of some of his old acid. 'Shows you got a heart in the right place, don't it? Never mind running down men what've done you no harm and breaking their ribs with the shafts, you looked after the horses – '

The boy who had been driving reddened. 'That was unfortunate,' he muttered. 'He riled me. I only wanted to help people get to their destinations, that was all. Doing my bit, don't you know.'

'I know,' the sergeant said grimly. 'I've dealt with a few sprigs like you this past few days and no error. Thick as they come, think it's all a great lark and never imagine what it's like for the people stuck in the middle of it all. Just another bit o' fun for you, ain't it? And you – ' And he glared at Chloe, who had been standing silently pulling on her hat again and resetting her shoes and trying generally to tidy herself. 'I'll have something to say to you, miss, in just a moment. Right now, what I wants is names and addresses from you two, and the address of the owner of this 'ere van so as they can be reported to on the state of their vehicle and be told where to make their application for damages – '

The boy who had been driving whitened. 'What do you mean, damages? It's none of my affair – I was just pulling my weight, damn it – '

'We'll have no bad language, young man, if you please, there is ladies present. Well, one as dresses to look like one, that is.' And again he looked sharply at Chloe who for the first time felt a prick of shame. Had what they had done been so dreadful? So far she had not thought so; a great adventure, a blow for freedom and all

18

that, but nothing *wrong*. That was how Joe and Teddy had described it when they told her what they were planning to do and of course she had begged to join in, and indeed had pleaded and nagged them so hard that at last today they had relented and let her go along for the ride. But surely it hadn't been so wicked a thing to do? Staring now at this large and clearly disgusted policeman Chloe was beginning to feel some tremors of doubt.

'Names,' the sergeant said implacably and after a moment they sulkily obliged. 'Joseph Randall,' said the boy who had been driving. '7, Crompton Street, Maida Vale. And this is my cousin from Croydon who is staying with us at present. He's Teddy – Edward Randall – '

'I can get your Dad at this address, I imagine?' the sergeant said and looked at the boy again with a little lift of one lip that set his wide whiskers askew. 'I don't see you as the sort that pays their own way. Live at home with Mummy and Daddy, I imagine, too busy with your social life to get a job – '

'I'm at University,' Joe burst out, furiously. 'If it's any of your affair! I came up specially for – to muck in and pull my weight and so forth, with this wretched Strike, and so did Teddy – '

'Yes, well,' the sergeant said and closed his notebook. 'That's as may be. You be on your way now. Where'd you say you got this van?'

'Carter Patterson's yard off Wapping High Street,' Joe said. 'You needn't worry, I'll take it back – '

'Oh, no you won't,' the sergeant said with great satisfaction. 'They'll have to send and fetch it for themselves. I want someone what knows what's what in charge of those horses. You've treated 'em shamefully, for all your feeding and watering. I saw your whip and the state they was in. Drew blood on that offside beast, you did, do you know that? No, it's time for the owners to get their hands on 'em again. And it's my guess that once they've had to

19

put themselves out to retrieve their property these people at Carter Pattersons'll think twice before they let bleedin' amateurs take their vehicles out to use as buses for strike-breakers. All right, you two, be on your way. You won't have heard the last of this, and never you think it, but right now, get out of my sight, the pair of you. And don't think you can get out of it for good an' all. I'm not so green as you might think. I'll know you two again when I see you, so watch your step.' And he nodded heavily at them and then turned away very pointedly and stared at Chloe.

'Now young lady, we come to you.'

'You leave her alone!' Joe said hotly and pushed forwards. 'She's done no harm to any – '

'Still doing our bit, sir? Still meddling in matters what don't concern us and we don't fully understand, are we? Take my advice and sling your 'ook, young man. I'll deal with this young lady and see she gets 'ome safe enough. You want to make it easy for 'er, you'll get going like I said. Now, be told, will you? Or do you want me to take you in charge 'ere and now?'

Joe hesitated and Chloe said swiftly, 'It's all right, Joe darling. You go, you and Teddy. I'll be fine. I can walk home from here, easily, well almost, and anyway, I'm sure this nice policeman won't be too hard on me.' And she smiled winningly at the large sergeant. She disliked him cordially, but that didn't mean she didn't know how to deal with him. And she made the best of herself that she could, peeping up at him from beneath her thick and lightly mascara'd lashes and making that little pouting mischievous smile that she knew set dimples at the corners of her mouth, because she'd practised it often enough in front of a mirror to know exactly how to do it.

'Yes, you be on your way,' the sergeant said, not taking his eyes from her but also not cracking a hint of a smile or showing any signs of being mollified by the carefully displayed dimples. 'Like I said, you're in enough trouble already without making a bad matter worse.'

Joe hesitated and then after another quick grimace from Chloe pulled on Teddy's elbow and the two boys moved away. Chloe saw them disappear into the crowd on the pavement and watched for only another second or two before returning her attention and all her efforts to the policeman.

'Now *dear* Inspector,' she cooed. 'You really mustn't be cross with me. I – really – '

'I'm a sergeant, miss, as anyone can see what uses their eyes,' he said, totally unmoved by her efforts. 'I want your name for a start.'

'But why, Ins – Sergeant?' It was getting harder to be sweet and nice in the face of quite such adamantine resistance. 'I mean, I did no harm. I wasn't doing anything but just going along for the ride you know and – '

'Name,' the sergeant said and she hesitated, trying to decide what to do. Refuse? But then he'd probably drag her to the police station and they'd search her handbag and she had her visiting cards in there as well as sundry other items such as letters which had her name and address on them. He'd be sure to find out then. The whole degrading scene flashed across her imagination and she bit her lip trying to think what to do for the best

'I'm Chloe Bradman,' she said after a long moment, and now her voice was somewhat less charming than it had been. 'I live at number twenty two Norland Square, Holland Park.'

'With your parents?'

She hesitated. 'I don't see that – '

'With your parents?' He was quite immovable.

'My stepmother,' Chloe said sulkily, quite abandoning any attempt to charm the brute. He was quite clearly beyond reach.

'I see. Your stepmother. And her name?'

'Poppy Bradman,' she said and let the contempt she felt for Poppy show in the way she said the name, and the sergeant gave her a bird-bright and very knowing flick of a glance and then returned his attention to his notebook.

'No father – ' he said, as he wrote a little laboriously.

'Killed in the war,' Chloe said shortly.

'Yes. Well, I'm sorry to hear it,' the sergeant said and closed his notebook. 'Well, if it's a stepmother we must talk to, it's a stepmother. We'll be on our way then – '

Chloe stared at him. 'On our way? What do you mean? You're not taking me to the police station, are you? I mean, I only went along for the ride, because it was all such a lark and – '

The policeman raised his very thick eyebrows at her, so that they disappeared under the brim of his helmet. 'Police station? Why would we want to go cluttering up our police station with the likes of you? Of course not. I'm taking you home, that's what I'm doing. So come along now, on our way. We'll use the car – '

She went white. 'You're taking me home in *that*?' she said and stared round at the large and obviously official car with the word 'Police' blazoned across the front of the indicator above the windscreen. 'You can't mean it! Why?'

'Whenever I finds children wandering I takes them home to their families,' the sergeant said heavily. 'Come along now – '

'Children?' Chloe's anger glowed fast and red. 'How dare you call me a child! I'm – I'm not a child! I'm – '

'Ho yes?' the sergeant said, as his large hand in the small of her back pushed her inexorably towards the car. 'And what are we? Seventeen is it, or even a bit younger? Hey?'

'I am not seventeen!' Chloe said furiously. 'I'm eighteen and – '

'And an infant in the eyes of the law, until you're

22

twenty one and reach your majority, young woman,' the
sergeant said triumphantly. So there you are. I am an
officer of the law and I am protecting with my power an
infant under the law. So you get in the car and we'll see
you get home safe and sound. And see to it that your ma
keeps a closer eye on you in the future – '

Chloe got into the car. There was nothing else she
could do. But she was weeping tears of bitter fury as she
did so.

2

It had been, Poppy decided, quite the most beastly of mornings. A pig of a morning in fact, and she felt a little better as the childish phrase came into her mind. It was the sort of thing that Robin would say, besotted as she was with animals; things she liked she called kittens and rabbits; things she disliked were pigs and rats, and for a moment Poppy felt her lips curve as she contemplated her small daughter's ways of expressing herself. It would be much more agreeable to be at home with her than cooped up here in the office where everything that could go wrong was doing so. But then she sighed and reached again for the telephone. Robin, of course, was at school, as befitted an almost seven year old, and would be much too busy about her own affairs to be concerned about her mother's.

Once again the number she wanted was engaged and she almost snarled at the operator who conveyed this information in her falsely honeyed tones, but managed to control herself; it wasn't the girl's fault, after all. Every restaurant owner in London must be trying to get through to Smithfield market this morning. It was all very well for the Government and the TUC to make soothing noises and tell people that food supplies were protected in this strike and would get through and not to panic; inevitably people did. She herself had set out to get to the office fully an hour earlier than usual, managing to snatch a taxi from under the nose of an irate business-man in the middle of Holland Park Avenue, and ever since she had been here had been trying to ensure that their supplies for the day would be assured. But no meat had arrived, and that meant there was only one thing for it. Someone would have to go to Smithfield, fight their way through the inevitable crowds there and physically manhandle the stuff back to Cable Street in the East End. And after that, the same would have to be done at Billingsgate to get the fish.

At least she had her fruit and vegetables in; Barney Heinemann had come up trumps, the dear old buffer; he lived in the middle of Covent Garden at the end of Maiden Lane ('no more'n a spit and a cough from the market' as he told anyone who would listen) and with the aid of a couple of lads he had scooped up from the lounging crowds round the market porters' pub, had arrived triumphantly at seven o'clock this morning with an ample supply of all that Jessie needed to ensure the day's lunches and dinners for her devoted customers. So far there had been no diminution of demand for the restaurant's services; Jessie had been gloomily sure that the strike would hit business hard, but Poppy had reassured her, and had been right.

'They'll want to eat in restaurants more than ever,' she had told her aunt and patted her massive shoulder reassuringly. 'It'll be less trouble for them than shopping for themselves, you'll see.' And so it had been.

Which of course made the matter of the lack of meat and fish even more of a problem, and now Poppy sighed and got to her feet and left her office to the care of her little junior clerk, Maisie, to go clattering down the stairs to the kitchens to see who was available to go and fetch what they needed.

She stood for a moment at the entrance and looked around. It really was an amazing sight, a vast space glittering with chrome, white tiles and glossy cream paint. There were the long preparation tables in the middle, and big gas hobs and ovens all round the walls, while above them gaped open the cupboards full of pans and pots and bains-marie and serving dishes and all the other impedimenta of an establishment that not only served several hundred covers a day but also ran a lively trade in prepared food for delicatessen shops all over the East End and even further afield.

Already the main preparation table was piled high with the vast crocks of chopped herring and chopped liver and prepared egg and onion mixtures that would be collected soon by the shopowners who would resell it (at what Jessie often considered to be wickedly inflated prices) to their own customers who bought it in tiny portions to liven up their otherwise dull tables.

Behind the three girls who were sweating busily over the delicatessen orders the hobs steamed furiously as great pieces of brisket were boiled in pans full of saltpetre and spices and garlic to make Jessie's famous salt beef. Today they were cooking their usual thirty seven sides and it was essential that at least the same amount should be prepared from fresh beef and put into pickle ready to be used next week. If that didn't happen then there would be in due course an uproar from the restaurant's customers, most of whom came to eat salt beef sandwiches at lunch time or salt beef platters at dinner time (when they supplemented the great mounds of delicate pink meat with the establishment's most famous side dish; potato latkes, crisp and meltingly delicious little pancakes that were regarded for miles around as the best of their kind anywhere in the world). It really was essential that someone go to Smithfield with some sort of transport, and went there fast.

Poppy could see Jessie at the far side of the kitchen, her bare arms flashing beneath her rolled up sleeves as she manipulated vast sheets of very thin pastry to make the other great favorite of the restaurant: Jessie's famous apple strudels. Poppy stood and watched her for a while as with expert flicks of her heavy wrists she slapped the sheets of pastry, so fine that light shone through them, flat down on a smoothly spread white cloth and then spread each one with prepared apples, plump sultanas and brown sugar and cinnamon before rolling it up, using the white cloth on which it lay as a tool; she moved so swiftly it was almost impossible to see what she was doing, until within a matter of moments there lay the long crescent of a curved roll, ready to be flicked on to the oiled baking tray, painted over with an egg glaze and put into the hot oven waiting for it; ultimately, after baking, to be dredged with drifts of icing sugar. One of Jessie's assistants was already putting a strudel in as Poppy made her way down the kitchen past the toiling workers, as Jessie herself started on the next piece of pastry, pulling and rolling it to thin it out ready to be filled and rolled in its turn. The whole system was like a beautifully oiled engine, with each person working flat out and seeming absorbed in what she was doing, yet managing to dovetail her efforts precisely into the pattern of her neighbour's. No one had to wait for anyone else, no time was wasted, and a steady stream of dishes went into and out of the ovens as the day's supplies were built up.

'Poppy!' Jessie cried as her niece came up to stand beside her. 'Where you been? I'm going crazy here, no fish! I've got Millie and Gertie with everything ready to start frying and I got no fish! Well, a coupla pieces of halibut and a cod what I had in the cold room, but I'm not happy using 'em, I'll tell you that. Not for frying. They'd be better for the chopped fish. It's got to be today's fresh to be fried, you know that! So where's my fish?'

'God knows,' Poppy said succinctly. 'Listen, can I ask Barney to go over to Billingsgate to pick it up? I can't get through on the phone and the only way has to be to send someone. If you can spare one of the girls to take over in the restaurant, setting it up for lunch, and let Davy from the yard go with him, Barney should be able to bring enough fresh supplies for today and tomorrow – and enough to make the chopped fish, too, for Friday.'

'So send him.' Jessie had not lifted her eyes from her work, and already another strudel was rolled and ready for the oven and her helper had slipped it expertly from under her hands as Jessie started on yet another piece of pastry from the little row of balls of it that lay ready waiting for her. 'And take my car – ' And she swelled a little as she said it.

Poppy hid a smile. That car was Jessie's most prized possession, a small Singer four-seater for which she had paid the stupendous sum of £225; stupendous because of course she couldn't drive and had no intention of learning. But Bernie could drive and often did, and seemed willing enough to ferry his mother about from time to time in exchange for the use of the vehicle, which was, Poppy had often told herself sardonically, a considerable step forward for Bernie, who normally did what he wanted, when he wanted, with anyone else's property he wanted, and never thought twice about anyone's convenience but his own. But he was better with his mother than he was with other people, which was something to be glad of. Who was Poppy to tell her much loved aunt that she was a fool to keep and run so expensive a vehicle mainly for Bernie's convenience? First of all it was Jessie's money and she had the right to spend it as she chose, and secondly Jessie wouldn't listen anyway. She never did listen to any word of complaint about her beloved Bernie.

'It's all right if Davy drives it? Bernie isn't here – '

Poppy almost added, 'of course' but bit it back; of course he should be helping his mother and her business out in what was undoubtedly an emergency situation, but Poppy had known he wouldn't be, even though Jessie had said brightly at the weekend, when it was obvious the strike was definitely on, that of course he'd be standing by ready to help. She hadn't said a word about him since, even though he had been totally invisible for the past four days. No doubt he'd turn up when it was over, bringing a pile of his filthy laundry to be dealt with by Jessie and she would smile brilliantly at him and fuss over him and feed him as though he were a naughty ten year old instead of a man of twenty five, and offer no words of reproach for letting her down. Again.

'Sure.' Jessie straightened her back as she reached for the final little knob of dough ready to make her last strudel. 'There's plenty of petrol, thank God – I got it filled up only on Saturday. We'll get through at least two weeks before we're in trouble. I got a coupla cans in the garage. Listen, Poppy, about meat – '

'I'll send them to Smithfield too,' Poppy said, already on her way to the far door that led through to the restaurant. 'I know what you want. Forty fowls, fifty sides of brisket to pickle, fifteen pounds of stewing beef, a tub of lambs' tongues – ' she rattled through the list as Jessie listened, nodding firmly at each item, and then shot a bright little glance at her as she dusted off her floury hands and the last strudel slid into the oven.

'I sometimes wonder what I'm doing here, Poppela,' she said, and began to roll down her sleeves. 'You know this business inside out and back again. There ain't nothing you couldn't do here – '

'Except make strudels and chop the fish,' Poppy retorted and grinned back at her. It was always a pleasure to her to be with her aunt. Over sixty and as large as she had ever been, she now looked even bigger in the fashions of 1926 which did nothing to enhance her luscious and, some would say, over-generous curves. What had looked delightfully voluptuous in *fin de siècle* frills and billows in rich crimson looked less appetizing in rose *crêpe de chine*, but that didn't matter. Jessie was what anyone would call a fine figure of a woman. With her once dark hair now dressed in a handsome silver shingle she exuded an air of competence and common sense and vigour that was as exhilarating as it had been when Poppy had first met her – or at least first remembered meeting her. There had been a time, long ago, in Poppy's infancy, when she and Jessie had been very close, but that had been followed by a long gap during which Poppy had totally forgotten she had an aunt called Jessie. But that had all come to an end fifteen years ago when they had found each other again; and since then there had grown between the two women a closeness and an understanding that sustained Poppy no matter what happened.

Life was interesting and busy for Poppy Bradman, but far from easy; not only was there the imperative need to earn her own living (for as a portionless widow what else could she do?) but she had so many responsibilities for what sometimes seemed to her so many people; her beloved Robin, of course, though she was no burden. She was all the joy and the delight she could possibly be, which made her quite unlike her mother's other dependant, Goosey, who was so much more than just a servant, and Chloe – and her face straightened grimly as she thought of her stepdaughter and then firmly set her out of her mind – and her mother Mildred, who though not a financial burden was undoubtedly an emotional one. Without Jessie to lean on, to share with, to enjoy simply as herself, Poppy sometimes thought, she would never cope, and then would grimace a little as she remembered that in many ways Jessie made her worry more than the others put together. Not because she herself was any sort of burden, but because she was so blind about her dreadful son. One of these days there would be such trouble over Bernie; Poppy knew that as surely as she knew the sun would rise in the east tomorrow morning. So far there had been only small explosions: the discovery of casual embezzlements, doubts about the provenance of the money he splashed about so lavishly, and which must surely, Poppy would think, have been stolen or certainly illegally obtained, and late night visits to the flat he shared with his mother from men who frightened Jessie by their manner, but whom Bernie seemed able to deal with well enough at present. But one day, Poppy knew, something awful would happen, and she grieved for her dear Jessie when she thought about that and felt powerless to do anything to prevent whatever disaster it was that was brewing inside the unspeakable, if incredibly good-looking, Bernie.

'Even that you could learn to do,' Jessie said. 'How to make a strudel is no problem. You just stretch a little, spread a little, roll a little and bake it. Phht, it's done. Listen, I'll take over in the restaurant, tell Barney. I'll be through in a minute. Get him on his way fast will you? As long as the fish is here by noon, we can put fried fish on the menu as usual. The chips we've already cut and started – so see them on their way, do me a favour. And then wait in the restaurant. I gotta talk to you – '

Poppy smiled at her and went and spent the next ten minutes making sure that Barney and Davy were absolutely clear in their understanding of their instructions and had all the money they needed before consigning them to the risks of London's streets. And she sighed as she watched them go and tried to contain her irritation at the way her life had been turned upside down by this wretched strike. Damned Government, she thought bitterly, not for the first time, backing the mine owners against the men. What had they expected? That they'd just touch their forelocks and say, 'Yes sir, no sir, three bags full sir,' and settle for longer hours and less pay? Poppy was a worker herself and she knew what it was like to put in long hard days pushing herself until her back ached abominably with bending over her ledgers and her head spun with the effort of trying to keep all her many tasks in her control.

'And I,' as she had been telling anyone who would listen around the restaurant, 'I'm just an office worker. I don't have to crawl underground and dig out coal with virtually my bare hands. It must be hell down there – '

And the people who worked in the restaurant had nodded and agreed, for weren't they all workers and didn't they all feel an uneasy closeness to the men who were striking? It was damned inconvenient, it made their own lives extremely complicated, but there it was; the miners deserved to win their case.

With Barney and Davy safely on their way in the Singer, Poppy stopped in the restaurant to help the other waiters set up the tables. There were only two of them and they always worked exceedingly hard, for the turn-over of customers when lunch-time came was phenomenal. The restaurant was immensely popular and successful, and made a good deal of money for Jessie and both she and Poppy, her general manager and book-keeper, were well aware of the value of their staff. Indeed, they had tried many times to persuade Barney to have extra waiters, but he had always refused.

'I got enough trouble watching the two I got,' he would growl. 'What do I want more for to fall over between the tables? We can manage. You look after your side of it, keep the food coming and me, I'll see to it the customers get their bellyfuls and pay up. We don't want more waiters – '

And neither Poppy nor Jessie would argue with the old

man, for hadn't he been part of the business from very early days before the war when it had been just a little delicatessen shop, before it had grown into the great enterprise it now was? How they would manage without him Poppy could not imagine, though she knew she ought to think about it. The old boy must be past seventy five, though you'd never guess it, so sprightly and full of life and bad temper was he, and one day must surely have to give up work. Then big changes would have to be made, no doubt, just as they would if ever Lily, who ran the original delicatessen shop next door to the restaurant, decided to give up. But she was a lively and hard-working fifty year old and it would be a long time before she willingly left Jessie's employ. Which was just as well because no one but Lily could possibly find anything in the small cluttered shop which attracted customers for its delicacies from all over North London, and even, sometimes, from the other side of the water. Which was funny, really, because Lily always treated people from south of London's river as though they were foreigners and not Londoners at all. She'd have set custom sheds on the bridges, given her head, Poppy would tell her sometimes. And Lily would laugh her raucous laugh and shout, 'Why not?' before plunging back into the intricacies of cutting herrings and weighing out cream cheese for her regular customers.

Poppy moved now from table to table, smoothing the snowy white cloths and setting the heavy bone-handled knives and forks in place, thinking about all the years that lay behind them. It didn't seem possible that so much had happened in so short a space of time, she told herself, polishing the glasses that had to be set at each place with a thick white linen napkin twisted into them. And yet, what is there to say about what has happened? It's seven years now since Bobby died and Robin came, and I'm thirty-one. Thirty-one – and she rolled the syllables around in her mind and tried to feel like a thirty-one year old.

But she couldn't. She was still Poppy, the same as she had been as a headstrong sixteen year old who had defied her mother and refused to prepare for university, the Poppy who had demonstrated with suffragettes, who had set out to find her own antecedents – and found them, the Poppy who had joined the FANYs in 1914 and gone to war as an ambulance driver and come back a sobered and much changed person; the same Poppy who had been married and widowed in so short a space of time.

But it was not to be thought of and Poppy refused to do so; instead she concentrated on setting the tables as she waited for Jessie to come through from the kitchens with whatever it was she wanted to talk about and thought instead of the way the business had developed and grown this past seven years since she had returned to work full-time after Robin's birth. Like the huge growth of the sell-out foods, as Jessie always called them, that now threatened to overtake the restaurant, busy though it was.

Each day Jessie and her small army of girls and women in the big kitchens and the smokehouse that had grown behind the restaurant, by dint of taking over property after property along Cable Street and Pinchin Street which lay behind and parallel, prepared great masses of food, including special sausages and wieners and liverwursts, for resale to the whole of London's delicatessens. Even the great West End stores bought from Mrs Braham, and, Jessie had told Poppy shrewdly, 'It's my guess there's a good many West End restaurants as buys my stuff there and add on even bigger mark-ups and still make a profit out of it.'

It was indeed a remarkable success story and Poppy could preen as much as Jessie over it, for she, with her skills with the bookkeeping and control of money and bills and ledgers, was as essential to it all as Jessie herself was. It was a good feeling to be so useful as well as self-reliant, Poppy told herself as she set the last glass in place. People can sneer at me if they like – and she tried not to remember Chloe as she thought that – because I work for a living, but at least it's work I can take a pride in. I don't have to be a bullied schoolteacher or a harassed typist in a bank like so many other women left without a man's supporting arm after the War.

She felt a little rush of hot food-scented air as the door that led to the kitchen blew open and Jessie came bustling in. She had tidied herself ready for the lunch-time rush and had reapplied her make-up and Poppy smiled as she looked at her well rouged cheeks and her rosy lips sticky with lipstick. Poppy, who rarely used make-up herself, little more than a dab of Tokalon face powder on a shiny nose, was amused by Jessie's strong determination to be fashionable at all costs. She bought outrageously expensive clothes in georgettes and crêpes, silks and very expensive voiles and tussores, always in shades of her favourite reds and pinks and then wore them to shreds in her hot kitchen, scorning the use of aprons. She often made Poppy feel very dowdy for she chose to stick always to sensible blues and greys made into neat coats and skirts or, in hot weather, simple linen dresses with neat low waists and round collars, but still in quiet colours like beige and deep lavender, and many were the times when Jessie would try to persuade her to dress more adventurously.

'Come with me to Mary Bee!' she would cry. 'She's the best dressmaker in London! Get something to do yourself justice with – '

'No,' Poppy would laugh. 'Too expensive, too silly – ' And Jessie would try to persuade her to let her buy dresses for her, but always Poppy refused, gently and with laughter but very definitely, and now Jessie didn't

35

nag so much, though occasionally she would return to the fray. But not this morning. She was bearing down on Poppy with a look in her eyes that meant business talk and Poppy smiled at her and went to meet her, so that they could stand together at the back of the restaurant and leave the waiters to finish off the preparations for serving lunch.

'I'll tell you what it is, Poppy,' Jessie said with no preamble. 'I'm sick of the way everyone else is makin' more money out of what I make than I make.'

Poppy lifted her brows. 'But we're doing very well, Jessie! The last financial year's figures were very healthy – seventeen per cent up on the profits of the year before, and I'm beginning to think that this year we'll beat even that growth. The capital's excellent and the return is even better – '

'It's not that I want to make more money exactly,' Jessie said and then shook her head. 'Well, of course I do. Everyone does. No, it's more than that. It's just that it makes me so – I was out last night with Hannah – you remember my friend from the next flat to me? It was her birthday, so *punkt*, she won't have it but I got to take the evening off and go up West with her – '

'And very good too,' Poppy said warmly. 'You work far too many late nights as it is – '

Jessie waved that aside. 'So, we go to the theatre, and see those two whatsernames – Astaires, you know? It's a show called *Lady be Good* or something. Anyway, after, we go to the Trocadero for a bite of supper and would you believe, there on the menu is my chopped liver! Oh, they call it something fancy like *Pâté de Campagne* and Hannah ordered it or I'd never have known. But I'd know my own chopped liver anywhere, and as soon as it come up, I took one look and I knew. And you know what they wanted for a portion no bigger than my thumb, believe me? Half a crown! It's the truth, half a crown! I never saw such *chutzpah*! And I'm thinking if the Trocadero can make that sort of money when I didn't charge no more'n tuppence to make that amount, I swear to you, then it's time we moved up West.'

Poppy blinked. 'Moved?' she said carefully. 'Leave Cable Street?'

'Good God no, what a thought!' Jessie looked scandalized. 'O' course not. I mean we *expand* up West, all right? I want a smart restaurant, Piccadilly, maybe, or somewhere near there, where the people with the money'll come. We'll have the best restaurant in the whole West End, and charge the same crazy prices everyone else does, and then we'll make our own profit out of our own efforts. What do you say?'

'What do I say?' Poppy said. 'But – what is it to do with me? I mean, it's your business, Jessie. Me, I just work for you. You want another restaurant, then fair enough. Am I to start a new set of ledgers, find the staff and pay the bills? What else is new?'

She crinkled her eyes then in laughter.

'It'll be the same as when you took over the Pinchin Street shops to expand the kitchens. All hell let loose for a while but then we settle down and it's business as usual.'

Jessie laughed. 'Not this time. This'll be different. Because this time I want you to run the place. I can't be there and here, can I? I want you to be there more than here, once I've found the place, that is. I've got the house agents looking for me. But I told 'em, my partner's got to see the place as well as me. She's got to decide too – '

'Partner?' Poppy gaped at her. 'But Jessie – '

'No buts,' Jessie said flatly. 'You been an employee long enough. It's time for partnerships. You got Robin to think of, remember, so don't go making no arguments with me. You'll work hard enough for what you'll get out of it, believe me.' And then her face softened and she leaned over and put one large arm across Poppy's shoulders. 'Like you always have. Don't turn me down, dolly. I made my mind up, believe me – '

The door from the kitchen opened again before Poppy could say another word and young Maisie from her office upstairs was staring at her goggle-eyed.

'Ooh, Mrs Bradman, miss,' she breathed, full of agreeable terror. 'Please, miss, there's a telephone call for you upstairs. It's a policeman, Mrs Bradman, miss, and he says as how he has to talk to you about Miss Chloe, miss, and oh, dear, I do hope she isn't dead nor anything!'

3

Chloe was lying sprawled on the long sofa in the drawing room, her head on a pile of multicoloured cushions and her feet up on the arm at the other end, looking as though she hadn't a care in the world. Poppy stood at the drawing-room door staring at her and all she could think was, absurdly, 'There she goes again, with her muddy shoes all over the loose covers – ' and bit back the rebuke which rose to her lips.

'Good afternoon, Chloe,' was all she said, but that came acid enough and Chloe threw her a glance from beneath lowered lashes, ran her hand through the tumble of curls on her forehead, and produced an exaggeratedly patient sigh.

'Well, all *right*, Poppy!' she said. 'Let's get it over with! The sooner you start ranting at me the sooner you'll stop, I suppose, and then we can forget it – '

'Forget it!' Poppy said, and came into the room to drop her bag and gloves on the chair by the door and pull off her own hat. Her thick dark hair was as elegantly bobbed as Chloe's, but looked, she knew, far less appealing, and not for the first time she felt that pinch of confused feeling she so often got when looking at this infuriating child who was her stepdaughter, admiration of her blue-eyed blonde prettiness, so chocolate-boxy and yet so full of vivacity that she had a fascination mere prettiness could never provide, and resentment of her

silliness and selfishness and underneath all that a hint of
– what was it? Jealousy, probably, Poppy would admit to
herself in her private hours; jealousy not of her looks but
of her youth and her freedom and her capacity to shrug
off any sense of responsibility for anyone, including
herself. To Poppy, burdened as she seemed to have been
for as long as she could remember with a great deal of
responsibility for a great many other people, this was
indeed an enviable quality.

'I can hardly forget it until I know what's been going
on,' she snapped. 'What on earth have you been doing
that I should receive a telephone call from the police
about you? Have you any idea how alarmed I was? For
all I knew you could have been hurt or – or – ' And she
swallowed and stopped.

Because she had indeed been terrified; how she had
managed to make the running journey from the
restaurant up the two flights of stairs to her office to pick
up the earpiece of the phone she would never know. Her
legs had felt as though they had been filled with iced
water, and her knees had barely held her up as she ran,
deeply aware of Jessie panting along behind her, and the
wide-eyed stare of Maisie who brought up the rear. Chloe
was dead, she had found herself thinking. She's killed
herself in that wretched little car of hers, driving like a
mad thing as usual, Chloe's dead – and underneath her
fear had been, very deep down, a little flicker of thought
that murmured 'and serve her right. A little peace and
quiet now without her – ' and it had been the sheer evil of
that thought that had distressed her most. It had been
almost a relief when the measured tones of the policeman
at the other end had told her a little about what had
happened, and she had hung up, after promising him she
would come straight home to discuss the matter with
him, almost light-headed with relief and guilt over the
way she had been thinking.

But all that had changed on the journey home. As she had battled her way to Aldgate Pump to find a taxi and then had sat on the edge of the battered leather seat as the vehicle pushed its way through the appalling traffic westwards to Holland Park, anger had begun to simmer in her, and she had luxuriated in that, almost fanning the flames as she went over and over again in her head the list of Chloe's sins. To waste Poppy's precious time like this, to get herself involved with the police – and to act as a strikebreaker; Poppy's lips had tightened most of all at that thought as she had sat staring out over the cabbie's head at the road ahead and the scattered groups of marching men and their placards.

Because she had a great deal of sympathy for them. It wasn't only that she shared the concerned feeling of almost anyone who worked at Jessie's restaurant and kitchens; it went deeper than that. It was the way the men looked. It had been almost ten years now since she had nursed soldiers in France, ten years since she had learned to live alongside and very close to the Tommies who had endured the years of mud and misery and blood that had been the War, but she had never forgotten them and never would. Working-class men of a sort she, in her protected Leinster Terrace upbringing under Mildred's close watch, had hardly ever seen, let alone met. They had at first seemed to her to be alien, almost exotic, but within a matter of weeks in France she had discovered them to be the sort of people she liked and trusted; honest, direct, vivid of speech and action; and she had come to care for them with a fierce protectiveness. So now, at the sight of an obviously underfed, hard-labouring man in rough clothes, with a fag-end drooping from his lips and his eyes wrinkled against the rising acrid smoke and that all-too-familiar look of resigned exhaustion on his face, she felt an immediate *frisson* of concern. She wanted to take hold of him and bath him and put him to bed and look after him, to feed him delicacies and rebuild his strength and make him smile again. It was absurd and she knew it, because by no means all the marching strikers she had seen around London in this past four days had been soldiers. Some of them were patently too old, and some of them were so young that they must have been schoolchildren during the War. Yet still they could create this reaction in her.

And Chloe, Bobby's daughter Chloe, the child whose own father had reported on that War for his newspaper, and who had suffered and died in it as sure as any of the Tommies, had gone out and behaved as a strikebreaker in such a way that she had been arrested – the thought of it made rage rise in Poppy so swiftly that she could almost have slapped that complacent and pretty little face framed by the coloured cushions; and that was a very unusual reaction in Poppy. She had never regarded herself as in any way a violent person, yet this small person, fully nine inches shorter and much more delicately built than Poppy herself, who was a statuesque five feet ten, made her feel murderous. It was a painful experience.

Now she took a deep breath and, holding her fists tightly closed behind her, said sharply, 'Get up at once, Chloe. Where is this policeman who brought you home? I thought he wanted to speak to me?'

Chloe made no effort to move. 'Oh, he does,' she said easily, with no trace of anxiety or concern. 'So I left him in the kitchen with Goosey. Isn't that where policemen always hang about? Sucking up to cooks in kitchens? You didn't expect to find him in the *drawing-room* did you?' And she yawned widely, her sharp little teeth gleaming in her mouth like a lazy kitten's.

It was more than flesh and blood could bear and certainly too much for Poppy's. She uncurled her fists and reached down and took Chloe by the arm, just at the soft part by the row of half a dozen gold slave bangles she was wearing above her elbow, and pulled hard. Chloe yelled and tried to pull away, but failed and was hauled ignominiously to her feet to stand glaring up at Poppy with tears of fury and pain forming in her eyes as she rubbed her arm.

'You've bruised me!' she cried shrilly. 'You hateful, horrid – you've bruised me – '

'High time someone did, madam, if you ask me.' The heavy voice came from behind Poppy and she turned to stare, shaking a little with reaction to her own behaviour.

To have handled anyone cruelly like that, and particularly this child for whom she was responsible; it was dreadful, quite dreadful, and she hated herself for it. But beneath the self-hatred was an even stronger loathing for Chloe, who had driven her to react so.

'If you ask me, madam, the trouble with this young lady is that no one never makes it clear to her what's right behaviour and what's wrong,' the police sergeant said heavily. 'If I might make so bold.'

'No, you might not!' It was Goosey, who had arrived behind him and who was panting with the effort of having climbed the stairs, and she came pushing past the man to come fussing over to Poppy and Chloe, her old stays creaking audibly under the heavy grey serge of her dress, and the starch in her white apron almost crackling with disapproval. 'I'm sorry, Mrs Poppy madam, I really am. I tried to keep him down in the kitchen as was right and proper until you rung to say you was home and ready for him, but he heard you come in and come up those stairs there and wouldn't have it any other way but he was going to come up and speak right away, ready for him or not. I don't know what the world is coming to what with these nasty strikers and now strange men pushing their way in where they got no right to be – '

43

'I am an officer of the law, madam, and my time is not to be wasted,' the policeman said heavily and came forward to stand in front of Poppy. 'It is my duty to warn you, madam, that you are responsible for this young person's behaviour, her being a minor, an infant under the law, like. I'd be in my rights to bring a charge at the police station against her which you would have to answer, being her nearest guardian, as it were.'

'Really, sergeant,' Poppy said, aware that her voice was tight and strained but unable to do anything about it. 'There is no need to be quite so – censorious with me. I am well aware of how wrong Chloe was to get involved with this matter and I intend fully to tell her so and see that there is no repetition of such behaviour – '

'Wrong? Why was it wrong?' Chloe burst out. 'Everyone's doing it! Not just Joe and Teddy but all my friends – some of the boys are being special policemen – sensible ones too – ' And she threw a look of pure hate at the burly sergeant. ' – and lots of the girls are running coffee stalls for the volunteers and there are people doing all sorts of useful things to help out. I wasn't wrong! I was – I was being public-spirited and – '

'It is not public-spirited, Chloe,' Poppy said austerely, 'to meddle in affairs you don't understand. These men who are marching and striking have a case that needs to be answered by the Government and must be answered fairly. Having silly young people like you and your friends meddling does not help in the least – '

The sergeant looked at her sharply. 'Do I take it you're in sympathy with the strikers, madam?' he asked.

'I fail to see that that is any affair of yours,' Poppy said sharply and then looked at him and saw the expression on his face. 'But well, yes, since you ask. It seems to me iniquitous that men who work in such appalling conditions to keep this country's supplies of coal going should be so misused. To lengthen their hours and cut their earnings by so high a percentage – it is fully thirteen per cent or more, I believe – seems to me decidedly wrong. After all that these men, or men very like them, suffered in the War to make the land fit for heroes we were all promised – well, I cannot but sympathize with their anger.'

'Ah!' The sergeant took a deep breath and smiled, and then pulled out the helmet that he had been holding under one tree trunk of an arm. 'That's all right, then. I'll be on my way, madam, then.'

Poppy stared at him. 'But I thought you were going to prefer charges?'

He grinned at that and his whiskers perked up with the movement. 'No, madam, I said I would be in my *rights* to do so. But no need now. Not now I can see you've got the rights of it yourself as it were, I dare say you'll see this silly young lady learns the error of her ways.'

He nodded affably and moved towards the door leaving Chloe and Goosey staring at him as Poppy, after one more startled movement, moved to follow him.

'I know what it's like with young ones, o' course, seein' as I've a few of my own. Seen the side of my hand more often than not they have, believe me, madam. You have to be hard on 'em for their own good, haven't you? How else will they learn? Good day to you, madam. No need to come down, I can see myself out, thank you.'

And with one more magisterial nod at Chloe, who was still standing gaping at him, he set his helmet firmly on his head, tugged it into place and went stomping down the stairs to the front hall and the door, and went out, banging it firmly closed behind him. And Poppy stood half dazed at the top of the stairs and watched him go, speechless with surprise.

'Well!' Goosey said at length, and plopped herself down on the sofa. 'Well I never did! And there he was sitting in my kitchen and saying as how Chloe ought to be put in gaol for a few hours to learn the error of her ways, and me shaking in my shoes for you, my little love. Well, I never did – '

'Chloe!' Poppy said as she came back into the drawing-room. 'You've been exceedingly foolish – and exceedingly lucky. What on earth were you thinking about to – '

'Now, please, Poppy, do stop it! I'm madly fagged and in no mood for one of your jawing sessions. It's over and done with so *do* forget it.' Chloe stopped rubbing her arm and peered at the soft round pinkness looking for marks. There were no bruises, and only a redness that could have been due to her own efforts as much as to Poppy's determined tugging. 'Though my arm still hurts dreadfully – '

'Your arm hurts?' Goosey, who was less acute of hearing than she had once been still never missed any murmur of complaint from her beloved Chloe. 'What happened? Were you hurt, my love? Show your Goosey now, and – '

'No, Goosey,' Poppy said loudly. 'Chloe was not hurt in the slightest. Now, please, go downstairs, will you, and make me some tea? And for Chloe. I must go back to the office of course, once I've had mine, but I have to talk to Chloe now. So off you go, Goosey.' And this time handling herself gently, Poppy took the old woman's hand and led her to the door, though she went unwillingly, staring back over her shoulder at Chloe with her papery old cheeks deeply creased with anxiety.

When they heard her heavy footsteps creaking down the stairs again Poppy turned back to Chloe and looked at her grimly. 'Now, young lady,' she began, but Chloe was in no mood to listen. She threw herself back onto the vivid sofa and its cushions, put her arms up behind her head and stared mulishly at Poppy.

'I'm in no mood to be nagged, Poppy, and so I tell you,' she said shrilly. 'The policeman's gone and there's an end of it – '

'The reason he's gone is because he trusted me to make it clear to you that your behaviour was not permissible,' Poppy said wrathfully. 'It was not so that you might be allowed to be let off scot-free – '

'He went because of the fact that he worked out all about you,' Chloe said and still she lay there staring up with her bright blue eyes, which glittered a little in the sunlight from the tall windows at each end of the double drawing-room. 'He knows you're just another Red, like the marchers, and himself too, it seems. I'm surprised a man like that's allowed to be a policeman, let alone a sergeant, being so obviously against law and order.'

Poppy stood and stared at her, feeling the hateful sensation rise in her. She was doing it again, this wretched, hateful, impossible child, digging deeply and painfully to the very roots of Poppy's self-doubts and personal shames, and she knew from bitter experience that there was no way she could stop her. She'd go on and on, now, jeering and digging until Poppy's head spun and she was filled with confusion and self-loathing at the fact that she could feel that way at all.

' – but then, I dare say he's from the East End too, just like you. Not an alien, of course, like the people you're related to, eh Poppy? He looks English enough, though you can never tell for sure, of course, can you? You look English enough, until you start to talk and everyone around discovers that really you're not at all one of us, are you? You're just a half and halfer – I can't imagine how my father ever – '

'That is enough!' Poppy managed and moved towards the sofa again and for the first time Chloe looked alarmed and shrank back against the cushions a little, her eyes watchful. 'I won't tolerate this sort of thing another moment. I tell you, Chloe, that you are not allowed out for the rest of this strike. Do you hear me? And don't think you can get round Goosey when I'm not

47

here and get her to break the rules, because as you know perfectly well, once I get it across to Goosey that this is to protect you she'll be even more careful than I am when I'm here. So you may as well bite on the bullet. You are to stay at home now until this strike is over and you are no longer tempted to treat – to behave so stupidly again. Do you understand?'

'It's not fair!' Chloe began to whine and now sat up and set her hands one on each side of her, and leaned forwards to stare at Poppy beseechingly. It was always like this; she slid from jeering to begging with such swiftness that sometimes it bewildered Poppy. Certainly she was well able to bewilder her old nurse, Goosey, who therefore let her do almost entirely as she wished. But this time Poppy was determined.

'It's no use saying that,' she said now, implacably. 'Fair or not doesn't come into it. I am not prepared to be fetched home again by irate police sergeants just because you haven't the sense to look after yourself. Believe it or not, Chloe, I am trying to protect you, not make life hard for you. This strike won't go on much longer. I'd like to see the miners win their case, and I don't deny it, but I'm a realist. I'm quite sure they'll give in before this obstinate Government does and it will be over, and the poor men will be worse off than ever. But that's beside the point. What is to the point is that I'm determined that you shall not go out of this house until such time as it is safe for you to do so. You may have your friends to visit as much as you choose, so you need not be lonely or bored. But here you stay. And there's an end of it.'

Chloe stared at her with her lower lip pouted outwards, clearly thinking. To Poppy, painfully experienced in her ways, it was almost as though she could hear her thoughts spoken aloud. Should she cry? Or rant and rave? Or face the inevitable and put up with it? And she watched her as the thoughts moved her small expressive face and then drew an almost imperceptible sigh of relief. Chloe had at least a streak of common sense, enough to know when Poppy was not to be shifted, and she looked sulky now and shrugged her shoulders. And Poppy leaned forwards and patted her knee and said briefly, 'Sensible girl. As long as you're wise and do as you're bid, then I'll say no more about it – '

'I'm going to Goosey in the kitchen,' Chloe said loudly and got to her feet to go flouncing across the room. 'I know where I am with her. *She* doesn't set herself up to be anything other than what she is – not like some – I hate you, Poppy, and I always will, so there!' And she went running swiftly down the stairs to leave Poppy standing in the middle of her vividly colourful drawing-room, exhausted with the strain of the last few minutes.

Slowly she sat down and looked around the room which she had left untouched in all the years she had lived here. Bobby had decorated it in the style of Leon Bakst long ago, years before the War, when he had first fallen in love with the Russian ballet in Paris and had come under the influence of the great designer and painter. She remembered the first time he had shown her the room, when she had come to this house the first time as a shy sixteen-year-old visitor, how she had gasped at the richly draped fabric wall hangings in rich deep jewel colours of heavy gold and sultry blue and luscious crimsons and greens, at the matching piles of cushions on the sumptuous Persian carpets and the huge low sofa that was almost the only piece of real furniture in the room, apart from low tables and leather covered stools and lattice work lamps in pierced brass, and sighed again.

It all looked a little shabby now, almost commonplace. One day she would have to redecorate, would have to buy little chrome and glass tables and angular furniture made of ebony and decorated in the jazzy art deco look that was all the rage now, but she didn't want to until she had to, however much Chloe nagged. This was really all she had left of Bobby, the last memory of the good days, before the War had come along and spoiled everything.

But not Chloe, she thought now, unable to keep at bay any longer her feelings about the girl. Chloe was spoiled even before the War. Bobby had spoiled her because her mother had died, and she felt a sudden jolt of anger as she thought of that long dead woman. Ultimately she had come between Poppy and the man she had loved so much, for he had told her bluntly he would always care most for his first love, his Barbara, and because of Barbara would always put Chloe first. And she had accepted that at the time, but now – now she knew that that had been the foundation of much of the trouble Chloe was causing now. Because Bobby had left her all his estate, every penny, and though it had seemed at first to be a small amount, it had turned out to be a great deal.

Poppy leaned forwards to the little brass table beside the sofa and picked it up, the copy of Bobby's book that always lay there. She couldn't bear to read it nowadays; it brought him back too vividly and brought back, too, the painful dreadful days of the battle of Verdun where she had fought and worked as hard as any of the men in British khaki or the blue of the French *poilus*; but enough people had read it to make Chloe a good deal richer than was good for her. The book, published just six months after Bobby's death, by an astute publisher who knew how to open people's pockets with clever advertising that harped on the dead man's superb war record, had been a great bestseller. The money it earned, all of which had gone to ten-year-old Chloe with no restrictions on her use of it despite her age, had been considerable, many thousands of pounds. And, since she had been fifteen or so and had realized how much there was, there had been no controlling her.

Clothes, the little red car which she so adored and

which she had bought the moment she was allowed to (and it had been her Uncle George, amazingly, who had overcome Poppy's doubts about the wisdom of such permission) and all sorts of silly nonsenses had gone through her fingers like corn through a miller's.

Her Uncle George had at least had the wit to make sure she only had access to her income and that the capital was left safely invested and intact, and that was something to be grateful for, Poppy would think sourly as she watched her stepdaughter preening over some new piece of expensive nonsense, but that was all that was good about the situation. For as the years had gone on, Chloe had become ever more difficult, headstrong and spoiled; even Goosey said so sometimes, setting aside her adoration to let a glimpse of common sense in, and so did Uncle George.

But it was hard to get anywhere with George. Even long ago, when he had been a young man and wooing Bobby's sister Mable, who had been Poppy's dear friend in those days, he had been a dry dismal stick of a man; now, after years of widowerhood and determined meddling in the affairs of his dead wife's only niece, he was impossible. Just another of the tedious crosses Poppy had to bear. What he would have to say about this latest exploit didn't bear thinking about; and as usual, it would be Poppy he would berate for Chloe's sins, for he in his own way spoiled the child as much as everyone else did.

Even I do, Poppy thought miserably, staring down at the pattern on the Persian rug and moving the toe of her sensible shoe along the lines of the design. I should insist she pays something towards her keep here, and doesn't leave it all to me, for she has a much greater income than I have, and no one but herself to spend it on. I should insist she takes up some sort of occupation, since she so resolutely refuses to be a student of any kind. I should – I should –

But I don't, she told herself drearily and got to her feet. Just like everyone else, I let Chloe get away with murder. One of these days something awful will happen because we don't control her. And that will be our fault too. And it's all because she can be so cruel to me about who I am, about Jessie and poor dead Lizah, my father —

But it didn't help to let her thoughts run along those tracks. It would lead her nowhere except to a morass of guilt and self dislike. She should be able to take pride and pleasure in her parentage, as other people did in theirs. Should find delight in the fact that her father had been so unusual a partner for her mother, that polite and oh-so-proper lady who lived in such quiet elegance in Leinster Terrace. There was no shame to Poppy herself in having a little Jewish boxer as a father, nor in having the exuberant and so very Jewish Jessie as her much loved aunt and benefactor, for how would she have lived and maintained her household if it hadn't been for Jessie's unswerving support and her provision of a well-paid occupation for her? But the fact was that she could not feel these good things. Somewhere deep inside stirred embarrassment and dislike of the fact that she was so very oddly parented and connected. Where that feeling came from she could not be sure; possibly Mildred, her mother — but how could she know? It had been many years since Mildred had spoken to her daughter of anything but the merest commonplaces. Any attempt on Poppy's part to get her mother to speak to her of the past and her life with the long gone Lizah, who had died just a few days before Bobby of the same awful flu that had killed Bobby and his sister Mabel too, always failed completely. Possibly in Poppy's now long forgotten childhood Mildred had planted the seeds of dislike of Jewishness and East End life in her daughter who had inherited so large a part of it? Perhaps that was why still Chloe was able to taunt her so successfully? One day,

Poppy thought fiercely, one day I'll cure myself of this. One day I'll learn how to be whole and how not to feel so dreadful about myself. And other people. People I love and owe so much to. People like Jessie –

She got to her feet then. There was still a lot to be done today. Somehow she had to get back to the restaurant, and catch up with the day's work, make sure that Barney and Davy had managed to get the supplies from Smithfield and Billingsgate, somehow she had to forget all that Chloe had done – yet again.

And she went heavily down the stairs and to the front door, just as Goosey came panting in from the kitchen below with her tea on a tray. She stood in the hall drinking it thirstily, refusing to sit down properly in the morning-room as Goosey tried to insist she did, and making it very clear indeed to the old woman why Chloe was not to be allowed out. On *any* account.

And when at last she was sure that Goosey did understand and would make an efficient jailer – and heaven knew she'd had enough experience with Chloe over the years, who often required such controls – she walked out into Norland Square wearily, to seek a taxi to get back to the East End and work.

Sometimes, she thought as she went along the street towards the busyness of Holland Park Avenue, sometimes I think that's all there is to life. Work.

4

'It's not much to ask,' Chloe hissed, and glared at her with that awful look she put on sometimes and which Robin so hated. Not that she'd let Chloe know she hated it; if she knew she'd probably do it even more. As long as Robin could remember, Chloe had been like that. 'It's something you usually like doing, anyway.'

'No,' Robin said in the best voice she could manage, but it came out small and silly, and that made her feel bad too. But it couldn't be helped. She knew that when Chloe begged her to do something, that was a very good reason not to do it. So she wouldn't. 'No,' she said again.

'Listen,' Chloe said, suddenly sounding as sweet as a lollipop, and slid to her knees in front of Robin, who was standing there in the hall just inside the front door with her school straw hat still on and with her satchel hanging from her shoulder. 'Listen. I waited for you to come home specially to talk to you about this – you do this for me and not only will I let you do it any time *you* like, any other time at all, but I'll buy you a bag of gobstoppers – great big ones. The ones she won't let you have.'

Robin wavered. Gobstoppers. Ever since Cynthia Louper at school had brought a bagful of them and shared them out and Robin had discovered the delights of sucking the huge things and taking them out to see what colour they had changed to, red to green, green to yellow, yellow to blue, blue to orange, orange to red again, smaller and smaller down to the tiny chewy nut in the very middle – ever since then she had yearned for a supply of her very own. Mummy had said no, absolutely not, they were cheap and nasty and would ruin her teeth, but all the same Robin still wanted them. Badly. And now here was Chloe not only begging her to play her gramophone for her when usually she screamed at her like a mad creature if Robin so much as touched the thing but offering her a bag of gobstoppers –

She looked at her stepsister for a long moment and then said bluntly, 'Why?'

'Oh, drat you!' said Chloe furiously, all likeness to a lollipop vanishing, and sat back on her heels. 'Why are you such a beastly child? As if it were any of your business! I just want you to sit there in my room and play the gramophone all the time until I come and let you out again – '

'Let me out again?' Now Robin was really alarmed. 'What do you mean, let me out?'

'Well, I'd have to lock the door, wouldn't I? Till I came back. Otherwise, Goosey'd come in when I didn't answer and see it was you and then the fat would be well and truly in the fire – '

Light burst on Robin like a shower of rain in a thunderstorm. 'No!' she said, very loudly this time and turned and went galloping down the stairs to the kitchen, her satchel bouncing on her bottom in a way that she usually found comforting but which now worried her because she was afraid it would slow her down, and then Chloe would be able to catch her and give her one of those horrid painful pinches she was so good at –

But Chloe didn't run after her. She just shouted something unintelligible and went running furiously upstairs to her own room and Robin reached the kitchen landing unimpeded and stopped, a little breathlessly, at the top of the last flight, and caught her breath as she looked down

55

into the reassurance of its dear comforting familiarity.

Their kitchen wasn't quite like anyone else's she had ever seen; it wasn't like Grandmama Amberly's or Cynthia Louper's or anyone's because theirs had this funny little flight of stairs that ran down inside it from the landing, all open at the side so that you could see right into the kitchen from up above so that it was laid out like a map, and Robin liked that.

There in the middle, like a continent all of its own, was the big square wooden table, with ridges and patterns on it where it had been used to chop and slice things, and been scrubbed and then scrubbed again. Just like a continent, with, in the middle of it, the mountain range that was the bowl of apples that was always there. Mummy always said that people ought to be able to have a little something if they needed it, and the best little something was an apple, so there was always the bowl, a deep copper bowl, full of yellow and green apples, good to look at as well as to eat.

And then there were the old peninsulas that were around the walls; Robin had liked thinking of them as peninsulas ever since she had learned the word in Miss Scoular's geography class, even though they weren't really; the big white sink stuck out from the wall only a little way, as did the draining-board alongside, but still a bit like a peninsula. And then the dresser, scrubbed wood like the table, but dressed with blue and white plates and saucers, with cups hanging on gold coloured hooks, and lots of jugs and bowls of all kinds; and the shelves on the cream painted walls on which the saucepans were arranged, their shiny copper sides glinting in the firelight and their black bottoms upwards. Not really peninsulas either, but sort of.

Last of all, on the rag rug that lay on the stone slabs of the floor which were scrubbed as white as the table, in front of the big open range with its glowing coal fire and looking like a sea made of red and blue and green water, all higgledy piddledy, an island: Goosey's big battered old armchair. Today Goosey was in it, her head back on the cushions, her mouth a little open, fast asleep. Not an unusual sight, and Robin smiled when she saw it. It was almost as good as seeing Mummy there – not that she ever would be in that chair, and certainly not fast asleep in the middle of the day – not quite, but almost.

Robin looked back over her shoulder once more to make sure Chloe wasn't coming after her and then went sedately down the steps, but stamping a little on each one to make a noise enough to wake Goosey, so she could pretend she hadn't been asleep at all.

It worked, for as Robin reached the fifth step Goosey stirred, opened her eyes and saw her and at once dragged herself to her feet, talking as she went.

'Bless us, is it half past four already? Where does the day go? And me so busy I don't know which way to turn – I'll never get it all done – '

Robin didn't smile at that. It was what Goosey always said, even when she wasn't doing much work at all. It was just part of Goosey, like the smell of her; she always smelled a little bit of new bread and a little bit of fried eggs and bacon. A good comforting smell that Robin liked a lot. Nicer than Chloe's smell of thick perfume, but not quite as nice as Mummy's smell of ink and Poudre Tokalon. But a good smell all the same.

She raised her face obediently for Goosey's smacking kiss and then let her take off her coat and hat for her. Robin was perfectly well able to do that for herself, but she liked to be kind to Goosey, who got flustered if she wasn't allowed to, and she stood there thinking as Goosey, exclaiming and chattering, took her things and hung them on the hook on the back of the kitchen door until she had time to take them upstairs to Robin's room and then went and fetched her coming-home-from-school-and-tide-you-over-till-supper-time milk and bread and butter and cake; for today Goosey had been baking. Ginger cakes and chocolate cakes; Robin could smell them. She liked smells, always had, and it was fun to work out what had been happening at home when she was away, just by using her nose.

But today was a little different and she ate her bread and butter and drank her milk quietly as Goosey talked on and on about nothing. And then said in an ordinary sort of voice, so that Goosey wouldn't be startled. 'Why isn't Chloe allowed to go out?'

'She's been a right limb of Satan, she has,' Goosey said, responding exactly as Robin had hoped she would, with an honest answer to an apparently casual question. 'Getting herself all mixed up with them – '

But Goosey was no fool, even though she was getting rather old and she stopped now and looked sharply at Robin.

'And you're another young limb. How d'you know that, Miss Nosey Parker?'

Robin lifted eyes, limpid with innocence, to look at Goosey as she chewed her cake. It was very good cake. She waited until she had swallowed it, for politeness' sake, and said, 'Well, she is, isn't she? Kept in? Isn't she?'

'That's as may be,' Goosey said. 'And none of your affair, young madam.'

'Why not? She's my big sister, isn't she? If she'd done something she shouldn't you ought to tell me what it is so that I don't do it too. That's how people learn, Miss Scoular says. They learn from other people's mistakes.'

'Well, that's all very well for your Miss Scoular,' said Goosey, who loathed having any of the teachers Robin dealt with quoted at her as sources of wisdom. 'I'm telling you it's none of your concern. Sister or no, Miss Chloe's a grown-up, and you're not – '

'She's not really a grown-up,' Robin said and finished

the last crumbs of her cake before sliding off her chair. 'If she was she wouldn't be kept in, would she? People who are grown up don't get kept in.'

'That's all you know, Miss Smarty,' Goosey said repressively. 'As you'll find out if you keep your tongue between your teeth and your eyes and ears open as befits the young.'

'Yes, Goosey,' Robin said and went and sat on the rug in front of the big fire. It wasn't a cold day, but there was something very cosy about sitting on the rag tufts and running your fingers through them while the glow of the coals warmed your back. 'Goosey, why is Chloe a grown-up? *If* she is – '

Goosey had cleared Robin's tea things and was pulling down bowls and platters to start making their evening meal. 'Of course she is,' she said and shook her head over the carrots she had fetched from the larder. 'Will you look at these, now? As tired as any I've ever seen, but I have to use them on account of who knows how long it'll be this strike'll go on and food hard to come by? Mrs Poppy said we got to be careful – but it's a waste of time peeling these and so I tell you – ' And she began to scrape furiously at the carrots.

'Well, why is she?' Robin persisted, and tugged on one of the pieces of green rag in the rug, which began to move. It was fun pulling pieces out and then burning them on the fire and watching them throw up multicoloured flames. She'd learned how to do that even before she'd started at school, and still managed to do it, and Goosey had never noticed.

'Why? Such questions you do ask,' Goosey said, her head down over the carrots. 'Because she is, that's all. She's eighteen. Almost grown up, in all consequence. Why, there's some as are married at her age.'

Robin contemplated that possibility with some awe. Chloe married? It didn't seem at all likely. 'Well, why is she eighteen, then?' she demanded and Goosey lifted her head now and looked at her in exasperation.

'Because she was born in 1908, that's why! Such silly questions – '

'Not silly!' Robin protested. 'My friend Cynthia, she's got two sisters and one of them is one and a half years more than she is, and one of them is two years less, and the little one, she's coming to school next term, Cynthia said, and she's awful. All spoiled and silly. And then there's my other friend, Molly, she's got a sister and she's eleven and that's ever so old, because she's going to Godolphin School, where all the big girls go. But no one else I know has a sister as old as Chloe is! I mean, eighteen is ever so, *ever so* old! So, why is my sister so old when everyone else's isn't?'

Goosey laughed comfortably and set the carrots in a saucepan and filled it with water and then slapped it down on the gas cooker. 'Bless the child, how its little mind does work! I've told you over and over, Miss Chloe's your stepsister. You had the same dad but her Ma was different. Died when Miss Chloe was a baby, poor little motherless scrap.'

'She's not motherless!' Robin said indignantly. 'She's my sister, so she's got Mummy!'

'Yes,' Goosey said after a moment and slid her eyes sideways to look at Robin and then started mixing pastry in a big yellow bowl. 'Well, yes. But it's not the same. Anyway, your Ma didn't come along till Chloe was – well, older than you. A big girl she was, when your Ma and Pa got wed.' She stopped then, her hands in the bowl and flour streaking her wizened old arms as she stared into the distance over Robin's head. 'Poor little thing. Didn't understand one bit, she didn't – '

'Didn't understand what?' Robin was getting so interested she had stopped tugging the green strand out of the rag rug.

'About your Ma,' Goosey said and started to knead her pastry again. 'I mean, how could she? Had her Dad and her Auntie Mabel all to herself all that time and me, o' course, and then along comes your Ma and well, it was different after that. Not that she hadn't known her of course. Your Ma had been coming to this house for – oh, years, before they got married. Let me see – it must have been – ' She wrinkled her eyes as she stared back down the years. 'Chloe couldn't have been no more'n three or so, as I recall, when your Ma and poor dear Mabel got to be friends.'

Robin wasn't at all interested in poor dear Mabel. She'd heard Goosey go on about her a lot and seen the photographs of her. An ordinary looking person, a bit dull really, Robin had thought privately as she had let Goosey show her the pictures and weep over them as Goosey always did. Not as nice looking as Miss Scoular, and a bit like Miss Trent, the headmistress, and you can't look more ordinary than that. Anyway, Mabel was dead, Robin knew that. She'd died of the flu, just before Robin herself had been born. She knew that because Mummy had told her, long ago. But Mummy had never talked much about why her big sister Chloe was so very old. Maybe once Robin knew why, she told herself now, Chloe would stop being so hateful to her. She was very hateful, often, much too fond of pinching her with those hard little fingers with the sharp little nails.

'Why was it all different after Mummy came along?' she said now. 'Mummy's – well, she's Mummy. Nice.'

There was a little pause and then Goosey said, 'Of course she's nice! A real lady, your Ma, and I'm the first to say so. Done wonders for your poor dear Pa, she did, for all he died so young – ' And now Goosey turned her head and lifted one shoulder so that she could rub her eyes and nose on her rolled up sleeve, while still kneading her pastry.

'He was a hero,' Robin said.

'Yes,' Goosey said. 'That he was. Died for his country, he did.'

'Like Cynthia Louper's uncle,' Robin went on. 'He was at Mons.'

'Like more good young men than the world could spare and that's the truth of it.' Goosey again mopped her eyes and nose in her sleeve. 'Now, young miss, just you come over here and make yourself useful. You can butter that there pie dish for me, after you've washed your hands. Chicken pie we got tonight, using the last bits from yesterday. I can stretch it a bit with potato and that. It's as bad as the war, this is, making food stretch. I thought we'd seen the last of those bad old days, and here we go again with all these nasty strikes and all that – '

But Robin was not to be deflected. She came obediently to wash her hands and then to the table to kneel up on a chair and to take a knob of butter to rub over the earthenware pie dish Goosey had waiting, but went on talking.

'You said Chloe didn't understand,' she said. 'What didn't she understand?'

'What?' Goosey looked puzzled.

'About Mummy coming along,' Robin said patiently. 'What didn't she understand?'

'That she couldn't have her Dad to herself no more, that's what.' Goosey said and began to roll the pastry, scattering flour about in a little shower and slapping her heavy wooden rolling pin down with satisfyingly loud thumps. 'It's always like that for children when there's second marriages.'

'How do you mean?' Robin was rubbing in the butter so well that it was getting all watery. It was fun, almost as much fun as painting was, or playing with plasticine.

'Oh, the questions you do ask!' Goosey said. 'Look here, you leave that dish alone. You'll rub it to death. I'll give you some pastry and you can make a little pie of your own. Only stop asking questions.'

'Mummy said asking questions is what makes you wise,' Robin said but got down in a hurry and went to fetch her piece of pastry. Maybe this time she could make a pie that wouldn't look quite so grey. If she was careful. 'What can I put in my pie. Can it be a sweet one?'

'It's never anything else, is it? Raspberry jam, in the larder. The jar with a bit at the bottom. That'll be enough – you won't need more'n that – '

Robin fetched the jam and took the small rolling pin that Goosey gave her and set to work, busily, and for a little while there was a comfortable silence in the big kitchen with the firelight glowing on the ceiling and the long beams of the afternoon sun moving across the stone floor from the tall windows, behind the sink and draining-board, which looked out to the area railings. This was the only time of day when the westering sun managed to reach the dark kitchen, the rays piercing the tracery of the tree branches in the square and coming through the area railings in broad bars, and it was a time that Robin loved. Home from school, and waiting for Mummy and the comfortableness of Goosey and the quietness of the house; it was lovely.

But today was different. Today she was uneasy because Chloe had been so very insistent and had tried so hard to make her do what she wanted, even though she knew it was wrong. It felt bad when Chloe was so nasty. It was the only bit of being at home that Robin didn't like. And it might be easier to deal with, she thought in a confused sort of way, if she knew why Chloe was so nasty.

'Goosey,' she said after a while. 'Cynthia told me her auntie, the one who was married to the uncle who was killed at Mons, Cynthia said she's getting married again.'

'Is she indeed?' Goosey was well used to Robin's chatter about her best friend at school and paid only half

63

her attention to it, busy now chopping up cooked chicken and potato for her pie, and setting about the making of a white sauce to bind it. 'Clever woman, then. God knows there's enough poor widows around as'd give a lot for the same opportunity. And few enough likely to get it, with so many good men lying there in France and Flanders – pass me that nutmeg, Robin, there's a dear child.'

Robin passed her the nutmeg and wondered if it might be a good idea to use some to sprinkle her raspberry jam pie, which was looking a bit grey after all. 'Cynthia said that her cousin's ever so pleased.'

'Her cousin?' Goosey was at the stove now, stirring her white sauce and watching it anxiously for lumps. 'Is that a fact?'

'His name's Gilbert and he's ten, Cynthia said,' Robin went on, and began to make pretty cuts in her pie, to decorate it. 'Will he understand, do you think?'

'Understand what?' Goosey began to stir the chicken and potatoes in the steaming white sauce and an agreeable scent began to pervade the kitchen. Suppery smells, thought Robin, nice smells which mean Mummy'll be home soon.

'You said that Chloe didn't understand about Mummy coming along,' Robin said. 'Well, will Gilbert understand about the new – I suppose he'll be a new father, won't he? – coming along?'

'How you do go on, child,' Goosey said and looked at her sharply. It never failed to amaze her how Robin could stick at things, how she could worry and worry away at something until she had all the answers she wanted. Not like other children who were so easily distracted, according to Goosey's experience. And hadn't she reared not only dear dear Mr Bobby and Miss Mabel, but Miss Chloe too? With her experience, Goosey felt herself a very knowledgeable person about children. But she had never met one quite as sharp as this little round-eyed creature who was staring at her so solemnly. And Goosey looked down at her, at the dark curly hair that was so like her mother's and the lustrous dark eyes and determined little chin that were so very much her own, and sighed.

'Well, Goosey, will he?' Robin said and then smiled at her. It was a singularly bewitching smile, and she didn't often display it. Robin had always been a solemn child, from her earliest infancy, much given to looking and listening as well as asking questions with all the tenacity of a cat with a bird between its paws; and Goosey melted at the sight of it and set down the pie dish she had picked up ready to put in the oven and bent to pick up Robin and hug her in her floury old arms.

'I don't know, child, and don't suppose I ever shall. Maybe he will and maybe he won't. It's never easy for a child when there's a second marriage, as maybe you'll find out one day for yourself. But don't you fret your little head over it. People rub along well enough whatever happens at the beginning. Look at us! Whatever it was like for Miss Chloe at the start, or your Ma, or Mr Bobby, we do well enough now, don't we? She's a young limb, I don't deny, but so are you in your own way. It's what you young things are born for, if you ask me – to give us old ones a run. Keeps us alive. Now – 'And she set Robin on her feet again and dusted her down, leaving even more specks of flour on her. 'You run away and play with your toys now, and I'll call you when your Ma gets home and supper's ready. I'll see to it your pie gets baked, too, so don't you fret over that. And stop all your worrying. Such a one for worrying as you are! *You've* nothing to worry over, that's for sure.'

But Robin was not so sure. She made her way upstairs to her room, and its collection of toys and above all its paint boxes and easel with lots of drawing paper to use on it which Mummy had given her, knowing how passionately she liked making pictures, feeling much less comfortable than she had hoped she would after talking to Goosey.

Chloe was horrid to her because of Mummy, that much was clear. It wasn't Mummy's fault, of course. It was just that she was a second marriage. And maybe, Goosey had said, maybe she'd find out for herself one day that it was never easy for a child when there was a second marriage.

This was the first time in all her life Robin had ever thought of the possibility of her mother getting married. But tonight she thought about it a lot.

5

'What that girl needs is a man around the house to keep a bit of a control on her,' Jessie said. 'That'd show her how to behave.'

'Jessie, for heaven's sake!' Poppy put down the Smithfield and Billingsgate lists she had been checking against the number of chickens and trays of fish Barney and David had loaded into the cold room. 'She's barely out of school! Marrying her off at her age – anyway, she's far too fickle. As far as I can tell there's a new young man every week to add to her quiverful. And she never lets go of any of them. Dozens of them buzzing around like flies in the summer – '

'I wasn't talking about *her* being married!' Jessie said and shut the cold room door with a slam, and jerked her head at one of her girls who went off with a load of halibut and soles to be gutted, cleaned and fried in egg and matzo meal, as Jessie herself set to work to draw half a dozen birds ready to boil them for the day's supply of soup. 'I'm talking about a man. Not a husband for her – a father! It's you who ought to be getting married and making sure there's someone there to deal with that little madam, when she gets into one of her flounces. Children need a firm man's hand – '

'She's hardly a child,' Poppy said drily. 'Not yet an adult, I grant you, but not a child. As for a man's hand, dear Jessie, don't start that again. And anyway, you didn't have one around, did you?'

And doesn't it show, too, when you look at Bernie, a secret voice whispered deep inside her head. If ever a boy had needed a bit of firm handling, it was the young Bernie. Too late now, of course –

'Well, I can't deny it would have helped,' Jessie said, and kept her head down over her malodorous task, tumbling gizzards and livers and unlaid eggs in little golden globules out of the carcass of the bird in front of her. 'Those were hard days. But I managed well enough. And Bernie's really grown up now, of course – out on his own – '

Her voice drifted away and she began to concentrate fiercely on what she was doing and Poppy felt a sharp stab of compunction. It was unkind of her to press Jessie on the subject of Bernie; her aunt was no fool and knew perfectly well that he left a lot to be desired in the matter of behaviour and simple honesty. And even though it was irritating when Jessie started on again about the need for Poppy to find herself a new husband, she, Poppy, had no right to take out her own sense of frustration on her. The dear old love meant well enough, after all. And in all fairness it had been a long time since she had talked about the matter. The last time had been – Poppy squinted at her lists as she tried to remember – it must have been over a year ago, when that customer in the restaurant had taken to coming every day at the same time Poppy took her own lunch, so that he could sit and moon at her lugubriously from the far corner. Poppy hadn't noticed him at all until Jessie, highly delighted, had pointed him out as a would-be suitor.

'He really likes you,' she had said complacently, looking at the man, a tall and rather bulky person in an expensive suit and with a very large thick gold watch chain across his incipient paunch. 'I can tell. You should encourage him. He's told us all about himself. He's got a nice business in the mantle trade, doing very well. He'd make a lovely husband. Been a bachelor these many years, but now his old mother's died he's free to live his own life. And it don't take no crystal gazer to see he'd as soon live it with you as anyone – '

Poppy had laughed at first but then became irritated and finally extremely angry as day after day Jessie had urged her and nagged her and made a point of being exceedingly charming to her persistent customer, revealed now as a Mr Daniel Marcus, aged forty-five and very well off indeed, thank you, more than just comfortable. Until, on the day that Jessie had graciously invited him to come and take dinner that evening with herself and her niece, Poppy had finally cracked.

'I'm not going to be here for dinner,' she had hissed furiously at Jessie behind the kitchen door as soon as she could detach her from Daniel Marcus' side. 'Not now or ever, if you're going to behave in this ridiculous fashion! Do you hear me, Jessie? I won't have it. It's – it's dreadful!'

'What's so dreadful about being a *shadcan*?' Jessie had said and then grinned as Poppy stared at her in angry incomprehension. 'A matchmaker, dolly! They're traditional and they do good work. To bring a couple together is a *mitzvah* – a blessing!'

'Then give yourself a blessing,' Poppy had snapped. 'And leave me out of it – '

'Believe me, if I could I would!' Jessie had said mournfully. 'But me? Who'd want me now? Sixty-two, that's me – who'd want an old goat of such an age? Not this fella, twenty years younger – but now? He'd laugh at me. No, it's you he's after – '

'Well, he's out of luck,' Poppy had said and marched out, and for the next month had flatly refused to eat her lunch in the restaurant at all, insisting on sandwiches being sent up to her office. Until at last Mr Marcus, somewhat ruffled at being given his *congé* so firmly, chose to eat his lunch elsewhere, and Jessie, one customer worse off, had found the wisdom to keep her tongue between her teeth on the subject of Poppy and men.

Until now; and Poppy went upstairs to her office to deal with the afternoon's work and to make sure that everything was organized for the evening before she went home at last to Robin and whatever trouble Chloe had managed to brew for her, with a sense of depression hanging over her.

Was she really such a failure as a mother that it was obvious to everyone, including Jessie in whose eyes generally she could do no wrong, that she needed to find someone to help her? Poppy took her responsibilities towards Chloe very seriously, and had done so even before her father had died in 1919; more even than the responsibility to her own dear Robin. The difference is of course, she told herself with the sort of painful insight that so often afflicted her, it's easy with Robin. I love her so comfortably; it's all so natural. But with Chloe it's anything but natural. I care for her passionately as Bobby's daughter, but I don't love her. I can't. I don't even like her very much. And how can it be easy to look after and make the best decisions for someone about whom you feel such contradictory things? Am I a failure because I can't? Do I have the added responsibility to go and find a man to marry simply so that Chloe will be better cared for? And if I do, what about Robin? And what, dammit all, about me? Do I have to tie myself to some gold-dripping businessman simply in order to take care of two children? Surely not –

None of her questions were answered by the time she had finished the afternoon's work, and she pushed them to the back of her mind and went to find Jessie. It had turned out to be an exhausting day, one way and another, and it wasn't over yet. On Wednesdays she always called to see her mother in Leinster Terrace. The fact that there

70

was a General Strike would make no difference to Mildred; she would be sitting there in her drawing-room, her back as straight as a yardstick, waiting for her. And Poppy would have to sit and talk to her for half an hour before at last escaping to the bliss of home and supper with Robin and then, if she was lucky, a long quiet evening in her own drawing-room with her feet tucked beneath her on the huge sofa and perhaps the earphones from her radio on so that she could hear some music. A little Beethoven was promised tonight, she seemed to remember —

But that was a long way away, and she clattered down the stairs back to the kitchen to find her aunt; and then stopped at the doorway at the sight that greeted her.

The kitchen was at its quietest at this end of the afternoon. The girls who had toiled so busily all morning to fill the orders for the sell-outs had vanished, as had the cooks whose job it was to sweat over the rapid fire of lunch-time orders. They'd be back tonight to get the dinner trade running, as would the overnight workers who had the job of preparing the foods ready for the morning workers to cook, but right now, there were just the long empty rows of preparation tables and the softly hissing steam cookers and the shelves full of steaming pots. And in the middle, there was Jessie, and sitting on the table beside her, with his heels swinging and kicking the chrome legs carelessly, was Bernie.

Poppy stood in the shadows of the doorway and looked at him, wanting to arrange her expression into a smooth non-committal one before facing him. It had been a long time now since she had first caught Bernie out in one of his casual depredations on his mother's cash, and had forced him to make repayment. Since then he had been much more careful and had managed to arrange matters so that when he did raid Jessie's resources he left no evidence to be found in the books anywhere. Poppy

71

knew he did it, and suspected that Jessie did too, but it was unprovable. She had to admit that for all his dislikeable qualities, the boy was clever, too damned clever for his own good, she would say to herself sometimes, feeling exactly like old Goosey who was much given to making statements like that about all sorts of people. But about Bernie it was true. Too clever and too beautiful for his own good.

And what is he doing here now, she wondered. Usually when he wants anything he comes when his mother isn't here and just helps himself to what he needs. Sometimes items from the storerooms that he could sell, for that was his favourite way of taking cash out of the business, knowing that his mother would shrug her shoulders and write off her losses as normal wastage of highly perishable goods; and sometimes cash from the restaurant till, which the waiters knew about but found ways of covering up for him. They in their own way wanted to protect Jessie from hurt too, and preferred to do it by keeping her unaware of the fact that she was being robbed than by making her face up to the facts about her beloved son. Poor vulnerable Jessie, Poppy thought now. We all do it. Because she loves that creature so and we love her, we do all we can to make life easy for him. We must be mad –

She took a little extra breath and then walked composedly into the kitchen, making her way down between the preparation tables to the area where Jessie and Bernie were side by side in the pool of light thrown by the only overhead lamp that was burning. They looked up at her as she came up to them and both gave her a blank-eyed stare that made her feel a moment of chill; they were closing her out, didn't want her there, she thought wearily, and after all why shouldn't they? It's their life, not mine; their business, not mine. And then she remembered, suddenly, her conversation with Jessie this morning – only this morning? It felt like half a lifetime ago – about partnerships. Maybe it's my business after all, she told herself as she looked back at them with her own face schooled into impassivity. Maybe I have as much right as Jessie to show an interest in why this wretched boy is here.

And then it all altered. Jessie's face broke into a familiar grin and she put one massive arm across the boy's shoulder and said to Poppy, 'See who's here! My little Bernie!'

'Lay off, Ma, for Gawd's sake,' Bernie said, wriggling his shoulders slightly so that Jessie had to take her arm away, and turning his face to Poppy, 'I ask you, calling me that at my age!'

'She calls me Poppela sometimes, and I'm older than you,' Poppy said equably. 'Actually, I quite like it. It sounds friendly. How are you, Bernie?'

'Well enough, thanks,' he said and grinned at her. 'Long time no see and all that.'

He was wearing a dark suit of a fabric that was clearly very expensive; it shone with a rich dark sheen in the bright light and the high collared silk shirt above the line of the immaculate waistcoat with its tasteful jet buttons was blindingly white and clearly even more costly. He was wearing a purple satin tie and a matching handkerchief protruded with studied carelessness from the breast pocket of his jacket. The requisite inch or so of white cuff, embellished with heavy gold links, protruded from his sleeves, and his long tapering white hands were emblazoned with a heavy gold and onyx signet ring. His hair gleamed sumptuously with brilliantine over his broad white forehead, his dark eyes crinkled with easy charm above a most beautifully modelled nose and a plump Turkish cigarette depended with insouciant rakishness from his perfectly formed mouth behind which even white teeth gleamed softly. He had a small cleft in his square chin and a hint of a dimple at one corner of his mouth. He looked every inch the young girl's dream of a rich and handsome young man-about-town and Poppy thought he was repellent.

'I've been here,' she said tartly. 'If you'd wanted to see me – or your mother – you always knew where to find us.'

'Ah, indeed I did. But maybe I didn't want to see you, dear cousin. The way you go on being so unpleasant to me, why should I? But there, I'm a forgiving sort of chap. So I'm here now. How are you coping with the strike, hmm? Need anything? I've got access to eggs and butter and some great cheese if you're having any problems – '

'I could always use extra butter,' Jessie broke in eagerly, riding over the waves of hostility between the two of them, as she always did. 'And cheese – '

'We don't need any strikebreaker's goods,' Poppy said sharply. 'We've got a supply that'll see us through the next fortnight and if we look like running low after that, Mr Hawking has promised me we'll be priority customers. We don't need to use the black market. We're not war profiteer types – '

'Please yourself,' Bernie said easily, well aware of the dig in the words. Poppy had been so disgusted when she had discovered, not long after the war, just how Bernie had made his money – which was by 1919 quite a considerable sum – that she had told him roundly what her opinion was not only of shirkers like him (he had bought his way out of the army with forged medical papers, claiming to be tuberculous) but of people who used a war in which other men were dying for their principles as a way of lining their pockets. He had looked at her incredulously and laughed in her face at her stupidity, and she had lost her temper spectacularly and slapped his face. He had never forgotten that and, Poppy suspected, never would. She could herself still remember the chill she had felt as he had stood there and stared at her over the slowly reddening marks on his cheek which showed clearly where her fingers had made contact and felt the hatred in him. But he had only smiled thinly at her and said nothing.

Now he smiled again with his usual sleek charm and went on, 'As long as Ma's happy, I'm happy. If she says she don't want no butter or cheese, so be it. But if she does – ' He slid his eyes at his mother now. 'It's her business, after all, eh Ma?'

Jessie opened her mouth to speak and then looked at Poppy and closed it again and doubt moved across her mobile round features so fast that Poppy could have laughed.

'Of course it is,' she said swiftly before Jessie could speak. This was no time for them to recommence any discussion of a partnership for Poppy. She and Jessie alone would have to hammer out the details of that; it was not something that Bernie could or should be part of; and she looked at Jessie with her eyes as wide and expressionless as ever. But Jessie, mercifully, got the message and said only, 'Well, if Poppy says we got enough, we got enough. She's the one who runs that side. So Bernie, you were telling me – you've got a new venture?'

He slid to his feet and stood there with his hands thrust into his pockets, looking more elegant than ever and grinned at his mother as the smoke from his cigarette wreathed itself upwards round his head, softening his perfect features into even greater beauty.

'We don't want to talk about that now,' he said easily. 'Some other time, Ma. I'll take you and show you, maybe. If it's a suitable thing for you to see.'

He laughed then and bent over and swiftly kissed the heavy old cheek and Jessie flushed like a child and put a hand up to touch the place his lips had brushed.

'Well, Ma, I must be going. Just thought I'd drop by,

you know – thanks for all the – well, ta anyway. Be seeing you!' And he grinned at Poppy, and went sauntering away down the kitchen towards the door, picking up his heavy camel overcoat as he passed the place where he had left it thrown down, and hanging it over his shoulders with a practised twist of his wrists. At once he looked like an advertisement plate for men's tailoring, Poppy thought sourly. Everything The Well Dressed Young Gentleman Could Possibly Need – and she felt her lip curl with disdain as she watched him go.

'He's looking well, eh Poppela?' Jessie said eagerly behind her as the door slammed behind him, and again Poppy had to smooth her face before turning round to answer her. Poor old Jessie, so besotted with so worthless a person.

'Yes indeed,' she said heartily and smiled and Jessie took a tremulous little breath and looked relieved.

'He was tellin' me, he's really puttin' himself about these days! Still involved in the agency of course – '

'Agency?' Poppy murmured.

'Well, you know, buying and selling this and that,' Jessie said vaguely. 'But now it looks like he's on to a really good thing. He's got his own place!'

Poppy looked puzzled. 'But he's lived there for weeks, now,' she said. 'The flat – '

Jessie laughed flatly. 'Oh, I didn't mean the flat! Sure he's got that. And now he's got a manservant there to look after him. How's that, eh? A flat in Sloane Street and a manservant. Not bad, eh? No, I mean he's got his own place – like this – '

Poppy gaped. 'Like this? A restaurant?'

Jessie shook her head. 'Not exactly,' she said. 'He told me, but I didn't follow it all. It's more a night place, you know? A bar o' course and music – '

'Ah,' Poppy said dampeningly. 'A night-club. I see.'

It wasn't surprising, she thought. It was in fact exactly

what she would have expected him to find interesting. London was full of them, seedy cellars tricked out in chrome and low blue and red lights with walls covered with weird paintings and a jazz band tucked in a cramped corner and making a lot of noise and cocktails, cocktails, cocktails. She'd never been to any of them herself of course, but she knew about them well enough. The newspapers reported on them avidly, and on the people who frequented them; how could anyone not know about the night-clubs, from the Bag o' Nails where the Prince of Wales spent so much time, downwards, and about the things that went on in them? Far from respectable establishments, whoever went to them.

'And what's wrong with a night-club?' Jessie said with a hint of her usual pugnacity. 'It's a business, ain't it? Like this one. People like to eat and drink and – '

'Not like this one,' Poppy said quickly. 'This is – you sell your heart here, Jessie. You cook like an angel, always did, and here you feed people good food at sensible prices. You don't fill them up with cheap gin and – and Old Fashioneds or whatever they call their horrible concoctions – '

Jessie grinned suddenly. 'Oh, you, Poppy! Always so nice to me! Sure it's not the same as a night-club – we don't even sell wine here. But in the new place, the one you'll run for me – there we'll have a licence and learn about wine so we can sell that with the food. No cocktails, though, what do you say? Or do you think they'll expect it, West End customers? Here they got more sense. Here they want a decent bowl of chicken soup, properly cooked salt beef, and my strudel and it's enough. But in the West End – you see why you got to run it, Poppy? From where should I know such things, eh, boobalah?'

Poppy softened at the sound of the familiar old endearment, and leaned forward and took one of Jessie's plump hands between both of hers.

'Darling, I haven't had a chance to even think about that,' she said. 'What with Chloe and everything – but I promise I will. It's a loving and generous offer – but we ought to go over the books together. And you ought, I suppose, to talk to Bernie. It's his inheritance, after all – '

Jessie went red suddenly. 'Inheritance? For Gawd's sake, Poppy, don't talk about such things! Are you trying to get rid of me?'

'Jessie, of course not!' Poppy was horrified. 'How could you think such a – it's just that he *is* your son. And even though it's no secret I worry about some of the things he does – well, he's your *son*. He has a right to be consulted in what you do, surely?'

Jessie relaxed a little. 'Well, all right, I suppose – but don't go talking of such things as inheritances.' And she turned her head to one side and mimed spitting three times in the time honoured way of the East End streets to keep away the evil eye. 'You don't have to think of such things. Only about how we can make the business better and give more people good food. I need you for that, Poppy. And we can do it. I don't see the books that much, now I got you to look after all that, but I ain't stupid, I know how to read a balance sheet as good as anyone. We're making money here, a lot of it, and it's crazy not to invest it in another business. Everyone's growing these days. Have you seen the way the ABC tea shops is spreading? Like measles they are. And the Lyons people – believe me, Poppy, anything they can do, I can do. Only I'll do it classy, really classy. Nothing cheap – '

Poppy laughed. 'Of course you will; I don't doubt that for a moment. It's just that – ' Her face straightened. 'I doubt myself, to tell the truth. Can I cope with another lot of responsibility? Running another place – and still doing what I do – it'll take a lot of time. And there's Robin who I don't see as much of as I'd like as it is – and

78

Chloe – ' And her voice drifted away as she thought about Chloe.

'You being there at home all the time won't make no difference to that one,' Jessie said with a great practicality. 'It'll just make you more mad with her than ever. You'll be able to see what she's like all the time. As for Robin – that baby's a happy soul. She's fine, whether you're there all the time or not. Leave that to Goosey. She's the best one to look after the children. Till you get a man around that is – ' And she gave her a wicked little grin. 'No, I promise not another word! I want to think about my new place and my new partner. My *old* new partner – what do you say, dolly? You got to say yes! How can you turn me down?'

6

'I can't possibly turn her down,' Poppy said and shook her head as Mildred put out her hand interrogatively towards her tea cup. 'No thank you, Mamma. No more. You must see, Mamma, that I can't turn her down.'

'It's entirely up to you, of course,' Mildred said and carefully poured another cup of tea for herself. Watching her, Poppy thought – is she eating enough? She looks positively haggard these days. I sometimes think she just lives on tea and toast. 'I have never been entirely happy with your – um – connection with Jessie and her affairs,' Mildred went on. 'As you well know. There has never been any need for it, after all. There's all this – ' And she waved one hand comprehensively to indicate the house beyond the drawing-room in which they sat. ' – as I have told you many times. You could stop this occupation that so wears you down and let that poky little house go and settle in here nicely – all three of you – '

Poppy didn't answer her, but sat and stared down at her ankles, crossed in front of her on the dark red turkey carpet. How long had that carpet been here, she found herself wondering. It was here when I was very young and came to this house for the first time; and she looked back down the long telescope of the years to her own small self wearing a white fur hat and muff and standing staring up at a woman with yellow curls wrapped in lots of frills and lace, sitting on the sofa with her feet on a hassock, and tall men in black clothes, very tall men who looked down at her and despised her; and closed her eyes against the memory.

To live in this house with Mamma; could she do it? There had been times, many of them over the past years, when she had considered it. When Bobby had died and left her alone and pregnant it had been a tempting prospect to crawl into the dim luxury of this great house with its labyrinth of richly carpeted and furnished rooms and its great fireplaces kept spruce and well filled by soft footed maids ruled with iron by the redoubtable Queenie who had worked here since time unremembered. When she was so bone tired that the thought of not having to get up in the morning to do anything more effortful than arrange flowers or go shopping or play with Robin had seemed deeply desirable. Mamma had offered her all that and went on offering it, over and over again, but over and over again Poppy had refused, choosing instead to spend long work-filled days in the tight-packed noisy squalor of an East End factory and restaurant, in a cramped little office where she carried an enormous responsibility, and to spend her precious free time in a small cluttered house in Holland Park where there was all too little space for her to escape from Chloe's tiresomeness or to find any peace and quiet of her own. She must be quite mad –

But even as the temptation spread and grew and wove its tentacles into her mind she heard her own voice rejecting it. 'It is good of you, Mamma, but no. I must earn my own living, you know that. It matters to me. It did to you once.'

Mildred bent her head and said nothing. How could she? She had indeed once run away from this house herself to earn her own living and had succeeded for a while, but the place and the people had sucked her back and here she now sat, long after the people had vanished, living in this house with their ghosts and not much more. Only Poppy who came once a week and filled Mildred's empty grey life with the only colour and warmth that existed. Not that she would have let Poppy know that; that was not Mildred's style. All she ever did was welcome her with a thin smile and a ready tea-tray and talk to her of the small commonplaces of her daily life, and sometimes listened to Poppy speak of hers. She did not often do so, and it was to Mildred an indication now of how agitated her daughter was at present that she had spoken to her of Jessie's offer. Poppy knew perfectly well of the old rivalry that still existed between these two women, who had once been so close but were now so aloof. She herself was the core of it, and there was nothing she could do about that, but she could be peaceable and loyal, and not speak to either of them about the other. And generally that was how it was.

But now, on this May evening as the sun lengthened its rays across the terrace and the faint scent of daffodils came blowing up from Hyde Park on the other side of the nearby Bayswater Road, Poppy had broken her self-imposed rule, and spoken to her mother of Jessie, seeking advice. And Mildred sat and watched her daughter over the rim of her Crown Derby tea cup and had the sense to bite her tongue. Whatever she said, Poppy would do as she thought fit. Any opposition from Mildred, she knew, would only harden her resolve towards Jessie.

'Well,' Poppy said now, and stretched a little. 'I suppose I ought to be making for home. It's been a difficult day – '

'Oh?' Mildred said non-commitally.

Poppy grimaced. 'Chloe,' she said shortly. 'I don't know what to do for the best about that child. She causes me more – well, let be. Just take it I've had a bad day with her. And I think I should get home soon to see what she's up to.'

Mildred lifted her brows at that. 'You startle me,' she said rather surprisingly. 'I find her reasonable enough.'

It was Poppy's turn to look surprised. 'How do you mean?'

'Oh, she calls on me sometimes,' Mildred said. 'During the afternoon, you know, when it is proper to pay morning calls. It is rather agreeable to find so young a gel so interested in the old ways of doing things.'

Poppy looked at her, not too surprised to notice and be a little amused by her mother's Edwardian pronunciation of the word 'girl' but taken aback all the same. Chloe, paying calls on a dull old lady? She had no illusions about the attractions of her mother; she could be interesting and somewhere lurking under her stiff manner was a strong will with a sharp mind and an interesting past. But she had spent so long keeping up what she regarded as appearances that now there seemed to the casual observer little beyond those surface appearances.

'I had no idea,' was all she said and Mildred permitted herself a thin smile.

'Well, she has the time of course, as you should if you were – well, never mind. But since she lives in leisure at home as a well-bred gel should she has the opportunity to observe the social niceties. It is agreeable, as I say, to see a modern miss behave so. I cannot pretend I like her clothes or her face painting – ' She gave a little grimace here. ' – for she is a pretty enough child and does not need it. But there, I cannot fight fashion. But we talk a little – '

'What about?'

'Oh, nothing much. The past. A little. She is interested in how life was before the War.' Mildred managed to look, just for a moment, wistful. 'It was a very different world then. I sometimes think we did more than put an end to German imperialism in 1918. We put an end to the whole of decent living.'

'Oh, Mamma, such stuff!' Poppy said and then stopped short. 'Does she quiz you about me?' she said then and her voice had taken on an edge.

'About you? However do you mean?' Mildred looked genuinely surprised.

'I – ' Poppy reddened. 'Well, if I cannot say it to you, whom can I? She is often – disagreeable to me about – about my background.'

'Background?' Mildred said non-commitally.

'She taunts me with my lack of class and my strange relations, as she calls them.' Poppy said bitterly. 'It makes it very difficult to deal with her when she's being headstrong.'

'I can imagine it would.' Mildred looked quite impassive and glancing at her thin composed face, Poppy thought with a moment of bitterness – she doesn't care. It was she and her passion for Lizah that made it all happen. If she had not chosen to go to him – then she bit her lip at her own wickedness. Lizah, poor dead Lizah, had not had a good life, yet he had loved her, his daughter, dearly, and been so very proud of her. They had spent little enough time together, heaven knew, because of what had happened between her mother and him, but what time there had been had been sweet enough. To be angry now because he had been her father was wickedly disloyal; and Poppy rubbed her hand across her forehead as the thoughts buffeted about her mind. It was always the same. Even talking about Chloe and the way she taunted Poppy about her antecedents could hurl her into this confusion of feeling.

'I can assure you,' Mildred said after a moment, 'that we do not discuss you, either in the present or in the past. I am saddened you should consider it a possibility, Poppy. I would never behave so ill.'

'No, Mamma, I'm sorry. I should have known – ' Poppy said wearily. 'Forgive me. It is just that I am so

84

puzzled by Chloe coming to call on you. I would not have thought so giddy, and well – selfish a girl could behave so.'

'There are often aspects of other people's characters which we do not understand,' Mildred said a little reprovingly. 'It is arrogant to think any of us can know another person totally.'

Poppy looked at her and managed a smile. How right she was! Even after all this time Poppy had no real understanding of what made Mildred be the way she was, of the tides that ran in her or the thoughts that filled her. She knew the surface facts of her life, of course, or most of them, or she thought she did; (sometimes she wasn't even sure of that) but no more than that. There were still many mysteries about Mildred. And not least of them now was the attraction she bore for her step-grand-daughter. Poppy shook her head to clear the confusion as best she could, and got to her feet.

'Well, Mamma, I dare say you are right. You often are. I must go, I'm afraid. However Chloe is with you, when I am about she is less biddable. And after this morning's fracas – no, I shall not bother you with it now, it is too silly – I expect sulks at the very least and temper tantrums at worst. I had better face it now if I am to have any peace left of the evening. Goodnight, Mamma. I shall come to see you again as usual next Wednesday. If there are any matters that concern you before that, see to it that Queenie telephones. Good evening, Mamma – ' And she kissed her mother's papery old cheek and went, following the same pattern as every Wednesday evening, calling in at the kitchen to speak to Queenie and make sure that all was well below stairs and then walking home along the traffic-clotted Bayswater Road to Holland Park. And whatever awaited her there.

In fact, it wasn't nearly as bad as she had feared. The

house felt and smelled good as she let herself in and she stood in the neat little hallway, her head up, taking it in. There was the rich reek of the polish on the parquet floor and flower scents from the big bowl of hyacinths growing on the table in the corner and the fragrance of baking – a savoury pie of some sort – and mixed in with it all the distant odour of the violet soda crystals and soap that Robin so loved in her bath; and Poppy felt her tense shoulders loosen and relax as for the first time that day she looked forward to the evening with some pleasure. Robin in her nightdress and her blue dressing gown, sitting opposite her at the kitchen table – for when there were only themselves they did not bother Goosey with trailing up the stairs to serve dinner in the dining-room – and Goosey padding about as she looked after them, however much Poppy tried to persuade her to sit still and let her do it, and the contented hiss of the fire behind its bars and the soft dripping of the tap in the sink which they kept talking about getting fixed but never got round to – lovely.

She could hear them then, Robin's chattering and laughing upstairs and the deeper sound of Goosey's loving scolding voice and also – and now her spirits sank a little – the thin wail of jazz music. Chloe was in her room, then, playing that wretched gramophone of hers which she so loved. At least it was a bearable sound; not so loud that people would have to shout to be heard above it. But that meant that she was in her room with the door tightly shut, and that was not good news.

When Chloe was on reasonable terms with the household she never thought of closing her bedroom door, leaving it swinging wide open to show the tangle of clothes and the litter of cosmetics that Goosey, no matter how hard she tried, could never put to rights, and caring nothing for anyone else's convenience or opinion. But when she was sulking, then her door remained very firmly closed indeed; and Poppy had learned the hard way not to try to coax her out. It was always better to let her have her sulk out and then reappear when she was ready. Which she usually did after a day or so, behaving as though nothing at all had happened.

Well, tiresome though it would be if she was going into one of her sulks and uncomfortable though Poppy found it, at least it meant that this evening would be a peaceful one, and Poppy put her hat on the stand and added her coat and went upstairs to put her head round Robin's door to say hello and exchange hugs before going to her own room to wash and change into a comfortable loose dress for the evening. Getting out of her office clothes, which, however careful she was always managed to smell of Jessie's cooking, was the first thing she did every evening. It marked the transition of Poppy the worker to Poppy the person; and also restored some of her spent energy.

Supper was as pleasant a meal as it could be. Goosey had spread the pretty embroidered tablecloth she had herself made for Poppy as a birthday present last year and the striped blue and white kitchen china made a brave display on it. The mushroom soup Goosey had prepared was delicate and delicious and the chicken pie as meltingly savoury as anyone could wish. Robin ate all her carrots without a murmur of complaint – which made Goosey bridle with pleasure, because she had done them with a 'little sugar and butter as a glaze, Mrs Poppy, just to tempt her – ' And so the hour they spent over the meal was tranquil in the extreme. And when Robin saw that Poppy ate some of her raspberry jam pie with her coffee – nobly ignoring the hints of overhandling that showed in the small fingermarks that could still be seen in the pastry – her cup of happiness was full.

She chattered all through supper with both Poppy and Goosey murmuring responses as they ate, and enjoying watching the vivid little face as she went on and on about school and about what Miss Scoular had and hadn't said, about her friends Cynthia and Molly and what they had done in this afternoon's painting class and similar items of vital news and Goosey watched her carefully throughout. But she said nothing at all about such matters as uncles and cousins and people getting married and seemed to have quite forgotten their afternoon conversation. So Goosey smiled at her and murmured fondly to Poppy in an undertone, 'Little lamb!' and Poppy flashed her a smiling response and thought that indeed yes, her Robin was a perfect lamb in every way.

But later, when she had taken Robin to bed and supervised her teeth cleaning and had sat on the edge of her bed and talked a little longer, with Robin getting steadily more sleepy, some of the comfort of the evening drifted away. She could still hear Chloe's gramophone grinding out its music, and she stood outside her door for a brief moment contemplating going in to ask her if she wanted some supper. There was plenty of pie left, and she would not have to sit with Poppy if she didn't choose to; but then she thought better of it. To behave so would make Chloe think she was trying to be conciliatory, which she was not; she was still very angry with her behaviour. That she could also be concerned that her stepdaughter should have her food while retaining her anger would not be something that Chloe would understand at all, and the last thing Poppy wanted to do was to let the child think she had only to sit and sulk to have her elders come sheepishly to her to coax her out of it.

She would come to no harm missing a meal, Poppy told herself shrewdly as she went down the stairs to the drawing-room on the first floor, and anyway she's perfectly well able to find her way to the kitchen to help herself to anything she might need. And it is very likely that Goosey will fetch something up to her as she goes to

88

bed; she could never let her beloved nursling go without anything for long.

The drawing-room was quiet and comfortable, with the fire burning cheerfully in the grate and only a few of the pierced brass lamps burning, which was the way Poppy best liked it, and she kicked off her slippers and curled up in the corner of the huge sofa and stretched her hand out to the flames. She had some hard thinking to do and it could no longer be avoided.

Was she or was she not going to become Jessie's partner rather than her employee? And what effect would that have on her relationship with Jessie if she did? Because as a partner, Poppy told herself now, as the flames in the fire danced before her eyes and dazzled her vision, I won't be able to bite my tongue when Bernie starts his tricks. If he robs Jessie now I feel bad about it; but she allows herself to be robbed and that is her choice. However, if I become a partner then he will be robbing me as well, and I won't be willing to allow it in the same way. And if I confront Bernie with his depredations and demand repayment how will Jessie feel about me then?

It was all very painful, very difficult, and she sat there watching the patterns in the fire and tried to see as far forward as she could. That had always been her way, planning and organizing; she had discovered when she had been a FANY during the war that you couldn't just lurch from situation to situation without giving some thought to how matters might turn out. You could never be sure your forward planning would work, of course, and it was useful always to have an alternative plan, just in case; she had run her complicated life tolerably successfully now for the past ten years using such a technique. But now when she needed it so badly, it let her down.

Because she could not see a way out of her impasse, could not visualize an alternative plan. It was a simple either/or; if she accepted Jessie's offer, good though it would be for Robin's future – for she would obviously earn more money than she did now – she risked causing a rift between herself and Jessie over Bernie. Indeed it was more than a risk, she thought now; it was a certainty. But if she refused Jessie, would things ever be the same? The offer had been made out of a loving heart, Poppy knew that; yes, there would be benefits for Jessie, who was as shrewd a business woman as anyone could be; she knew that with Poppy taking an even more active part, her business would grow, and though half of it would belong to Poppy, the greater growth would ensure that the loaf they sliced between them would be that much bigger. Jessie could end up richer than ever as a result. Poppy was no fool and had a clear and honest awareness of her own abilities. She knew that though it would be hard work she could make a great success of a new restaurant; indeed, could grow it into more than one. The idea was exhilarating and was growing ever more attractive. And yet, always there was Bernie; whatever she did, whichever way she looked, he loomed up in front of her like some sort of wicked goblin in a Christmas pantomime. And she sighed and closed her eyes against the dazzle of the flames in order to think more clearly.

The result was inevitable. She woke suddenly two hours later as a log, burned almost to a charcoal cinder, collapsed into a little flurry of dead ash, and shivered as she stared at the dullness there in the grate and then looked at her watch. One o'clock – heavens, how silly! She had been sitting here all this time when she should long ago have been in bed, like everyone else.

She got to her feet stiffly, hopping a little awkwardly, for one foot had gone to sleep and was tingling dreadfully, and set the night guard in front of the fireplace, almost dead though it was, turned off the lamp and limped her way up the dim staircase towards her room and bed.

She stopped as she always did outside Robin's door, which was held partly open by the small sausage of fabric which was tied round the two doorknobs; they had done this since Robin's infancy when she had been prone to night terrors. It had been a long time now since she had had one of her nightmares, but it helped her to know she could be heard and now Poppy stood and listened to the rather heavy breathing coming from inside and thought – she sounds fine. It's nothing like as noisy as it used to be; the doctor said her tonsils would stop bothering her once the better weather came, and it seems he was right. The croupiness she had suffered last winter seemed almost gone now.

She moved on, satisfied, to pass Chloe's door and then stopped uncertainly. To look in on Chloe was not something she had done for a long time. When she had first married Bobby and Chloe had been very young she had always done so, until one night Chloe had been dreadfully rude to her and forbade her ever to do it again because she 'didn't like being spied on'. And Poppy, though hurt, had put that down to the fact that Chloe was going through the stormy days of adolescence and learning to live with her new womanhood and had said nothing. But she had never checked on her well-being at night ever again.

But tonight she felt somehow that she should. She had set a harsh punishment on the girl; to be locked up at home for so long a period would be misery for her, as Poppy well knew. She had the prospect of that to think of as she had spent the whole evening alone and probably had no supper and the least Poppy could do, she felt obscurely, was to make sure she was comfortably asleep after so long a day.

She opened the door very gently and pushed it open. A wash of cosmetic and perfume scents came out, rather sickly and heavy, and Poppy wrinkled her nose a little as she pushed the door further so that the light from the small hall lamp, which always burned all night, could penetrate. She could see Chloe's bed, and in it the humped shape of the girl sleeping there and she stood for a moment, her head up and looking and listening. It was hard to be sure she could hear her breathing, for she could still hear Robin; her tonsils might be causing less croup but still her breathing was rather loud. Surely that was Chloe's softer quieter breathing she could hear beneath it?

It was, she decided, and gently pulled the door to, closed it and went to bed, reasonably content. Chloe might still be angry and sulky, but at least she was safely where she ought to be; here at home in bed.

7

Chloe could not have been in a fouler mood. She sat in
the half darkness and glowered like a small angry animal,
and the few people drifting past who might have considered stopping to talk to her took one look and
wandered on. This was no pleasant party acquaintance to
be made, that was for sure.

Chloe, oblivious of them, sat and hugged her anger.
The situation she was in was all the worse because it had
all started out rather well. Yes, the day had been beastly
after the policeman had got involved, though the
beginning had been quite brilliant; she had enjoyed that
mad rush along the length of Oxford Street in that great
van more than she could remember enjoying anything for
years. But once the policeman came – well, never mind
that. Policemen were by their very nature likely to be a
nuisance to one.

But then Poppy, the pig, had been as hateful as only
she could so the rest of the day had been misery. Even
that horrid Robin had been against her; and sitting now
thinking of the day, Chloe's eyes glittered with tears of
self-pity. It shouldn't have happened so, it really
shouldn't. It wasn't fair.

But then she had had that brilliant notion and it had
got a lot more cheerful. She had sat there in her room
playing her gramophone, furious because Robin had
refused to do it so that she could sneak out, and then had
had this much better notion. To arrange her bed so that

93

anyone who looked in – and she knew Goosey did that – would think she was asleep, instead of just sneaking out for the afternoon to show them – well, to show Poppy really – how stupid they were, but actually to go out to a party and stay out for ages. All night maybe – that would be grand!

It had taken a lot of working out. First she had to sneak downstairs while they were all pigging themselves in the kitchen over supper to phone Teddy and then Dickie because Teddy was a misery and wouldn't go out (Chloe got the distinct impression he had been gated by his family, too) and to make a plan to meet him. That had been a deliciously scary thing to do because Poppy might have heard the ting of the telephone bell at any moment and come to see what was happening. But Chloe had heard Robin chattering on and on in that silly high voice of hers and for the first time had been grateful to her. If she hadn't talked so much it was a sure thing that Poppy would have heard her phoning.

And then making her room look right and, after hearing Goosey go to bed, creaking up the stairs to the attic after peering in at Chloe – as she had known she would – slipping out of the house. It had been a bad moment when she had passed the drawing-room door and seen Poppy sitting there; she had been very afraid she would turn her head and see her and ask her where she was going in her new silver tissue evening dress and the little white fur-collared matching coat, but that surge of fear had passed when she had realized that Poppy was asleep. And she had stood in the drawing-room doorway hugging her coat around her and liking the feel of her silver sequinned cap with the swinging silver beads around the edge which covered all her hair, and wanted to laugh aloud. But of course she hadn't. She had just crept down the stairs and out of the front door, and gone to meet Dickie.

But from then on it had all been hateful. Dickie, whom

she had only called because Teddy hadn't been able to take her out, had been perfectly ridiculous, thoroughly bumptious and above himself, making a grab at her the moment they were in the taxi, as though she were the sort of girl to behave like that. Of course she wasn't a silly namby pamby; she had done her share of kissing and flirting – and why not – but more than that she was not interested in, and certainly not with someone like Dickie, who was all rather pink and white and had such silly thin hair the colour of dust. Not at all interesting, though useful sometimes. And to think he thought – well, he had deserved to have his silly face slapped, and to have sulked the way he had after that had been really monstrous and childish too. She had been glad to be rid of him once they got to the party he had told her he had been invited to.

But the party had been quite, quite ghastly. It was in a house in St John's Wood which was almost, if not quite, as bad as living in Holland Park. At least Norland Square was within a reasonable reach of Knightsbridge and was near the Park. This place was dreadful, full of refugees and war profiteers, she had told herself, looking round the rather over-furnished drawing-room of the house they were in. Lots of people horrid Poppy would be at home with, she told herself sourly as she saw a rather beautiful, very dark-haired girl with particularly rich and flashing dark eyes go by; they probably started out in the East End just as she did. And she had lifted her nose in a sneer as Dickie had brought her a drink, which was something they called cider cup and was perfectly frightful, and he had gone off in a huff again.

She had ostentatiously left her glass of cider cup on a table after sipping it and discovering it tasted as dull as it looked – all fruit juice and sugar – and making a face, and been glad rather than embarrassed when she realized that the hostess – a much too large woman in gold fringing whose insipid daughter, it seemed, was having an insipid birthday – had seen her distaste. Serve her right, she had thought furiously, and wandered off to see who else there was to talk to. She certainly wasn't going to waste another moment on a creature like Dickie Tanden, that was for certain.

There had been one or two tolerable looking boys, she discovered at last, one of them rather dashing in a green brocade waistcoat under his evening coat, and she had watched him covertly for a while. He was smoking a cigarette through a long green holder and looked wonderfully bored. And then Chloe had seen her hostess throw him a look of suspicious dislike and that had settled it; he was the one for her to go for, though he wasn't perfect; really rather a make-do. First of all, he wasn't quite as bright as he was pretending to be; Chloe could see that, because there was an anxious look about his eyes and he was much too aware of the impression he was trying to make. Secondly, he lacked the true devil-may-care casualness that Chloe so adored in boys; but at least he was trying and making not too bad a fist of it, so she had gone over to him, swinging her hips a little so that the silver tissue of her frock moved sinuously against her legs and made her look very *femme fatale*, and said to him in the most bored voice she could muster, 'I say, what a ghastly affair this is, isn't it?'

'Ghastly,' the young man said at once and looked at her coolly; but not quite coolly enough. He was delighted she had spoken to him, Chloe could tell that, and at once that set him down another peg in her estimation. He should look really as though she had crawled out of a piece of cheese to be properly interesting. But, as she was quite sure after looking around at her fellow guests one more time, and seeing them giggling and carrying on like a bunch of twelve year olds at their first dance, there was no one any better. So she would have to make do with him, as she had thought.

'Shall you stay?' she said and didn't look at him, standing alongside and keeping her gaze firmly ahead and her face as bored as ever. But she could still see him perfectly well, without looking directly at him and she saw him flick a glance at her before trying to emulate her facial expression.

'Doubt it,' he drawled. 'You?'

'Couldn't bear it,' she said and gave a little catlike yawn. 'Too, too uninterestingly dreary.'

There was a little silence then and she wondered for a moment whether he really was too stupid after all to understand what was expected of him; but fortunately he spoke at last.

'Shall we toddle, then?' he said and she lifted one tired brow and favoured him with a look.

'Might as well,' she murmured and went drifting across the room to the hallway where coats had been left piled on an ottoman. She got a glimpse of Dickie standing leaning against the wall beside the table where the cider cup – ugh! – was being dispensed by a maid, and not even a manservant! What sort of party was this, for heaven's sake? – and stared at him until he tried a weak smile which she could magnificently ignore as she went out, her head high, to pick up her coat and go down the stairs as she trailed it negligently behind her. It was, she knew, a superb performance, and she could feel the young man who walked with equal *hauteur* beside her preening himself on having picked up so splendid a representative of the genus flapper all for himself.

He hailed a taxi as soon as they were out in Avenue Road, waving his glossy topper lazily and settled her in it and then said something unintelligible to the driver and came to sit beside her.

For the first time she had begun to feel a *frisson* of anxiety. He was, after all, a total stranger and what if she had misread the situation? Suppose he really were as

97

soigné and man-about-town as he seemed? Suppose he expected her to be as devil-may-care as flappers these days were supposed to be? She had slapped poor old Dickie's face quite hard for just trying to kiss her; suppose this rather large young man – as she now saw he was – tried to be even more fast?

But she need not have worried. He leaned back in his corner of the cab with the same bored expression on his face and his topper tipped over his nose and she pulled her snowy fur collar up to her own nose and snuggled into it, feeling safe. And then, as the cab wheeled and turned into Maida Vale to go rattling along towards Marble Arch and the West End, felt the time was reasonable for some comment.

'Where are we goin'?' she drawled, as easily as he had himself earlier.

'Mm? Oh, amusin' little place – rather new, don't you know? Only been open a few weeks. Quite wicked as night-clubs go – some gambling and so forth – run by a chap some friends of mine know – friends of friends and so forth – '

'New, you say?' She sounded bored still even though inside she was thrilled to the marrow. A new night-club? She had never yet been to a really wicked one. In fact she'd never been to a real one at all. Teddy and his crowd simply hadn't enough money, because they were at university, and though there were some cafés and restaurants where one could dance, a really wicked night-club would be an enormous adventure. Not that she would let the piece of elegance beside her know that, of course.

'What's it called?' she asked.

'Hmm? Oh, the Rat Trap. Tedious, I suppose, but you know how it is with these places. Such silly names – '

She had to gamble now. 'Mm, I can't say I've heard of it – '

'Well, as I say, madly new. Might take off, might not.

One never can tell. These places all get so boring after a while, don't they?'

'Oh, yes,' she said. 'Ghastly.'

'Mmm. Ghastly,' he echoed and from then on they sat in silence, each making sure the other was made as aware as possible of how sophisticated they were, and how hard to please and how anything but enthusiastic. To be enthusiastic about anything would be the utter dregs, of course.

It should have been all right, she thought now, looking round the dim room and glowering still. The place was a cellar, which was a good beginning, and there had actually been a sliding panel in the door which a man had opened to look at them through, just like in the films, and then he had unlocked it to let them in when her escort had said lazily, 'Roger Dennis, Member – '

Inside it had seemed hopeful at first. Smoky and agreeably noisy with a jazz band somewhere making a great deal of showy play with 'Honeysuckle Rose' on a saxophone a piano and drums and, she rather thought, a clarinet. When they had been led through the first of what turned out to be a network of small cellar rooms to the far one where the bar was she saw the band was made up entirely of black men, and had cheered up greatly. She had heard that all the best jazz was played by Americans, and the best of all by black Americans, and this was the first such band she had seen. Not that they seemed to be playing as well as some of her records sounded. However, there were two or three couples dancing in a desultory sort of fashion on the minute dance floor, which seemed positively crowded with them, but they weren't at all excited by the music either. They looked to be actually as bored as Chloe was pretending to be.

But it wasn't long before she was bored in all truth. Her escort brought her a drink – and very daringly she had ordered an Old Fashioned, thinking it sounded like an exciting sort of cocktail to be seen sipping – and they had sat side by side at the minuscule black glass table on matching glass stools, sipping and watching the band.

And that was all. Her escort went on smoking his cigarettes through his long holder, and went on looking wonderfully bored and dripping with fashionable ennui, but that was as far as it went. He said nothing at all, and only responded to her occasional sallies with a profound, 'Umm – yerss – ' and no more. Clearly he had used up all his conversational possibilities already and had nothing left.

And there she sat, bored and she could not deny, feeling a bit sick. The smokiness was beginning to be very disagreeable and the cocktail, which she had swallowed rather more swiftly than perhaps she should have done, combined with a total absence of any food since this morning – for she had been far too annoyed with Poppy and Goosey to gratify them by eating any lunch, let alone dinner – was beginning to have a nasty effect on her.

So nasty that after a while she got to her feet, still gamely playing the role of the madly bored fashionable creature, to go drifting off to the powder room. She found it – a rather dimly lit little hole in the wall of one of the cellars where there was just one lavatory, one wash basin, a flecked mirror, and nowhere to sit down at all.

But after a while of sitting perched on the lavatory and breathing deeply she began to feel a little better. She would go back to her escort, she decided, whoever he was – and maybe it would be an idea to get to know more about him than just his name, Roger Dennis – and make him buy her something to eat. A solid ham sandwich could do much to restore her.

But when she had returned to the table, still trailing her silver and fur coat, he had vanished, and she had sat down after staring at the space where he had been, and tried to pretend it didn't matter; that she was used to being on her own in night-clubs with names like The Rat Trap and wasn't at all put out when people stared at her. Anyway, she told herself, he'll be back soon. Probably went to his own version of the powder room –

But he didn't come back, and she sat there getting angrier and angrier and glowering more and more, not caring at all any more what people might think. How dare this hateful boy do such a thing to her? To bring her here and dump her – it was too bad of him!

And she felt a little worm of anxiety crawl in her belly as she wondered how she was to get home. All she had in her little silver beaded bag was a threepenny bit, in case she had to leave a tip in the powder room (which she hadn't left, of course, since there was no attendant there to leave it for), her compact and lipstick and her front door key. She had fetched no money, because she had never dreamed she would need it. Just as boys always took one out, so they always took one home again. But she had left reliable boring old Dickie at that horrid party in St John's Wood and all this was his fault for taking her somewhere so absolutely foul – and there was no guarantee that Roger Dennis would take her home. After all, he had abandoned her already, and her eyes in spite of herself began to fill with tears. It was getting dreadfully late – well past twelve – and she really was awfully tired. It had been, after all, a horrid day and horrid days always left one feeling positively wrung out –

Someone slid into the seat adjoining and she stiffened. He'd come back. The hateful wretch had come back and she sat there staring ahead of her at the jazz band, which had now launched itself into a soulful rendering of 'Ill Wind', a melody that at the best of times made her feel rather doleful, trying to plan what she would say to him. Bored unawareness of the fact he had been away at all? Anger at being abandoned and a sharp telling-off? Or even – and it was a measure of her fatigue that she considered it – a tearful announcement that she was miserable and wanted to be taken home at once.

He said nothing and she took a deep breath, opting for the first of her list of possible choices. Bored unawareness that he had been away, that was the ticket, and she said in the slowest drawl she could manage, 'I think a ham sandwich would be useful. Do get me one – '

And then turned her head to look at him. But it wasn't him and she sat there actually feeling her eyes widen, aware of the fact that the pupils were enlarging as she stared.

He really was, she thought, as she felt her chest tighten with the excitement of it, the most incredibly good-looking boy she had ever seen. No, not a boy. A man. This wasn't the pale imitation of sophisticated worldliness she had thought she was with. This was the real, the unmistakeable, original article. The sleek hair, the long lashed dark eyes, the perfect skin (Roger Dennis, she had noticed, had a few acne scars across his forehead), the chin with its cleft and the hint of a dimple at the corner of the perfectly modelled mouth – she caught her breath and said, without any artifice at all, 'Oh! Hello!'

'I've been watching you,' he said and his voice brought her back a little closer to earth. Not exactly the voice she would have expected to emerge from those chiselled lips; it had a nasal quality and a decided London twang to it that in another man she would have found a complete negation of all his other qualities. But in this one it was not important. It was just part of him and did not detract at all from his beauty.

And again all she could say was, 'Oh!'

'You really do it awfully well,' he said, and already it seemed to her that his London accent was less obvious.

He was drawling as nicely as any one of her friends did.

'Do what?'

'Look as though everything beneath your pretty little nose smells quite Godawful. Real stinkers everywhere, according to your nose.'

'Really?' She was beginning to revive her defences. 'Perhaps that is because this place makes me aware of it. It really is a frightful dump, isn't it?'

'Oh, do you think so? I'm rather pleased with it. You should have seen it last month before I opened it.'

'Before – ' she managed.

'Oh yes,' he said and smiled, the most devastatingly wonderful smile she could ever remember seeing on any man's face. 'It's mine. A poor thing, I know, but it'll get better. You just watch me. This is just for openers – '

'Openers,' she said.

'American, ducky. You must forgive me if I sound American sometimes. I used to live there – '

At once his voice seemed to her to be exciting and interesting and not at all *déclassé*. It wasn't a London twang after all; this was the real thing, an American, and she opened her eyes even wider to look even more closely. She had read about such men in the papers and of course had seen them on the films, lovely creatures who lived outrageous lives in extraordinary places and with extraordinary people. To hear one actually speak was really very exciting.

'Did you? Where?'

'Baltimore,' he said and smiled again his heartrending smile. 'And then the Rock – '

'The Rock?' she said, puzzled.

'Manhattan. The only place to be. Not bad here though. I'm sorry you don't like my place – '

'I'm sorry.' She was mortified. It was after all a wonderful place. 'I didn't mean it – just being – you know – '

He laughed then. 'I know. Just being madly *sophistiqué* – too too boring, eh ducks? Well, that's all very well for those who don't know how to do better. Listen, you said you wanted a sandwich, hmm?'

It didn't matter at all any more. She felt wonderful now and not a bit sick and not a bit hungry. But she knew better than to say so.

'Please,' she said. 'I haven't eaten all day and if I have any more of this without something I'm liable to be – well, it won't be nice.'

'It's my guess it would be lovely,' he said and leaned forwards and took her hand from its resting place on the table and squeezed it hard and it was as though he had taken her heart in that hand and squeezed it. She could hardly breathe with the wonder of it.

He got to his feet and because he did not let go of her hand, she had to do the same. 'Come on,' he said. 'Come and see the real part of the club. I agree with you about it here. Madly dreary. But there's more than this, you know. Much more. I'll show you and give you your sandwich – lobster suit you? Good – and then perhaps you'll see why The Rat Trap is a good place to be after all.'

And he led her away, pulling on her hand, towards the dark place behind the band and she followed him willingly. The day was turning out to be anything but miserable after all.

8

Until then Chloe had thought that she was in the very end
room of the network of cellars that was The Rat Trap
Club, but now, as her eyes became accustomed to the
gloom, she realized that the place was far more extensive.
He led her through a small corridor and pushed on a door
at the end and after a moment it opened and she followed
him, blinking a little at the brightness, into a sizeable
room beyond.

Here the atmosphere was quite different. There were
still the black glass tables and stools around the edge of
the room but the overhead lights were much brighter,
there was a black glass piano providing the only music –
in agreeable contrast to the wail of the jazz band outside
– the floor was heavily carpeted and the walls panelled in
blonde wood. But above all, in the middle were four large
tables covered in green baize and one of them was fitted
with a roulette wheel. Chloe knew that was what it was,
for she had seen pictures of the Season at Monte Carlo in
her illustrated magazines, but this was the first time she
had ever seen a real one. And she caught her breath as she
looked at it.

'I'm treating you as a very special person,' he
murmured in her ear as she stood and stared. 'This isn't
precisely legal, you understand me? I'm trusting you – '

'Trusting me to what?' she breathed, still watching the
table with the roulette wheel. There were half a dozen
people sitting round it on low stools, and a tall man was

standing behind it spinning it and the clack of the little white ball that he threw in it made an agreeable sound. The patterns of numbers and colours on the green baize fascinated her too and she wanted to go closer to look.

'To stay shtoom,' he said and then grinned as she turned startled eyes on him. 'To keep quiet,' he amended. 'To say nothing to anyone about my little secret playground.'

'Of course not,' she said and looked even more eagerly around again, all pretence of bored sophistication quite gone. 'What's happening over there?'

'That's blackjack,' he said, indicating one table. 'And that's *chemin de fer*,' pointing to another. 'And the last one – I'm very proud of that. I dare say there isn't another like it in all London. Craps, direct from America.' And he grinned at her and she felt herself go a little dizzy at the effect that the row of gleaming white teeth had on her.

'Craps?' she repeated, slightly dazed.

'Dice. A simple and very fast game involving dice. Now, what will you do? Would you like to play? I'll order a drink and a sandwich for you at the table. Just say which you – '

She looked back at the tables. 'Play?' she said. 'But isn't it with money?'

He laughed with real delight at that. 'Bless the little duck. Of course it's with money! What'd be the point if it wasn't? This is gambling, sweetie, wicked old gambling! Will you play?'

She felt the tide of red slide up her face as she remembered the contents of her bag. A threepenny bit wouldn't be of much use, she imagined. She hadn't even the price of her taxi home –

'Uh – well, I can't,' she blurted, too put out to stop in time to concoct a face-saving excuse. 'I've no money with me – '

'And quite right too,' he said approvingly. 'A princess like you shouldn't ever carry money, believe me – listen, let me stake you, hmm? A few chips – hold on – ' And he patted her arm and went across to the far side of the room where she saw for the first time that there was a little grille in the corner and a discreet sign above it that read 'Cashier'.

She watched him and took a deep breath. This really was the most extraordinary thing that had ever happened to her; to start the evening being locked in and end it in a gambling den; too too delicious.

'Oh, hello! a voice drawled beside her. 'How did you find me? I was just about to toddle back to you, actually – '

She turned her head and saw Roger Dennis peering down at her over the smoke curling up from his long cigarette holder and she stared at him as though she'd never seen him before; and indeed she hadn't really looked at him properly until now. She saw a long thin face that in this bright light looked far less appetizing than it had in the badly lit St John's Wood drawing room or outside in the almost dark bar. There were more acne scars than she had at first noticed, and it was clear he was very young, not much older than she was herself really. His green waistcoat looked rather childish now, not at all dramatic, and the cigarette holder was a stupid toy and not in the least glamorous. And she tilted her nose and said coolly, 'Were you? I wonder why you bother.'

'Well, I mean, damn it all, I brought you here, what? But when you sloped off as you did for a while I thought – just pop in here, see what's what, don't you know. Not bad, eh? My brother brought me to The Rat Trap first. He's rather long in the tooth, of course, so it's easier for him to join jolly places. But then he went off to work in Malaya so he passed on his membership to me. Quite ripping, really, isn't it?'

'Is it?' she said coldly, and flicked her eyes away to

look at the back of the man still standing at the small grille.

'Oh, yes, frightfully ripping. But pricey, mind you.' He gave a sudden high-pitched giggle. 'I mean, lost a packet I did. Three pounds right down the old drain. Too frightful – '

'Then you'd better toddle off home, hadn't you?' Chloe said icily and flicked one more glance at him, full of scorn this time. 'I'd hate to be the cause of any greater waste of your money – ' And she went sauntering off towards her new friend, who was now coming back towards her across the heavy carpet.

'But, here, I say – ' Roger breathed but she ignored him, and smiled brilliantly at the other.

He smiled easily back and held out a hand. 'Here, take these,' he said and she held out one hand obediently and he put into it a collection of large coloured celluloid counters which made her laugh, for they looked for all the world like the tiddly winks she had used to play with when she was small, only they were much larger.

'What fun!' she cried. 'So pretty – '

'Twenty five pounds worth,' he said expansively. 'See? These are worth pounds and these are ten shillings and these are a dollar – five shillings to you. Now come along and I'll show you what you do. Roulette, I think, for a starter like you – ' And he tucked his hand into her elbow, where the touch of his warmth against her bare skin made her want to shiver, and led her towards the central table.

'Here, I say – ' Roger said again, but she waved one dismissive hand at him over her shoulder, not even bothering to turn round, and her companion looked at him quizzically but said nothing. And together they went to the roulette table, leaving Roger standing disconsolate and alone.

She forgot about him completely in the next blissful

half hour. Her new friend leaned over her and showed her what to do, and she wasn't sure what was the most exciting; his warm breath on her bare shoulder and sometimes on her cheek, or the way the game worked out. All she had to do was choose numbers and colours, and where she would put her chips, as he told her the counters were called. Sometimes she put one on just the centre of a number but, more often, she chose to put it on the lines that defined the spaces so that she stood to win something from two or four possible numbers; and using this method, in which he schooled her carefully, the tall thin man with the rake and the little white ball began to push extra counters towards her; the very small number she had had to start with (and it amazed her that they should be worth twenty five pounds for, extravagant though she was, even she could not imagine gambling that vast sum so easily) began to grow. More and more of the red chips and then the striped blue ones came to build up in a little heap in front of her and she laughed delightedly at each call of the results. The sandwich and her drink that had been ordered for her remained untouched at her side as a few more people came drifting over to watch what was going on.

'Beginner's luck,' someone said behind her and she lifted her chin and laughed aloud, a peal of giggles which she knew sounded childish, but didn't care; not with all those counters in front of her. If the first had been worth twenty five pounds, these must be worth – well, hundreds, she told herself gleefully.

She turned her flushed face to her companion and said breathlessly, 'Have I won lots?'

'Lots,' he said solemnly and then laughed at her eagerness. 'Do you want to keep it or do you want to go on?'

'Oh, go on, of course!' she cried.

'I wouldn't, my dear.' A woman in a rather grubby

blue dress leaned over her bringing with her a miasma of gin and chypre perfume and unwashed body. 'You'll lose the lot. Get out now while you're doing so well. Beginner's luck needs to be made the best of – eh, Bernie?' And she laughed up at Chloe's companion and shoved at him with one plump shoulder.

'You could be right,' he said after a moment, and then smiled at Chloe. 'My – ah – friend, Mrs Argent here thinks I'll encourage you to go on and lose it all again because I'm the owner and therefore stand to lose if you win. She doesn't know me very well, my dear. Stop now. We shall go and eat your sandwich and drink your drink while I cash in for you. There'll be other times to play again – ' And he took her elbow and lifted her from her seat so firmly that she could not resist him.

'Here's what you do,' he said then and took one of her counters and tossed it across the table to the tall thin man, who nodded without for a moment smiling or looking up and then murmured, '*Faites vos jeux*' as he threw the ball back into the wheel again.

Chloe allowed herself to be led to a table and then sat while he went to collect her money for her.

'I shan't be long,' he promised. 'Eat your sandwich – ' and she did, almost gobbling it, for it was very delicious with a great deal of lobster mayonnaise on it, and she was, she now realized, extremely empty.

When he came back he was smiling widely and he sat down beside her and lifted his chin at her, holding out his closed fists invitingly. She looked up at him, and then held out one hand, but he shook his head and nodded at the other hand, so she held out both, with the fingers cupped, and he reached forwards and opened his own fists over them.

And left her gasping. For there in her grasp was a little wad of five pound notes, white and crisp, as well as some one pounds and ten shilling notes, and she put it all down on the table and counted it, her fingers shaking a little with excitement.

'Oh my goodness,' she said, and looked up at him in awe. 'There's ninety-seven pounds and ten shillings here -

'So there is,' he said and laughed. 'Fun, hmm?'

'Oh, wonderful! Please, when can I do it again?'

He shook his head. 'Don't think you always win, you know. You heard that old bat Mrs Argent. She's left a lot of her money here, one way and another. Some of that probably started out in her purse.' And he nodded at the money that Chloe was now counting again, not able to believe what was there.

'Oh, I won't lose!' she said and giggled. 'Not with someone like you to teach me.'

'Never you think it,' he said, and now his face was quite straight. 'Even I can lose. That's why I don't play myself no more – '

'You don't? But how can you bear not to?' she cried, looking over at the now crowded roulette table. More and more people had come drifting in through the anonymous door in the corner that led to the bar and the jazz band.

'Because I'm on the permanently winning side now. It's my place, ducks. I'm the bank. I win when everyone else loses, and I make sure I'm a winner. I just wanted you to have a little fun, that's all. I like fun and I can always tell when I meet someone else who does, too.' And he leaned a little closer towards her.

She felt herself go red as for the first time a tiny warning bell rang somewhere deep inside her head. Young as she was, and as carefully protected as her stepmother tried to make sure she was, Chloe was a child of her times. She sat and giggled and gossiped with her girlfriends, especially Mary Challoner, often enough and daringly enough to know perfectly well that there were men around who were a danger to young girls, men who were not unwilling to make what they could of a silly one, and leave her high and dry. They all remembered Susan Gore-Maddern with whom they'd been at school, and how she'd got herself involved with some old friend of her brother's who turned out to be a bounder and no good to anyone. She had quietly disappeared into the country and no one ever talked about her any more. But they all knew pretty shrewdly what had happened to her.

And now here was Chloe in a night-club where she had been illegally gambling, with a man she didn't know who had made a point of giving her a great deal of money. Yes, she'd won it, but after all he'd given her the money to gamble with in the first place, so it really wasn't her winnings. And maybe he'd want something back for it –

She looked at the white fivers in her hand and then, unwillingly, held it all out to him.

'I can't,' she said in a small voice. 'I can't take this. It was super fun winning, really it was, but I must give it to you. It's yours. It was your money to start with so the winnings are yours too – '

He closed his hand warmly over hers. 'I wouldn't hear of it,' he said softly. 'It's yours. *You* won it – '

'No,' she said and tried to pull her hand away, leaving the cash behind. 'It really wouldn't be right – '

'Your Mummy wouldn't like it – ' he said and looked at her rather mockingly and she reddened again at the hint of scorn in his voice.

'It's nothing to do with – I haven't got such a – I mean, there's only my stepmother and I don't give a fig for her! It's not that – it wouldn't be right – '

'Then give it to charity,' he said apparently off-handedly, and with one swift movement took the money from her hand and reached for her silver bag which was lying on the table beside her crumb-filled plate.

She tried to reach out and stop him but she couldn't, for he turned his body half away from her, grinning at her over his shoulder and opened her bag, and shook out the contents on to the table. Then he shoved the money in firmly and began to put the other things back on top of it. But he stopped as he reached the powder compact, for when he picked it up it glinted in the bright light and he saw it more clearly and then bent his head to peer at it.

'This is pretty,' he said after a moment. 'A birthday present, I see.'

'Yes,' she said, a little sulkily, not liking the way he had taken over so firmly. 'Look, I really can't take that – '

'A pretty name,' he said and looked at her. 'Chloe Bradman. Whose name is this? The one who gave it to you?'

'You can see it for yourself,' Chloe said crossly and again reached for her property but he shook his head and pulled it away.

'Tell me and then I'll think again about the money,' he said. 'Who is this Poppy?'

'My stepmother,' Chloe said sulkily. 'As if it mattered!'

'Everything about you matters, my pretty little duck,' he said and slowly put her bag down on the table. 'Everything.'

'Why?'

'Because you're so – pretty. And interesting. Madly interesting – ' And he bent his head a little and gave her a sideways little grin that once again made her dizzy. Somewhere deep inside she knew that he had done it deliberately, that he was well aware that he was turning on his charm. Who, after all should know better than Chloe, who was so very good at doing that sort of thing herself. But deliberate or not, it didn't matter. He made her feel wonderful, and especially so now as he pushed her bag towards her.

'Here you are, ducky. Do what you like with it.'

She smiled at him gratefully. 'I'm so glad – you do

understand, don't you? It really wouldn't be – well, I couldn't – ' And she shook out the bag's contents again and picked up the money and handed it back to him and then hesitated.

'Actually, could I keep one of the ten shilling notes? I – well, to be perfectly honest, I've no more than a three-penny bit with me and that stupid creature who brought me here has gone and I'm not sure how to get home. I need the taxi fare. I'll put the change in the charity box. How would that be?'

'That would be wonderful,' he said solemnly and held out his hand and she gave him the money, except for one crumpled ten shilling note, and he smiled and bent his head in a mock salute and took it, tucking it into a wallet which he pulled from his breast pocket.

'There,' he said lightly. 'Honour is satisfied, Miss Bradman, Miss Chloe Bradman of the devastating eyes and mysterious hair. What are you? A blonde or brunette or a redhead? That silver cap is quite devastating but very mysterious.'

She dimpled at him. 'I don't think I shall tell you,' she said and bent her head to look down at her fingers on her bag. This was better; this was the sort of badinage she could understand and could cope with easily.

'No? Why not? To tease me?' He understood the game as well as she did. 'It's too cruel of you to be so very mysterious.'

'You're just as mysterious as I am,' she said and threw him a challenging stare. 'I don't even know your name, though you know mine. Except for Bernie, of course.'

He was silent for a moment, sitting looking at her with a slightly calculating look on his face and she stared, wide-eyed with knowing innocence, and then he smiled.

'You really are a naughty child, aren't you?' he said. 'Full of wickedness – '

'As full as an egg is of meat,' she said promptly,

quoting one of Goosey's favourite sayings. 'But don't change the subject. I still don't know your name.'

'Bernie,' he said. 'You heard what Mrs Argent called me.'

'It's an odd name,' she said.

'I'm an odd person.' He laughed. 'It's an American name, okay? Does that help? An American nickname – '

'You mean it isn't your real name?'

'Who knows what is real?' he declaimed and threw out one hand in mock heroics. 'I answer when people say Bernie. What could be more real than that?'

'Well, all right. So it's Bernie. Bernie what?'

'Ah,' he said and got to his feet and held out both hands towards her invitingly. 'That would be telling, wouldn't it? Come along, you pretty little object. It's time you went home.'

'I say, don't treat me like a child!' she protested, but rather liking his masterful way all the same. 'I'll go home when I'm ready.'

'And you're ready now.' He leaned forwards and took her hand from the table and pulled her easily to her feet. 'It's almost half past one, you wicked creature. Little ducks should be safe in their home ponds well before that, or they wake up looking like scrawny old hens and that'd be a tragedy, hmm?'

She looked horrified. 'Never! It can't be so late – '

'It is,' he assured her. 'Will the – ah – stepmother, the wicked old stepmother, be waiting up with a whip to punish you?' His tone was light but there was real curiosity in it.

'Not at all,' she said shortly. 'I do as I please and never mind her!' But she was uneasy all the same. She had never been out quite so late before and it could take a long time to get home. Maybe someone had woken and discovered she had gone. Maybe there was already a hue and cry out for her –

She didn't argue any more as he led her out to the now packed night-club. It was indeed late and though the evening had been rather marvellous it was time to end it. And she sighed and looked up at him and said almost timidly, 'Shall I – I mean, could I – '

'Play the wheel again?' He smiled down at her. 'Why not? But I leave it to you. Just call me on this number.' And he inserted his thumb and forefinger into his breast pocket and brought out a small square of pasteboard to give her – and then with a second thought pulled it back and took out a fountain pen and scribbled hard with it on the square before this time putting it into her hand.

'Call me any time. And then we'll make plans, hmm? But don't take too long to call me. Because I'll come and find you if you don't.'

She shivered a little, rather more excited than scared, but a little of that too. 'You can't. You won't know where to find me.'

'Oh, Miss Chloe Bradman, never think it. There isn't much that Bernie can't do, believe me! Whatever he wants, he gets. You'll see – '

And he took her out into the dark silent street and whistled loudly and a taxi appeared, it seemed almost from nowhere, and he handed her into it.

'Good night,' he said solemnly and then leaned forwards through the open window, and very swiftly and gently kissed her cheek and then lifted one hand and turned and disappeared again into the door of his club, which closed behind him with a little snap.

She was almost home after giving the driver the address, sitting in the corner of the cab in a sort of dream, before she remembered to look at the pasteboard he had given her, which was still clutched in one hand. She peered at it in the dim light of the passing street lamps and saw that he had scratched out the surname. It just read 'Bernie' and then 'The Rat Trap, Haunch of

Venison Yard, London W1.' And a Mayfair phone number.

And then she hugged herself with delight. What a marvellous adventure! What a super evening! Everything about this extraordinary day had turned out all right after all. Or as far as she could tell – because she still wasn't home. And there was always what people at home did and thought to worry about.

9

Poppy got home just after six, which was rather earlier than usual and opened the front door and let herself in gratefully. It had been a hectic day, with the restaurant jam-packed with people celebrating the fact that the strike was over, and the kitchens in an uproar because of the sudden upsurge in orders for the sell-outs once the news flashed around London that life was to get back to normal – or normal for everyone but the miners, who were still grimly holding out. Poppy had heard the broadcasts on Jessie's fancy new wireless set and felt a great wash of anger on their behalf. It was too bad, the way they had been let down by their own fellow workers, she thought furiously and almost opened her mouth to say so. And then had closed it again, for Jessie, for all her lack of snobbery – the emotion which it seemed to Poppy fired most people who expressed opinions against the strikers – could be very scathing about anyone who made things difficult for her business. It really wasn't worth getting into a political argument with her. Poppy had simply put her head down and got on with work, gloomily certain that she would have to stay until all hours to get things sorted out.

But in the event, they had managed to catch up very well. The customers had all been so good-natured and un-demanding that there had been none of the all too common episodes of arguments over bills (Poppy sometimes thought sourly that arguing about paying a bill after you've eaten your head off was a popular East End sport) and everyone on the staff had beavered away cheerfully. So, by five thirty she had been able to close her account books, snap the cashbox shut and go home.

And there was no need to be apprehensive about home either, she had thought with a sense of real contentment as she sat in the crowded underground train that swayed noisily through the darkness towards the West. Chloe had been really remarkably sweet this past week. Poppy had been sure she would sulk for weeks, and also be rebellious, but after that day when she had fallen foul of the police at Marble Arch, she had been a perfect lamb. She had come down to breakfast, in fact, the following morning, looking rather wan and with violet shadows under her eyes but at least had joined the family table, which was rare in itself, and had told Poppy gruffly that she hadn't meant to cause such a fuss the day before, which for her represented the most handsome, indeed grovelling, of apologies. And ever since had been, as Goosey also marvelled, as good as gold.

'Sat and snoozed in the drawing room, Miss Poppy, she did, most of the day,' Goosey had reported when Poppy returned home that evening, 'and then sat with me and read to me from the picture papers while I cleaned the silver. Really sweet, she was. I told you she meant no harm, now didn't I?'

'Yes, Goosey,' Poppy had said and smiled, so glad to be grateful for Chloe's sudden attack of biddableness, that she didn't mind Goosey taking sides quite so blatantly. And ever since, life in Norland Square had been very peaceful. Chloe hadn't nagged to go out, and had seemed content to have her friends to visit, and by the end of that week Poppy had happily lifted her ban. So Chloe had gone buzzing about in her usual way, shopping madly for even more evening dresses on the Saturday, and showing them off to Robin and Goosey and Poppy with enormous glee (and though Poppy had thought privately that she was being outrageously extravagant, she had wisely bitten her tongue; it was Chloe's own money after all) and going off to a party at her friend Mary Challoner's house on the Sunday in a high good humour. Yesterday she had still been cheerful and friendly, even reading a story to Robin at bedtime, which she rarely did. Could it be that Chloe was undergoing a change of heart? Could she actually be growing up at last and starting to find life at home less chafing as a result? Poppy felt hope stir in her, for there was no doubt that of all her problems Chloe was the most difficult. It would be wonderful to think that life could go on as tranquilly as it had this past week.

She bathed and changed as usual, and then went to find the rest of the family in the kitchen, but only Goosey and Robin were there, and Poppy stood for a moment at the top of the stairs looking down on her daughter's bent head as she sat at the table, busily drawing. Lately all she had drawn had been buildings; houses and shops and churches, and Poppy was entranced by her work; it looked like a child's work, of course, but was remarkably detailed and real for someone who wouldn't be seven for another five weeks (and really, Poppy thought, I must do something about her birthday party soon) and showed a fine sense of balance. She'll do well in the world one day, she thought contentedly and came downstairs.

Robin lifted her head and saw her and smiled widely at her mother and Poppy's heart melted, for she'd lost another tooth and the gappy grin was very endearing.

'Hello, Mummy! The tooth fairy'll have to come tonight!' she carolled and then tilted her head on one side and looked at her mother consideringly. 'I like your dress,' she said then. 'It looks like melted jelly. Lovely.'

Poppy laughed and looked down at herself. She was

wearing a long sleeved robe in very fine wool jersey in dark shades of blurred red, blue and green. Beneath a deep square neckline it was held in snugly at the waist with a wide belt, and fell in soft pleats to her feet. It was wonderfully comfortable as well as pretty and Poppy had been delighted with it when Jessie had given it to her. Jessie had several friends who were dressmakers and was much given to buying lengths of fabric that caught her eye and having them made up for Poppy, without even consulting her. Poppy had tried to protest at first, but had long ago given up doing so, simply accepting the generous gifts with a smile and hug. It gave Jessie so much more pleasure to give than it gave Poppy discomfort to accept that she had to be generous in her own way, and bend gracefully.

Now she smiled at Robin and said easily, 'I'm glad you like it. Not too dark?'

'Nice dark,' Robin said after another considering moment. 'Like under a tree when the sun's ever so bright,' and Poppy marvelled not for the first time at the imagery that this child of hers could use.

'Hello, Goosey,' she said then, and went over to peer over the old woman's shoulder at the pot she was stirring on the stove. 'What's for supper?'

'Kedgeree,' Goosey said crossly and Poppy took a deep breath of the savour of the dish; smoked haddock and butter and mixed curry spices of all sorts, and rice coloured a rich yellow by the turmeric.

'Lovely,' she said. 'You like it too, don't you, Robin?'

Robin was back at her drawing and vouchsafed only a vague 'mmm' and Goosey picked up the pan and slapped it down on the top of the range and began to spoon the steaming mixture into a wide earthenware dish.

'And so does Chloe,' Poppy went on, wondering what had upset Goosey this evening. A spat with the butcher or the fishmonger? Or was it the baker's boy being his usual cheeky self? Goosey had a great gift for taking umbrage with such visitors. 'You'll be popular tonight.'

'That's as may be,' Goosey grunted and pushed her dish of kedgeree into the warming oven to keep hot as she turned her attention to the pan of clear vegetable broth that was clearly designed to be the first course of their supper. 'I dare say them as eats it'll enjoy it well enough.'

Robin lifted her head then and caught Poppy's eye and lifted her brows at her with such a comical imitation of an adult making an unspoken comment that Poppy choked with a little burst of suppressed laughter.

'I'm sure we all will, Goosey,' she said heartily, much as she would to encourage a child even younger than Robin. There were times, she thought, when Goosey behaved in a positively infantlike way.

'You will and Miss Robin will, no doubt,' Goosey said and slammed the soup pan down so that it splashed and some of the contents hissed softly on the hot metal of the range. 'But not Miss Chloe, oh dear me no – '

Poppy's heart seemed literally to sink, so sharp was the internal sensation the words gave her.

'Oh?' she said guardedly after a moment. 'Why not?'

'On account she ain't here,' Goosey snapped. 'On account she went marching out of here dressed up like a – well, far be it for me to use the words what come into my mind but I didn't like the way she was dressed – and painted – and so I tell you. Downright common, it was. And no supper she says, cool as you please, not nothing. She's off to her friend's house, she says, and then she's going to a party, she says, and when I asks her where she'd go dressed in such a fashion she got very nasty indeed, very nasty – '

Goosey lifted her head then from her soup pan and Poppy saw the tears in the milky blue eyes and felt a great surge of fury at Chloe. Unkind as were the things she did to Poppy and Robin, when she felt in that sort of mood,

122

they were nothing like as cruel as the things she did to Goosey who adored her so, and who had looked after her from her birth. No one, Poppy thought wrathfully, has the right to treat anyone as that child treats Goosey. And here was I thinking she'd changed; more fool me!

'Oh, Goosey,' she said now. 'I am sorry. But I've told you before, my dear – you really shouldn't let her get at you this way. She's just a silly thoughtless child, no more, and means no harm I'm sure. She just doesn't think – '

'I'm a child and I'm never so rude to Goosey,' Robin said complacently from the table and Poppy looked at her and raised one eyebrow.

'We'll have no pertness from you, young lady!' she said firmly and quelled Robin with a look. 'This is not a matter with which you need concern yourself.'

Robin looked mulish. 'Why not? My friend Molly talks all the time about *her* sister. Why can't I?'

'Because in this instance it is none of your business,' Poppy said firmly. 'So we'll have no crowing or other forms of meddling, if you don't mind, miss! Now, go away and put away your drawing things for now, and we'll have supper. Wash your hands and you can come and help set the table – ' And as Robin went, not a little sulkily, Poppy turned back to Goosey.

'My dear, really you mustn't upset yourself. You must understand that she likes the modern fashions. I agree, some of them are a bit extreme, but it's only fashion. And you can't expect a young girl not to enjoy it, if she can – '

Goosey sniffed richly. 'Well, that's as may be. All I know is that seeing a respectably reared young lady in a dress what shows as much of her shoulders and bust as does that new lilac chiffon of hers, and with her stockings rolled to the knees in that style so anyone can see her legs above, well it's disgusting if you ask me, and so I told her. Someone has to. You're too easy on her, Mrs Poppy, and so I tell you to your face. She needs a firm hand, does Miss Chloe – '

Poppy sighed. They had had this discussion before, and now she launched herself patiently yet again into an account of her reasoning. 'Goosey, dear, she is an intelligent and spirited girl. You only make her resentful and difficult when you try to force her. She has to be coaxed and gentled along. I see no reason to make a great fuss over what she wears even if I do think she uses more powder and rouge than she needs, because like clothes, such matters are not important enough to make a fuss over. If I say, "no" to everything she pays no attention when I say, "no" for good reason. Look at what happened over that affair with the policeman! I put my foot down then, didn't I? And didn't it work? She's been perfectly charming this past week – '

'Hmmph,' Goosey said and threw the cloth on the table to start setting it for supper. 'Until now – '

And Poppy said no more. It was true of course. No matter what technique she used, whether the firm hands or the softly-softly-catchee-monkey approach she had always believed to be better, the result was the same. Chloe set the household on its ears.

They ate supper in silence and then it was Robin's turn to flounce a little as she went off to bed, clearly still annoyed with her mother for chiding her over her comments about Chloe, and Poppy thought, as she went up to bid her goodnight and to make her peace with her, how typical it was of Chloe to set everyone else in the house at each other's ears over her. If only they could all face her silliness with equanimity, how much more agreeable it would be!

Goosey went early to bed, too, as she so often did these days. Poppy had given her her own wireless set for Christmas and she liked nothing better than to arrange herself in bed against her piles of pillows, wrapped in her

124

old baby blue shawl and with her thin grey hair in tidy plaits over her shoulders, to listen agog to the dance music from the Savoy Hotel, humming along tunelessly as she did so. She'd be all right by morning, Poppy told herself as she made her way back to the drawing-room, after settling Robin with a kiss and receiving a forgiving hug in return so that they were friends again. We all will be, and Chloe will come home in the small hours and sleep tomorrow morning away as usual and never know what a pest she has been. I wish, oh how I wish, I had the answer to Chloe!

But she didn't, and there was no point, she told herself sensibly, in sitting here and thinking about her. No doubt they would come to words again sometime soon; that much was inevitable. But tonight all was peaceful and she would enjoy it. And she sat in her deep sofa, listening to the house settle down about her with the odd creak and cracks of old wood, while outside the sky was a deep rich blue, a springlike blue that was mirrored, she told herself, in her warm new robe. And she ran her fingers down one of the rich folds and thought kindly of Jessie. It was a much more unusual garment than she would have chosen for herself, with her own rather spartan taste, but she had to admit she liked it. It made her feel soft and vulnerable in a way that made a change from feeling as she normally had to, firm and resilient and ever capable.

It would be nice, she told herself, dreamily staring into the fire, to have someone else to be all those sensible things for me. To be able to be as other women are and sit on a cushion and sew a fine seam and feed upon strawberries, sugar and cream, while another person was strong and hard-working for her and for her children. A man who would know when she was tired without having to be told and who would come and sit with her and hold her safe and warm and –

She sat up a little more upright. Such silly notions to

get into her head! It was all Jessie's fault really. She had started again today about Poppy's lonely life, as she was pleased to call it ('And me with three people in the household, none of whom seem able to do anything properly unless I watch over them!' Poppy had said with some asperity), and need for more pleasures.

'There's any number of nice people comes here to the restaurant as'd be really glad to take you on the town, boobalah!' she had said. 'Go and see a picture maybe, or a revue at the theatre, have a bit of dinner somewhere West End and smart. Give you a chance to look over the opposition that would, ready for when we start our new place!' And Poppy glowered a little, for she had still not been able to make up her mind about that; and Jessie knew it and was turning the screws even more tightly with all her chatter.

No, she thought now, and reached for her book. She had bought Somerset Maugham's new one, *The Casuarina Tree*, for herself, for she did try, as much as she could with the limited time she had available, to keep up with the newest publications, and settled down to read. Maybe tonight she would be able to last half an hour or so before dozing off? It would be all too easy just to go to bed, even though it was not yet half past nine; but that way, she knew, lay real disaster. What would Jessie say to her then if she knew her evenings were so arid that all that offered was the loneliness of her sheets and pillows?

She read for a while as the fire flickered and murmured in the grate and had almost decided that this one was not for her, and not as interesting as his last one, *The Painted Veil*, when she heard a sound that made her raise her head sharply to listen hard. Surely that had been a rapping? And she sat very still with her head up, and her eyes closed as she concentrated. She had almost decided that it was just another part of the old house's night-time noises when she heard it again, and this time she got to her feet and went out of the drawing-room to stand at the head of the stairs and look down.

She could see the front door, with its coloured glass panels which looked very dark, for the hall light was burning and so blackened the outside sky, and she almost thought she could see a shadow against the panes. Was someone standing there and knocking? But who could be coming to the door at this time of night? And she slid her arms around herself in a hug, not liking to admit she was afraid. There were after all only two women and a small child in the house, with no men to take care of them. And there had been so many stories lately of ill-intentioned men breaking into well-off houses to rob them. Some of the papers this very day had thundered on about the lawlessness that followed uncontrolled strikes by the likes of selfish miners and that had made her angry and scornful; but now, standing looking down into her empty hallway and what seemed to be a shadow on the glass panes of her front door, her scorn seemed to melt away and leave only fear behind.

And then another possibility slid into her mind and that was almost worse; was this another policeman coming to tell her of yet more of Chloe's peccadilloes? She had got her little car back from the mechanic only yesterday after the last time she had damaged it so badly, just before the strike, and Poppy knew, from what Goosey had told her on the way to bed, that Chloe had taken it out tonight. Had she crashed again? Even hurt herself? And she felt the fear inside increase. Either this was a policeman, or she had let her imagination run away with her.

And then she was sure she had not imagined the figure behind the glass, because whoever it was was suddenly illuminated in a great lift of light and she realized that the person had struck a match. She could see the glitter of the

127

brief flare outline a tall shape, clearly male, for it was bulky and wearing a man's hat, but equally clearly not a policeman, for there was no familiar helmet shape; and then the light flickered and died and all she could see again was the glass panels.

But now the bell pealed through the quiet house and she almost jumped and then realized what had happened. Whoever it was had struck the match to find the bell pull – which she had to admit was rather hidden by an overgrowth of ivy from the tub in the area creeping up the old bricks to the front door – which having been identified had been used. She could hear the bell pinging and jangling from below in the kitchen and wished she had closed the kitchen door when she had come up. If she had, the bell would have been muffled and disturbed no one. But as it was, it could be heard very clearly, and she lifted her head and stared up behind her, trying to strain to hear if Robin had been wakened by the unusual sound. It was true she no longer suffered her night terrors, but maybe they could be triggered again by this unexpected din. It was possible –

Once again the bell jangled, and now Poppy became angry. She didn't want to answer her door to a stranger. She wanted to run and hide away from whoever this intruder was; and she hated herself for her own timidity. To be so feeble – it was ridiculous. Why should she allow herself to be railroaded into terror just because she was a woman in charge of a household and had no man to help her, and because silly newspapers spread fear and loathing of harmless miners? It was too bad; and she took hold of her anger and relished it, turning it about in her mind and making it grow for all the world like yeasty dough, and redirecting it so that instead of being angry with herself she could wallow in anger at the man who stood at her door and made her feel so dreadful.

She marched downstairs and across the hall floor, her

slippers flapping softly on the parquet, and pulled at the door fastening and then, just before turning the knob prudently reached out and took from the hall hatstand her long umbrella. It was silly, really, and she knew it was, but it comforted her to have it firmly held in the hand that was hidden behind the door as she pulled it partly open and stood and peered out into the dark street beyond.

'Good evening.' The voice was low and somehow odd, and she struggled to place it, for there was a sound about it that she knew. Or did she? And then she thought – he's not English. She didn't know why she could be so sure from just hearing two words, but she knew it was so, and she pushed the door a little closer to the jamb, leaving only the smallest space out of which to peer. And behind the door her hand tightened on the umbrella.

'Who is that?' she said firmly and was furious because it came out as a frightened sort of bleat and she spoke again, even more firmly this time, and it came out in a snap. 'What do you want and who are you? Making such a noise so late – '

'I'm sorry,' the soft voice said and a hand went up in the darkness and the hat was removed from the shadowy head as she peered and tried to see more clearly. 'I really wouldn't bother you, but I'm looking for Mr and Mrs Bobby Bradman? I wonder if you can help me. I had the address, you see, but then I kinda – well, mislaid it, and I just had to rely on memory. If I have the wrong house, I'm very sorry – '

She stood there and stared out at the dark shape as memory pushed and jostled in her, shouting and jumping inside her head like an excited child. Once again she saw dark male figures outlined in brilliant light, just as this one had been by the struck match; but that had been far away in Verdun and the lights had been the coldness of Very lights.

And she pulled the door open more widely and stepped back a little so that her face could be seen more clearly in the lamplit hall and let go of the umbrella which clattered to the parquet behind the front door.

'Wow!' the man on the doorstep cried. 'I didn't forget! Well, would you believe it? I found you. If that doesn't beat all – I remembered! Poppy, how *are* you? Dear old Poppy. You look great, really great. More beautiful than ever. And old Bobby – how's old Bobby? Gosh, you'll never know how much I've looked forward to this moment! I've been thinking about it all the way over on the ship.'

And he stepped forwards and into the house and pushed the door closed behind him and stood there smiling down at her; and Poppy looked up into David Deveen's face and to her horror and eternal shame, burst into a flood of tears.

10

She would not have believed she could weep so much. It was as though she was crying properly for the first time for Bobby, now, seven years after his death; it was as though the long time of mourning had never happened, and the pain was as raw as on the day it had first been inflicted. She stood there in the hall, making no attempt to stop the tears – indeed, she could not have done so – with her hands clenched in front of her and her head bent and he stood there beside her with one arm across her shoulders simply holding her. He said nothing, made no sound of any kind, and for that she was deeply grateful. He did exactly what she needed, which was to provide a wall against which she could hurl her tide of grief and shock.

It came to an end at last, and she was in control again, or almost; just the occasional sob hiccuped out of her and she was able to lift both hands and with fingers spread wide wipe her wet cheeks with the palms. And then took a deep rather shaky breath.

'I do beg your pardon,' she said huskily. 'It was the shock, you see. I couldn't imagine who it was, and I was so afraid and then it was you – and then you spoke of Bobby.'

He let go of her shoulders then and stood looking down at her, and began to turn his hat between his hands, rhythmically. It was a soft and rather battered grey one, quite unlike any that Poppy had seen on men's heads in London and she stood and stared at it, not wanting to look into his face.

'Because I spoke of Bobby – ' he said carefully. 'I see. Does that mean that – ?'

There was a silence and then she said wearily. 'Yes. I'm sorry, David. Bobby died of flu, not long after the Armistice – just a few days later. I didn't write to you then – I was ill myself for a long time. And then – well, when I did write in the summer to tell you the news, my letter came back. It said on the envelope you'd gone away. And that was all – no new address.'

Now she did lift her head to look at him. His face was very still and she stared at it consideringly. Still the same face, really, of the cheerful funny man she had met so long ago when the battle of Verdun was raging and she had been at the hospital in Revigny where he had helped her find his friend Bobby, for whom she had been looking for so long. Still the face of the man who had helped her get Bobby out after he was gassed, and onto the troopship home to England.

Yet it was not the same at all. This face was thin where eight years ago it had been round, even rather plump. There were shadows under the eyes and in the temples and hard lines about the jaw and mouth she had not seen before. And yet, he remained the essence of the man she remembered, the bouncy American newspaper correspondent who had kept calm and so cheerful all through that dreadful bombardment, and with a sudden lift of her spirits she said, impulsively, 'Oh, David, it *is* good to see you!'

'It's – you'll never know how good it is to see you,' he said gravely and then smiled. And at once it was as though the past eight years had not happened. He was of course the happy person she remembered so gratefully. 'I was so sorry to lose touch. But I can explain why and give

you all the news, and perhaps you can give me yours.'
And he looked beyond her into the hall, consideringly,
and at once she was aware of her own social ineptitude
and became almost flustered.

'Oh, my dear, do come in and – come up to the
drawing-room. Take off your coat, please – and give me
your hat. We'll leave them here – have you had supper?
Shall I fetch you some coffee or tea or cocoa perhaps? Or
would you prefer some whisky? I have some in the
drawing-room and – '

He laughed and began to shrug off his heavy overcoat.
'Bless you, Poppy, I don't want a thing! Don't you dare
to go worrying over me! Well, okay, maybe a small
Scotch – I remember how good Scotch can be in this
country. But that's all – '

She took the long skirts of her soft robe between both
hands and almost ran up the stairs to the drawing-room,
leaving him to follow her, and once there hurried round
to switch on extra lights to make it more cheerful and
threw a couple of logs on the fire and stirred the embers
to wake them up. It mattered to her very much suddenly
that she should be seen to be the soul of hospitality.

He laughed then and held out both hands to her.
'Honey, for heaven's sake!' he said and she looked at
him almost shyly and then, dodging him as casually as
she could, went over to the table against the wall where
the decanters and glasses stood.

'I have soda if you want it,' she said, not looking at
him as she busied herself with pouring his drink. 'Would
you care for some?'

'If I can't have it on the rocks I'll have it straight,' he
said and then, as she threw him a puzzled look over her
shoulder, laughed again. 'Over ice, Poppy. As I recall ice
is the one thing you don't have a great deal of here. Anyway, I like it straight and warm, English style. Aren't you
joining me?'

She had given him his glass and had been about to come over to the sofa but now she stopped and after a moment turned back to the decanters.

'Perhaps some sherry,' she murmured and somewhere deep inside herself was scornful. Not to be able to cope with seeing an old friend without a glass in her hand? How ridiculous! But she stifled that thought and filled her glass and bore it carefully across the room.

'Do sit down,' she said and at once he came and sat at the other end of the sofa and leaned back into the cushions with a little wriggle, almost like a dog guiltily settling himself where it should not be. And smiled at her again and lifted his glass.

'To merry meetings,' he said. 'Isn't that the proper toast on such an occasion?'

'I don't know.' She lifted her own glass to him, a little awkwardly. 'But it's a nice one. To merry meetings – ' And drank. And then bit her lip. 'Not very merry when you get a flood of tears hurled at you,' she said and kept her head down, staring into the deep honey coloured sherry. 'I am so sorry.'

'Oh, you British!' There was the kindest of mockery in his voice. 'Always apologizing, always so frightfully sorry – it was no sin, my dear. I startled you and reminded you – ' He stopped then and she was almost forced to look up and meet his gaze. 'And in a way it was a great compliment. It means we are old friends. That you can trust me, hmm? You can only cry with someone you trust.'

'I don't know,' she said and looked away. 'As I say, you surprised me and I'd been scared – '

'Scared?'

She blushed, to her own annoyance. 'I'd got this silly notion you were a – a burglar or something of the sort. There are only Goosey and Robin and me here, you see, and – '

'Goosey,' he said appreciatively. 'Heavens, Goosey – I remember her! Such a – well, such an English sort of person to have around your house. Almost like a Southern Mammy in Georgia. You know what I mean?'

'Not really,' she said and he laughed.

'Well, one day I'll explain. Who is Robin?'

She lifted her head then and stared at him almost in surprise. It seemed so absurd somehow that he didn't know. But why should he, after all?

'I explained about her when I wrote to you that summer and the letter came back. Robin is my daughter.'

He smiled then, a wide gentle sort of smile that felt almost like being stroked, and she felt her shoulders relax as the warmth of it enveloped her. 'A daughter! You and Bobby, a daughter? Oh, that's so – I can't tell you how pleased I am. It would have been so – such a tragedy if Bobby had not left a child for you. And little girls are so much more agreeable than boys.'

'I'm glad you think so,' she managed, so taken aback was she by the way he made her feel.

'I know so! I was a small boy. Pretty disgusting, small boys, I'm here to tell you. How old is she? And does she look like you or Bobby? And is she cheerful or cross? Clever or couldn't care less about school? I want to know all there is to know.'

'She's all you'd expect of an almost seven year old,' Poppy said and laughed. 'And perhaps a bit more. Rather solemn, you know, being the only child in the house. It makes children rather old, that does. I think she's pretty and clever and sweet, but then I would, wouldn't I? As for who she looks like – like herself really. You'll see, I hope – '

'And the other child? Bobby's other daughter? As I recall, not the easiest of little minxes. Has she improved with keeping like this excellent whisky?' And he drank again and his eyes glinted at her over the edge of his glass.

Perhaps it was the sherry, for in her nervousness she had already swallowed half of it, or perhaps it was something about David himself; whatever it was she felt more relaxed now than she would have thought possible, almost sleepy, and somewhere inside herself she pondered on that. Maybe it was the effect of that storm of tears? It really had been a most overwhelming flood of emotion and she still needed to think about it and why it had happened quite so violently. And also why now she felt so very – well, the only word that came to mind was comfortable.

'Still a minx,' she said and lifted her brows. 'I like the word. It's not unkind but it's pretty accurate. A minx – '

'Bobby spoiled her dreadfully,' David said. 'I remember telling him that. He had so much guilt about that kid. Ridiculous really, because she'd have been fine, motherless or not, if he'd just kept off her a bit. But there, in some things Bobby was very stubborn. Always set out to get his own way – '

He stopped then and leaned his head back on the cushions even further so that he was sprawled very comfortably. But his eyes were bright and considering as he looked at her and she thought – he's not at all as relaxed as he's pretending to be.

'Mind you, not as stubborn as you. As I recall. You set out for him, didn't you? And it worked – '

Her face flamed at that. 'I don't know what you – '

'Oh, Poppy, my dear Poppy, this is David, remember me? I was there all the time. I was the one who went looking for him for you and – oh, I was jealous of that guy! He was my friend and I thought the very world of him but I was so *jealous*! To have a girl like you plainly crazy about him and so determined on his behalf – '

'I – you make me sound positively predatory,' she said and finished her sherry and after a moment went recklessly to refill her glass. 'A downright harpy.'

'Oh, such stuff!' He held out his glass to her to be refilled as well. 'I mean no such thing. Just that you were a girl very much in love and determined with it. I was jealous, that's all. I'd have liked to be in his shoes – oh boy, I'd have liked that. But it's no insult to tell you that was how you were. A compliment really. As far as I'm concerned anyway. I like people to have firm ideas about what they want and to go and get it. Whether they're men or women –'

She stood beside the sofa looking down at him and then gave him his glass. 'Well, maybe,' she said after a moment, wanting to be honest. It mattered suddenly that she be honest with him. To have a friend she could talk to about whatever worried her, someone she could rely on to be always the same no matter what she said. It would be a great comfort. And she was remembering in great washes of recollection that this was how this man had been long ago, when she had been so very young and so very adoring of Bobby. She remembered sitting in the little café in Revigny eating *lapin aux pruneaux* with both of them, remembered the way he had helped her through those dreadful days after Bobby's gassing and could have hugged him with the sheer delight of seeing him sitting there.

He lifted his head then and looked up at her and she felt herself redden again and went back a little hurriedly to her own corner of the sofa.

'Never mind all that now,' she said. 'I want to know about you. What happened? Why did my letter come back? And the others – I wrote a couple of times and every time they came back. Gone away it said. Gone away where?'

He twisted his mouth a little. 'Hospital,' he said shortly. 'Goddamn it, call it how it is. Sanatorium. Tuberculosis, Poppy. Would you believe? I went through that lousy war without being hurt – at least not hurt so that anyone could see it – and then got hit with a goddamn plague like that – forgive my language but I get so mad when I think of it. I was so disgusting they had to keep me locked away from other people for – oh, it was a mess. I got the flu, you know, but then who didn't? And after I just didn't get better as I should. And then I bled – '

He looked ahead with half glazed eyes, clearly gazing at the past. 'It wasn't easy,' he said. 'They put me in this hospital and then shipped me to a damned sanitorium in Arizona and there I rotted for three years. Would you believe, three years?'

'Oh, David,' she said and leaned forwards and put one hand on his. 'I am sorry.'

'Yeah,' he said. 'Me too,' and grinned a little crookedly. 'To lose three years of your life when you are in your twenties is a misfortune. To lose them when you are in your thirties is carelessness – isn't that the way the quote goes?'

She smiled then. 'Almost. But the important thing is you just lost three years. I mean it might have been – '

'Yes,' he said. 'I might have followed Bobby, hmm? There were times I wanted to, believe me – '

'But why didn't you tell me? Write to me and let me know?'

He lifted his brows. 'I was too ill at first, to be honest, to do anything. The first year of it all I barely remember now. Fevers and bleeding and lying flat and waiting to die. Only not dying. A strange time – and then when that was over, well, it was so long I'd lost contact with everyone. The people I'd worked with, they'd all gone off and got married and had families and there I was, a left-over old bachelor, dumped on the shore to rot – '

'Oh, no,' she said and again touched his hand. 'That isn't the way you used to be. So bitter – I'd have expected you to be glad to be alive and to – well, get on with things – '

'I know,' he said. 'I'm sorry. It seems to happen to some people like me. They get melancholia with their TB. I still – it still happens sometimes. I'm sorry. It's a bit of a black dog that jumps on me when I'm not looking. I won't let it happen again – '

'I don't mind,' she said and then became aware that she still had one hand over his and pulled it away, in embarrassment. He seemed shy too, suddenly, and sat more upright.

'Anyway, tell me what you do now?' he said. 'Are you still a political person?'

'Political?' She stared at him in surprise and then realized what he meant. 'Oh, did I use to run on at you about votes for women and so forth? Heavens what a bore and a prig I must have seemed! No, I'm much too busy now. Anyway, women have the vote – '

'Almost,' he said. 'Only some do. Not the same as men yet – '

'Oh, I know,' she said and shook her head. 'It's all wrong, of course it is. And I should be involved I suppose, but I just can't. What with the house and the children – though Goosey is wonderful, she is getting rather old and need almost as much looking after as they do – and the office, I have so little time – '

'The office?' He looked interested and she launched herself into an account of what she did and how she did it, and even of the offer of a partnership that Jessie had made her, rattling on and on about it all, like an eager child. And he sat and watched her, listening and smiling a little and sipping from his glass until at last she ran out of words and almost of breath and shook her head at herself in annoyance.

'Oh, David, I'm sorry! Here I am talking your ears off – I really should be ashamed of myself. But it's – ' She bit her lip and then blurted it out. 'It's as though these eight years never happened. As thought you've been here all the time. It's so easy to talk to you. There aren't that many people around I *can* talk to so comfortably.'

'I'm glad,' he said and then gave a little shout of laughter. 'Oh, for Pete's sake, that sounded awful. I don't mean I'm glad you have no one to talk to comfortably. Only glad you can to me. Tell me more.'

She shook her head firmly. 'No more to tell. It's your turn. Tell me what you're doing. How is it you're here? How long will you be here? Is it just a flying visit or – ' And she would not admit to herself how much she hoped it wasn't.

'What am I doing? Well, I tried to write a book and failed totally.' He grimaced. 'It wasn't that bad a book, you understand, but by the time I got out of that damned sanatorium and was on the mend, everyone else and his brother had written their goddamned books about the war and mine just wasn't new enough for them. People have short memories, you know?' And he looked brooding for a moment but then cheered himself up again.

'Anyway, I managed to get back to work, slowly. Just in the newspaper darkrooms at first – they reckoned I'd been out of commission so long I was useless as a photographer, and of course there were all those young guys coming up full of themselves and all the new sorts of cameras and so forth – but there, I managed it in the end.'

Again he produced that crooked grin of his.

'I got a chance to work on the town beat of the old *Post* in Baltimore and after a year they said I could come and attach to the London Bureau. I got here three days ago, found a flat, started work and this has been the first chance I've had to come and look for you. I was scared at first – '

'Scared? To look for me?' she said. 'Oh, David, no! I'm not a person to scare anyone, surely – '

'Of course not. It was myself – or circumstance – I was scared of. Suppose I'd not remembered the address properly? Suppose I'd got it all wrong? Suppose you'd moved away? Suppose – well, suppose anything. When I saw you behind that door tonight I could have – well, you'll never know.'

'I think I do know,' she said. 'I felt – extraordinary when I saw you.' Again she made a little face. 'I mean, you must know that, I certainly behaved extraordinarily.'

'You were sweet,' he said. 'It made me feel – incredible to see you weep like that.'

'Thank you!'

'Aw, come on, Poppy! You know quite well what I mean. It was all so – so real and so – I mean, suppose you'd stared at me all hatchet-faced like so many of your compatriots do and looked down your nose at me and said, "And who maight you be, sir? I've nevah seen you evah in mai laife!" What would I have done then?'

She laughed at his attempt at an English accent and shook her head. 'You're as ridiculous as you ever were! Of course I wouldn't have done that.'

'No,' he said, serious again. 'No, I should have known. Oh, Poppy, isn't this great? Here you are, and here I am and we can be friends again. Just like we used to be.'

She was never to know quite why she said what she said then, but it seemed to emerge from her in words she had never thought, as a complete sentence created in someone else's brain.

'Not quite as we were,' she said. 'We can't be the same without Bobby, can we?'

And he leaned back and after a moment said in a rather colourless voice, 'No, of course. I should have realized. Without Bobby it can't be the same at all.'

11

Chloe had actually tried to be good for several days. She had woken up the morning after her adventure at The Rat Trap in a state of mild shock. Had she really behaved so very dangerously last night? Had she really sneaked out to go to a party with one boy, dropped him to pick up another, gone with him to so raffish a place as a night-club, then dropped him too? Had she actually gambled on a roulette wheel in a place that was illegal with the handsomest man she had ever seen in all her life? Had any of it happened?

She had lain there snugly under her covers staring out of the window at the sunlit branches of the trees in the square outside and remembered every single moment of the evening, over and over again, marvelling at her own temerity. Because for all her stubbornness and determination to do exactly what she wanted when she wanted, Chloe was a well-bred young woman who knew the difference between right and wrong. And last night had been definitely wrong. And she felt less than fully comfortable about it.

So, for the next few days she was a model of rectitude. She helped Goosey, she was kind to her small stepsister, she appeared at meals and was if not exactly polite to Poppy, at least not impertinent, and that was quite an achievement, for Poppy always managed to irritate her so very much. Altogether, she told herself a little smugly, she had been positively angelic.

Of course there had been compensations for her virtuousness. Poppy had allowed her to go out again at last and she had shopped blissfully, buying rather more evening dresses than perhaps she should, considering she was never going to The Rat Trap ever again. That was understood. But you never knew what might come up, after all, and a girl could never have too many evening frocks. So that was fun. Of course Goosey had fussed over what she had bought, calling it indecent, but then Goosey always did –

And then her good resolves were broken into shards and were blown away like leaves in autumn, by a telephone call. Just one phone call and what it could do! She had cradled the earpiece afterwards and stood looking at the dumb instrument, awed. And excited and scared and happy all at the same time.

She had been alone in the house, because Goosey had gone to meet Robin from school as it was such a sunny afternoon and she wanted the exercise, and at first Chloe had almost decided not to bother to answer the imperious ring; she was expecting no telephone calls herself and why should she bother to take messages for boring old Poppy? But it had gone on and on until at last she had been driven into the hall to pick it up, and snapped into the mouthpiece, 'Well?' not caring how ill-mannered she might seem to whoever was calling. Life was so boring at present that such things didn't seem to matter much actually.

'At last!' clacked the small voice in her ear and she had stood there holding the earpiece and with the handset cradled against her chest and stared at the brightly coloured glass in the front door. She knew that voice, even through the distortion of the telephone. Didn't she? And she said carefully, 'I beg your pardon?' needing to hear it again to be sure.

'I said, about time. I thought you were never going to answer.'

143

She knew now she had been right and was so glad to be alone. It meant that she could pull faces if she needed to do so, to relieve the tension, but could keep her voice cool and unencumbered.

'I might have been out,' she said, and screwed up her eyes at the stained glass front door. 'I usually am.'

'Oh, I rather thought you'd be there,' he said. 'Don't ask me how I knew. I just did.'

She frowned suddenly. 'And where is there?' she demanded.

'What is that supposed to mean?'

'What I say. You said you'd thought I'd be there – well, how did you know where there was? I didn't tell you where I lived. Or my telephone number.'

He laughed. 'Such an odd way you have of putting things, ducks! Of course I know where you live. That little house in Norland Square – '

She was so startled that she could say nothing and after a moment he said 'Are you there?'

'Yes,' she managed at length and then drew in a sharp little breath, suddenly rather frightened. This man who had made her misbehave so badly knew where she lived. It was a terrifying notion, though she would have been hard put to it to say why. 'How did you know?'

'I have my ways,' he said. 'Bernie does. You'll find out.'

'Find out what?'

'All about me. I thought I'd have seen you again by now. It's been a week, almost – '

'Why? I never said that I'd – '

'You didn't have to say. I saw how much fun you'd had, I was sure you'd have been back by now. Did she stop you?'

It did not occur to her to ask who he meant by 'she'. 'Of course not. Why should she?'

'Stepmothers. We all know about stepmothers.'

144

'What do we all know? I know nothing – '

'They're unkind and they beat you and they rob you and – '

'Oh, don't be silly,' she said, uncomfortable now. Poppy was irritating, of course she was, but no more than that. To say she beat and robbed her was more than Chloe could possibly allow. From a stranger too; and now she was annoyed and it was a good feeling, because it made her feel stronger, more in control of the situation.

'If you say stupid things like that,' she said then, sharply, 'I shall just hang up the phone and not talk to you.'

'Why is it foolish? Everyone knows how stepmothers behave – '

'Well, this one doesn't. She's just a nuisance sometimes. But she doesn't – none of the things you say about her are true. I wouldn't put up with it! So stop it.'

He gave a low whistle that prickled in her ear unpleasantly and she pulled the earpiece away from her face, and it let go with a little slap, for she had been pressing it so hard against her skin that she had left a sweaty little ring mark there.

'Don't do that!' she commanded.

'Did it bother you? Sorry. Listen, never mind your silly stepmother, or sainted stepmother or whatever it is she is. Tell me when you're coming back to The Rat Trap.'

'Never,' she said firmly.

'Well, that takes care of this week. What about next week?'

She giggled then; couldn't help it. 'You're a silly man!'

'Silly? We'll see about that! There are a lot of things I could be called, but silly isn't one of them.'

It was time to screw her face up again to keep herself calm and relaxed because the tone of his voice had changed, become rather caressing, and that made her face feel unusually hot.

'Like romantic,' he was saying now, and she knew he had deliberately lowered the level of his voice to tease her, but it still had the effect he wanted. 'Like interested in you. Like desperate to see you again – '

'Silly – ' she murmured again, but uncertainly now.

'Chloe Bradman, my dear Miss Chloe Bradman, this has gone on quite long enough,' he said with mock severity, though still his voice had that deliberately seductive burr in it. 'I have matters I must deal with and you'll need time to get ready – '

'Ready for what?'

'For the party you're dressing to go to. Time to take a bath and to climb into your wisp of satin camiknickers – ' She flushed scarlet at that. ' – and to roll your stockings to your knee and to paint your eyebrows, not to say your ruby lips. Wear your most divine evening dress and I'll meet you at the Cumberland Restaurant at Marble Arch in – let me see – about an hour and a half. Tell them at home you're going to a friend's house and then to a party. I'll do the rest. Make sure you're on time, Miss B, because it isn't far from the restaurant to your house and I can walk down in a matter of minutes. If you're not here then that's what I'll have to do. *A bientôt*, then – '

The telephone clicked in her ear and buzzed as he hung up and she stood there staring blankly at the glass panes of blue and green and crimson until the operator came on the line and demanded 'Are you *thrrrough*? Has your party disconnected?' in that absurd singsong voice that operators always used and she said, 'What? Oh yes,' and cradled the earpiece in its hook and set the phone down again on the table.

How long it took her to give in to it all she couldn't remember afterwards. It seemed to her that she stood there in the hall for a long time, thinking, staring at the

146

phone and remembering his voice in her ear, as intimate as though he had been standing beside her and touching her; and then there was a noise as the front gate creaked its familiar old whine and Robin's high voice said something about her friend Molly and Goosey's deeper more querulous tones answered, and at once she was galvanized, and turned and fled up the stairs to her room as fast as she could.

After that it all just happened. She bathed and changed and when she put on her underwear – a rather fetching set in apricot satin – she remembered his comments about wisps of camiknickers and blushed again at the memory and put on one of her newest dresses, the lilac chiffon with the handkerchief hem which was so daringly short in some places and so elegantly drooping in others. Then she brushed her hair until it shone, and took as long as she could over her make-up, even adding a hint of lilac shadow to her eyelids, very daringly indeed, and lots of dark mascara.

When she had finished she was delighted with herself, from the crown of her most elegantly shingled fair head to the toes of her lilac kid shoes, and including her matching silk stockings and her shawl coat in deeper lilac silk. It was rather early to be going out dressed quite so elegantly, but it couldn't be helped, and she turned and picked her way over the clothes she had left littering the floor when she went to bath and change, tucking her silver bag under her arm as she did so.

And then very deliberately, turned back to rummage in her private drawer, the only one to which she had a key, and pulled out some money. She wasn't going to be caught in the same sort of trap she had been the last time she had been with this man, and she folded two crisp white fivers from her special fund and tucked them into the hidden folds of her bag, where the secret purse was. Goosey had made the lining especially, telling her

147

everyone ought to have a place to hide things; she had jeered at her then, but now she was very glad of it, and she went down the stairs full of fear and excitement; a most heady and delightful if uncomfortable way to feel.

It was her bad luck that Goosey was coming toiling up the stairs from the kitchen with a tea-tray for her. Chloe hadn't wanted any tea and if Goosey had called up and asked she could have saved herself the trouble of making it, and the whole silly argument would never have happened. But there, that was Goosey all over. So they had stood at the foot of the stairs, with Goosey trying to stop her from making her way to the front door and out, arguing absurdly. Goosey nagged her about not having her tea, about the amount of make-up she had on, about her dress, about her coat and about her stockings most of all. Was it any wonder Chloe lost her temper and snapped at her for being a stupid old woman with addled brains who was fit only to sit in a corner and shut up? Of course it wasn't; and she had slammed out of the house furious with Goosey for spoiling the fun in this fashion. It was too bad for her, it really was.

But she was over the worst of it by the time she got to the Cumberland Restaurant, a large and somewhat shabbily grand place on the ground floor of the gloomy mansion flats which stood on the corner of Great Cumberland Place. She had walked along Bayswater Road, managing to ignore the occasional stares of passers-by who were still dressed in more ordinary afternoon clothes, but now she felt very uncomfortable. The place, full of people taking afternoon tea, was brightly lit under large crystal chandeliers, and there was a rich scent of Darjeeling and crumpets and cream cakes which went well with the string trio playing sprightly tunes in the corner; and it seemed to Chloe that almost everyone turned their heads to stare at her with insulting curiosity;

and she hovered in the doorway, mortified to be so very much out of place. It was an unusual experience for her, for generally she knew exactly what to wear and when; she had only dressed as she had because he had told her to, and a little voice inside demanded, 'Will you always do as he says? You who never pay attention to anyone?' But there was no answer to that.

And then suddenly it was all fine. He appeared at her elbow, looking quite breathtaking in perfect evening clothes, with his top coat hanging with wonderful insouciance over one arm, and a most glossy topper dangling from one negligent hand, to slide his other hand into her elbow.

'Just in time,' he murmured. 'Over here,' and led her to a corner table where she could sit with her back to the mirrored wall and survey the whole room without the other people finding it quite as easy to stare at her. An obsequious waiter took her satin wrap as well as Bernie's coat and hat and they settled themselves in place at the snowy white cloth with its glitter of silver and bone china under the fluttering attentions of no less a personage than the head waiter. Clearly, Chloe thought, impressed in spite of herself, her escort had some influence here, for it was obvious that he was being treated with more than usual deference and she became aware of the fact that when other customers of the restaurant looked at her now it was more with envy in their glances than anything else; and she began to feel quite marvellous.

He ordered tea and it arrived with remarkable promptitude, with chafing dishes full of buttery crumpets and muffins and plates of tiny sandwiches dripping with fine mustard and cress and cake stands bearing the most outrageously delicious cream bun and éclairs; and he laughed indulgently as she clapped her hands in childish delight.

'I'm so glad you have appetites, Chloe,' he said. 'I

149

can't bear these thin-blooded females who never eat or drink. And clearly never do anything else either.'

Again there was that seductive note in his voice, but she chose not to notice it this time. Maybe he was saying something she would rather he didn't, so it was simpler to pretend she didn't understand; simpler still deliberately *not* to understand. So she pushed away the thought that had come to her mind at his words and concentrated on the little smoked salmon sandwiches which were undoubtedly delicious.

By the time tea was over it was as though they had known each other for years. She chattered of her friends, her parties, the things she adored and the things she loathed, in music and the theatre and clothes, and he sat and watched her, a cigarette held between his fingers and the smoke rising lazily, with a hint of an indulgent smile on his face and his eyes warm and amused.

'Parties,' he said at length. 'You like parties.'

'If they're good ones.' She had finished eating now and was leaning back in her chair looking around at the other people. 'I say, what a dreary lot these are! All these silly women who've been out shopping and have nothing more exciting to do now than go home and have dinner with their even more dreary husbands,' and she shivered at such a hideous prospect.

'But don't you enjoy shopping? I thought you said you did.'

'Adore it – but not on its own. I mean there has to be something to do afterwards, doesn't there? Places to go where one can wear one's new things and so forth.'

'Parties,' he said again. 'You like parties.'

'Who doesn't? Don't you?'

'Not ordinary ones.'

'What do you call ordinary ones?' She was gazing at him now, instead of at the people at the other tables. He looked more handsome than ever with his polished black head and his rich dark eyes with their absurdly long lashes. She preened a little at sitting next to the man who was undoubtedly the best-looking in the room. She knew herself to be pretty of course – how could she not? – but there was no doubt in her mind that nothing enhanced a girl's looks more than a suitable escort. And Bernie was definitely very suitable, in spite of his odd accent and his rather thin voice. And even that was interesting and different; American, after all.

'Oh, parties where people eat and drink and dance, you know,' he said, watching her closely.

She wrinkled her nose. 'What else is there to do at parties? As long as there are jolly people there to do it with, surely it's fun?'

'Sometimes. But not always. Sometimes you need more.'

'More what?'

'More to do than eat and drink and dance.'

'Like what? Party games I suppose.' Now she looked a little disdainful. 'Some people do that. Charades and Clumps and so forth, and though that's all right if you're with a very jolly crowd it can be a bit juvenile with some people.'

He laughed at that. 'I wasn't thinking of Charades and Clumps,' he said. 'Something very different. But much more fun – '

'You're talking in riddles,' she said crossly. 'You really are – *what*, then? Don't just talk – '

'Shall I show you?'

'If you like.' She pretended not to care and reached for her little bag and pulled out her compact and began to powder her nose.

'I do like,' he said firmly and lifted one hand and at once the bill was put down beside him by the obsequious head waiter. 'We shall go now and you'll see what I mean.'

151

'Go? Where?' She stared at him over the rim of her mirror.

'To an unusual party – keep the change,' he instructed the waiter and then stood up invitingly. 'Are you ready? Here's your coat – ' as it arrived on a waiter's arm together with his coat and glossy topper. 'Come along – '

'Along where?'

'Such a child for questions!' he said and leaned forwards and urged her to her feet. 'Put away your bits and bobs now and we'll be on our way. That's it, good girl. Now, your coat – splendid – '

They were at the door and almost out into the street, which was beginning to glitter with lights as the sky above them deepened to an early evening richness, before she could get the words out.

'I'm not going with you until you tell me where,' she managed, and stood stock-still in the middle of the pavement and glared at him.

'To the best party you've ever been to in all your young life, ducky,' he said promptly. 'To an experience you'll never forget. No, don't look so frightened! You were brave enough at my Rat Trap the other night – and I didn't let you down, did I? Then I shan't now. I'm simply offering you the best party you've ever attended. Surely, you're not going to run home to your dear stepmamma and refuse are you? I thought better of you – '

12

Of course she didn't refuse. The challenge he had thrown at her might be an obvious one, designed to force her to accept, but it was also a very tempting prospect. She adored parties, always had, even those dull ones where they played Charades and Clumps. They were always such hopeful events; one never knew who one might meet and what might happen. So it would have been beyond possibility for her to turn her back on this one in spite of all her doubts and the warnings that kept bobbing up at the back of her mind about this handsome escort of hers. She didn't know his surname, knew only that he owned a raffish and highly illegal nightclub and he sometimes said things that were downright *risqué*. Goosey, she knew, would have a fit if she knew what sort of person her beloved Chloe was allowing to take her to a party. And yet – a party, an unusual party. And she pushed the warnings well down, shrugged her shoulders to make herself seem offhand and too terribly sophisticated to be enthusiastic, and allowed him to hand her into a taxi.

And to start with, was very glad she had. The party was in a house in Bloomsbury and that was exciting for a start. It sounded such a glamorous place, famous as it was for artists and painters and writers. Maybe she would even meet Virginia Woolf there? She had shivered inside with anticipation when she had heard Bernie give the taxi driver the address of a house just off Bloomsbury

Square, and settled down to have a marvellous time.

There was no disappointment on arrival, either. The house was one of a terrace, tall and narrow and not unlike her own home in Holland Park's Norland Square, but inside it was quite different, rather stark and dramatic and not at all cosy. The walls were covered in paintings and the lights were low and thrillingly coloured; there was an unusual smell in the air, on which she remarked and which Bernie told her in a whisper derived from incense sticks from India, and the whole place had an exotic look. It was a little like their own drawing-room at home, with its Bakst designs and oriental influences, but there was more to it than that; and she decided it had to be the people. Because they really were a very mixed collection indeed.

The men looked tolerably ordinary and were mostly in evening clothes, though there were one or two in soft tweeds and brightly coloured pullovers who were bearded and looked extremely intense, but it was the women who made most impact. There were plenty of the sort of frocks that Chloe understood, up-to-the-minute fashions with lots of softness and charm about them, much like her own lilac chiffon, but there were others which were the most extraordinary of garments, and she had to make a decided effort not to stare. One woman was wearing the skimpiest and tightest of black frocks with very bare arms and throat but also a plunging back that showed every knob of her spine (and it was, Chloe decided, a very knobbly one indeed) and had her hair cut so close that it was almost possible to see her scalp shining through. She had a slick of black hair across her forehead in a geometric curl and her face was made up startlingly white while her eyes were outlined in dark pencil (kohl, Chloe suspected, having read about it in her fashion bibles, the illustrated magazines) over lips painted so dark and bloody red that her mouth looked like a gash. She was smoking a cigarette through an exceedingly long black holder and looked too soulful, Chloe decided, for words; and she wondered briefly whether it was a style she could emulate, and decided she couldn't. This woman was a dark, sallow creature, she told herself a little waspishly, not a softly coloured blond like herself.

She looked further around as Bernie led her into the press of people – for it really was very crowded – and saw even more startling outfits. Several women were dressed so mannishly, in waistcoats and ties and with monocles screwed into their eyes, that the only way one knew they were women was because they had lip rouge and pencilled eyebrows and skirts, while others were wrapped in long draped robes in soft jewelled colours and wore their hair unfashionably long, drooping over their shoulders in serried waves. They, Chloe decided, were the Artistic Ones; short of having dabs of oil paint on their faces and fingers, they could not have announced themselves more clearly.

The conversation was very loud and as thrilling as the dramatic lighting; people talking about art and books and music; it was much more exciting, Chloe decided, than overhearing conversations about the arguments someone had had at the tennis club or the frightful way they had been cheated in a shop somewhere, which was what people at the parties she went to talked about, unless they were married, when they went on and on about the awfulness of servants, which was even worse. These people braying loudly about Marc Chagall and darling Augustus John's splendid portrait of dear Lady Ottoline and raving about the starkness of Epstein's new Draped Reclining Figure were much more interesting, and she listened hard, collecting things she could say herself at the next ordinary party she went to.

But it was hard to take it all in; a thin man with very dark eyes was lecturing a bored-looking woman in puce crêpe on 'the extraordinary tonality and harmonic colours' of something called, as far as Chloe could tell, *Wozzeck*, which she decided must be a mistake, while another couple were shouting at each other at the tops of their voices about Honneger's new opera *Judith*; and Chloe stored that away as possibly useful one day.

And then as they reached the centre of the room someone stopped Bernie and cried, 'My dear chap! What are you doing here? How marvellous to see you! But you're a long way from Haunch of Venison Yard, surely?'

'Not impossibly,' Bernie said. 'Good to see you – '

The man was middle-aged, Chloe decided, at least thirty-five and rather unhealthy; he looked pale and sweaty and his eyes seemed anxious. He had thinning mousy hair and a thick waist over a bulging paunch and was, she considered, most unappetizing; so much so that she was sure that Bernie would ignore him with some disdain.

But he didn't. The man set a hand on his arm and leaned forwards and murmured something inaudible to Chloe in Bernie's ear and Bernie listened and then smiled an odd little smile and turned his head to Chloe.

'My dear, let me get you a drink. There'll be champagne – there always is – and then be a duck and wait a moment while I sort something out for Arthur here. An old friend, Arthur, eh?'

'Mm? Oh, yes, yes, absolutely,' gabbled the fat man called Arthur and tugged on Bernie's arm rather urgently.

'In a moment,' he said, disengaging him. 'Chloe needs her champagne first and a corner in which to drink it.'

'I'll see to that,' Arthur said eagerly. 'You just well – you know – '

'Such a man,' sighed Bernie and winked at Chloe. 'Come along, my little duck. Sit you here – ' And he led her through the hubbub to a chair in the corner and set her down. 'Fetch me some bubbly, Arthur,' he commanded and the man bobbed his head and bustled away.

'I'll have to leave you for a moment,' Bernie murmured at her. 'I'm sorry, but it's business, you understand. And that has to be dealt with, you'll agree. Then I'll be back and concentrate totally on you –'

'But you're not going to leave me here all alone, are you?' Chloe protested as he straightened up and reached for the glass Arthur had brought, holding it in front of him with exaggerated care not to spill it.

'I told you, just for a moment,' and suddenly his thin voice seemed thinner than ever in her ears and she looked at him sharply. But he smiled and her moment of irritation passed. 'Just be patient, little duck – come along, Arthur, let's be quick about this –'

And there she was left among a great many people she did not know at all with a glass of champagne clutched in one hand and her eyes smarting a little from the smoke that was really everywhere. The room was blue with it and though she smoked a cigarette occasionally – who didn't, these days? – she was by no means so accustomed to it that she was comfortable in such an atmosphere; and she sipped some of the champagne – which was rather strong and sour and made her screw up her nose – and let sulkiness move into her.

It was a rotten thing to do, to leave someone alone, just sitting, at a party. She'd only come because he'd persuaded her and now to treat her so – it was too bad, really too utterly bad of him! And she drank some more, sour or not – and it tasted a bit better this time – and brooded on Bernie's all round awfulness.

Except that he really was so dreadfully handsome; and she sat and sipped at her drink steadily and thought about his handsomeness and felt what was becoming a familiar little shiver of excitement come back and felt better. He did make life so very interesting, that was the thing. She'd only met him a few days ago, and already look at the difference he had made to her. She had gambled, she was at a party in Bloomsbury where people talked about Augustus John as though he were their next door neighbour, and where women wore clothes that made your eyes pop out of your head and some of the men had shaggy beards; to be annoyed with him for leaving her alone for a while when he'd already done so much for her was hardly fair.

But it wasn't fair to do it all the same, she told herself then and tipped up her glass to drain it. And now she'd had her drink and he wasn't back, so she'd go and find him and tell him what she thought of people who left people all alone with a lot of strangers; and she put the glass down on the table beside her and got to her feet, and began to push her way through, flashing smiles and murmuring apologies as she went.

Not that it made much difference; people went on talking to each other busily over her head as she went by, quite ignoring her, and that piqued her not a little. At the parties she usually went to she was accustomed to being rather special; often the prettiest and the most vivacious girl there, she took it for granted that people – well, boys, really – would notice her and come drifting across to cluster round her, usually within a half hour or so. But not here; at this party, she might as well have been invisible for all the attention paid to her. She realized that most of the people were frightfully old, of course, certainly much older than she was, but even so, that didn't permit them to be so very nasty and rude –

She reached the hallway where there were not quite so many people and looked about her. There was no sign of Bernie or Arthur, and she peered hopefully along the corridor towards the green baize door at the end. But he was not there and there was no possibility he was behind the green baize door, for that was the servants' quarters. So she made for the stairs, and picking her way over the little cluster of people who were sitting on them, went up to where she imagined the drawing-room must be. The room she had been in had, it appeared to her, been the dining-room; certainly that was what it would be in any ordinary house, though in this one it was hard to tell what the rooms were used for, so full of people were they. But upstairs it was quiet, and she found a door and opened it and looked in, and there was no one there. It was as sparsely furnished as the room downstairs, though it had as many pictures on the walls, and as she caught sight of one of them her face went pink. It was very explicit indeed, showing a very large and faithfully painted naked man picking apples from a small tree. The man was standing very pugnaciously facing forwards and she had never seen anything quite so – well, outspoken was the only word that came to her mind. She had seen some interesting pictures with her friend Mary Challoner (who had a friend who had a brother who had a friend who sometimes loaned out French books and magazines) but she had never seen anything like this. And she left the room and closed the door sharply behind her and looked further.

There was a cry from below that sounded like 'Supper!' and the few people who were on the stairs got to their feet with alacrity and went wandering away and left her alone on the first floor; and after a moment she went to another door and then another, and pushed them open, looking.

Each of the three rooms she looked into was empty and dark and she was about to go downstairs again, in an increasingly ill humour, when she saw another door tucked behind the bannisters at the side of the stairs that led up to the bedroom floor above, and she marched over to it

159

and without stopping to take her time and peep, as she had with the other doors, pushed it open and marched in.

And then stopped short. It was a small bedroom, she realized, with a single bed in it and a few pieces of rather cheap ordinary-looking furniture. A servant's room in other words. And sitting on the bed, with a newspaper in his lap, was Arthur. He lifted his head sharply as she came in and after a moment grinned at her widely. His face was still sweaty but he no longer had the pasty ill look he had had; now he seemed relaxed and comfortable and glowing with good humour and he smiled at her contentedly and said, 'Ah! The little lady!'

'Well, look at you,' said a voice from the other side of the room and she turned her head sharply. Bernie was leaning against the wall, both hands in his trouser pockets and his head resting back easily against the wallpaper. He smiled lazily at her and said, 'So you couldn't wait for me?'

'I'm bored,' she said after a moment. 'All those strangers! I thought you said you were taking me to an unusual party, one I would enjoy? This one isn't so special. Just a lot of people I don't know – ' and she hurled a look at Arthur and added spitefully, '*old* people, boring old fat people – '

'Like me,' Arthur said and giggled and then, oddly, bent his head and lifted the spread newspaper up towards his face at the same time. Chloe looked at him, frowning, and then flicked her gaze away back to Bernie.

'I'm bored,' she said again.

'You're a spoiled madam,' Bernie said easily and then laughed. 'I wonder just how bored you are?'

'I told you. Very. Are you staying here in this housemaid's bedroom with him? – ' And she jerked her chin towards Arthur. 'Or are you coming downstairs again? They said it was supper – madly early, isn't it, for supper? What sort of a party is this, that people have supper so early? And what sort of business is it you have here with that – well, what sort can it be? Business is very boring and it is miserable of you to leave me alone for it –'

She blinked then and wondered for a moment why her head felt a bit strange. Everything she looked at was a bit glittery and she didn't usually feel as reckless as she did now. It seemed to her it didn't matter at all whether she was rude to Bernie or not, and she shook her head a little as she thought that.

'Arthur, was that just champagne you gave our little duck here?' Bernie said.

Arthur giggled again, a soft little sound that bubbled in his throat. 'Mmm? Oh, yes. Mostly.'

'Mostly,' Bernie said and it wasn't a question; there was a resigned note in his voice.

'Well, some brandy too, of course!' Arthur said. 'What's a glass of champagne without its bit of brandy?'

'I suspect you're feeling it a little, Chloe,' Bernie said then. 'This naughty man has slipped you a mickey –'

Chloe stared. 'Done what?'

'Given you a rather stronger drink than you should have. It's made you a little – different.'

Chloe blinked. 'Did you?' she said and looked at Arthur. 'Why?'

He looked back at her owlishly. 'Why not? What's a glass of champagne, say I, without some bones in it? Wasn't it nice?'

'It tasted sour,' Chloe said and suddenly giggled for no reason she could imagine. She was still annoyed with Bernie, still didn't like this man, but all the same she giggled.

'Next time I'll put a sugar lump in. I should have done anyway,' Arthur said. 'Would you like some of my snow now, to make up for it?'

'Your what?'

'Shut up, Arthur,' Bernie said sharply and for the first time moved to come across the room to stand beside the other man. 'Do you hear me? Shut up – '

'Why? What've I done wrong now? Nice girl, nice manners, thought I'd give her a little treat,' Arthur said and held out his newspaper to Chloe with an inviting lift of his brows. 'A little snow to make up for the sugar – '

Chloe moved closer and looked curiously at the newspaper. Now she could see it more clearly and saw a thin line of whitish material straggling across the black type, in the opposite direction to the printing, and she put out one finger to touch it, puzzled, but Arthur pulled the paper away from her reach.

'What's that?' she said and looked at Bernie. He was standing staring at her now, his face quite expressionless, but there was a wary look in his eyes and she saw it and said again, 'What is that?'

'Illegal,' he said briefly. 'Wicked stuff. Not for little girls.'

'Lovely,' Arthur said. 'Lovely stuff. Good for little Arthur – ' and again he bent his head and as Chloe watched, her eyes wide with surprise, he set his nose to the newspaper near the white line and sniffed hard.

The line of powder, which she could now see was what it was, shifted and began to disappear into his nostrils and with a practised gesture he pulled the paper towards him so that his nose travelled along the white line, and in a moment or less it had all disappeared and Arthur was sitting staring at her, his mouth partly open and his face rather flushed now as well as sweating and staring at her. He looked the same as he had before, and yet not the same; more relaxed and apparently deeply content.

'What on earth is he doing?' she said and looked at Bernie again. And then suddenly, she knew. She had read stories about villains and detectives, swallowing Edgar

Wallace and E. Phillips Oppenheim books whole, and had learned a good deal of useful slang from reading such stuff. Snow, she remembered now, was a drug and she turned and looked at Arthur with some awe. He had seemed such a dull fellow, fat and old and not at all romantic. People who used drugs, surely, were rather romantic figures?

He looked back at her contentedly and then smiled, a wide beatific smile and almost against her will she found herself smiling back. He was so very much at peace with himself it seemed impossible to do otherwise.

'He's a drug fiend,' she breathed and Bernie laughed.

'Hardly a fiend,' he said. 'Just an ordinary sort of man who rather likes it. Learned about it in Paris –'

She looked at him then. 'Do they use it a lot in Paris, then?'

'Quite a lot,' he said gravely. 'About as much as here in London.'

Her eyes widened. 'Then it isn't just in stories –'

'Oh, by no means, not just in stories.' He was leaning against the brass foot rail of the bedstead now, looking at her consideringly. 'And most of the people who use it are no different from you or me. Or Arthur.' He looked down at Arthur who was now lying back on the bed, the newspaper cast aside, and staring happily into middle space. 'He has this sort of reaction – gets a little sleepy, you know. Other people are different – some of them get very excited and lively and jump about, some of them –' He stopped very deliberately. 'Some of them get particularly – shall we say, friendly?'

'Oh,' was all she could manage and looked again at Arthur. But he hadn't changed at all. He looked still the rather dreary middle-aged person she had thought him all along.

'Of course getting it is the problem,' Bernie said then. 'People who like it need to have a way of obtaining it.

163

You can't just buy it in shops, you see. Not legal. Silly isn't it, when it's so harmless?'

'Harmless? But I thought it was dangerous. I read in one book where – '

He waved one hand dismissively. 'My dear child, you don't want to believe all you read in books! Most of them are simply made-up stories based on no real knowledge at all. I, on the other hand, have real knowledge of real situations. And I know it to be quite harmless. Why, people hurt themselves more with champagne and brandy than they do with a little cocaine – have you come to any harm from your drink? Of course not! Well, the same applies to Arthur's snow. Just a little agreeable something to pass a dull time away.'

She shook her head dubiously. 'If it's harmless, why is it illegal? If drinks aren't why aren't they illegal?'

'A wise question,' he said. 'Because of money, my duck. The government here makes a great deal of money out of drinks. Taxes, you know, and excise duty. In America they are trying to do without it, and have Prohibition. Alcohol is forbidden, just as cocaine is here. It makes no difference of course. Americans drink their illegal gin and we sniff our illegal cocaine – '

'It must be more than money. Everyone always fusses so about such stuff. They don't fuss about drink that way,' she protested.

'Believe me, child, believe me. It's money. Everything always is, as you'll find out one day, when you need some of your own and can no longer rely on your stepmamma.'

'I have my own money,' she said sharply. 'More than she has. I take nothing from her, or ever would.'

He lifted his brows at that and said, 'Really? That's interesting.'

'Why is it interesting? It's no business of anyone else but – '

'It's good to know what a free agent you are,' he said.

164

'You can buy for yourself anything you want, clearly. Even snow. It's quite expensive of course.'

'I don't want any,' she said hotly. 'It's wrong to use that – ' Again she looked at Arthur, but he was now curled up against the pillows and was fast asleep. 'I wouldn't want to be like that, anyway.'

'I told you. Some people have a totally different response. People vary so. It feels wonderful, of course, quite wonderful. Being like that is what he most likes. There are some people I know however who dance the whole night away and never feel in the least sleepy because they've had the help of a little high quality cocaine. And it does them no harm at all. Why, I could tell you of people who use it, really famous people, who are living busily and happily and never come to any harm at all. And they've been using it for many years too. You'd be surprised.'

'How do you know?' she said challengingly. 'You say a lot about what you know, but how do you? Why should I believe you?'

He smiled, a slow very sweet smile that brought the excitement back into her belly, and then put his hand in his jacket pocket.

'Because I deal in it,' he said. 'I have the best stuff in all London. That was the business that Arthur was so eager to transact, you see, and I hadn't the heart to refuse him.'

He pulled his hand out of his pocket then and opened it and on the palm she could see a little white packet that looked for all the world like one of the headache powders Goosey gave her when she felt low. 'There, you see?' he said softly. 'The best quality that, and an excellent price. Would you care to try some? My treat, of course.'

13

Robin's birthday party was extra big this year, much to that young person's satisfaction. At first.

'When it happens to fall on a Sunday, darling,' her mother had explained. 'It's so much easier for everyone – and it means Auntie Jessie can come too, which she can't if it's any other day of the week. Because of work you see.' And that had made Robin very happy because she was particularly attached to her Great Aunt Jessie, who was so big and noisy and who always wore such jolly frocks in such a shocking sort of red and who smelled wonderful, a mixture of flowery scent and fried fish and apples. 'And I'll tell you what else I can do,' her mother had continued. 'I can invite some extra grown-ups to keep some of the mothers company. They'll like that, I'm sure.'

Robin had sighed deeply with pleasure at that. At other parties some of her friends' mothers had been an awful nuisance, interfering at tea-time and fussing over party frocks getting grubby and generally being *there*. Mummy never did that, but Molly's mother did and so did Cynthia's a bit. So it would be lovely this year if they had other grown-ups to occupy them.

And at first it had all been lovely. The entertainer who had come to give them a conjurer's show had been very clever, Robin thought, for he had pulled strings of glorious coloured handkerchiefs out of her ear – though Robin hadn't felt a thing while he did it – and had made a beautiful cake in his topper. That had been the best bit of his show, Robin had decided, after he had mixed eggs and sugar and flour and milk in the tall glossy hat and then held it over a candle and waved it about and pulled out a proper little cake with her name written on it in pink icing. Real magic.

But then it had all gone wrong, and that wasn't fair at a person's birthday party. Tea had been nice, of course. Goosey had set the table in the dining-room with all the best china and trimmed it with streamers and pompoms and there had been tiny sandwiches filled with mashed banana which Robin loved, as well as ordinary ones of sardine and tomato and cucumber and so forth, and jellies and blancmange and chocolate biscuits and tiny cup cakes as well as the most magnificent big birthday cake shaped like a seven covered in white icing with yellow rosettes and 'Now Robin is Seven' on it in curly letters. She had blown out her candles in one magnificent blow and wished and everyone had sung to her, but it had stopped being fun by then because Cynthia and Molly were really being hateful. They kept whispering to each other and giggling and wouldn't tell Robin what it was all about when she asked them and that made her very angry indeed. They were supposed to be her best friends, both of them, better than any of the other nine little girls and boys at the party (well the boys couldn't be friends at all, of course, being boys. Mummy had insisted Robin invite some so she had, but of course she didn't like them. No one sensible liked *boys*).

So, after tea, when Poppy took everyone up to the drawing-room for musical cushions (better than chairs because you had to bump down hard on your bottom to get a place and it made everyone shout and giggle a lot) she only agreed to play because everyone had to to start with, but she made sure she was out after the second go. She wasn't going to play the same game as Cynthia and

Molly if they were going to whisper and giggle like that, not she, and she went to watch them all, sitting against the wall next to Auntie Jessie and her mother, her knees up and her arms round them, watching everyone gloomily.

Just let them wait till tomorrow, that was all; she'd take her best birthday presents to school, the way everyone always did, and she'd make sure she didn't take Cynthia's or Molly's, even though usually she did because that was what you always did when you had best friends. She'd take the doll that man with the curly hair had brought her, even though it wasn't her favourite present (though she quite liked it; it had eyes that opened and shut and it made a 'Maaa' sound when you tipped it over) and she'd take the new paint-box her mother had given her. No one would see Cynthia's painting book (even though Robin really liked it a lot) or Molly's Little Knitter's Set which she didn't like one bit anyway. So there.

The man with the curly hair who had bought the doll was the one working the gramophone for musical cushions while Molly's mother, who had a lot of very yellow hair pinned up on her head in a bun instead of being shingled like almost everyone else, and who was wearing a rather silly dress of pink frills (which is just what you'd expect Molly's mother to wear of course), was looking after the cushions, taking one away each time and laughing a lot, all high and tinkly. The curly man didn't like her much, Robin could tell, even though Molly's mother obviously liked *him*, and that pleased her.

He seemed a nice man, really. She didn't know him very well, of course. He'd been here once before, Robin remembered, when he had collected Mummy to take her to the opera one night. Robin had been sitting by the kitchen fire with Goosey, having her supper, and Mummy had brought him and introduced him (though

Robin had forgotten his name at once) and he'd been polite and sensible, shaking hands with her like a person and not patting her head and calling her 'little girl' or anything stupid like that the way so many grown-ups did. She watched him now as he pounced on the gramophone to stop it and catch someone without a cushion; he was playing the game with lots of energy as though he were really enjoying himself. Robin liked that; so many grown-ups acted as though they were terribly bored with children's games even if they weren't really.

'A lovely man,' Auntie Jessie said above her head and she turned and looked up. Clearly Auntie Jessie hadn't noticed Robin was there and she hugged her knees even more tightly to make herself smaller so that she wouldn't notice her now. It was always so interesting to listen to grown-ups talking when they didn't know you were listening.

'Nice-looking but better than that,' Auntie Jessie went on, staring across the room towards the gramophone. 'Look at him laughing there like a boy! So tell me, how long you known him?'

'Jessie, behave!' That was Mummy and Robin thought, I can't see her without looking, and then she'll see me and they'll stop talking. 'I want none of your prodding.'

'Who's prodding?' Jessie said comfortably. 'I notice a man is nice and he's a new friend to you, so naturally I ask –'

Poppy sighed, but laughed all the same. 'Jessie, you really are impossible. All right – if I don't tell you what little there is to tell, you'll give me no peace. So, his name's David Deveen. I told you that already, didn't I? I've known him for – oh, years.'

'Years?' Jessie turned to stare at her, her brows raised. 'How come I don't know him then?'

'We were in France together. At Verdun,' Poppy said

and now Robin did take a risk and leaned forwards a little to peer round Auntie Jessie's comfortable bulk to stare at her mother. She was sitting very straight, her hands folded on her lap and staring at nothing the way she did sometimes and Robin thought – she always looks like that when anyone says anything about France. It's strange. Miss Scoular says France is beautiful and they grow lavender there at a place called Grasse, which is funny, and the children all speak French as soon as they're born and that's funny too. France sounds nice but Mummy always looks as though she's gone away somewhere dreary when she talks about it. Very strange.

'Verdun, eh? He was a soldier?'

Poppy sighed and came back from wherever she had been inside her head. 'Not a soldier, Jessie. A newspaper man.'

'Ah! like Bobby, hey? A writer – '

'And a photographer. He's American – '

Jessie seemed to sit up more straight. 'Is that a fact? Where from? A New Yorker, maybe?'

Poppy shook here head. 'Baltimore, now,' she said. 'He used to live in New York, I know. I used to write to him there – just after we got back – '

'Baltimore?' Jessie slapped her fat lap in delight. 'My old town! That's where I lived with Nathan, rest his poor old soul in peace. Maybe your friend knows my old shop? You must ask him to come talk – I must talk to him, Poppy! It'll be like the old days, talking to someone from Baltimore – '

'Oh, yes,' Poppy said. 'I'd forgotten. Well, you shall talk to him later. Let him finish the children's game – '

'So who's trying to stop him? Of course he can finish! So tell me, Poppy, how come he's here in London, if he's a Baltimore man?'

'He's working for the Baltimore paper's London Bureau. Based here for some time, I think – '

'And the first thing he does when he gets here is to find you?' Jessie said and sighed sentimentally. 'That's very encouraging, Poppy – '

'Encouraging?' Poppy looked at her sideways. 'Jessie, I warned you – '

'So you warned me,' Jessie said comfortably. 'So I'm warned. But I still have a head to think and a tongue to talk, all right? And I tell you it's wonderful you got a nice man friend, really wonderful. I told you, I keep on telling you, not that you listen, that a woman needs more to her life than house and work and children. She needs a nice man. A husband! I could do with a nice man myself, believe me, but me, I'm not so lucky to find one as'd be any good for me. But you're just a kid, and it's easier for you – '

'A kid?' Poppy said and laughed. 'My dear Jessie, I have to remind you – again – that I am past thirty, hardly a child – '

'And I'm twice your age and then a bit and like I said if I could find the right man, I'd be there in a whistle. Trouble is, you get older, you get choosier. And I've got a few bob to my name nowadays and that brings all the wrong ones sniffing round.' She nodded then at her own shrewdness. 'Me, I got to be careful who comes calling. But you? You're a girl, believe me, no more than a girl, and you don't have to be so fussy. Anyway, this is a man, looking at him, even a fussy person would consider. Nicely set up, old friend, got an interesting job, likes children, and likes you – I see the way he keeps looking over here and smiling at you. I tell you, Poppela, that man likes you the way a man ought to like a woman, I feel it in my bones, this is the one for you – maybe this year a wedding – '

'Jessie, if you don't stop such silly chatter I shall personally fetch a piece of cake and push it into your wicked mouth!' Poppy said but she wasn't really annoyed. Robin could tell that. She was laughing inside

171

and really quite liked what Auntie Jessie was saying.

But Robin did not, and now she leaned further back against the wall, and bent her head so that her chin was resting on her knees and watched the last rounds of musical cushions, trying not to think about what Auntie Jessie had said. Everyone was shouting and jumping up and down now, because there were only three people left in the game, Cynthia and Molly and a rather small but very agile boy called Arnold who had managed to get this far by wriggling his way past all the other players with such speed and eel-like grace that he had not failed to grab a cushion every time. Now, as the music stopped with a sudden screech of needle on record – which made the curly man grimace across the room at Poppy and then laugh – he succeeded again. It was Cynthia who was left standing disgruntled, as Molly seized the other cushion and fell on it with great triumph.

Cynthia was red with chagrin and Robin noticed that; serve her right, she thought. And then as the music began again, Cynthia came stamping across the room to throw herself down on Robin's other side and hiss in her ear, 'I shall never speak to that Molly again, not ever! She cheated, did you see, she cheated? She pulled the cushion away so that she could sit on it and you're supposed to leave it where it is – '

'Really?' Robin said loftily and tilted her chin in the air and wouldn't look at her.

'She did, she did! Didn't you see? I shan't ever be her friend again, not ever. Don't you be her friend either, Robin. It'll be just you and me and never Molly ever again. I hate her.'

'Then why were you giggling and whispering before and not telling me why?' Robin said and looked at her sideways.

'That wasn't my fault!' Cynthia said and smoothed down her blue tulle frock with careful hands, not looking

172

at Robin. 'That was Molly's fault. She kept whispering at me and I had to be polite, didn't I?'

'Hmmph,' Robin said and sniffed. 'You weren't very polite to me, were you?'

'I'm sorry, Robin, honestly I am,' Cynthia said, all contrition. 'Shall I fetch you an ice to save you going? Will that make up for it?'

'Maybe,' Robin said, her nose in the air again and Cynthia at once got to her feet and went running across the room to the door, to which the other people were being shepherded by a flustered Goosey, to fetch ices from downstairs which they could eat from little dishes with tiny spoons while they cooled down from the heating excitement of the musical cushions game, and got their breath back ready to play Blind Man's Bluff. She walked past Molly with her own chin well in the air, at which Molly, who had lost the last cushion to the highly determined Arnold, looked thoroughly downcast. Robin watched them, knowing that a little while ago seeing that would have made her feel much better. She would have laughed, really, to see what had happened to the silly whisperers and been glad.

But now she was not glad at all and she shifted her gaze to the other side of the room where her mother and Auntie Jessie were standing talking very animatedly to the curly man. David Deveen, Robin thought. I suppose I shall have to call him Mr Deveen. Or even –

But she refused to think any more about him or about her mother. Nor would she think about what happened to children when their mothers got married. Mummy wasn't getting married. No one had said Mummy was getting married. Of course she wasn't. But all the same, Robin understood a good deal more of what Auntie Jessie hadn't said from what she *had* said, and she watched her mother now, a little pink and looking shiny somehow as she talked to the Deveen man.

And looked away and saw her grandmother Amberly on the high-backed chair in the corner, brought in specially from the study for her to sit on. She too was watching Poppy and David Deveen and her face had a sort of wooden look on it that Robin had seen before. She always looked like that when she saw people she didn't like very much or people who were misbehaving. She sometimes had that sort of face on when Chloe was being silly; and now she was looking at Mummy's new man friend like it. And he wasn't behaving in a silly way at all.

Robin suddenly felt that dull flat dead feeling inside which she got sometimes. It always made her think that nothing nice would ever happen again. It was a feeling that came over her for no reason usually, and she always hated it. If she was on her own she could go and find a book and read that until the feeling went away, or persuade Goosey to give her something nice to eat; that mostly helped. But today she wasn't hungry at all, after so much birthday tea, and nothing surely could be as much fun as her own birthday party. Reading a book couldn't possibly be better and even if she could manage, it certainly couldn't make the dull dead inside feeling go away. It felt too big for that.

Cynthia reappeared at the door, carefully balancing two ice cream dishes in her hands and began to come over the room towards her, and Robin got to her feet and headed for the door the long way round, making her way well out of Cynthia's sight. She didn't want ice cream and she didn't want Cynthia. She wanted – she didn't know what. But the first step to getting it was to be outside this room and well away from Mummy and Auntie Jessie and David Deveen and Grandmamma looking wooden.

Just as she reached the door Goosey appeared in it and she couldn't get past her, though she tried, attempting to push her way through, but Goosey put a firm hand on her shoulder and said, 'Where are you going, Miss Robin? You can't leave your guests you know – and didn't your little friend fetch you an ice cream? Yes, there she is. Go along now and thank her nicely for her trouble – '

'No,' Robin said and swallowed hard. The feeling was getting worse, and to make it extra hateful there were sharp needles in her throat. They were tears, she knew that, and it was imperative she got out of the room before they pushed their horrid way up to her nose and burst out of her eyes. It wasn't often it happened, crying, but when it did it was dreadfully shaming. And she swallowed again and shook her head and Goosey bent down, all concern and anxiety and said, 'Why, Miss Robin, whatever is it? Are you all right, my little dear?'

Robin shook her head and tried to push past again and Goosey let out a little yelp as she almost toppled and then, suddenly, everyone in the room was looking at them, and Robin wanted to die a little bit. More than a little bit, in fact. She wanted to die altogether.

'Whatever is the matter?' That was Mummy standing behind her, and then to Robin's horror there was the man with his curly hair crouching down beside her, so that his face was at the same level as her own.

'Everything all right, then?' he said easily. 'Sure it is. Hey, I'll fix it shall I?' And then he was standing up and reaching down and picking her up; she Robin, seven years old today, being picked up like a baby!

'We'll be back in a moment,' he said easily over his shoulder to the people in the drawing-room who were staring. 'Just a spill on a party frock – finish your ices and we'll be back to start the games going in a trice – '

And he carried Robin out of the drawing-room, with Mummy and Goosey following anxiously and as he set her on her feet, which to do him credit, he did very quickly, he reached back swiftly and closed the door so that no one in the room could see them.

175

'There,' he said in a comfortable voice. 'Now, you can sort it out in decent obscurity, hmm? Whatever it is that's upset you, Robin, you don't need other people muscling in – '

Robin said nothing. She couldn't, because somewhere between the drawing-room and here in the hallway the tears had started and she was so angry with herself and so miserable she would have shouted if she'd had any breath to spare. But it took all the air she had in her to stop herself from crying out loud as the scalding tears slid down her face and made her mouth crumple.

'Not to worry,' David Deveen said cheerfully to Poppy. 'Just a bit too much party, I reckon. It always used to take me this way. What with the presents and the candles and the games – it's more than any sensible person can handle without feeling a bit stirred up.'

'But it's never happened to Robin at her parties before – ' Poppy said anxiously and now it was her turn to crouch in front of Robin.

'What is it, darling?' she murmured and took a hanky from her sleeve and began to mop at Robin's hot eyes. 'Are you feeling ill?'

Robin shook her head and tried to speak but the words wouldn't come out properly. All she managed was a squeak. 'I'm all right,' was what she tried to say but Poppy still looked worried.

'Was someone nasty to you? I saw Cynthia and Molly talking. Did they leave you out of their game?'

Robin seized on that. Mummy was always good at things you never thought grown-ups would be good at, and she nodded now, very grateful to have something to nod about.

'Ah!' Poppy's face cleared. 'Well, I did think – well, there it is, my love. People can be silly sometimes, but they mean no harm, I'm sure if you go back into the drawing-room Cynthia will be just as friendly as ever. I saw Molly pushing her when she tried to get onto a cushion and of course her foolish mother pretended she hadn't noticed! I dare say they'll be on bad terms now. Wipe your face, darling – that's right. Good. You look much better. Try a smile – well done!' as Robin managed a watery sort of grin. 'And we'll go back. You can't leave guests, you see, however upset you may be over something. You have to make an effort. Don't you?' And she looked up at the other two grown-ups for agreement.

It was David who answered. 'Of course,' he said. 'Robin can do it, I know she can. Hey, Robin?' And he put one hand on her shoulder.

Robin almost tore herself away from him, she moved so fast, turning to her mother and then wriggling so that she stood well out of reach.

'I'm all right,' she said with all the dignity she could. It was easier now, for the tears had, at last, stopped. 'I can't think what all the fuss is about – '

Poppy laughed and straightened her knees to stand up and then bent to brush the dust from her frock, which was a rich green and did rather show any marks. 'Really, you sound older than Grandma Amberly sometimes,' she said. 'One of these days, my darling, I'll understand what goes on inside your head, but I won't pretend there aren't times you confuse me a great deal – Oh, well, if you're all right, we'll go back to the party. Come along – '

And then she stopped and turned her head and listened and went to the head of the stairs to peer down.

'Who's that?' she called and then her voice altered. 'Oh,' she said. 'Hello Chloe. I wondered if you'd get here – '

14

Chloe hadn't meant to forget Robin's birthday party; she had been given ample reminders, after all. When she had got up in the morning the whole house had been in a fuss of balloon-blowing and cake-making and Goosey had been bustling about quite absurdly. It had all been too much, Chloe had thought. There had been a moment when standing in her dressing gown at the top of the kitchen stairs and peering down looking for signs of breakfast, she had remembered her own young birthday parties. Forever ago, of course, twelve years or more, when Daddy had been here – and she had sniffed hard and run down the stairs and said loudly, 'For heaven's sake! Can't a person get coffee and toast in this wretched kitchen?' And that of course had made Goosey stop her cake-making and set about her breakfast, which was only right and proper. It wasn't fair, people fussing over this birthday party, rather than one of her own –

But then she had gone out and her irritation had been washed away in fun. Bernie had invited her to a summer lunch party and had added mysteriously, 'I shan't tell you where, but be at Charing Cross Pier on the Embankment at half past ten this Sunday morning to meet me and all will be revealed.' And then said that it was to be al fresco – in the open air. So, she had put on her newest and prettiest voile frock in the palest primrose and her new summer straw hat with the tilted brim which set off

178

her small face so perfectly and had felt all the rage; and when she had seen the sharp-eyed stares of the other girls on the boat that it turned out Bernie had hired to take them all down the Thames to Greenwich, she had positively preened.

Oh, it had been a wonderful party! All morning, as the hot June sun warmed the decks and made the men take off their blazers, they had danced to the sound of the newest jazz on the gramophone and drunk champagne and then lunched on lobster salad and been very, very silly. And then when a special few had gone below to have their special fun (and it had been marvellous of course, though sometimes Chloe worried about how much it was all costing. It was only the twentieth of the month and already her allowance had gone; she'd have to draw on some of her capital soon at this rate) it had been even better. She sat there curled up in the corner with Bernie's arm set casually across her shoulders and known herself to be exceedingly fortunate. Here she was at the most divinely sophisticated party with the best-looking man in the entire world and having a most unbelievably exciting time; and she had thought dreamily of her old friends, those silly Marys and Rogers and Joes and Teddys and pitied them for their boringness and for not being here to see her and admire her. It really couldn't be better –

But then it *had* got better, because Bernie had begun to murmur in her ear about his new venture and she had listened, bewildered at first and then with increasing excitement. It had never been any part of her plan to *work* at all, to take a job anywhere. Only dreary people did things like that. There were jobs of course that one could consider, being on the wireless, perhaps, or acting on the films so that people stared at you in the streets and asked for your autograph. That would be worth doing and not a bit like work. And here was Bernie offering her that sort of job; it seemed too unbelievably good to be true. But it was true. He made that very clear.

'It's as handsome a set-up as you ever saw,' he said. 'Just off the Rue Montmartre, in the most elegant quarter of all Paris. A cellar of course – the best places always are – and massive? You never saw one so huge. Stage all set with bronze mirrors and glass and lit from below as well as overhead, chrome everywhere, real sumptuous.'

'As nice as the gaming room at The Rat Trap?' Chloe asked.

'Better ducks, better. Me, I never go backwards and I don't ever stand still neither. A new place means a new look. A better look. A richer look. So Armand and I, we chose only the most unusual stuff we could find – '

'Armand?'

He waved a hand dismissively. 'My French partner. Does the donkey work. I'm the brains, of course, and I'm in charge. Anyway, we made it the best we knew how. And the show we'll put on will be the best, too. Lovely girls, lovely frocks, real eyecatchers. You'd be perfect. Are you interested?'

She had widened her eyes and twisted her head to stare at him, though it was difficult to focus; her head was still a little muzzy from their last bit of fun. 'Interested in what?'

He had laughed then. 'Joining us, ducks, joining us! I told you, we want gorgeous girls in gorgeous frocks for the show. Dancers and singers and *girls* – '

'I can't sing or dance,' she said. 'I mean, I can, but only in the ordinary sort of way. Not on a stage – '

'I didn't imagine you would,' he said. 'For the dancing and singing we want professionals, none but the best. I've got Margaret Kelly – Miss Bluebell, you know?' Chloe didn't, but that didn't matter. ' – She's looking out for me. Says she can train 'em as long as we don't use her

180

name, because they'll go mad at the Folies if they find out. Don't you see? Only the best. As for singers – coming from America they are, and black as the ace of spades. It's the line-up I want you for. The gorgeous girls in the gorgeous frocks who come out at the start of the show, move around among the punters – the customers – and again at the end and persuade 'em to go back to the gaming rooms. Even the losers start again once they've see a good show, had a few drinks, found a pretty girl on their laps for a moment of two. What do you say?'

'I don't know,' she had said and shaken her head in confusion. 'I mean, me in a show? In *Paris*? How could I? Where would I live?'

'Oh,' he had said casually. 'That'd be no problem. I've taken a house – big one, lots of space. You could live there, I could find you a really nice room, good decor, make it dainty for you. There'll be some of the other girls staying there too. I'll pay you three quid a week and the chances are you'd get more. The punters can be really nice to girls they like the look of. You could clear over a fiver easy. Maybe even double it if you make a special effort.'

Her eyes had widened at that. Her income was a good one and more than enough for her needs – or had been until she had started sharing Bernie's interests as she had but had only been around five pounds every week. That had kept her in frocks and *maquillage* and petrol and repairs for her little car well enough; but how would it be to have more than twice that? She couldn't imagine it. And for doing something that was so much fun, too; walking about on a stage in pretty clothes and having people look at you and admire you; and to do it in Paris! It seemed unbelievable.

Then for a moment her basic commonsense lifted its head and peered out through her eyes and stared at him.

Could he be trusted? Was he telling the truth? After all, she had heard all the tales about white slavers who stole girls away and turned them into the dregs of society. She had read too many shilling shockers and steeped herself in too much Edgar Wallace and Oppenheim not to know that. But he stared back at her, his eyes wide and candid and she thought – I'm being silly. This is Bernie. He cares for me. He wouldn't do a thing like that. Anyway, it's always strangers who do that to girls in the stories. They snatch them up in the night or spirit them away. It's not something that happens with people they know. And I could make sure –

'Could I go and see for myself, first?' she said then, and was surprised at her own shrewdness. 'Could I go and look at the place and at the house where I'd live and so forth? After all, it might turn out to be awful.'

'Of course! You'd be a fool if you didn't,' he said. 'If you hadn't the wit to look at all the options before you started I'd think you were a complete ass. And I don't want complete asses on my payroll, ducks, take it from me. Come on. Up on deck, or we'll have all the Caspar Milktoast types coming down and wanting to know what's happening. And that'd be a nuisance.' He had got to his feet. 'I'm going over tomorrow for a couple of days. You can come if you like. The seven o'clock crossing from Dover to Calais and a fast train up to Gay Paree. You could have lunch in a Montmartre bistro, have a good look round and be home again in safe and sunny Holland Park by bedtime – phone me later tonight and let me know if you're coming. I've got other people to talk to, you see, if you're not interested – '

That had been the thing that had convinced her. That he was willing to show her what the job meant – and she had giggled inside her head at that thought; she, Chloe Bradman, with a job? – and then had made it clear that he was not going to attempt to persuade her to take it, made all the difference. No one who was planning to do something awful would ever behave like that, it was obvious. So she had gone back on deck and enjoyed the party till the boat arrived back at Charing Cross Pier, and then climbed into her car and buzzed back to Norland Square as fast as she could.

She had to tell Poppy about it; and she had actually looked fowards to seeing her stepmother. There had been so many times when Poppy had hinted – or even downright said – that Chloe ought to have an occupation. Well, she was going to have one, once she had been to Paris to make sure it was what she wanted. It would earn a lot of money and that surely should impress her. Altogether it would be very agreeable to have Poppy and Goosey smile at her admiringly for a change instead of always looking so exasperated. And she had positively glowed with satisfaction as she pulled the car into the curb with a squeal of brakes and ran up the steps to the front door.

And straight into that wretched child's birthday party. She stood in the hall staring at Poppy looking down at her, her keys still in her hand, and felt her heart sink. Oh, hell and damnation! And she would have liked to say it aloud, except that it wouldn't be worth the fuss over what they pleased to call bad language.

'I would have thought you could be back sooner than this, Chloe,' Poppy said and her voice was cool to the point of frostiness. 'It's only one a year after all, and everyone else is here.'

Chloe looked at the balloons festooned over the hat-stand and the wreck of the birthday tea visible through the open dining-room door and heard the high voices of the children in the drawing-room above, and in her chagrin said the first thing that came into her head.

'Even Uncle George?'

Poppy reddened. 'You know perfectly well that your

Uncle does not attend such events as Robin's parties,' she said stiffly. 'He only comes to yours – '

'I can't imagine why,' Chloe muttered and pushed her keys into her pocket and began to pull off her gloves. She knew of course that Poppy found George Pringle difficult; their relationship was remote to say the least; he had been the husband of Poppy's sister-in-law, no more, and once Mabel had died there had been little to bind them. Except Chloe. George had been one of the executors of Bobby's will and had always meddled in Chloe's affairs as a result, seeming to think, as Poppy sometimes said wrathfully, that he was Chloe's guardian when he was nothing of the sort, and only her uncle by marriage anyway. They had had enough disagreements over the years regarding Chloe for there to be cool blood between them and Chloe was well aware of it. To taunt Poppy now with George's absence from her beloved Robin's party was hardly the way to start a good conversation with her, and somewhere at the back of her mind Chloe regretted having done so. She had so much wanted Poppy to be glad about her new opportunity, and now it had all gone wrong.

And she set her lower lip into a mulish line and went marching up the stairs looking as cool as she could.

'Well, I'm here now,' she snapped as she swept past Poppy and went to the next flight. 'But don't bother with any tea for me, for I shan't be here to take it. I'm going to my room.' And up she marched, leaving Poppy alone on the landing staring up at her.

And glad to be on her own. David had with great tact withdrawn into the drawing-room with Robin, urging Goosey to go too, and Poppy had been aware of his hand on the door as he closed it, and had been grateful to him for his good sense. At least no one else knew that once again Poppy and her stepdaughter had clashed swords, and her eyes pricked with sudden tears of anger and regret as the door above slammed noisily. Why did it always have to be this way? Why couldn't they be friends, at least? They had both loved Bobby so very much, had both been so desolated by his death, they should have found some comfort together. But all that had ever been there between them was suspicion and sudden flurries of anger.

And Poppy couldn't pretend it was all Chloe's fault. Yes, the child was thoughtless sometimes and dreadfully spoiled and headstrong but there was good in her somewhere. There were times when she could be very sweet and genuinely caring, when her usual selfishness dissolved into an awareness of other's needs; and after all she was only nineteen, little more than a child.

But then Poppy remembered herself at nineteen, an ambulance driver in France seeing heaven knew what miseries, and bearing responsibilities so heavy they were almost unbearable; Chloe wasn't that young. But Poppy herself was often difficult, she was sure; a lonely widow beset with anxieties about her own small child and the importance of making a living for her, and somewhere deep inside bitterly resentful of the way her stepdaughter frittered money that should at least have been shared equally with Bobby's other child — no, the pair of them had never really had a chance to be on good terms. And Poppy regretted that so very much.

Now she turned to go back to the drawing room and her guests, schooling her face to show no hint of any problems (for Molly's tiresome mother would be the first to come and twitter round her and ask impertinent questions and generally make a nuisance of herself if she could) and tried to stop thinking about Chloe and what she would have to do to sort out this present disagreement. They would have to make friends again, eventually, somehow —

Up in her room, Chloe too was brooding over what

had happened. Why did Poppy always have to make such a fuss over everything? If she hadn't been so sharp about forgetting the party, had made some sort of joke about Chloe arriving so late, it would have been so much easier. Chloe could have laughed and been sorry and said so, and would have gone running up to her room to fetch the present she had brought for her small stepsister (a large china doll with a great many clothes to put on and take off, including real underwear) and joined in the silly games with the children. Then afterwards they could have talked and it all would have been so nice –

But Poppy as usual had turned it into a fight with her sharp tongue and her wretched hurry over everything. Just because she had to go to work and that meant she had a lot to do she didn't have to rush everyone else, Chloe thought resentfully. One of these days Poppy would rush something important out of her life, that was what would happen. And then she would be sorry.

And perhaps, Chloe thought then, sitting up in her bed instead of lying sprawled on it in angry tears, perhaps that time is now? Perhaps I ought to do what I want to do and never even tell Poppy about it? Not till afterwards, anyway.

She sat and thought for a long time, and then got to her feet and went to the door and peered out. All she could hear was the sound of singing from below and the piano in the drawing-room thumping out 'Oranges and Lemons' and she could imagine them all there, the children in a row ducking under the linked hands of two of them, with the grown-ups joining in and pretending they were only doing it for the children but really loving it for themselves, and for a moment almost wished she could go down and just walk in and take her place in the line as well. But then as the children's voices rose into, 'And here comes a candle to light you to bed, and here comes a chopper to – chop – off – your – HEAD!' she steeled herself. That was silly stuff, children's stuff, Norland Square stuff. She was going to do better than that. She was going to Paris to live in a house with lots of other jolly girls and to be a gorgeous creature in gorgeous frocks on a stage. She had the chance to have a better life than this and she was going to take it.

She slipped down the stairs again and out of the house, and hurried to the car. There always seemed the risk someone would look out and see her, but no one seemed to be aware at all of what she was doing and somehow that added to her determination. She had made up her mind and if anyone tried to stop her there would be trouble; yet it would have shown someone cared if there had been a face at the drawing-room window, a waving hand to stop her, someone looking concerned about her.

She scowled a little as she pushed the car through the traffic, heading for Mayfair and Haunch of Venison Yard, but as the road spun away beneath her wheels she began to feel better, excited and hopeful, and she thought – please let him be there. Please make sure he's there. Because if he isn't and I have to wait to tell him, I'll die, I'll just die. I want to go now, I really do, and he may think I don't and take someone else, and that would be awful.

She parked the car in Bond Street and walked into the little yard and her heart tightened as she stared at the door of The Rat Trap. That was a padlock on it, surely? But she moved closer and then breathed more easily. The padlock was open, and it was clear there was someone inside, and she pulled the door open and stepped into the dimness, leaving the yellow late afternoon sunshine behind her, and called tentatively, 'Bernie? Are you here, Bernie? Bernie?'

There was no answer and she moved further into the dimness, knowing her way and feeling sure he was there somewhere. The place smelled different in the daytime.

None of the exciting promise of the night in the stuffy rooms now. Just stale cigar smoke and the remains of perfume dying in a sickly fall in the dusty air and the reek of spilled gin and whisky; and she wrinkled her nose a little and moved forwards more quickly.

The door at the end that led into the gaming room was open and she moved even more certainly now. He had an office on the other side, she knew that, and it was clear that was where he was, and she almost ran into the hidden room and looked round. The big tables were shrouded in holland covers and the mirrored bar was dark and she could just see her own shadowy figure reflected in it; and she stood still for a second, staring. It was an odd moment, for she felt suddenly that she was on the edge of something; that she was about to step over a great chasm into a totally different world. The shadowy shape that was herself stood and stared back at her, a slender figure with a neat head and she put up one hand to touch the waves at the side and the reflection imitated her almost mockingly. And she shook herself a little for being so silly and turned her head to look for where to go next and saw at the far side the door that clearly led to his office, for it was ajar and a light was shining through it to throw a wedge of bright yellow onto the carpet.

He was sitting sprawled on a long black sofa at the side of the well-furnished room, a cigar in one hand and a sheaf of papers in the other and he looked up quickly as she came in and stared at her blankly, as though she were a stranger, and she stared back, suddenly frightened. He looked different somehow, sharper and not quite as beautiful and she said hesitantly. 'Bernie? It's only me – '

He gazed back and then his face changed and became the one she knew and liked so much, warm and cheerful and smiling and she smiled too, in relief.

'Hey, I thought we left you at Charing Cross!' he said and set his papers down on the table to one side and left his cigar resting on an ashtray there. 'Didn't you go home after all?'

She made a face. 'I did. And wish I hadn't. Never mind that. Listen, Bernie, I'd love to work for you. I've thought about it, and I know it'll be all right. I'd love to do the job and I'll go with you tomorrow. And if you like I can stay there right away. Would you like that?'

He sat and looked at her and then slowly his face broadened into a wide smile that made his teeth glint and showed his dimples clearly.

'Would I like that?' he said softly and then opened his arms wide, 'Does a cat like cream? Come and try me, ducks. Just come and try me.'

And without being quite sure what she was walking into, Chloe went across to him and sat on the sofa beside him. And then found herself wrapped in his arms and somehow not sitting at all any more, but lying flat on her back and staring up at his face which was now closer to hers than it had ever been. And then being kissed in a way that was very unusual indeed, in Chloe's hitherto limited experience.

15

'I must say, it looks really classy,' Jessie said with huge satisfaction and stepped back even further to admire it even more. Her red silk coat strained a little round her ample haunches but still looked magnificent, her hair was piled high in the most elaborate of curled shingles under her crimson cloche and her face was exuberant with rouge and powder. She looked singularly pleased with herself and Poppy laughed aloud with pleasure at seeing so much obvious happiness.

'Look at that, Poppela!' Jessie cried and threw out one hand towards the fascia above the huge glass front of the establishment before which they stood. 'Did you ever see anything so smart, hey? No one can do anything better than that, not if they was to try a year and a half, believe me.'

'I know,' Poppy said, amused. 'Who chose it, darling Jessie, for heaven's sake?'

'And you done good, Poppy, you really did.' And now Jessie turned and hugged her, to the amusement of many of the people going past them in the busy street, and Poppy let her do it and didn't care at all what sort of an exhibition Jessie was making of them both. It wasn't every day a new restaurant opened, after all.

It really did look very good indeed. Behind the great glass spread of the window discreet curtains in the most pale of lilac net were lavishly draped, and shadowy tables on which small lamps burned could be seen through them. Above the window there was a wide bronze mirrored fascia and on it, in cursive handwriting, ran the legend 'Jessie's', each letter outlined in rich violet-coloured light. Even at this hour of the day, half an hour before lunch, the light was on and reflected against its background very effectively. The main door to the restaurant was a revolving one, and each panel of glass in it repeated, in careful engraving, the same flowing 'Jessie's'. Even Poppy, who had chosen every item of the design of the place and who had worked so many long hours making sure it was all ready for today, was gratified. She could not deny that she had, as Jessie had said, 'done good'. It made her feel better to have made so successful a job of her first major responsibility as a new partner in the company.

But then some of her pleasure was diluted as that thought came to her, and as Jessie went on staring up at her own name glowing so brightly and hopefully into the elegance of Duke Street, where so many very expensive potential customers passed by, she tried to push it away. But she couldn't. All week, even as the work here had reached a crescendo of busyness, she had been bothered about Chloe. The girl had been irritated, admittedly, at being told off for forgetting her sister's party, and had been tiresome enough in return, but surely that hadn't justified the way she had subsequently behaved? To have marched off as she had to spend a week with Mary Challoner had been downright sulky. Poppy had considered the possibility of going after her and making her come home and apologize to her sister as well as to her stepmother, but David had persuaded her that was not a good idea at all.

He had stayed long after the other guests had gone, taking their weary children with them, and after a somewhat subdued but apparently happy Robin had gone to bed with her new dolls to accompany her, to talk. And had let her go on a good deal about the difficulties of Chloe and how she felt about her, and said nothing, just listening and watching her through the smoke that curled from his ever present cigarette. That was one of the most comforting things about David, and something she had come to value deeply in the weeks since he had arrived in England. Not the visits to the theatre and opera, agreeable as they were, nor the quiet dinners in Soho restaurants, fun though they were, but these evenings at home after Robin was asleep and Goosey had climbed her early way to bed, when she could talk aloud and he would listen. It didn't matter what she talked about; it was simply that he was there to be talked to. Nor did it matter that he rarely offered any particular response to what she said. That wasn't what she wanted most of the time.

But sometimes he did make a response. He had when she had talked to him about Jessie's offer of a partnership. It had been he who had finally persuaded her that to refuse the opportunity would be madness.

'She's the perfect partner,' he had said. 'She loves you, she's an honest woman, but above all she is clearly a superb businesswoman. That set-up she's got – magnificent, really magnificent. Don't be unfair to everyone by refusing, Poppy. If she wants you then it has to be good for you as well as for her business, and at the same time, you'll be doing good for Robin – '

So, she had. And this time, when he once again gave her direct advice she once again took it.

'Don't run after Chloe, Poppy,' he had said and ground out his cigarette before reaching for another. 'She needs time, and so do you. She's gone to a friend? Fair enough. Let her cool her heels and you cool down too. The trouble with both of you, I reckon, is that you both have very short fuses. So lay off for a while – '

So she had but that hadn't prevented her from being

anxious and thinking about Chloe. She didn't phone and she didn't send messages, and to Goosey's particular hurt had actually locked her bedroom door.

'I only wanted to go and tidy up for her,' Goosey had said tearfully. 'I wouldn't have tried to open it otherwise. I wasn't prying or nothing nor would I touch anything she didn't want touched. Who should know better than me that's had the care of her all her life? And then she goes and locks her bedroom door on me. It's too bad – '

That had almost made her go to the phone to call Chloe at Mary's house, but she had remembered David's advice and stopped herself. It wouldn't help to call her to complain yet again. They had to meet next time on agreeable terms. That was the key; David had said so. And it was getting now that what David said went. Because he was so very obviously right.

'That's enough out here,' Jessie announced then and pulled Poppy out of her reverie. 'Inside, eh? We'll look at everything else – '

And look she did. She took off her coat and hat to reveal a matching red dress of such effulgence and so rich in folds, frills and pleats that it looked as though it would stand on its own without Jessie to hold it up, and marched all over her new establishment. She checked the hems on the lavender table cloths and held up to the light a large number of glasses to inspect them for fingerprints. She rubbed silver forks on a napkin and then checked that the napkins had been folded precisely as they should be. She peered under the serving tables for dust and inspected every waiter's hands for clean nails (and not one of the seven of them, lofty creatures that they were, objected at all, much to Poppy's relieved surprise) and then marched out to the kitchens to inspect there as well.

Poppy held her breath, for here the chef who reigned supreme, a tall dour man in his late forties, had put the fear of hell-fire into every one of his staff and had made

Poppy herself wary; she had been content to run every-thing else and to leave the kitchens to him once she had appointed him. But Jessie understood him for she took one look at him and cried, 'Harry!' and held her arms out and he grinned for the first time since Poppy had met him, and hugged her.

'I didn't know you knew each other!' Poppy said and Jessie grinned at her over her shoulder.

'Listen, do you think I'd have a chef in one of my restaurants I didn't know? At Cable Street I can be there, watch everything. Here I had to have someone who'd watch over everything the way I do. It's different food here, sure, more fancy, not so *heimische* – all right, homely, okay? – more fancy, maybe, but it's got to be *right*. So I sent one of my best old friends to see you when you began interviewing.' And she reached up and pinched the chef's leathery cheek affectionately.

'I give up,' Poppy said in a resigned voice. 'Here was I thinking that I was doing it all on my own, and all the time you were in the background twitching my strings.'

'Don't feel bad, dolly,' Jessie said and looked some-what shamefaced. 'Believe me, I meant no harm. I meddled with nothing else at all. But when it comes to chefs, I had to. Anyway, I wasn't so wicked. Did I tell you you had to have him? I did not. You told me you was interviewing chefs, so I sent him. I knew you'd choose him, because he's the best and got the best history. I knew it'd be all right – '

'And suppose I'd chosen someone else? Suppose I'd hated Harry's face?' Poppy said and grinned at Harry to make it clear she meant no insult. 'I took to him, obviously, but just suppose – would you have insisted?'

'Don't ask silly questions!' Jessie said airily. 'Who cares what might have been? It's what *is* that matters. You chose and you chose right. So show me, Harry, what's what. The menu – what you got for this first day

194

that's special? The usual menu I've seen already, and it's good. No fancy schmancy but good. But you'll have everyday specials according to the markets?'

Poppy left them. Jessie would spend the next half hour happily talking food with Harry and Poppy would be superfluous; and she needed time to think and make sure that all was ready in her department, in the front of the restaurant where the customers would be. It had been a hard pull since she had finally gone to Jessie and told her she would accept the partnership; they had worked all the hours there were, it sometimes seemed to Poppy, finding the right premises and then making the shopfitters sweat to get it ready. But they'd done it and here they were, ready to open barely a month after the partnership papers had been signed; and Poppy marvelled at how effective Jessie could be. She was herself a hard worker, but Jessie was, in her own words, a hustler; someone who made people dance to her piping. And she always piped fast.

'I can't sit around and wait for English gentlemen,' she had cried over and over again. 'We need a bit of American hustle here – so let's go!' And go they all had, from Poppy and Jessie via stuffy solicitors down to the most junior carpenter's mate and kitchen fitter.

She stood now in the pretty quietness of the restaurant, staring out of the shrouded windows at the street and the strollers there, and marvelled at how different it was from Cable Street. There the passers-by – and therefore the customers – were a much different crew; of all sorts of occupation and all sorts of language and accent. Here they were all very English and very much of one class; leisured and lazy and mostly rich. And a part of her thought – I like Cable Street people better; it's more vibrant and fun there. Here people are so drawling and dull –

But rich; and she thought of Robin and how fast she

was growing and her need for shoes and dresses, of the many corners of the Norland Square house which were dreadfully shabby, and of the way Goosey was getting old and frail before her eyes and really needed another servant to help her, and straightened her shoulders. Money had to be made and there was an end of it. And she, with dear Jessie to guide her, was going to make it here.

The big revolving door moved and began a slow spin and Poppy felt her heart lift into her throat, or so it seemed. Their first customer and they weren't supposed to be open for another fifteen minutes. But she would turn no one away of course and she moved forwards bravely, a professionally welcoming smile on her face.

And then stopped and relaxed as the smile converted to a genuinely pleased one.

'David!' she said and held out both hands. 'What are you doing here?'

'Come to launch you on your way, of course,' he said. 'And to do myself a bit of good.' He had his camera slung over one shoulder and he patted it. 'I'm doing a story about you!'

'A story about us?' She stared. 'I'm delighted, but why? I mean, what on earth can a Baltimore newspaper want with a story about a London restaurant?'

He laughed and looked very pleased with himself. 'I worried about that. I'd set my heart on doing it and couldn't find an angle, but then, when Jessie told me she'd had a place there, it was a cert. They'll love the idea. "Baltimore Deli Queen Wows London!" I got the go ahead this morning. So, is she here? I have to talk to Jessie of course and get pictures of her and the place and then I'll be able to relax and have some lunch myself. Okay?'

'Couldn't be better!' Poppy said and grinned too. 'Lunch on the house, of course.'

'Of course,' he said and looked round. 'It looks great. Very classy.'

'You Americans! Supposed to be above all that sort of thing, but you talk about class more than anyone here. That was what Jessie said too – '

'There's class and class,' David said and pulled his camera off his shoulder and began to fiddle with the various attachments, and to load magnesium powder into the fire bar. 'The sort we like is the sort you get for yourself, not the sort you're born with. Listen, let me get a shot while it's quiet and then later on, when there's a few customers in, would you mind?'

'As long as they don't,' Poppy said. 'If people are lunching with the wrong companions they might object – '

'I'll make sure I'm easily seen getting ready,' he promised. 'Then anyone who's got a bad conscience can move out of the way. How are you, Poppy? All right?'

She laughed. 'I'm about the same as I was last night,' she said gravely. 'After we got back from the concert. Which I loved, by the way.'

'Good. It seems a long time ago since we said good-night.' He threw a sharp little glance at her under his camera, with which he was now fiddling, under a dark cloth. 'It always seems ages between seeing you.'

'It's never that long these days,' she said as lightly as she could, though it wasn't easy. It was ridiculous how this man could make her chest tighten when he looked at her. She thought briefly and confusedly of Bobby and how he had been able to make her feel, and tried to push that away; there was no disloyalty here, surely? 'We seem to see each other every day.'

'Not often enough,' he said and then opened his mouth to say more; but the door from the kitchen flew open and Jessie surged out in a rustle of crimson and suddenly made the place feel smaller.

'Mr Deveen,' she cried after a short moment of

surprise and then beamed at both of them. 'There's a treat! A visit from an old friend, hey, Poppy? Ain't it grand when old friends turn out for you?'

'Grand,' said Poppy and went on hastily, seeing the roguish glint in Jessie's eye as she looked from one to the other of them. 'David's here to talk to you, Jessie. He's writing about us in his paper – '

Jessie was distracted at once, and was all business-woman. 'A story? Marvellous! Publicity we need badly. But we need it more in London than Baltimore. Can you get your article into another paper here as well?'

'Such gratitude!' he said and patted her shoulder. 'Of course I'll try to. I don't see why not. I'm doing a bit of freelancing on the side, and the London *Star* might be interested. Right now I need pictures of you and Poppy in the kitchen and then the chef and then maybe – '

He led her back to the kitchen talking busily and Poppy, after checking with her head waiter Horace that the wine was precisely as it should be (it was, of course, and Horace looked mortally wounded that she had thought it needful to ask), followed them.

The kitchen was now showing signs of edginess. Harry was standing ready behind his main hob and his *sous-chefs* and assorted assistants were standing poised and ready. Pans and ovens sizzled and hissed and all round were platters of prepared foods, just waiting to be ordered so that they could be cooked. Steaks spread on great wooden boards and staining them with their blood (Poppy had to avert her eyes from them) and rows of gutted scaled fish gleaming on metal trays, and vegetables and fruit salads and puddings all set waiting mutely for the moment of truth when the first real customers would arrive. Everyone looked as nervous as Poppy felt, except Jessie. She was chattering happily to David, who was scribbling at a great rate in his notebook, and seemed supremely confident, and that helped Poppy a good deal.

If Jessie was so sure customers would walk in to try the new establishment – and she most certainly was certain – then it would happen. Of that Poppy had no doubt, for Jessie had never been wrong yet, as far as she knew.

And she wasn't this time. Just as David had finished taking his photographs of Poppy and Jessie and Harry, half blinding them with the flash, one of the waiters came bustling through the service door, his face glowing with delight at being the first.

'The vichyssoise soup for one and the smoked salmon for one,' he shouted at the top of his voice even though the usual kitchen din was far from evident yet. 'And they'll follow with the salmon aspic and a chicken salad and there's three more tables giving orders right now –'

Poppy fled and emerged into her restaurant to find it transformed. It had looked delightful before, but in a somewhat lifeless way, like a wax doll rather than a living breathing creature, but now it was very much alive. Only four of the twenty six tables were occupied but that was enough to light up the big cool room with its walls covered in lilac silk hangings and its engraved bronze mirrors, for the occupants were the sort of people who made no efforts to modulate their tones at all; they spoke of their activities at the tops of their voices and had no shame whatever about it. So four tables could and did make a lot of cheerful sound.

Even as Poppy emerged into the restaurant the door revolved again and this time four more people came in and the noise level rose, and as they were divested of coats and hats and shown to tables more still came in, and soon the place was humming.

Poppy had little to do but to watch over everything. Her task had been the preparation and employment of the staff and now she kept a close eye on them all, and they were, to her immense relief, splendid. From Horace came the control the waiters needed and they worked as

199

an excellent team, and Minnie, the rather wispy blinking little bookkeeper Poppy had taken on as a cashier, trusting to a deep inner conviction that the woman was much brighter than she might look, proved a treasure, dealing with bills with such accuracy and despatch that Poppy felt herself physically relax. Working on the ledgers would be much easier with Minnie in the office here.

Jessie was of course in a state of total delight. She took a corner table for herself and David and tried to persuade Poppy to join them, but she was too nervous, preferring to remain out of sight behind Minnie's little corner, enclosed with its own engraved glass screen, from which she could watch everyone; so Jessie and David ate together, and obviously enjoyed themselves greatly. They laughed a lot and ate a lot too, Poppy noticed and she was glad of that. There was a gauntness still about David and that had worried her. Now he was well again, she had promised herself, she would see to it that he took care and was well-fed, and regained his old sturdy look; and she was amused at her own silliness as she watched them over the glass screen. A grown man like that needed no care – and then he looked up and caught her eye and winked a long slow wink, and the most extraordinary thing happened. Her belly tightened with exactly the same sort of breathless excitement she had known so long ago with Bobby, and her face flamed as she recognized what that sensation meant. And he stared at her across the tables full of braying shouting gluttons and saw it and an expression of happiness, deep certain happiness, moved across his face and he smiled at her and then bent his head as though he couldn't bear to look any longer, and she knew as surely as she knew she was standing there behind Minnie's chair that he had felt what she had felt and shared in it. It was a very special moment and one she was never to forget.

Or at least, not in the long term. Because then the telephone on Minnie's desk shrilled and Minnie picked it up and listened with a puzzled expression on her face and then turned to her.

'I think it's for you, Mrs Bradman,' she fluttered anxiously. 'It's someone a bit upset, but I think she asked for Mrs Poppy. That is you, isn't it?'

16

16

Goosey, thought Poppy in a wash of cold fear. Only Goosey calls me Mrs Poppy. And Goosey hates the phone, only ever uses it when there's an emergency; and memory broke over her in a sick wave, a memory of Goosey phoning her at the office on a November afternoon eight years ago and weeping frantically as she told of her finding Bobby so very ill in his chair. It was to be the same now, she was certain; something dreadful had happened to Robin, and she reached out with a hand that did not feel like her own to take the earpiece of the phone from Minnie and said carefully, 'Goosey?'

'Oh, Mrs Poppy!' wailed the familiar old voice at the end of the phone, thinned and distorted by the transmission, but still unmistakeably Goosey's. 'Oh, Mrs Poppy – ' and she began to weep, gulping noisily.

'Goosey, calm down,' Poppy said, trying to keep her own panic at manageable levels. 'Take a deep breath and tell me at once what has happened. At once, do you hear?'

'It's Miss Chloe, Mrs Poppy,' Goosey said. 'Oh, Mrs Poppy, what shall we do, what ever shall we do?'

Poppy did not know what was worse; the fear she had originally felt or the sickening guilt that followed immediately upon the relief that engulfed her as she realized that Robin was all right. She felt physically ill as she tried to get herself back on an even keel and had to breathe deeply on her own account to push the nausea away.

'What's happened?' she managed to say at last, as once again Goosey broke into a wail of tears. 'What is it?'

She had kept her voice low instinctively, still aware at some deeper level of where she was and the importance of not distressing the customers, but something of her agitation must have transmitted itself to the corner table for suddenly David was beside her and his hand was warm, high on her back, just below the nape of her neck. That touch steadied her and she lifted a shoulder towards him in gratitude. He did not move or speak but remained standing there as she said again, more sharply this time, 'What is it, Goosey? Tell me immediately.'

The authoritarian tone worked. Goosey took a shuddering breath and said, 'Mary Challoner, Miss Chloe's friend, Mrs Poppy. She just phoned and said as she had to talk to Miss Chloe and when I said, well wasn't she there with her then, she was all amazed and said no she wasn't and I said well where is she then, has she gone out and she said she didn't know what I meant and I said well isn't Miss Chloe staying with you all this week, and she said of course she wasn't, what would she have phoned for if Miss Chloe was staying there and what was old Chloe up to now the little wretch and well, then I went up to her room to see if she'd come back you see. I didn't know what to think and the door was still locked and oh, Mrs Poppy I'm that scared and – '

It went on and on, a gushing torrent of words that Poppy made no effort to stem. She just stood there with the phone held to her ear, feeling David's hand on her back and thinking confusedly – I'm wicked. I was glad when Goosey said it was Chloe, oh, I'm so wicked, and where is she, and I'm frightened too –

At last Goosey stopped talking as her breath and energy ran out and Poppy said crisply, 'Hold tight there, Goosey, I'll be on my way. Don't do anything or go anywhere. I'll be home before it's time to get Robin from

school and I'll sort everything out. Just wait for me – '
And she cradled the phone and turned to look at David.

His face was tight with concern and she managed to smile tremulously at him and say in a low voice, 'It's Chloe –'

And his face cleared at once and she thought almost wonderingly: then I'm not so wicked after all. He thought it was Robin too and he's glad it isn't. And that was the moment when she knew beyond any hint of any doubt that this man had moved from friendship at the edge of her life to a much more central position. There would never again be any uncertainty about that or about how she felt about him. But this was not the time even to contemplate the matter, let alone give it any real thought. So all she did was explain as briefly as she could the gist of Goosey's cascade of words. He listened carefully and then closed his eyes for one brief moment and said in a thick voice, 'Oh, God, was I ever wrong. I said not to go after her. Oh, God, Poppy, I was wrong.'

She reached up and touched his cheek. 'No need to blame yourself,' she said. 'It was good advice. You couldn't know about – how devious Chloe can be. It's nothing to get so agitated about, David. She'll come to no harm. She's involved in some crazy scrape or other – she hasn't the wit she was born with sometimes – but it will be no worse than that' – And I wish I really believed that, a corner of her mind thought. I wish I could be as certain as I'm sounding. 'I'll go and see what's happening,' she said then. 'I'll call you at your office, let you know – '

'Like hell you will,' he said strongly, and now he looked himself again, his rather gaunt face friendly and composed, if a little pale. 'I'll come with you – no, don't argue. I'm coming with you. Get your coat and I'll find a taxi.'

'Train should be faster,' she said. 'Where's Jessie?'

'Gone into the kitchen,' he was already on his way.

'Wanted to say something to Harry. I'll see you at the door. Don't worry – Jessie'll cope here.'

In the kitchen Harry and Jessie were deep in colloquy over a dish of egg and lemon sauce which Jessie was tasting by means of dipping her little finger delicately into it and then sucking it clean with a fine judicious air, and Poppy made her way through the hubbub of clashing pots and pans and bawling waiters to her side and said in her ear, 'Jessie, take over outside, will you? Panic at home. I've got to go now. I'll be back as soon as I can or I'll phone. Sorry to dump you.'

And Jessie, with all the good sense she had in her, didn't question or argue. She just nodded, put the dish of sauce back in Harry's hands and followed Poppy back out of the kitchen to the restaurant.

But she did ask one question as Poppy turned to leave. 'Robin?' she said briefly.

Poppy shook her head. 'Chloe.'

And the same thing happened. The tight anxious look that had appeared on Jessie's round face faded and a look of relief slid across it and Poppy thought with a deep pang of bitter sadness – poor Chloe, poor little Chloe. All of us feeling the same way, none of us caring enough. Poor Chloe. I am wicked after all. We all are –

There was a taxi waiting at the kerb as she came out of the revolving door, leaving the restaurant full of noisy customers who were still, almost to Poppy's amazement, eating and drinking and shouting at each other as though the phone call had never happened, and the knowledge that that was a silly response did not make any difference. She still felt surprise.

'Taxi will be quicker,' he said. 'I've checked with the map. Come on. I've told the driver it's an emergency.' And he bundled her in and followed her and she sat there in the corner of the cab trying to look calm and relaxed but shaking inside.

He took her hand and she held on to him tightly, but didn't look at him, staring out of the window at the street bucketting past as the cabbie, clearly taking his role as an emergency driver very seriously, took crazy risks and went screeching round corners and weaving through the traffic at a lunatic speed.

'It's all right, Poppy,' he said. 'I'm sure of it. She's been a silly child but we'll soon sort it all out.'

'She's not a silly child,' Poppy said with sudden intensity. 'She's a sad child, a pathetic one. Oh, God, David, we were all the same, me and you and Jessie, so glad it was Chloe – '

He was silent for a moment and then said, 'No. Just glad it wasn't Robin. That's rather different.' But he made no attempt to deny any guilt and she was grateful for that.

'She could be anywhere,' Poppy said. 'She's been gone over a week, and none of us did anything. We simply ignored her disappearance and did *nothing*. She could have died for all we know – '

'We'd know.' He sounded very certain. 'Take it from an old crime journalist, Poppy. Even in this country – it can't be all that different from back home – it isn't easy for people to die without being identified. If that had happened police would have been round long since. Dead she isn't – '

'Hurt then. Lost her memory, in a hospital somewhere – '

'Not likely,' he said after a moment. 'Possible, I suppose, but not likely – '

She managed a weak smile then. 'I suppose not. Maybe I have seen too many silly films at that. All right, she's not dead, you think, and not injured. Then what?'

'Run away? She was angry with you the last time you saw her, wasn't she? Robin's party – '

'There was nothing new in that.' Poppy knew she

sounded bitter and didn't care. 'She was always angry and so was I. Oh David, make me stop using the past tense, for God's sake!'

He let go of her hand and put his arm around her shoulders and she turned to him as naturally as if it were something she did every day of her life and held on tightly, her head tucked into the space at the root of his neck so that his chin rested on the top of her head.

'There, there,' he murmured. 'It's all right. Just take it easy, honey, very slow and easy. It's all right – we'll soon be there –'

She sat up after a while and lifted her hand to her rumpled hair and stared at him with her eyes wide and red-rimmed with unshed tears. 'I'm sorry,' she managed.

'Oh, phooey. What are you supposed to do? Trill like a bird and sing like an angel all the way home? Do shut up –' And he smiled at her amiably and again she managed to smile back. He really did make her feel so very much better.

'I'll be all right,' she said then. 'I'm sure you're right. She's gone banging out of the house in a temper before and always comes back –'

'Sure,' he said encouragingly. 'Of course she has.'

'Though never overnight. And without clothes Or maybe she did take clothes and that's why her room's locked.'

'Ah,' he nodded then and began to dig into his trouser pockets, writhing a little in the tight space as he tried to get his hands well down into them. 'That of course will be the first necessity – ah, here we are –' And he lifted up a set of odd looking keys with an air of triumph.

'What are they?'

'You'll never believe, but they're miniature skeleton keys. I made 'em up for myself – and for the other patients – while I was in the San. They used to keep us on godawful grub – lots of it but so damn dull – but they had

207

better stuff themselves, the nurses, locked in cupboards, all of it. So I used to steal it when I could – ' He rattled the keys and grinned. 'I kept them for sentimental reasons. To make sure I never got back there. We'll get tht door open, you see if we don't. I'm pretty good at a lock – '

'I'm glad you're a crook,' she said and then as the taxi screeched to a halt in front of the house held out a hand to him. 'And I'm so glad you came to help,' she said. 'So very glad.'

He smiled. 'It's what I'm for. Now, come on.' And he helped her out of the taxi and followed her up the steps after paying a highly gratified driver – he tipped him hugely – to where Goosey was standing in the open doorway where she had obviously been watching and waiting.

Poppy wasted no time and went straight upstairs to Chloe's room. David following behind in long-legged lopes of two steps at a time and Goosey came panting in the rear talking all the way in an unintelligible breathy monotone; but Poppy knew there was no more she could tell her than she already had. There would be time to take care of Goosey; right now there was more important work.

It took David over five minutes of fiddling to get the door to open, as the two women stood with barely contained impatience and watched him. Poppy had almost reached the stage of asking him to try to break the door down (even though she knew that it was a very strong one and that the likelihood of anyone being able to break it so easily was very small) when the tumblers at last clicked and he straightened his back and turned a flushed face towards them.

'Right,' he said. 'I'll go in – '

'I will too,' Poppy said and moved forwards, but he put up one hand.

'Absolutely not.' He sounded unusually determined and she stared at him in puzzlement as he opened the door, just enough to get himself through, and then closed it, leaving them both on the outside. Poppy stood and stared at the dumb panels in silence, shocked at the thought that had clearly prompted his action and behind her Goosey, who had also picked up the message, began to weep again.

But then the door opened wide and he stood back to let them in and she breathed easily again and with Goosey close behind her, walked in.

It was a shambles of course; it always was. Clothes were tumbled on the floor, the dirty dressing table was littered with hair grips and clouds of powder as well as a week's collected dust, and stockings dangled from the bed rail. The bed was unmade and the room frowsty and after a moment, Poppy went over to the window and pulled back the thin curtains to open it. A breath of the summer air came in to lift the dust a little and set it dancing in the sunlight.

Goosey began to bustle about, picking things up and tutting as she went, and taking them over to the wardrobe to hang them up; and then she stopped and peered into the mass of tightly packed clothes there and shook her head.

'Oh, dear, oh dear, oh dear me, she's taken a lot with her, oh, dear, oh dear – it's run off she has and caught by robbers and God knows who besides and never to come back to us again, oh dear, oh dear.' And the tears flowed again, faster than ever.

'Are you sure?' That was David and his voice was sharp, so sharp that Goosey stopped weeping and mopped her face with the corner of her apron and nodded miserably.

'Don't I have the care of her? Don't I wash and mend it all? Course I know! There's a lot gone. The marocain

209

and the two new voiles and the silk duster coat and any number of the summer frocks she got at the start of the season and look, shoes too, and her little handbags and – let me see – ' She waddled over to the tallboy to pull open drawers and peer in. 'And here's her underwear gone too – the pink crêpe de Chine and the peach silk and all the lemon lawns that I sewed for her, all gone, every bit of it – '

David shook his head. 'It's amazing you can tell,' he murmured and indeed, looking at the wardrobe with its crowded rails and the drawers that still seemed as full as they could be it seemed remarkable. But Goosey was certain and went on and on saying so in only marginally different words.

'Run away it is then,' David said in a low voice to Poppy under the cover of Goosey's monotone. 'She's taken enough to see her through for a while, obviously. And what about money? Will she have enough?'

'Oh, yes,' Poppy said a little bitterly. 'She has ample. She has full control of her own capital as well as the income. She has cheque books and so forth. She has no problems about money. Oh, David, what shall we do? This isn't an ordinary running away – a come-back-soon one. Not after a week, for heaven's sake!'

'No, I agree,' he said. 'We need to have a plan. Look, get Goosey to do something to keep her busy, and we'll sort things out on our own – ' And she nodded and turned to the old woman and went to hug her and murmur soothingly in her ear, for she was indeed deeply distressed. She looked shakier and frailer than ever and Poppy thought with compunction of how very old she was, well over seventy now. It was high time she had more help in the house. All this was too much for her.

'Dearest Goosey,' she said now. 'What we all need is some tea. Would you do that, while David and I see what is to be done?'

Goosey seemed cheered by that suggestion and mopped her face again and went heavily downstairs to the kitchen while David and Poppy went into the drawing-room to sit and stare at each other from each end of the sofa, and try to think.

'Hospitals and so forth seem out,' Poppy said at length. 'There's clearly no point in assuming she's ill. As I see it that only leaves the police – '

'Not yet,' David said after a moment. 'Such a drama that could cause. I think perhaps – look, is there anyone she might have gone to that you know of? Family perhaps?'

She shook her head. 'There's only us, really,' she began and then stopped. 'Well, not entirely. There is George, of course. George Pringle.'

'Oh?' He cocked an inquisitive eyebrow.

'He's her uncle. Bobby's sister Mabel, you remember her? Well, she married George Pringle.'

'Ah!' He remembered then. 'Of course. A rather stuffed shirt sort of chap who – oh, Lord! I'm sorry.'

She laughed a little then. 'No need to apologize. He is. He's everything you want to call him. So desperately pompous and such a bully. But he's a bit of a sad creature too. He never remarried after Mabel died and he lives on his own in the house they bought in Brondesbury, a great big place with room enough for the half a dozen children which Mabel always said she wanted. But they never had any – so he's a sad creature, as I say. I just wish he didn't meddle so with Chloe – '

'Has he any right to do so?'

She shook her head. 'He was an executor of Bobby's will and was furious when he found he didn't have any real control over her money once she'd inherited it. He told her he had, told her she could only have the income and not touch the capital but I've long suspected she found out very soon that she could get her hands on it if

211

she really wanted to. All she has to do is lean on her Uncle George. He had it arranged that he looked after her banking and so forth, and I let him. I had so much to do at the time I really couldn't face it – ' Her voice drifted away. 'I should have taken it on I suppose. But she was only ten at the time Bobby died and I couldn't imagine the day coming when it would cause problems, all her money. But there it is – '

'So, if she wanted to run a long way away she would have needed more money and might have gone to him about it? If he looked after her banking?' David said, and he sounded so practical and commonsensical that he pulled her out of her rather self-pitying state. 'Do you think she might have done that?'

She bit her lip, thinking hard. 'She might have done,' she said at length. 'I don't think she really cares much for him because he is so hard to care for – but she uses him a good deal to taunt me. She knows we don't get on and – well, never mind that. Yes, it's possible.'

'Then we talk to him,' David said firmly. 'Definitely. Do you have a number?'

'Yes,' she said unwillingly. 'I suppose we have to?'

'Yes,' David said. 'Better than starting a hare's run at this moment, hmm? Come on. Let me get the number for you and you talk to him. Be cagey – maybe he'll be okay – '

She got to her feet and went over to her little desk in the corner and rooted in it and found the book of numbers she kept there. There were very few of them, for she did most of her necessary telephoning at the office, but George's was one of them, and aware of her unwillingness, she held the book out to David. It was horrid to have to admit to that pompous man that she had failed so far with Chloe that the child had run away for so long a time, but she knew it had to be done. David, picking up her thought – and there was another moment of delight for her in realizing that fact – said gently, 'It'll be all right, Poppy. And he has to know, doesn't he?'

'I suppose so,' she said miserably and led the way to the stairs so that they could go down to the telephone in the hall below.

He put a hand on her arm as they reached the first stair and held her back.

'Poppy,' he said and she turned to look at him, a little surprised by the diffidence in his voice. 'I just want you to know that – if you'll let me – I'll always be here, you know. To take care of you and look after you. I want you to know that.'

Her breath tightened again in what was now an almost familiar way. 'Yes,' she said after a moment. 'Yes, I know.'

'Is that all right with you?' He looked at her earnestly in the somewhat dull light, for they were above the level where sunshine came tumbling in through the stained glass panel of the front door.

'Yes,' she said. 'Oh, yes. Very all right.'

'Always?'

'I – yes. Always.'

'That's settled then,' he said with great satisfaction and started down the stairs. And then turned and looked back up at her. 'I know this is one hell of a time to say so, Poppy, but my God, how much I love you! You'll never know. And I have for years. I'm going to spend the rest of my life trying to show you. I just thought you ought to know that.'

'I – well, yes,' she said breathless still. 'Yes. I'm glad that – yes.' And then smiled. 'Dear David,' she managed but that was all. 'Dear, dear David.'

'Good,' was all he said but his face was alight with happiness as he turned and went down the stairs to the telephone.

17

'Police?' George Pringle said. 'Absurd. Completely out of the question.' And he got to his feet and once again marched round the room before coming to sit down once more. He'd been doing that ever since he had arrived, puffing and fussing in a taxi, and Poppy thought – if he doesn't sit still I'll hit him, I swear I will. But David caught her eye and made a tiny grimace and she relaxed. Of course she wouldn't hit him; she could control her irritation better than that. With David there to help her.

'If we do that,' George went on, 'the girl will be ruined, quite ruined. What sort of reputation will she have, do you imagine? What decent sort of man will ever want to marry her? How you could allow her to destroy her chances in this way, Poppy, is really beyond me. A gel needs care and protection, not the sort of household that allows her to go on in this rackety fashion – '

'She has had excellent care and protection, sir,' David said crisply. 'I have seen enough of this household to know that. Mrs Bradman has been an excellent mother in every way, but Chloe is headstrong and has of course a good deal more money than is good for her. It makes it impossible for anyone to maintain reasonable controls. Would you have had the girl locked up?'

'Oh, of course not,' Pringle said and once again got to his feet. 'It would have been better, however, had you remained here to observe her doings, Poppy, instead of always being off about your own affairs – '

214

'My affairs, George, consist of earning a living for my child,' Poppy flared. 'You know better than anyone that Bobby left her completely unprovided for. It all went to Chloe and – '

'Well, yes, yes, enough of that,' George looked fussed and embarrassed now and becked his head a little and began to polish his thick glasses with a large handkerchief. His bent head showed the ring of baldness on the crown and the wispy greyness that surrounded it and Poppy felt a sudden and totally irrational wave of pity for him. He was growing old and he was alone and he was upset; so she spoke in a more conciliatory tone.

'I don't think we'll get anywhere by slanging each other, George, do you? I only called you because we thought she might have contacted you. I didn't mean to distress you – and you needn't have come rushing here that way – it's upset you – '

He lifted his head and peered at her myopically through pale eyes that looked worried and defenceless without their usual protection, and then put his glasses on again to become his usual dry and self-contained person. But his face had an unhealthy colour, pallid, but with spots of colour high on his cheeks, and his expression was bleak. 'Well, yes, that's as may be,' he grunted. 'The thing now is to decide what to do.'

'I still think we need professional help,' David said. 'The police will know how to make searches – '

'They're hand in glove with those damned newspaper people,' George said. 'It will be everywhere in all those rags if we do that. I can't permit it – '

Poppy stiffened. 'I don't see that you can forbid me – ' she began, but George ignored the interruption.

' – so I shall use the services of the man who – um – deals with some of the work that my junior partner has in the practice – I have never been happy that we deal with such unsavoury work as divorce cases, of course, but at

215

least at this juncture it ensures that I have access to um –
an investigator of some skill. Or so I am told – we will
set him to work – '

'A private investigator?' David said and looked at
Poppy. 'If they're anything like the American sort,
Poppy, they're very expensive. And far from reliable.
They sell all the stuff they get their hands on to the
highest bidder among the newspapers. Mine would never
use them of course, but then not all of *our* papers are
rags, are they?' And he looked sharply at George who
had the grace to redden.

'Well, that's as may be in America,' he said. 'I can
assure you that the man we use is – um – very discreet and
reliable. He will see what is to be seen and will report to
me. As for cost – I shall bear it myself and – '

'No!' Poppy said strongly. 'This is my responsibility,
not yours. I'll accept the man's services – there is something to be said for using such a one – but I'll pay for him
myself. That is to be clearly understood – '

'Hmmph,' George said, sounding more like a
caricature of a lawyer than ever. 'Well, we won't come to
blows over it. I dare say an arrangement can be reached
whereby the costs are kept low. The important thing is to
find her – '

'And once she is found, I'd suggest that Chloe be
expected to pay back the cost of the search from her own
pocket,' David said dryly. 'That might make her think
twice next time she thinks of putting you all through such
hoops.'

'Yes – an excellent idea,' George said, at the same time
that Poppy nodded and said, 'I agree, David – ' And
David looked from one to the other and smiled slightly.

'Good,' he said. 'Then at least we're all on terms about
it, even if we're not entirely happy. So, let's about it, Mr
Pringle, shall we? How do we get this man of yours to work?'

*   *   *

216

The next few days were hellish. George kept his word and set his investigator on to the case at once, and he sent back exhaustive reports listing in elaborate detail all he did, everywhere he went and how much he spent, and Poppy would stand and read the sheets of flimsy typing with deep distaste, hating the man's dreadful prolixity ('I interrogated in as casual a manner as possible in order not to excite undue remark several of the subject's acquaintances at a tennis club that meets in Kensington Gardens at regular intervals, to no avail. There has been no unusual observation among these persons which might indicate motives or causes for the disappearance of said subject on June 20th or 21st ult – ') and feeling soiled by the knowingness of the comments and the sleazy way he implied that Chloe might have gone off on some sexual adventure. Because Poppy was quite certain that whatever else her stepdaughter might do, she would not do that. She had always been perfectly open about her friendships with boys and had shown no prurience at all in any of her dealings with them. This was more than that, Poppy was convinced.

After four fruitless days, she and David sat over supper late in the kitchen, having sent a visibly wilting Goosey to bed ('and if this goes on much longer the poor old dear will collapse, David, really she will,' Poppy said worriedly) and talked interminably about the situation.

'I feel so damned helpless,' Poppy fretted. 'I go to work, and I keep my mind on it as best as I can – '

'At least everything there's going well. I saw a couple of excellent reports in the gossip columns about it,' David said.

'Mm? Oh, yes. It looks as though we're going to turn out to be the fashionable place to go. If a restaurant is going to take off like that, it usually does it at once – and we're booked out every night as well as lunch-time. Jessie's cock-a-hoop about it. But me, all I can do is get

217

through the work as best I can and worry all the time about Chloe, and where she is and what she's doing – ' She shook her head miserably. 'I hardly ever get a chance to spend time with Robin and she must be miserable too. But the only way I can get everything done is by staying late at work, till after she's gone to bed. Even when I'm here I'm always thinking about Chloe – '

'She's a tough little lass, your Robin,' David said. 'She'll cope. You've told her what's going on, I take it?'

Poppy looked horrified. 'David, of course not! How could I? Tell her Chloe's run away? It would be awful – '

'Then what have you told her?'

'Nothing. She hasn't asked, so I've said nothing – '

David shook his head. 'You're wrong, Poppy. Keeping secrets doesn't mean she won't know there's something up. She'll be more upset if you don't explain it all to her than if – '

'Please,' David,' Poppy said wearily. 'Let me know what is best for Robin. She's my child after all – '

He became very quiet then and said no more, but Poppy was too wrought up over her situation to be as aware of that as she might have been, and went rattling on as she sat and stared into her half-empty coffee cup.

'I can't see any sense in keeping this wretched man on any longer. He gets us nowhere – even George admits that – and his bills are ridiculous. Do you know, he demands two guineas a day? And then his expenses on top of it? And he makes sure he goes to all the best restaurants and hotels, too, so they're not neglible – '

'Well, that'll be Chloe's problem when she comes home,' David said. 'That's the least of the problem.'

'If she comes home – ' And Poppy couldn't look at him. 'I'm so afraid she won't, David.'

He leaned forwards and took her hand. 'That is silly thinking, Poppy. She can't be badly hurt, of that I'm sure. If she were we'd know, believe me. She'll be back eventually, you'll see. Sadder and wiser and all that, just as it says in all the books.'

'I wish I could be so sure – ' Poppy got to her feet and went to empty her cold coffee cup into the sink before refilling it with a hot brew. 'I just wish I knew where to turn next.'

'What does your mother say?' David said after a while, when they were both sipping coffee again. 'Has she any ideas?'

Poppy reddened. 'I haven't asked her,' she said after a moment, clearly uncomfortable.

He put his cup down in its saucer with a little clatter. 'Not told her? Oh, really Poppy, this is getting ridiculous. Why ever not?'

Poppy thought for a long time and then said unwillingly, 'I think – I'm so ashamed, David.' And she bent her head so that he couldn't see the tears that were glinting in her eyes. 'I drove her away, my own stepdaughter, Bobby's child. What sort of villain am I that she should do that? I feel like the sort of stepmother in fairy tales, wicked and evil and cruel – '

'Oh, such stuff!' he said. 'I thought better of you than that, I really did, Poppy! The girl has lost her temper and gone off on an adventure. How can that be a reflection on you?'

'Of course it can! It means I'm just not a suitable person to have care of a girl.'

'I think it's high time you talked to your mother,' he said after a pause. 'I have a good deal of respect for that lady. She says little but what she says is very much to the point. Go and see her, Poppy. Tell her what happened and let her reassure you. She'll do a better job than I can, clearly. For all I love you more than anyone else does.'

She managed a bleak little smile. 'I – we agreed, we wouldn't – that there'd be no talk like that until – I mean,

219

please, David. Let her get home. Then I can think about – other things.'

He smiled at her and patted her hand. 'I know. I promised and I mean to try to keep the promise. But don't be too hard on me if I find it difficult. It's not easy when you love someone as much as – oh, all right – ' He held up both hands in mock submission as she opened her mouth to speak. 'Not another word. Go and see your mother, please. I'll clear the kitchen so that Goosey needn't worry over it in the morning and I'll hold the fort here till you come back, in case Robin wakes again – '

She had got to her feet and was moving over to the door, willing to obey him. He was right; talking to Mildred about the situation might help; but at his words she stopped, suddenly uncertain. Robin had started having her night terrors again, over the last week or so, and she bit her lip, thinking. Could he be right about Robin too? Was the child reacting to the upset in the house over Chloe? And she felt a great wave of loathing for her stepdaughter as she thought that. She was just as much trouble when out of the house as when in it; if only she would leave them in peace. And then again felt guilt mixed up with concern for Robin and a deep sense of exhaustion, a most queasy mixture of emotion that made her shake her head irritably. Why did life have to be so messy all the time? Why could she not just throw up her hands and say, 'If Chloe wants to go, let her go,' and think no more about her? That would be the easiest thing in the world; and then she could concentrate on David, and all he had said and all he was wanting to say, and all that she herself wanted to say to him –

'Go along,' he said, watching her over the rim of his cup. 'There'll be time to sort out feelings later. Go and see your mother. You should have gone yesterday, shouldn't you? Don't you always go on Wednesdays?

She'll be wondering – ' And she nodded and went over to the stairs, marvelling a little at the rapport that already existed between them and his almost uncanny ability to know what she was thinking.

All the way to Mildred's house in the rather elderly taxi that was the only one plying for hire in Holland Park Avenue, she thought about that: his sensitivity, his ability to enter into her anxieties and feelings and the sheer comfort of him. To have someone around to share with; what more could any woman ask? And there was more too. He made her feel so good, made her so very aware of her own physical self. When Bobby had died she had thought that some of her life had died too. Their love-making had been so distressing for her for so long before Bobby died, so lacking in tenderness on his part as his war-created depression and misery made him more and more self-centred, that the loss of it had not been particularly painful. In many ways it had been a relief to be able to go to bed without fearing an onslaught from a depressed and angry husband; God knew the loss of Bobby had been anguish, but that had been the least of it.

But now, here was a man she had known as a friend, and liked as a friend, and yet felt towards as a lover. Even thinking about that, here in the frowsty interior of an old taxi, she felt a *frisson* move across her belly and deep inside her and was almost embarrassed by it, although it made her exultant too. It made her feel young and feminine in a way she had forgotten was possible.

And yet, and yet – and she closed her eyes against the glitter of the lights in the road outside and tried to think clearly. What right had she to upset life in Norland Square just to gratify herself? Robin needs security and peace; if she had started having night terrors again over Chloe, how would she react to David? Would she be upset again, have more nightmares, lose her happy good temper and become tense and awkward, just as Chloe had when her father had died? To make Robin a stepchild, just as Chloe was; would that be fair and loving? Would that be what a mother should do to a much loved child? And the thoughts swirled and twisted in her head as the taxi at last stopped outside her mother's house and she pushed them away with an almost physical effort and got out and paid. Time enough to worry about that when David spoke of taking their relationship further. He'd said he loved her, but no more than that. Chicken-counting, she thought sombrely as she went up the stone steps in the pool of light thrown by the street lamp at the kerb, is a stupid occupation for a grown woman. And especially one in my situation. I must think of first things first, and right now that is Chloe. Perhaps David is right; perhaps Mamma will have some suggestions, some ideas of what we can do to find Chloe.

She did. Poppy sat and stared at her mother sitting there in her usual straight-backed chair in her impeccable drawing-room with her hands folded neatly on her lap, and blinked with amazement.

'What did you say?' she said carefully. She had come in so uncertainly, full of apologies for her failure to visit the night before and then had launched herself into an account of why she had been so remiss, explaining in awkward words all there was to explain about Chloe's disappearance and Mildred had listened, her face quite smooth and calm and then had nodded and said, amazingly, 'I know. She is in Paris.'

And in the face of Poppy's patent amazement she had amplified that. 'She has work there. In a new establishment that is, I gather, partly a restaurant and partly a theatre. Certainly they do shows there.'

'How do you know all this? Have you the address? Is she all right? Why didn't you tell me?' Poppy cried and felt anger begin to bubble in her. 'I've been going out of

my mind with it all and you sit there calmly and tell me
you know where she is – '

'You didn't ask me,' Mildred said and smiled thinly. 'I
imagined she had after all told you herself. At first she
had said she would not, but I told her that would be
remiss of her. So she said she would consider it. When
you did not come as usual last evening, I considered
calling on you and asking, but then I thought that you
would come eventually and we could discuss it then. As
has indeed been the case, hasn't it?'

'Mamma, you really are – tell me everything! When
did you see her? And why didn't – oh, for heaven's sake,
tell me all there is to tell me! At once. When did she come
to see you and tell you all this?'

'She did not come at all,' Mildred said and lifted her
brows. 'I told her I thought it would be better if she did,
but Chloe, I need not tell you, is a headstrong gel and not
one who is easy to control. She told me she was travelling
to France with her new employer and would write to me
from there. I have to say she has not done so yet, but she
is hardly the sort of gel to be a careful correspondent. But
she did at least telephone me before she went – '

'But not me,' Poppy said dully. 'She didn't think it
necessary to tell me.'

'I didn't know that.' Mildred sounded regretful for the
first time. 'If I had, I would of course have telephoned
myself, much as I dislike communicating that way. It
seems so – it is not the way people should speak to each
other. But had I known – I was sure she would after we
had our discussion. And since I did not hear from you, I
took it for granted that all was well. You should have told
me.'

'Yes,' Poppy said and bent her head to look down at
her hands clasped on her lap. 'I suppose I should. It
seems I'm not very good at explaining things to people I
care about, at all. Am I? I didn't want to worry you, I

223

suppose. No, I can't even say it was that.' She looked at her mother then, and went on with painful honesty. 'I didn't think of you at all. I just fretted over Chloe and over myself. I'm so ashamed that she behaved so. It has to be all my fault – '

'Nonsense,' Mildred said crisply. 'You cannot be responsible for everyting. You are not the Deity and it is arrogant of you in the extreme to imagine you are so important and so powerful. She is a person who must do what she wishes to do. As you did once – ' She smiled thinly then. 'If I had my way you would have attended a university, and would have been a most respected academic. As it was, you chose to go to war and then to – involve yourself in that restaurant and shop in the East End. Hardly what I would have regarded as a suitable choice for you. Yet you made that choice and I do not take to myself any guilt for that. I did all I could, and could do no more. And you must be sure to behave in the same way about Chloe. I am sure you have done your best for her. Now she has made her own choice.'

She stopped then and looked down at Poppy's bent head and then went on almost reflectively. 'As I did once.'

Poppy looked up then at her mother, but the face seemed as smooth and lacking in expression as ever, just its usual calm and imperturbable self.

'I left this house a good many years ago to seek my own occupation,' Mildred said after a long pause. 'You know little of those days, because I never regarded that as in any way as your affair. But now, you are a woman grown and I am old – well, it is ancient history. I had my own ideas and my own plans for my life and for good or ill I followed them. And when I heard Chloe tell me of her plans and ideas, I remembered how I had been and I felt – I felt for her.'

'Is that why you said nothing to me?' Poppy said.

'Because you *felt* for her? What about me and my anxiety?'

'I knew nothing of it,' Mildred pointed out reasonably. 'You did not come and tell me that you were concerned. As I said, I assumed you knew where she was. Why should I think otherwise?'

Poppy got to her feet and drew on her gloves, very decisively. 'Well, I did not know. But let that pass. Tell me the address, now, and I will go to Paris and fetch her home. There is no sense now in talking about who did or did not speak to whom, or why. Just tell me what I need to know and we'll leave it at that.'

'Ah, there I can't help you,' Mildred said as calmly as ever, and now her stillness began to anger Poppy.

'Why not?' she snapped. 'Too much fellow feeling for Chloe? Do you think she needs protection against me as her stepmother?'

'Of course not,' Mildred said. 'Any more than I did. I too had a stepmamma, you know. It seems to be a pattern in this family. But I see no need for you to become so – well, let be. No, the reason I cannot help is that I do not know where she is precisely. Only that she is in Paris. She gave me no further information than that I have already given you. So I'm afraid when it comes to fetching her back, I can be of no assistance at all.'

18

'I want to go now,' Poppy said. 'Tonight. I have to find her, David! Paris, for heaven's sake – she could be in all sorts of trouble. I have to go – '

'Of course you do. But not until you know where you're going and what the situation is. You could wander around forever and never find her. But with my contacts maybe we'll have tracked her down in twenty four hours. Less even. That'll give you time to get organized here, and to take the right care for Robin – and I promise you, when I have traced her, I'll come with you to bring her home.'

'You can't do that! I can't let you use up time that way. You've your own work to do – '

He grinned a little crookedly. 'Of course I have. And so I shall. I'll get a story out of this – '

She froze for a moment and he saw and frowned.

'You don't really think I'll write about Chloe, do you?' he demanded and she blushed.

'I'm sorry,' she mumbled. 'I should know better – but you did say – '

'A story about English people working in Paris is one thing, a story naming Chloe quite another. Heavens, you have got yourself in a state to get ideas like that about me! Poppy, please, go to bed, will you? I'll telegraph Paris as soon as possible, get Greg Sessions there to start a hunt. He'll know where to look – '

'How? If it would take me forever to find her, why not him?'

'Paris is his beat. He's been there for years. He'll know where everything is. And everybody. You say Mildred said that the place Chloe had gone to was a new one? With an English owner?'

'She said it was new, but nothing about the identity of the owner – '

'Well, it's a reasonable guess. If the man was taking Chloe there, that must mean that he started from here, I imagine. A Frenchman wouldn't come to England just to find someone to work in his place. He'd use the agents there are – dozens of 'em. I wonder what sort of work she's doing? Has she any sort of training?'

He was shrugging into his overcoat now, at the front door, and Poppy watched him, wishing he didn't have to go. It helped so much just having the bulk of him there, reassuring and comforting her.

'She has no training for anything,' she said without bitterness. 'I could never persuade her that having an occupation would be more agreeable for her than having nothing to do and all day to do it in. But she wouldn't listen. All she cared about was being decorative.'

'Ah,' he said in great satisfaction. 'Then she'll be very easy to find. She's in a place that's a restaurant-theatre, you say? Or Mildred said?'

'Yes.'

'Then she's a showgirl of some kind.'

'A – what sort of girl?'

'Showgirl. They wear costumes, walk around to be looked at, persuade the customers to buy them drinks. You know the sort of thing.'

'I don't,' Poppy said and swallowed. 'It sounds – rather cheap and nasty.'

He shook his head. 'Not in Paris. There it's a perfectly respectable way to make a living. Usually. I'll call you in

227

the morning, Poppy. Will you go to the office as usual?'

'I must. We're so busy – call me there?'

'I will. I promise.' He was out and halfway down the front steps now, looking up at the indigo of the summer sky, and pulling up the collar of his coat. 'It's colder out than I expected. Goodnight, Poppy – ' He turned and looked back at her standing on the doorstep and then came back, both arms held out to her.

'My dear one, don't look so woebegone! It'll be fine, really it will. We'll find out where she is and then I'll book a crossing for both of us and we'll go and fetch her. Just you be sure you're ready – ' And he bent his head and kissed her nose, and then tapped it with one long forefinger. 'You have my word for it everything will be just fine and dandy.' And then he was gone, loping away across the Square towards Holland Park Road and she watched him, feeling in spite of her misery and the undoubted chilliness of the air an inner glow. He said it would be all right. So it would be.

In the event it took Greg Sessions in Paris less than five hours to find the new restaurant showplace where Chloe was working.

'It's called *La Ratière*,' David told her on the telephone, his voice warm with excitement. 'Not madly appetizing, is it? Means a rat trap – even in France there are laws and this one seems to be suspected of being a bit cavalier about them – and popular with some people Greg doesn't think well of. I've booked a crossing tonight, at six o'clock. That way we can be in Paris before midnight when the place is going full tilt. Can you manage that?'

'Yes,' she said. 'Oh, yes. Thank you, David. You'll never know how grateful I am.'

'Don't thank me. Thank Greg. He'll meet us at the Gare du Nord and you can tell him yourself. He's a good guy. You'll like him – Poppy – at the risk of offending you – let me ask – will you tell Robin where you're going tonight?'

There was a little silence as she stood staring out over the top of Minnie's glass screen at the busy restaurant, trying to think as Minnie sat with elephantine tact, her head down over the bills. Then she said carefully, 'I'll think about that, David. I'll tell you later. Where shall I meet you?'

'Victoria, at four. Can you manage that? It's a bit of a rush, but the boat train gets so packed. We can't risk missing the crossing.'

'I'll be there,' she said. 'Jessie said she'd take over, I told her what was happening. She's been splendid over it all. She's a good guy too. Like your Greg Sessions.'

'Most people are in my experience,' he said and then dropped his voice a little. 'You are too, my love. Best of them all. I'll see you at the boat train platform then. Don't be late.' And he rang off. And she stood and looked at the dead telephone in her hand and tried to take it all in. Everything was going to be fine. Chloe had been found and was all right –

Or was she? Her brows creased as she cradled the phone. He hadn't said so; only that his friend had found the place where she was working – and that is was unsavoury. But how did he know she was there? After all, he didn't know Chloe. Only her name –

But there was no point in worrying over that; David clearly was certain Chloe was there and that they would fetch her home tonight, and her heart lifted with gratitude and relief and a new surge of anger at Chloe for making so many problems.

Jessie was angry too, and said so. 'A right little koorer!' she cried and then shook her head when Poppy demanded a translation. 'Never mind. Just take it from me it's what she is, the way she behaves, if not in real life you understand me.' Poppy didn't but she was used to Jessie's spattering of odd words. 'Just you wait till she gets back! I'll tell her a thing or two!'

'You'll do no such thing,' Poppy said firmly. 'I will, of course. But if everyone goes on at her she'll probably rush off again. I don't think I could cope with that.'

'Well, make sure you do tell her,' Jessie growled. 'Someone has to, because much more of this and we'll all be grey and in our graves, believe me.'

Poppy remembered that when she stood a few hours later at the top of a small flight of glass steps that led down into the main section of *La Ratière*, just off the Rue de Montmartre a few hours later, feeling very grey and gravelike indeed. She was exhausted, kept going only by nervous tension and anger. Her nerves felt as though they were twanging like fiddle strings at every movement, and her head ached with a sickening thudding that made her eyes tighten against the light. Not that there was a great deal in this place, which sported a number of red lamps and coloured Chinese lanterns and that was all, but there was enough chrome to create glittering flashes that assaulted her cruelly, and it was certainly noisy. A jazz band was wailing at the back somewhere and there was a lot of shrill chatter and shrieks of laughter from the customers packed around the black glass tables, and everywhere was a haze of cigarette smoke and the reek of brandy. She felt her gorge rise and with the same effort of will she had used on the steam packet which had bucketed its way through a summer rainstorm in a most sickening fashion, plunging and rocking in the waves till her head had spun, stopped it from going any further. She had only to hold on a little longer now, until they found Chloe, collected her and her belongings and went home. There was a crossing at six am, David had found, and they could with an effort get that, if they caught a train at the Gare du Nord just after three am. It was now almost one, and a lot had to be done to be sure they kept to their schedule, but Greg Sessions, an exceedingly large and convivial man, had assured her it was possible.

If she'll come, of course,' he'd added cheerfully. 'She's a determined puss, isn't she?'

'You've spoken to her?' Poppy had asked eagerly as they went careering in a mad taxi ride from the station towards the light and noise of Montmartre, while she clung like grim death to the leather strap beside her. 'Is she all right?'

'I've spoken to her. Had to make sure she was the lady you wanted, didn't I? As for how she is – I don't know what "all right" is for her, do I?' Greg said, reasonably enough. 'I can just tell you I went there this morning when places like this never look up to much, and she was rehearsing. Well, walking round the way the fella told her – Armand, his name is –'

'A Frenchman? I was wrong about that then,' David said and made a face. 'I keep on making a lot of damn fool mistakes lately. I was sure it'd be an Englishman who arranged it –'

'I don't know any details,' Greg said. 'Just that she's a showgirl –'

'I was right about that at least,' David said with some satisfaction.

' – and she's a bit upset about something. Not sure what. Could be the place she's living in. I checked up. It's a pretty sleazy sort of house not too far away from *La Ratière* – ' He stopped then and flicked a glance at Poppy, who was staring out of the taxi window and then lifted a warning brow at David. 'Let's just say it could be more delicious than it is. I don't think she's best impressed, hmm? I thought the kid looked tired too, but as I say, maybe she always does. I've no way of comparing.'

Now they were here in the club, though, Poppy could

231

see he was right. There was Chloe across the big room –
and she felt a lift of excitement as she saw her mixed with
a sense of deep relief that made the exhaustion that was
hovering over her step back a little – and it was clear that
she had lost much of her energy and bounce. She was
wearing a dress that consisted mainly of gilded fringe –
and not much of it – and Poppy tried not to look too
closely at it, for it was so very skimpy and showed so
much more of Chloe's slender body than was seemly that
it embarrassed her, and her face was carefully made up.
But there was a dreaminess about her movements, a sort
of heaviness that betrayed her, and even at this distance
and in spite of the make-up Poppy could see the shadows
beneath her eyes.

She waited no longer, but went plunging away down
the steps towards Chloe, in her hurry pushing dancers
aside with more firmness than was perhaps entirely necessary, and some people protested in loud machine-gun-
fast French that quite defeated her. Not that she was
particularly interested in paying much attention to them,
for all her concentration was centred on Chloe who was
sitting at a table with five men, most of whom looked to
be at least twice her age, if not more. She was staring listlessly at her drink, a tall glass of something that seemed
to bubble, and seemed unaware of the fact that one of the
men had a heavy much-beringed hand on her knee and
that another was stroking the back of her neck.

Poppy's own throat tightened as she looked at her and
she stopped for a moment, just long enough to allow
David and Greg to catch up with her.

'Poppy, don't be too hasty,' David murmured swiftly
in her ear. 'Don't just jump in, please – '

But he was too late. All the protectiveness she had in
her came welling up and she went plunging across the last
few yards of glass dance floor to stand beside Chloe's
chair. And Chloe looked up and blinked and then peered

at her in the glittering darkness and then just sat and stared.

Her expression was a confused one, as thoughts chased across her mind and left their imprint on her face. She was startled of course, very taken aback, but there was something more there than that; a sort of – was it gratitude, an enormous relief at seeing her stepmother? At any other time and in any other circumstances Poppy might have been a little more circumspect, would have taken her time, but the mixture of the way she was feeling, her headache and the long days of anxiety that had led up to this moment swept aside any caution that might have been in her. She leaned forwards, took Chloe by the arm just above the row of gold slave bangles she wore there and yanked.

And Chloe came to her feet with a little yelp of pain and pulled her arm away and cried loudly, 'Don't do that! Leave me alone!'

The men at the table had stared at Poppy in amazement, one or two with their mouths hanging open in classic surprise so that they looked positively comical, but Poppy was indulging her bad temper and fatigue now and paid them no attention at all.

'I will not leave you alone,' she said now, loudly, and some of the people at adjoining tables turned to crane their necks and stare and one or two laughed. At that moment the jazz band, which had been playing throughout, came to the end of a set and stopped, and the little burst of desultory applause that resulted petered out and left the place quiet enough for every word that was said by the two of them to be clearly audible.

'You are to leave this place at once, Chloe. It is disgusting, quite disgusting, and you must be out of your mind to be here! We have come to fetch you home at once –'

'I shan't go and you can't make me!' Chloe cried shrilly, and then burst into loud and uncontrolled tears and some of the people nearby moved more closely and began to make warning sounds, chattering at each other loudly; and Poppy with one corner of her mind wished she had not lost most of her French in the eight years that had passed since she had spoken it so easily during the war, and then went on scolding at Chloe.

'Stop that silly display at once!' she said crisply. 'You should be ashamed to be so ill-mannered! Now, where is your coat? We cannot take you into the street in that dreadful garment. The sooner we can get some decent clothes on you the better. You look like a – well, I can't bring myself to tell you. You should know for yourself how disgusting such clothes are, and be ashamed. Now come along – '

'Hey, hey, what is happening here?' A small man in a very dapper suit and with hair so dark and so thoroughly brilliantined that his head looked as if it had been painted with black lacquer came pushing through the crowd now circling the little scene and full of buzz and chatter about the *petite anglaise*. 'What is all this disturbance in my restaurant? Hey? If zis is not ceased, at once, you comprehend, *tout de suite*, then all of you must be collected and put out into the street – hey?' And he looked ferociously at Poppy and then at Chloe and jerked his head at her sharply, indicating the curtains at the side of the minuscule stage, which clearly led to the dressing rooms, and she flicked a frightened glance at him and tried to turn away to obey.

And then Poppy got very angry. She moved forwards, even as David's hand came down and set itself on her arm, and said crisply to Chloe, 'Are you frightened of this man?'

Chloe stared back at her with eyes that seemed opaque, they were so dark and then she said breathlessly, 'He's the boss here – he gets a bit cross – '

'Then leave,' Poppy said. 'You don't have to stay. You

understand me? If he is unkind then you must leave. It is wrong to stay. Come away with us now.'

Chloe looked beyond her to David and Greg who were now standing each side of Poppy, looking watchful, and then again at the man Armand and now there was real anxiety in her eyes, even fear, and Poppy said with sudden concern, 'Oh, my dear! You don't have to be frightened! This place isn't for you. Do come home. We want you to come home – '

Chloe's face seemed to crumple then. She looked like a very frightened child, and not at all like the blasé painted creature she had seemed and tears collected in her eyes and began to trickle down her nose and she sniffed dolorously. And Poppy saw not Chloe, not the spoiled young woman who had made life so complicated for her, but a crumpled infant, not all that much older than her own small Robin; and she put out a hand and with a rough sort of tenderness tugged at her and led her away, back through the crowds to the door, scolding all the way.

'You silly girl, getting involved with such people as these! This man Armand is repellent, he makes me think of a slug. I can't imagine how you came to know him or to agree to work for him!'

Chloe sniffed hard and turned her head to look at her and opening her mouth to speak, but Poppy ran on. 'I shall have to be more careful about the places you go and the people you meet, my dear, to avoid such an awful thing happening to you again. It just isn't right that a young girl as protected as you have always been should come to be in such a place. I have given you too much freedom, I'm afraid, just as everyone said I did, and they were right, clearly – '

'It's not just his fault. Armand, I mean,' Chloe said, and her voice was small and not at all combative. 'I mean – there was – '

'I really don't want to know,' Poppy said firmly. 'I just want you to collect your clothes and come home. You need looking after. And Goosey and I will do just that. Come along, now. This is all over. We'll hear no more of it.'

They reached the street outside then, with Greg and David close behind them to make sure they were well-protected, and she turned to Chloe, now shrugging into the coat that David had picked up for her and held out her arms and Chloe with one last despairing sniff came towards her and let herself be hugged.

And Poppy looked over her head at David and grinned widely. It was all right, after all. It had been a perfectly dreadful few days but they were over. Chloe had been through a miserable time but she had learned from it, Poppy was certain. From now on all would be lovely between them. Poppy held her stepdaughter close and was absolutely certain of that.

19

But she was wrong of course. Within a fairly short time life at Norland Square had settled down to being much the same as it had before Chloe had caused such consternation.

At first she had been a very subdued and unhappy person, drooping about the house like an invalid, allowing Goosey to fuss over her and cook her little delicious messes without complaining once, and indeed she did look rather invalidish. She was pale and seemed to have an almost permanent head cold (certainly she was always blowing her nose) and was slow and heavy in her movements. She seemed to have lost much of her old energy, too, for though she spent some of her evenings at her friends' homes, most of the time she remained at home, playing listlessly with Robin until it was her bedtime, and seeming to tolerate Ludo and Halma and Snakes and Ladders well enough. And for a while Poppy managed to convince herself that this lowness in Chloe was an inevitable reaction to her Paris adventure, soon to pass, and was content enough.

All would be well now, she promised herself; Chloe was a changed person who would behave sensibly in future, once she felt better; the new restaurant was doing very well, and things were running smoothly at the Cable Street office and restaurant too, where the sell-out trade had increased yet again, much to Jessie's delight. And of course there was David, with whom she was becoming ever more at peace, ever more comfortable. There was a rich physical delight in being with him; just seeing him could give her a *frisson* of excitement and when he held her hand or set his arm across her shoulders or kissed her on greeting and parting, she felt marvellous. But it was the peace and comfort which mattered most; it was quite different from the emotional turmoil she had experienced with Bobby and in so many ways so much better.

But her contentment did not last. As July limped, hot and breathless, into a glowing August and the park drowsed under its yellow parched grass Chloe began to be restless. When Robin wanted to play – and she had more time to do so once her school had broken up for the long summer holidays – Chloe snapped at her, and that made Robin mope about the house and become irritable herself. Most of her schoolfriends had gone away to the seaside for their family vacations, but this was not a pattern of life that obtained in the Norland Square household. Poppy had to work all through the summer weeks, for even though London was undoubtedly quieter than it was at other times of the year, still the restaurants were as busy as ever and so were the Cable Street kitchens; for, as Jessie said sapiently, 'When the thermometer starts to climb people don't fancy cooking for themselves. In summer we make money, and we make it good – ' Poppy had suggested to Robin that she should go with Goosey to stay on her brother's farm in Dorset, for that would give old Goosey a rest too, but Robin wept and clung to Poppy at the mere suggestion. She wanted to go nowhere that her mother did not, and Poppy had to give in, seeing no point in forcing the child to have a holiday she would not enjoy; so neither she nor Goosey got away. And Chloe became snappier and sulkier and more and more horrid and Poppy knew, with a sinking heart, that the good changes in her stepdaughter which she had so optimistically told herself were for always were in fact very temporary indeed.

She discussed the situation with David one evening, late, when he took her to dine at Rules' restaurant in Maiden Lane, in Covent Garden, sitting close together in the panelled dimness over chicken aspic and a bottle of good Chablis. She should have been happy; the business, to Jessie's jubilation, was showing a twelve per cent increase in income since this time last year and that meant that Poppy would have a bumper bank balance too, come the end of the year when the new partnership's accounts were cast and the profit shared out. But she was not happy and she told David so, in some detail.

He listened with the quiet solidity he always showed, not interrupting while letting her pour out all her irritation and worry over Chloe, and then said, 'Is there anything you can do to change things, do you think?'

She thought for a moment and then made a face. 'I suppose not. I can't lock her up. I know George is always on about taking more care of her, sending her away for a rest and so forth – and half the time I feel he's more interested in goading me than in Chloe's wellbeing – but when I tell her that's what he says she just shrugs her shoulders and refuses, so what can I do? I can't make her do anything she doesn't want to. No one can. That's always been the trouble.'

'Then,' he said calmly, 'the best thing to do is nothing.'

'Nothing?'

'Precisely nothing. She is as she is. Perhaps the problem is that too many people fuss over her and worry over her and it makes her think she's exceedingly important.'

'Well, of course she is! How can she be otherwise when she plagues poor Goosey so with her bad temper and makes Robin so cross and edgy and – '

239

'Wrong sort of important. She's been made to feel troublesome – '

'Are you surprised?'

' – so troublesome is what she is,' he finished as though she had not spoken. 'Better surely to be relaxed and sunny about her, take it for granted she'll behave herself and see if that works. It mightn't – but you can't be any worse off than you are if you try it, can you?'

She sighed. 'You make it sound so reasonable.'

'Well, isn't it?'

'Where did you learn to – well, to work things out in that sort of way?'

'Try spending months on end in a sanitorium with a bunch of guys who don't know whether you're going to live or die, and who act up because of their TB anyway,' he said a little grimly. 'It'll concentrate *your* mind wonderfully too.'

She reached across the table to hold his hand and for a while they said nothing, sipping their wine and just being peaceable together. How did I manage before him? she asked herself. How could I have been so lonely and not known it? I will do it his way, because he's right. I'm getting nowhere with her my way, so I might as well try –

Chloe sat on the edge of her bed and thought about what to do. For weeks now she had been trying to work out how on earth she was to get in touch with him again, but it had been impossible. Poppy had seemed to have eyes in the back of her head, and Goosey too was much more watchful than she used to be. When Chloe went to visit Mary Challoner in the evening, one or other of them insisted on accompanying her there and arranged with Mary's father to fetch her home afterwards. There had been no hope of any subterfuge there.

And to tell the truth Chloe had not been sure she wanted to go against Poppy at present. Paris had been absolutely dreadful, once Bernie had gone back to London. The first few days when he had been there and shown her *La Ratière* – and it had been such fun that it was really the same name as in London – she had been entranced at the whole wonderful adventure, and though she had been dubious and uncomfortable about the skimpy costume she had to wear, she had managed to cope with that well enough. But then, once she was settled, Bernie had gone back to London and suddenly it had been no fun at all any more. Armand had been quite hateful, shouting and screaming at her if she did the walking round the restaurant wrong, and getting even angrier if she wasn't what he called 'Nice to all customers in the way the customers expect a sensible girl to be nice', and that meant being pawed and even kissed sometimes, which she hated. The other girls too had been horrid, ignoring her, being unfriendly and obviously sneering at her.

Before the end of the first week she had wanted to go home and would have done if she hadn't been too frightened of Armand. There was something about him that made her shake inside; and anyway he was the one who gave her her stuff now that Bernie was back in London. So that had been part of it too. All very, very miserable.

So that was why, when she had seen Poppy standing there with that American friend of hers, David, and that other man, the one who had come round asking questions saying he was from a newspaper but who had obviously been their lookout, she had felt – well, glad. It was amazing but there it was. She had been glad. And so she had come back to London with them, feeling safer once she was out of Armand's way. Even for the chance to get some stuff, it wasn't worth it. Armand was totally, utterly disgusting and she hated him; to go home to Holland Park had seemed like a good thing to do.

But now it was all different. Now she had been back in

Norland Square for so long she wanted to scream it was so awful. Nothing but Goosey nagging and Poppy watching and that wretched child and her silly games –

But today it had become suddenly easier and she thought, Poppy had been different. She hadn't gone on at her when she said she wanted to go out this afternoon, hadn't even asked where she was going. She had just said in a vague sort of way, 'Have a nice time, dear,' and then started talking to Robin. Was it a trick to try to catch her out doing what she wanted to do? Or was Poppy really going to be as she had used to be, just letting her do as she wanted when she wanted? It was a difficult question to answer.

If only Bernie would answer her, she thought then. All those letters and phone calls and messages she had left, even the telegrams she had sent him, all ignored, every one of them. Was he angry because she had left the job in Paris? Why should he be? She'd tried and it hadn't been fun after all. No one had paid her any money so she didn't owe him anything, did she? So why should he be angry over that? It had to be something else, surely. Something she had to understand. And anyway she needed some more stuff. It was so dreary without any and there was nowhere else she could go for it but to Bernie. The question was, could she go?

She got to her feet and went to the landing outside her room to peer over and down the stairs. All was silent below; maybe Poppy had been telling the truth after all? She had said she was taking Robin to the theatre at Drury Lane as a treat, to see *Rose Marie* and Goosey of course had gone to bed early, as she nearly always did. It was now ten o'clock; surely if Poppy had meant to creep back to see if she could catch her, Chloe, up to something or other, she would have come by now?

She made up her mind quickly. It had to be now or not at all, and she ran into her room and snatched up her bag and stuffed some money into it from her little cache which she left hidden in her stocking drawer, and pulled on her cream tussore coat and the small straw hat to match. Quite the wrong clothes for this time of night, of course, and totally disastrous for a night club, but she didn't care. She was going to see him and couldn't waste her time changing. If he wouldn't answer her phone calls or her letters, what else could she do? She had to see him – because it wasn't just the stuff she missed so dreadfully. It was Bernie himself, Bernie with the marvellous face and the touch that could make her shiver and the kisses that were so very special and made her do things she would never have imagined possible. She had to see him, no matter what.

'Don't be a bloody fool, Arthur,' Bernie snapped. 'I've got more sense than to try a trick like that, even if you haven't. And anyway why should I? I'm the best bloody man they've ever had here and it's high time the bastards knew it. I've made a fortune for 'em here, a fortune. And I've got a bit of information they mightn't like spread around. That'll be useful too to remind 'em that they can't dump me that easily. Stop getting yourself worked up, Arthur, for God's sake.'

The other man was sitting in the armchair opposite his desk, his hands on his plump knees and his chin tilted so that he could look at Bernie more easily. He was sweating in the bright light and looked pale and uneasy.

'I don't like it, Bernie. I really don't. It's no use you saying you're not worried. I am, and there it is. I want to get out of this now, right away – '

'Well, you can't,' Bernie said sharply and reached for a cigarette. He helped himself from the silver box and then ostentatiously closed it with a little snap as the other reached to help himself too. 'You're in this up to your arse as much as I am. It was your money that got the first lot in, remember? And anyway, if you get out, where are you going to get your stuff in future? Don't be such a bloody fool. I told you that. It's what you are and what you'll always be, but for once in your stupid life try to think and act like a mensch, will you? Pretend you're a man, not the lump of jelly you look like.'

Arthur got to his feet and stood there in the vivid light with his hands clenched at his sides and his face even whiter than it had been.

'That is it,' he said a little breathlessly. 'That's enough. I'm not putting up with your nastiness as well as everything else. As for stuff – I'm not as stupid as you think I am. I can get what I want when I want it. But I'm going now and I'm going to tell them all that they – '

The door behind him rattled and clattered and suddenly the room seemed to be full as Arthur turned his head and looked and then whimpered. Three men, all in heavy coats in spite of the weather and all staring at him owlishly were there and once again he whimpered and seemed to shrink a little.

'I'm just going,' he gabbled. 'Just going. It's nothing to do with me, nothing at all. I've only just found out about Paris and I'd have told him if I'd known, he shouldn't do it and it's nothing to do with me. The police are after him too, you know, and I want no part of it. He'll split on you, you know that, you tell Armand, and tell him too, he'll split on you and then where'll we all be? It's nothing to do with me, it's all him – '

'If you believe that you'll believe anything,' Bernie said easily and got to his feet. 'Hi, John. And Theo! Haven't seen you in an age. Not since Ascot, eh? Good day we had there. And you must be Oliver. Heard them speak of you, heard them speak.'

He moved across the room and held his hand out to them and they stood, all of them, staring at him and then at Arthur, their faces quite blank; and Arthur whimpered again and said in a shrill little voice. 'Don't you believe him, whatever you do don't believe him. He's lying, he always lies, you ought to know that, it's him, not me. It's him, believe me – '

Bernie shot a contemptuous look over his shoulder at the now heavily sweating Arthur. 'Doesn't he make you sick?' he said dispassionately. 'I've been after him for weeks now and I've uncovered some stuff about this man – he's been milking the Paris books, you know that? Calls himself an accountant, so he knows how to do it, I suppose, but he made the mistake of thinking I wouldn't understand. I'm no accountant, thank God, but I understand – oh, I understand.'

'No, no!' squealed Arthur. 'It's not like that at all, it's not – it was him, believe me it was him – '

The three men moved further into the room and came towards the sofa behind the obviously terrified Arthur. Two of them sat down and the third, a thin man who looked as though he would break in a high wind, but yet who seemed to have a wiriness about him that promised more energy than was at first apparent, stood to one side, watchful and alert, both hands in his overcoat pockets.

'It's money of course,' the one called Theo said, and sounded a little sad. 'It's always money, ain't it, Bernie? Here you are, chucking the stuff around we've been told and where is it coming from, we want to know? Cars like that three litre Alvis you got out there don't come for tuppence ha'penny and a couple of cigarette coupons, do they? No, they don't. So he was saying, our friend was, when he said we should visit you, that he reckoned it's got to be coming from somewhere and he reckons it's his pocket. You see? So what are we to tell him? That's the thing. What are we to tell him?'

'It's all him,' Arthur began again, and now the sweat was running down his face so that he looked as though he were weeping and maybe he was at that. The man called

Theo looked at him for a moment and then flicked his eyes away and back to Bernie, who was standing by the door, leaning against the wall.

'Seems to be sure about it, doesn't he?' Theo said in a conversational tone. 'Maybe he ought to talk to him, at that. He's very good at sorting out things like that, he is – '

'He'll understand, he'll believe me!' Arthur said. 'And about the police being on to him as well. He'll see – '

There was a little silence and then the door rattled again and opened.

She had no trouble getting into the club, crowded though it was. She had her special membership card, and it had been signed by Bernie himself and he'd fixed a gold star in one corner. That meant she was a special customer, and no one had said a word when she had left her coat and her hat in the cloakroom and gone walking through to the special room through the door behind the band's small stand. Some of the women she had been sure had stared at her day frock as she passed but she hadn't cared about that; they were all frumps, anyway, she told herself, her head up. All dreary frumps. I look better in what I'm wearing than anyone of them in their fancy evening frocks. Much better –

She had sat for a while in the corner of the big room with the roulette wheel and the card tables, trying to decide what to do, for her courage had abandoned her. Send a message in and wait for him to come out? And it might be easier to start talking out here where there were other people –

But then she had shaken her head at herself. No, they had to talk privately. She would have to go into the office to do that. He had to be there; she could see the light beneath the door, even in this brightly lit room, because it was a bad fit, always had been. So he had to be there. But she was uneasy, and deeply unwilling to make the last part of her journey. She had come this far and it was only a matter of yards now to be with him, to be standing there looking at that marvellous face of his; and yet, she was frightened.

And it was ridiculous, of course it was. She had come so far and it was ridiculous to fuss about the rest of it. And then she saw across the room a couple of people hunched, heads together, over one of the small glass tables and saw the small box flash in the woman's hand and her nose suddenly ached, and she thought – I'm going in there *now*. I'll say it all very simply – I don't want to see *him* at all really. I won't let him know I care about him, why should I? He went away and left me with that hateful man in Paris and why should I be nice to him now? I shall just tell him it's some stuff I want and that's why I'm here. No other reason. He's just a sort of shop-keeper as far as I'm concerned. That'll show him –

And she got to her feet and somehow managed to walk the rest of the way across the room to the door in the corner. And opened it and walked in without knocking.

20

The smell of the hospital was comforting and she halted
for a brief moment in the big echoing hall and closed her
eyes and lifted her head to take it in; ether and carbolic
and the rich undertow of lysol and suddenly she was back
at the field hospital in Revigny, unloading her ambulance
of battered men brought from the front at Verdun and
feeling the weariness of long sleepless hardworking hours
aching in their bones. But when she opened her eyes she
was at once back in the present in London, in the
tesselated grey and white waiting room of the casualty
department of St George's hospital, with its rows of
chairs filled with dispirited looking people and the light
glinting from the chrome trolleys and shelves. But the
weariness remained, compounded not just of the lateness
of the hour – for it was now almost midnight – but also
of the certainty that here again was major trouble with
Chloe. Certainly never before had she been summoned to
a hospital to collect her.

She looked around and saw a Sister on the far side of
the big space and went across to her, very aware of her
shoes clacking on the tiled floor, and also of her clothes.
It was rare she had occasion to wear evening dress, for
when she dined out with David they usually went to
pleasant small restaurants where day clothes were
perfectly suitable. But tonight, taking Robin to the
theatre as a special treat, she had decided they should be

248

dressed up, she and her small daughter, and now being in a hospital in a froth of apricot coloured chiffon under a matching velvet coat she felt out of place at best, frivolous and silly at worst.

'Miss Bradman?' Sister said when she had managed to explain what she wanted. 'You were sent for, you say? Ah, yes. The – ah – people who came in at ten o'clock.' She looked at the fob watch on her apron breast and then sharply at Poppy, her eyes glinting behind her round tortoiseshell-rimmed spectacles. 'A rather nasty affair, I gather. Miss Bradman – she was admitted, I believe – '

'So I was told when I was telephoned,' Poppy said and bit back the retort that had risen to her lips at the Sister's obvious scorn. 'Perhaps you can tell me where I will find her.'

'Oh, Fitzwilliam Ward,' Sister said. 'I can't imagine why they should permit you to visit her at such an hour. It is probably simply to get particulars from you that they have sent for you. She is of course under age – '

'She's almost nineteen,' Poppy said sharply, painfully aware of the criticism in the Sister's voice. 'Hardly a child to be watched at all times.'

'Still, under age.' The Sister tucked her fob watch back into its case with a little snap. 'Fitzwilliam Ward, second floor, the stairs are to your right – ' And she was gone, bustling busily away across the waiting hall, her veil flapping and her heels tapping importantly. Poppy wanted to go after her, to stop her and explain to her how it was a well brought up and cared-for girl of Chloe's age had arrived at hospital in need of emergency treatment, but she did not. It would have done no good, of course it wouldn't. But it was an indication of her state of mind that she should even consider it.

Wretched Chloe, she thought now as she made her way through the dim hospital to the ward on the second floor. Whatever I do, however hard I try, she creates problems all the time. Why can't she just leave us in peace? Why does Robin have to be all upset, and Goosey too – for of course both of them had shown great alarm when the telephone had rung so late at night and woken them, and even more when they had heard that Chloe was in a hospital – and why did she herself have to be always busy about Chloe's affairs? Didn't she have enough to deal with, enough to worry over, what with the restaurant and the office? It was a very self-pitying Poppy who arrived at the door of the ward and peered in hesitantly to look for her stepdaughter.

But her self-pity disappeared as soon as she saw Chloe. There was a tall girl in the uniform of Staff Nurse sitting at the desk in the middle of the darkened ward, only her head illuminated by a low lamp which was shrouded in a red cloth, and she got to her feet at once when she saw Poppy hovering and came towards her.

'Miss Bradman? Yes, she's here. You her mother?'

'Her stepmother,' Poppy said. 'Someone phoned me and said she was here at St George's. How is she? May I see her?'

'Not too bad, considering. She's been rather weepy, but that's natural enough,' the nurse said. 'Of course you can see her. Just be nice and quiet. Maybe she'll get some sleep once she sees you, poor thing. She is upset, I'm afraid –'

'What happened?' Poppy asked and the nurse shook her head.

'I'm afraid I've no idea how she was hurt, if that's what you mean. I can only tell you she has a fractured tibia and fibula, but fortunately it's a simple one and needed only minimal reduction – not too painful. She has a plaster of course and tomorrow I imagine they'll decide what else might be needed –'

'How did she manage to do that?' Poppy said and again the nurse shook her head. 'You can ask her. And if

250

you can settle her to get some sleep, I'll be grateful. I'm quite busy tonight – ' And then she turned her head, as someone wailed, 'Nurse,' from down the ward, and went hurrying away. 'She's in bed twelve – there on the right – behind the screens – ' she called softly over her shoulder.

Chloe was lying propped up on two pillows and her left leg was also propped up, her toes pink and pathetic against the slab of white plaster that encased her leg to her knee and halfway up her thigh. The blankets and counterpane were carefully arranged to cover the rest of her and she looked extremely uncomfortable as she lay there with her eyes closed. Her hair was rumpled and her face, washed clean of her usual make-up, looked rather pale, though there was a high flush over the cheekbones and violet shadows beneath the eyes. Poppy stood at the front of the bed and looked at her and felt a stirring of deep pity. She looked helpless and lonely and very miserable.

As though she felt Poppy's gaze on her Chloe stirred and opened her eyes and then peered and blinked and peered again, and her face cleared as she saw Poppy, and then crumpled into tears.

'Oh, Poppy,' she said and that was all that seemed willing to emerge from her. 'Oh, Poppy, oh, *Poppy* – ' And Poppy came through the screens to the side of the bed and stood there and put out one hand and took Chloe's and she lay there with tears running down her cheeks and sniffing miserably. And all Poppy's anger melted away in a great rush of concern.

'There, there,' she murmured and bent and mopped at the small face with a handkerchief taken from her coat pocket. 'It's all right, my love, it's all right, there, there – ' And she went on crooning until at last the tears stopped with one last doleful sniff.

Poppy looked around, saw a chair against the wall and

brought it to sit next to Chloe, who clung to her hand tightly, unwilling to let her go even to fetch the chair, watching her movements with big eyes.

'Well, tell me what happened,' Poppy said then, and leaned forwards so that her whispers could be heard. She was very aware of the ward stretching out beyond them in the dimness, of the soft breathing of some of the other people in the beds that ran in rows on each side, and of the snuffles and odd gasping sounds made by others. She could hear the nurse murmuring to someone at the far end of the ward, and a faint clatter of chrome and steel as a trolley was moved, and it was all very familiar, deeply achingly familiar, a remembrance of her own young days, when she had been Chloe's age and had been working in wards much like this one, if less well-appointed and warm, and filled with injured soldiers rather than women.

'It wasn't my fault, honestly,' Chloe said. 'Truly it wasn't – '

'Hush, my love,' Poppy murmured. 'Try to whisper or you'll wake the others and nurse will come and make me leave – '

Obediently Chloe dropped her voice. 'I only wanted to tell him – to see him – to make sure he wasn't angry because I'd left the job – '

Poppy stiffened. 'Who?'

Chloe seemed not to notice the interruption. ' – That was why I went, honestly it was. I didn't know he was in there with other people. I just went into his office to tell him you'd brought me home and anyway it wasn't nice there, and there were all these people there too and they were hateful, really hateful, and when I tried to go one of them said I couldn't but *he* said it was silly me staying there and then it all started – ' Her face crumpled again, as the tears began once more. 'I was so frightened. I tried keeping out of the way, but they were so horrible, really

252

hitting each other but especially hitting him, it was awful, and then I tried to get behind the desk to be out of the way and one of them just tipped it up and it landed on me and my leg does hurt so – it's awful – and when they brought us here it hurt even more and they cut off my stockings with huge scissors and the doctor was so horrid – oh, Poppy, oh, Poppy – '

Poppy, highly confused, stroked her gently until at last the tears stopped once more, and then leaned closer.

'Who are you talking about, Chloe, love? Where were you?' she whispered.

'At The Rat Trap,' Chloe said and then suddenly yawned hugely and looking at her in the dim light thrown by the shrouded overhead lamp Poppy thought, they've drugged her. Her eyes show that, with such small pupils. They've drugged her for the pain and that's making her mind wander. And yet, she seems to be making some sort of sense.

'The Rat Trap?' she said carefully.

'His club,' Chloe said. 'The same name as the one in Paris. *La Ratière*. It's his club. Or I thought it was, but the things those men were shouting I think now it isn't. I think he just works there. I don't know about Arthur, he was there too, the man from the party in Bloomsbury, that one, a silly man, horrible, but he got out, I think. He wasn't there afterwards, when the men had gone away and we were both left there and I was crying because my leg hurt so dreadfully and the people came in from the club and called an ambulance and everything. Oh, Poppy – Oh – Po – '

'Hush now,' Poppy said firmly. 'You're getting over-wrought. You need to sleep. They've given you something for the pain in your leg?'

'Something?' Chloe said. 'What something?'

'They gave you an injection because of your broken leg – '

Again Chloe's eyes filmed with tears. 'I won't be able to walk, will I? I'll never be able to walk – '

'Nonsense,' Poppy said as robustly as she could in a whisper. 'Of course you will. It will take time, but it will heal as good as new. Listen, Chloe, you must explain more carefully. Who is this man you're talking about? What's his name? And how do you know a man who has a night-club here in London? It all sounds very odd – '

'You'll be angry and hateful now,' Chloe said in a little whimper and rolled her head on the pillow. 'I meant no harm, it was just fun. I went there with one of the boys and I met him and he was so handsome and – Oh, Poppy!'

'You went there with one of the boys you know and you met someone handsome,' Poppy said and then sighed as pieces began to click into place. 'And this is the man who told you he could get you a job in Paris and you just agreed to go – '

Chloe rolled her head on the pillow again and said drowsily, 'It sounded such fun – ' and then closed her eyes. Clearly the drug she had been given – morphine? Probably, Poppy thought – had taken over again and she was on the edge of sleep, and the remnants of the nurse that remained alive deep inside Poppy took over and she patted Chloe's hand, and then smoothed the sheets and blankets over her and leaned back and sat there watching her as she slept.

There was clearly a great deal to find out about what Chloe had been up to but questioning would have to wait, though Poppy felt she had a shadowy idea enough. The silly child had been taken to some raffish establishment by one of her young friends from the tennis club, who should have known better than to go to such a place with a nice girl, and Chloe had thought it highly sophisticated no doubt and been swept along by this awful man she met there, whoever he was, and who thought it clever to persuade well brought up girls who were as silly as they were spoiled to run off to work in even more raffish establishments in Paris. Though perhaps it wasn't entirely his fault, whoever he was, Poppy thought, trying to be just. Maybe George and the Sister down in Casualty had been right and Poppy had neglected Chloe, had allowed her too much freedom. And yet David had said that trying to tie the child down wouldn't work any better; and surely he was right too. And she sighed again and got to her feet.

No point in thinking about it any more now. Tomorrow, when she found out just how severe Chloe's injury was, decisions would have to be made. Certainly life with Chloe could not be allowed to go on hurtling from crisis to crisis in this fashion.

She stood there for one last look at Chloe, who was now snoring softly, she was so deeply asleep, and then slipped out between the screens and made her way to the door of the ward. The Staff Nurse lifted her head as she went past and came after her.

'All right?' she murmured. 'You feel better about her now? You've had a nasty shock.'

Poppy's heart glowed; for the first time someone had shown some concern for how *she* was feeling and she smiled brilliantly at the nurse and said gratefully, 'Oh, yes. It's so dreadful to get late calls telling you people are hurt – you think of heaven knows what till you've seen for yourself.'

The nurse nodded sympathetically. 'I know. That's why I always allow visiting at whatever time people arrive, even if some of the others don't. It helps the patient too, actually, once they know their relations feel a bit better. You'll find that Nurse Jennings on Arthur Wellesley Ward is just the same. She'll have allowed the other one's visitor to see him – '

'The other one?' Poppy said.

255

'The young man who was admitted at the same time as your stepdaughter,' the nurse explained and then turned her head as again someone called plaintively, 'Nurse,' at the end of the ward. 'Arthur Wellesley Ward – on the floor above this. Just go up the stairs at the other end of the corridor. I dare say Nurse Jennings won't mind letting you see him as he's a family friend – she's a dear. Tell her I sent you – I must go – ' And she went hurrying away, her uniform whispering its starchiness as she went.

Poppy stood thinking. Whoever he was, he was no friend of hers, of course. What she'd like to do to this young man was wring his neck for creating such problems for Chloe. And anyway, maybe this wasn't the time to see him. She looked at her watch; it was now gone midnight, and she bit her lower lip. Sleep was what she most needed; and yet there was the man who had led Chloe into all this trouble. Maybe tomorrow when the place was bristling with nurses and sisters and doctors, she wouldn't be allowed to visit him. She didn't after all, even know his name. No doubt Chloe would tell her, but –

She made up her mind quickly. He was here and putting things off was never of much use. Pulling her coat closer, she went quickly along the corridor and hurried up the stairs at the end to find her way to an identical ward above the one where Chloe was now sleeping. Standing in the doorway for a moment listening, she was momentarily diverted; the women in the ward below had snuffled and whimpered in their sleep, but here the sounds were much more definite and loud as men snored and snorted and generally breathed like beached whales. And where downstairs the smell of hospital had been strong enough to overwhelm everything else, here the reek of tobacco from hand-rolled cigarettes was thick and disagreeable. It was even more familiar here than it had been downstairs, for this was the way sick soldiers had smelled.

She peered in, pushing away her memories, looking for the nurse. She could just see at the end of the ward two figures with their heads together and she peered even harder, as the couple separated and moved. One of them – the nurse, for now Poppy could see her cap bouncing on her head – went to the far end, and the other came towards her.

Poppy hesitated a little longer, not wanting to walk all the way up to the ward to find the nurse, as the other shape came towards her and then, as it passed the central table with its dimmed light she frowned, screwed up her eyes and stared hard.

The figure came closer, reached the door and came through it and Poppy opened her eyes wide and stared harder than ever. She was so amazed that it didn't seem possible to her that she could be seeing what she thought she was seeing. It had to be an error, a trick of the light, a nonsense –

But it wasn't. For the other stopped and stared at her as the two of them came level and shook her head and said wonderingly, 'Poppy?' just as Poppy managed to say in the same tone of voice precisely, 'Jessie?' And then they spoke together in such complete unison that it would have been very funny, if either of them had been in the mood for laughter.

'What on earth are *you* doing here?' they asked.

21

'What I can't get over,' Poppy said wearily, 'is the fact that neither of us had any idea they'd ever met.' She stirred her coffee abstractedly, turning the spoon in the cup for far longer than was needed to mix in the milk, and Jessie watched her and nodded agreement.

'If you ask me, the funny thing is they never did before,' she said. 'I mean, they're almost relations – '

They were in the empty restaurant, an hour before the lunch rush was due to begin, sitting slumped on each side of one of the small tables, their coffee in front of them, and both looking as they were feeling, tired, anxious and dispirited.

'Relations?' Poppy lifted her head sharply. 'Of course they're not. She was Bobby's daughter, remember, not mine. I'm her – '

Jessie waved that away. 'I know, I know. Not blood, of course, not blood! But like *mechatunim* – you know what they are – '

'No,' Poppy said shortly.

'They're your children's parents-in-law, that's who they are. Not related by blood, of course not. But how can you be closer to people than to have their child marry yours? It's an important relationship, ain't it? Sure it is. Well, your child and my child may not be related directly, on account of she isn't exactly your child, and they're not married of course, but all the same – you and me are

258

close. More than auntie and niece, hmm? So our children – '

'Jessie,' Poppy began almost desperately and then stopped. How could she say what she wanted to say to her? There she sat, looking so very tired and a little old, which was a thought that rarely came to Poppy regarding Jessie. Somehow Jessie had always seemed ageless. But not this morning; this morning she looked dreadful. This was no time for Poppy to speak her mind about Bernie and his influence on Chloe. But all the same something had to be said.

'Jessie,' she said again, carefully this time. 'We have to talk about this situation. It's all very difficult – '

'Difficult?' Jessie said loudly. 'Difficult? That's a hell of a word to use, with your boobalah lying there in the hospital covered in plaster and mine with concussion. I never saw a boy look so terrible. And his face all bruised – ' Her eyes looked bleak. 'You should see, Poppy. It's terrible. His cheekbone, here, all blue it is, and with a cut. Please God there shouldn't be any scar – '

'You told me the nurse said no more harm was done. That the concussion would soon be all right and that his skull isn't broken or anything like that,' Poppy said.

'That's right. But concussion – it's very bad.'

'Not that bad,' Poppy said firmly. 'So don't you go thinking it. The important thing is that his skull is intact. He'll have a few days of headaches and that'll be the end of it. As for the bruising – that'll go as well. He'll heal and so will Chloe. It may take a few weeks, but she'll get over it – they both will.'

'It's how it happened worries me,' Jessie said fretfully. 'All my Bernie'll say is there were some jealous business rivals. Rivalry – this, I can understand. But beating up? That's something else. It worries me – did Chloe say anything about it?'

'Not to me,' Poppy said. 'She just said there was some

259

sort of argument going on, and someone pushed the desk over on her and that was how her leg was broken. I know nothing else. It all sounded – ' She hesitated. 'It sounded like some sort of a film story. Not like real life at all.'

'Believe me, life can be like stories sometimes,' Jessie said. 'It's what Bernie said it was, then. Just jealousy.' She brooded for a moment and then said, 'You're sure they'll both be all right? You did nursing in the war – you understand these things. They'll be all right?'

'They'll be fine,' Poppy said reassuringly. 'Truly they will. What's more important, frankly, is what happens after they're both well again.'

'What should happen?' Jessie said and leaned forwards to pick up her cup. 'They'll be better, and what could be more important than that?'

'Of course that matters,' Poppy said. 'But we have to think of other things.' She was picking her words very carefully now, trying to convince herself she had not earlier seen that gleam in Jessie's eye that she thought she had. 'But just as important is this business of their – of their knowing each other. Not friends precisely but – '

Jessie was leaning back in her chair again, her chin up. 'So why shouldn't they be friends? All right, they're not related but they're still family. What could be nicer than everyone's friendly?'

'Jessie, you're not making this easy.' Poppy felt she was almost being goaded. Generally she and her aunt were on the most amiable of terms, liking each other cordially as well as being linked by a bond of love which in Jessie's case went back to Poppy's childhood, and in Poppy's own had certainly had time to grow over the past fifteen years since she had first come into contact with her in her adult life; but at this moment Poppy felt a sliver of cold dislike move into her. And hated it.

'What's to make difficult?' Jessie sounded defensive.

'You're always so touchy, Poppela. Why are you being touchy now? What you upset over?'

It didn't help when Jessie used her pet name either, and Poppy had to steel herself to say what she had to say.

'I don't think that – it's a suitable friendship for Chloe,' she said, and then cursed herself. So much for tact. Even in her own ears that had sounded blunt to the point of rudeness.

It was inevitable that Jessie should flare up, and it was a formidable sight when she did. She sat very upright and fixed her gaze on Poppy, her face so suffused with suppressed anger that it was almost as red as her summer blouse.

'Not a suitable friendship? What are you saying? That my Bernie isn't good enough to speak to your Chloe? That he's some sort of riff-raff that is so far beneath her that – '

'Jessie, Jessie, for heaven's sake!' Poppy got to her feet and came round the table to stand behind her aunt and bend over her and put her arms around her, so that the older woman's head rested against her chest. It was affectionate and it had the additional benefit of ensuring that Poppy didn't have to look in Jessie's face as she spoke.

'Listen to me, darling,' she said gently. 'Please listen and don't interrupt, all right? I can't deny that over the years your Bernie and I have not been – well, we've had our arguments. You know I think you've spoiled him. It's no secret that I get upset when he doesn't treat you right, when he doesn't call for weeks on end – '

She felt the brawny shoulders tighten beneath her grip and leaned even further forwards so that she could set her cheek against Jessie's. 'And he isn't the only one who's spoiled. Chloe is too, and don't I know it. Not entirely my fault, mind you. It all started long before I came on the scene – '

Jessie's shoulders tightened even more. 'Are you saying that you did a better job than me, then, that I spoiled my Bernie all on my own?' she demanded gruffly.

Poppy bit her tongue and then made a grimace into Jessie's warm hair. No point in trying to wriggle out of that piece of monumental tactlessness, she told herself. It wouldn't be possible.

'Well, yes, darling,' she said candidly. 'You know you did. But that isn't the point. What I'm trying to say is that these two would not be good for each other. What your Bernie needs is a nice sensible set of friends who'd stop him from doing some of the things he does. He – his imagination runs away with him sometimes, he gets over enthusiastic and things go wrong. Who knows what happened at this Rat Trap place last night? He says rivalry and maybe it was that, but it's not the first time he's been in scrapes, and frankly on present showing it's unlikely to be the last. What he needs, you see, is someone to put on the brakes, make him see sense. And Chloe – heavens, that Chloe! She'd egg him on! She'd make him be – well, even more than ever what he was. She needs someone much tougher to keep her in line too. Some of her friends are so – well, indulgent to her, and it worries me. I wouldn't want to worry over Bernie the way I worry over some of them – '

The shoulders had eased a good deal now and there was a little silence and then Jessie said in a rather flat voice. 'I suppose so. I just thought there for a while – ' She shrugged and Poppy turned her head and kissed the lined old cheek and straightened her back to come and sit down again facing her. 'I got hopeful,' Jessie finished.

She grinned at Poppy then and her face for just a moment bore its usual warm affectionate look. 'I got so hopeful there for a minute that I was under the chuppah – the marriage canopy, you know? I thought – what could be nicer, my Bernie, your Chloe – but you're right.

262

They'd never suit, would they? Much too – what's the word? Mercurial, that's it. Much too mercurial, both of them.'

Poppy smiled at her, relief filling her. 'Yes, Jessie,' she said gratefully. 'That's really the right word. They're much too mercurial. So, what we have to do is try to cool them off a bit – not let them see each other.'

Jessie gave a little bark of laughter at that. 'And I wish you all the best of luck with that,' she said with a sardonic note in her voice. 'Did you ever try to make my Bernie do anything he didn't choose to do? Or stop him from what he wanted? He may be spoiled like you say – and I can't deny it and who can blame me when he's such a nosh and anyway the only chick I got – he may be spoiled, but a momma's boy he ain't. Nothing I say ever makes any odds with him, and I don't think you'll have any better luck. As for your Chloe – '

She hauled herself to her feet and stood there looking down at Poppy, a vast red shape in the cool pretty restaurant.

'Let's not kid ourselves any, dolly. That girl is as much a runaround as anything Bernie is. Every time I see you you got something to worry over. This week it's a broken leg, last week it was running away to Paris, no less – '

'At Bernie's instigation,' Poppy snapped and then wanted to bite her tongue yet again for Jessie looked for a moment as though she had pulled a curtain over her face, and had become rocklike with anger. 'I mean, it was his place she ran to – '

'That's as may be,' Jessie said, seeming to thaw a little. 'But the thing of it is, she went, eh? And you couldn't stop that. So if she wants to go on being my Bernie's friend then that's what she'll be, and you won't be able to prevent her.'

There was a little silence and then Poppy said unwillingly, 'I know. Of course I know that. You're absolutely right. But we still ought to try, surely, to keep them apart?'

'Poppy, Poppy, when will you understand about people, hey?' Jessie said. 'Did you ever hear of the mother went shopping one morning, said to her kids, "Listen, be good. I'll be home soon. Just be good and whatever you do, don't go putting no peas up your noses, all right?" So she goes shopping and when she comes back she finds the kids with their noses full of peas. It's human nature! Tell a young one not to do something and you put ideas in his head. And into hers. Lay off, Poppy. You're trying too hard. I agree, Bernie and Chloe ain't maybe cut out for each other, but I'll tell you this – if it's meant, it's meant and there won't be a thing we can do about it. All right?'

And she turned and went off to the kitchen, leaving the door swinging behind her with a soft sigh as Poppy sat and stared at it and tried to think sensibly about what to do next.

It was just as well, she decided, that St George's agreed to keep Chloe in Fitzwilliam Ward and said she'd be there for almost a month. The fracture, the doctor told Poppy when she went to see him that afternoon, was a straightforward one, but her knee had been injured too. That was why she had so large a plaster on.

'You won't be able to manage her easily at home,' he said. 'Unless you have your own private nurse perhaps? Miss Bradman tells me that her old Nanny is still with you and that she is very caring – '

'Oh, not Goosey,' Poppy said hastily. 'She's over seventy and in no state to nurse someone in a heavy plaster. May Chloe stay here? It might be as well. She'll get so bored at home and so – '

The doctor grinned. 'Having had her here for just one day, I suspect I know what you mean, Mrs Bradman. Of course she may stay. I'm interested in knees and her injury is the sort that can do very well as long as great care is taken. Leave her with us and we'll see to it that she'll be as good as new when we return her to you.'

So Poppy was given time to make the plans she wanted to. No matter what Jessie said about the intractability of both Bernie and Chloe, she was determined to sort out matters so that they were at least kept well apart in the future. That was the reverse, she told herself stoutly, of putting ideas in their heads. No peas up noses, here.

She said as much to David when he came to have supper with her the day after it had all happened, an evening so hot, since it was now the very end of August, that she had on an impulse set a table in the garden and put candles around to light the dusk and to keep the moths and flies bobbing around their flames and well away from the food. Goosey had made one of her celebrated chaud-froids of chicken and some special peach ice cream, and David had looked at the lace-clad table and the gleaming silver and glass in the soft summer twilight and grinned a smile of pure delight.

'You have all the right ideas, my love,' he said. 'Exactly the setting a man needs to speak of love –'

She shook her head at that. 'Dearest David, that isn't why I did it. I mean, I – it's wonderful to hear you speak so, but not at present.'

He looked at her sideways in the dimness as she settled herself at the table and began to serve the food which Goosey had left ready for them under muslin covers.

'Will there ever be a time when I may be allowed to speak of us?' he said as he sat down, and began to open the bottle of wine which Poppy had left in an ice bucket beside his chair. 'It is difficult for a man to make any headway when the lady of his life and heart is so busy about everything but him.'

She laughed at that. 'I know. I'm sorry, truly I am. But

it is difficult right now. You must see that. What with the new restaurant – '

' – which is doing so well it almost runs itself – ' he put in.

'Well, yes, but there is an enormous amount of paperwork to do. Anyway what with that, and Chloe – really, it's so difficult. I wanted to talk to you about that, actually – '

'About Chloe?' He was eating his chicken and looked up for a moment and said, 'This is magic. I must tell Goosey how much I love her, and how much more my stomach does. She won't mind such romantic talk, even if you do. What's happened now?'

She sighed and told him, leaving nothing out, including the doubts she had about what had happened at The Rat Trap and Chloe's great distress. And he listened in the serious way that she found so very comforting and said nothing till she had finished.

'And you think Jessie is trying to match them?' he said at length.

She nodded. 'I know it sounds stupid, but, well, Jessie's like that. When you first came back and she saw you – ' She reddened suddenly. 'Well, she was all set to marry us off.'

He laughed. 'And she wasn't wrong, was she? Could she be right this time?'

Her face became very still and she stared at him. 'Oh, David,' she said at length. 'I do hope not.'

'Why?'

'Why? Because he's a disaster, that's why,' she cried. 'He's cheated his mother as long as I've known him, he's a spoiled wretch who cares for no one but himself and – '

'And is very like Chloe,' David finished. 'Jessie could have a point.'

'Well, she hasn't,' Poppy said flatly. 'I won't have it.'

'Oh dear,' David said. 'I do seem to have found myself a very managing sort of lady, don't I?'

Again she felt her face go hot. 'Do you mean I'm a – busybody? A – meddler who – '

'No,' he said calmly. 'Just what I said. A managing sort of lady. It doesn't usually work, you know. People do what they want to do, no matter what others try to make them do. I think you should step back and leave them be. She'll be in hospital for a while you say – '

'About a month – '

'A month's a long time in a girl's life. And she's had a nasty time at his hands. Maybe the whole thing will die on its own.'

'And maybe it won't,' she said grimly. 'I have to help it die, surely?'

He sighed. 'If you're determined then you are. Look, what do you want me to say? I can't see the answer to this. As we've said before, this girl is as she is. You can't force her to be otherwise – '

'I don't understand it,' Poppy burst out. 'I really don't. I never gave my mother such trouble and – ' She stopped then very suddenly and sat and stared at him and he gazed back, his brows slightly raised, and said nothing. All round them the dark garden scented the air with late tobacco flowers while the moths danced in the flames of the guttering candles and the distant hum of traffic mixed with the whispering of the leaves on the trees that shaded the end of the garden to make a music of its own.

'You've remembered,' he said at length and she made a little face.

'I suppose it's all a matter of comparison,' she said in a small voice. 'I went off to the FANY and she wasn't at all pleased about that.'

'Did she try to stop you?'

'I wouldn't have let her,' Poppy said and then laughed a little shamefacedly.

He smiled too. 'Then you see the situation you're in?

267

Chloe is as she is. All you can do is go on as you are, I think. Perhaps learn to love her a little more – '

She was very silent for a long time, and then said painfully, 'I find that very difficult. I always have.'

'Even for Bobby?'

'Even for Bobby.'

'Well, thank God for honesty.' He leaned forwards and took her hand. 'It would be much worse if you lied to yourself about it. Some people do in such circumstances. You know what I think the answer here is? It's for you two to have some time for each other. To go away on a holiday, perhaps, so that you aren't always in a rush and she isn't diverted by outside people and interests here in London. Why not arrange it? Take some time, and the two girls and maybe Goosey too, and go away for a couple of weeks. Take her on her own and she'll get suspicious and withdrawn – she'll think you're up to something. So make it a family affair, but with extra time for Chloe and you to talk. I suspect it would make a big difference – '

She sat and looked at him for a while and then said slowly, 'It's an idea. You could be right. Maybe if I weren't always so busy we could talk properly. I could – she isn't all bad, you know.'

'Of course I know! It's just that she's headstrong and awkward. She's a girl,' he said and then smiled. 'As awkward as you can be.'

She lifted her brows at that. 'I'm not at all awkward!'

'Oh, yes you are. I remember you in Revigny, a proper termagant you were. And I've watched you in action here in London. A strong-minded lady with a will of her own and a rather impatient manner. It can make things difficult, especially when you're dealing with someone who's very like you. And though she's your stepdaughter and not your own child, she is very like you in many ways. Believe it or not.'

268

'I find it difficult,' she said. 'I wonder if I could do as you say? Take her away, get to know her better – she'll need to convalesce – '

'Of course she will.'

'But what about Robin? I'd hate to have to leave her behind. It would be so miserable – '

'No need. Take her away too. She'll love it.'

'But there's school,' Poppy objected. 'She goes back in a couple of weeks and the hospital says Chloe must stay there for a month or so – '

He waved a hand. 'Get permission to take her away for a while. They'll give her books to read I dare say, and she'll soon catch up when she returns. She's a bright child and she is after all, only seven. Hardly going to ruin her education to miss a couple of weeks at this age, is it?'

'I suppose not – ' Poppy said slowly. 'I'll talk to Jessie about it.'

'Taking her too?'

'Jessie – ' Poppy looked startled. 'Hardly! Who'd be in charge here at the restaurant and at the office if we both went away? It can't be done – '

'I don't see why not,' David said. 'It would do her no harm to have a holiday and it's a bad business that won't run itself for a couple of weeks with the people who work for it for heaven's sake! It would make Chloe feel very – cherished, I rather think, to have you both take her away. And, while you're at it.' He warmed to his theme. 'Why not include your mother? A real woman's trip, you know? It could be very good for all of you. A chance for Chloe to feel herself part of a real family. I suspect now she often feels a bit shut out, what with one thing and another. Well, do this and you'll be bringing her into the family more, won't you?'

'And with so many of us there, and so far from Bernie, she'll not be able to see him and that will be a good idea too, won't it?'

He laughed. 'There you go again, managing! The object of this holiday is to give you all time to give Chloe what she needs – a bit of attention and the feeling that a lot of people care for her and about her. You're not trying to hide her away. Remember that.'

She smiled. 'I'll remember that. Oh, David,' And she leaned forwards and set her hand over his on the lace tablecloth. 'I am so grateful to you. You do talk so much sense. And you make me feel so much better.'

'Then can we now talk about – '

She shook her head. 'If you mean you want to talk about – what you said you wanted to talk about earlier, please don't.'

'You did seem to say you cared about me before,' he said in a low voice. 'At least that was what I thought you said – '

'I do care about you. Honestly, I do. But – ' She pulled her hand away. 'Don't rush me, David, please. I've got an awful lot to think about, truly I have.'

He made a face. 'Including a long holiday away from London. I must be mad to suggest that. It means I won't see you for – how long?'

She smiled. 'I don't know. What shall we say? A week, two weeks?'

'At least. I'll miss you like the very devil, but it could solve some of your problems. And that means when you come back we will be able to talk about us. Is that a deal?'

She laughed aloud. 'You'll make an American of me yet. Yes, it's a deal.'

22

Robin sat in her sand armchair and ran the shells through her fingers, making them into piles around her feet. They looked lovely, she thought, glinting pinkly in the sunshine, and she let herself imagine what it might be like to live in a house made of such transparently thin rosy shells with delicate lines on them and all curly at the edges. It would be beautiful, she decided, and conjured up a bed made of shells to put inside it and a bath and wash basin and chest of drawers made of shells too, and then fitted the windows with sheets of bubbly pale green seaweed to be curtains and covered the floor with patterns made of sand, just like the sand she was sitting on.

But she soon got tired of that and let the house melt away inside her head and looked behind her at the others. Grandmamma was sitting on a sort of deckchair, but one with a straight back, and was reading a book, looking just as though she was sitting in her drawing-room at home, except that she had a hat on. Her dress was the same sort she wore at home and so were her shoes; imagine Grandmamma in sand shoes! And Robin wriggled her bare toes inside her own blue canvas sand shoes and giggled inside her head.

Auntie Jessie was lying asleep as usual, in a long deck chair that had a sort of canopy fixed on it, and she looked rather funny. She was wearing very bright red beach pyjamas, which looked funny because there was such a lot of Auntie Jessie, and the colour reflected from them on to her face and made her look redder than the lobster that they had had for lunch, and that was the funniest thing of all. So, Robin wondered, why didn't she laugh? And she looked at Mummy and she knew why she wasn't laughing.

Mummy was looking at Chloe, who was lying on the sand on a huge yellow towel and wearing a swimsuit that was also yellow, and looking very bored, even in her sleep. She shouldn't look like that when she had such a lovely swimsuit made of real smooth material, and not knitted like Robin's own blue one which sagged a bit over her bottom and made her feet itchy. Goosey had knitted it for her while they were waiting for Chloe to get better enough to go to the seaside and at first Robin had been very excited. She was to have a holiday after all, just like the other girls at school! But then the excitement had faded away because she had discovered all the things that were not at all nice about the holiday. First, she'd have to miss school, and that made her miserable; not to be there to know everything that happened was horrid. Secondly, Goosey wouldn't come with them; she was going to her brother's farm in Dorset, because as she had said firmly, 'I don't hold with going on nasty boats. That's all right for fishermen, but it's not for the likes of me. What do I want to go to foreign places for when I got a good English farm to visit? It's time I saw my own people anyway – ' And Robin was missing Goosey quite a lot.

But most of all what was not nice about the holiday was Mummy and now Robin started to sift the shells through her fingers, because she didn't want to look at Mummy. She was too cross with her to look at her, because ever since they had got here she had thought of nothing but rotten old Chloe. If Robin wanted to do something like run a race with Mummy along the beach she couldn't because it wasn't fair to leave Chloe. If

Robin needed Mummy to come and sit with her at bed-times she couldn't because of Chloe. It was too bad; and especially too bad when there were Auntie Jessie and Grandmamma to talk to Chloe if she had to be talked to. Robin was really feeling very scratchy indeed about her mother, almost as scratchy as she had been at home when David Deveen came visiting so much. At least he wasn't here; that was something to be glad about.

'Robin?' That was Mummy calling her, and she pretended not to hear. It was easier to sit there in her sand armchair that she had built this morning and play with her shells.

'Robin darling, let's go up to the Promenade des Anglais and find some ice cream, shall we?' Mummy was crouching beside her now and Robin had to look up. She was very pretty in her shady straw hat and her green cotton dress, and Robin frowned, trying to go on being cross with her, but it was getting harder.

'What about Chloe?' she said suspiciously.

Poppy looked back over her shoulder. 'Fast asleep,' she said. 'Like Auntie Jessie. Come along. Grandmamma will tell them where we are if they wake up. What would you like? Strawberry or vanilla or – '

'Praline,' said Robin decidedly and got to her feet, filled with huge forgiveness. Everything was lovely after all. 'In a sugar cone, not in a wafer.'

'Me too,' Mummy said and stood up and together they went toiling up the beach, after a murmured farewell to Grandmamma who was still reading, picking their way through the scattered people who sat there, most of them asleep just like Auntie Jessie and Chloe.

'Are you having fun, darling?' Poppy asked and Robin considered her answer carefully.

'Not very much,' she said at length. 'There's no one to play with.'

'Oh dear,' Poppy said. 'I know. I wish we could have

come earlier in the season when other children – but we couldn't. Chloe's plaster, you see, and – and of course I couldn't even know we could get away at all, could I? It's amazing that Jessie agreed, and really I wonder why we didn't do it before years ago – '

She's talking to herself, Robin thought, not to me at all, and tugged her sun hat closer round her ears and stomped on through the sand, all her scratchiness coming back. The ice cream that had seemed such a good idea a little while ago wasn't nearly so much fun to think about now.

'I'm sorry it's a little misery-making for you, darling,' Poppy said then. 'I suppose I should have realized that it might be and suggested to Cynthia's mother, or to Molly's even, that we bring someone along to keep you company. You'd have liked that – but that would have meant so many of us. Bad enough there are five in the party as it is – '

'We're called the *femmes anglaises* in the hotel. The waiters and the people at the desk,' Robin said. 'They look at us and laugh at us because we're all women.'

Poppy looked down at her and laughed. 'Darling, do they? Are you a woman too? I suppose so – '

'Of course I am,' Robin said indignantly. 'I'm not a boy, am I? Of course they mean me too. Even those people who sit at the table in the corner, they call us the *femmes anglaises*. The man said to me this morning that I have a good accent because I said "*Bonjour*" to him.'

'You have a very good accent,' Poppy said. 'I must tell them at school how well you are doing with your French. Then they'll agree it was well worth letting you miss a few days of school to come along. And you're looking very well, darling. Lovely and brown. Are you feeling well? Are you glad we came?'

Robin thought for a while as they negotiated the last

part of the beach and then climbed the steps to the Promenade above.

'I'm all right,' she said at length, but she didn't look at her mother because in fact she wasn't really. She didn't feel just scratchy but a bit achy too, and kept wanting to cry and she wasn't usually a crying sort of person. Not like Molly who cried like turning on the tap in the bathroom. As for being glad that they were here, she didn't want to answer that at all.

'There, look,' Poppy said. 'An ice cream man. Praline, you say? I shall have a lemon sorbet, I think – '

The man scooped out the pale golden ice cream and Robin watched him, trying to be excited to see it, but it didn't work the way it usually did. In fact, when the cone was put into her hands and she could look more closely at it she felt a bit sick and didn't want to lick it at all. But she didn't say so and when Poppy had paid over her handful of change, and they turned to go back to the others, she lagged behind a little so that Poppy shouldn't see her not eating it.

'Would you like a comic, darling?' Poppy asked brightly then as they passed the newspaper kiosk and Robin shook her head.

'I can only talk a bit of French,' she said, almost crossly. 'I can't read it properly yet.'

'But there are the pictures,' Poppy said. 'I'll find one where the words aren't so important – '

'Or maybe you could read it to me,' Robin said hopefully and considered licking her ice cream – which was beginning to drip down her hand. But she still felt a bit sick inside and didn't.

'Of course, darling,' Poppy said. 'That's a lovely idea – ' And when she had the comic tucked under her arm they went back down the beach towards the others, pushing their way through the soft sand as the ice cream went on dripping interestingly.

'I'm sorry you're not really having fun, darling,' Poppy said at length as they almost came up to the others and then she stopped. I did think you'd like to be here at the seaside.'

'If it was just us, I would,' Robin said and looked at her. Could she say what it was that was bothering her? Tell her about how glad she was to be away from David but how cross Chloe made her? How cross it made her even to have Grandmamma and Auntie Jessie there? And how much worse it was because of the way they both kept niggling at each other? She hadn't realized how much like the sillier girls at school a pair of grown-ups could be. But Poppy looked so worried and bothered that she decided not to say any of it.

'But it's all right,' she said and started to walk again. 'The shells are pretty. Oh!' And she accidentally on purpose dropped her ice cream cone which was melting a lot now and stood and looked at it lying in the sand, all covered in grit.

'Oh,' she said and began to cry. It helped to cry even though she'd done it on purpose, because it wasn't the ice cream she was crying about. She felt so miserable and so very cross that crying helped.

'Oh dear!' Poppy cried and crouched to look at it and then shook her head. 'Ruined! There, darling, have mine. I've had plenty, really I have – '

Robin shook her head and wept on. It really was very strange that she couldn't stop now she'd started. Her head was aching too now, and she couldn't think when that had begun and her throat was hot and dry and the crying went on and on till she began to hiccup.

Poppy, alarmed, dropped her own ice cream and bent to pick Robin up and lifted her into a cuddling sort of carry – rather shaming for a person of seven, Robin thought for a moment, but then didn't care any more because it felt so nice – and took her the rest of the way to join the others. Even before they got there Auntie Jessie was awake and on her feet and even Grandmamma was looking concerned.

'What's the matter, little one?' Auntie Jessie cried as they arrived, Poppy stumbling a little in the yielding sand. 'Has she hurt herself?'

'Dropped her ice,' Poppy said and then as Mildred leaned forwards to peer at her added, 'She'll be all right, I'm sure – '

Jessie reached out to pat Robin's cheek and then stopped and said anxiously, 'She's very hot, Poppy.'

Mildred touched her too and then nodded. 'Feverish,' she said briskly and turned to pick up her bag and put her book in it. 'We'd better take her back to the hotel. Not a good idea to remain here in the sun if she has a fever.'

Poppy sat down and held Robin close and set her cheek against her wet one, for Robin was still crying, if not quite so badly now. She was hiccuping softly and gulping a little.

'She is hot – ' she said anxiously, and then peered into Robin's face. 'Darling, why didn't you say you felt ill?'

Robin didn't bother to answer that. How could she? It wasn't till now that she knew she felt ill. Her headache was sitting there on the top of her sun hat and squeezing down and inside her throat was very hot and dry. It might have been nice to swallow some ice cream to make her feel better and when she thought of her cone lying dead in the sand she began to cry more loudly than ever at the sadness of it.

'I'll take her back,' Poppy said then and got to her feet. 'There's no need for all of you to come though. Just come up later when you're ready – no, Jessie, really. I mean it. Robin's just a bit off-colour, that's all. She'll be fine, I'm sure, by the time you all come up to change for the evening.'

Mildred sat down again obediently and said after a

moment, 'Jessie!' But Jessie was paying no attention at all and was busily packing her possessions into her over-sized beach bag, tossing nose protection cream and sun glasses and her magazine in in a fine tangle.

'I'm coming too,' she said firmly. 'The child's ill. Poppy needs help! You stay here, Mildred, and when Chloe wakes tell her what's up and bring her along, you hear?'

Mildred sighed, 'Such a fuss,' she murmured and picked up her book again. 'Really, Jessie, will you ever learn to be calm?'

'She's right, Jessie,' Poppy said even more firmly than Jessie had spoken. 'Sit down and let us be. I'll manage better alone, frankly. I'll see you later – ' And she turned and began to march up the beach, with Robin held in her arms and resting her wet face in the crook of her neck.

Jessie watched them go and then sat down again, un-willingly, just as Chloe stretched, opened her eyes and yawned.

'What's the matter?' she murmured and she looked round. 'Why are you both looking so all over the place?'

'The little one's ill,' Jessie said. 'Feverish – Poppy's taken her back to the hotel. We're to go up later. Doesn't want any help, she says – '

'What?' Chloe said and made a face. 'Oh, God, what a bore! As if all this wasn't dismal enough at the end of the season and no one here but old trouts, without that wretched child getting the grizzles! And I'm supposed to be convalescing!' And she threw herself down onto her towel again and rolled over onto her front to toast her back in the last afternoon hours of the early October sunshine. And Jessie looked down at her and bit her lip thoughtfully as Poppy, a diminishing figure in the distance, trudged her way back to the Hôtel des Pins with an increasingly miserable Robin.

* * *

'*Rougeole*,' Poppy said and rubbed her forehead worriedly. 'This *is* measles, isn't it? It certainly seems so. No rash yet, but the doctor says that'll show soon. She's frightfully hot, poor lamb, and clearly has the most ghastly headache. He's prepared a powder for her if I can get her to take it, but she's not herself at all. Not a bit easy to get on with, to tell the truth. She's been so cross and miserable – ' And she looked as though she were ready to weep herself.

'Cool sponging, that's the answer,' Jessie said. 'I know how – had to do it for Bernie when he had measles. I'll come and do it – ' She was standing in the hallway outside Poppy and Robin's room, trying to see over Poppy's shoulder into the dim interior, but Poppy shook her head and pushed her gently away.

'No need, darling. Believe me. I can manage fine. All I ask of you is that you keep Mamma and Chloe busy and happy. I can cope fine with Robin as long as I don't have to concern myself with them. Take them into dinner, there's a dear, and see if you can find some company for Chloe after dinner. That family who sit in the corner behind the biggest palm, you know the ones I mean – perhaps they'll be interesting?'

'Well, if you like,' Jessie said unwillingly. 'Believe me, I could make the child comfortable in no time at all – '

'So can I,' Poppy said. 'Please, Jessie. If you want to help, do as I ask you, will you?'

'What about your dinner then? You need to keep your strength up.'

Poppy grinned at that. 'So dramatic, darling! For heaven's sake, I'm not going to keel over for want of one dinner. Anyway, I'll have some sandwiches and coffee. You can arrange that, if you like. Will you? Then I can concentrate on poor little Robin.'

And at last Jessie nodded and turned to go, trailing her crimson evening frock and with her headful of shingled waves bobbing busily as she went down the stairs and Poppy went back into the bedroom in relief.

Downstairs in the bar Chloe was sitting hunched over a tall glass that seemed to contain a good deal of fruit and looking sulky. She also looked well for she glowed with a light tan. The long rest she had been taking had clearly agreed with her, and she had put on a little of the weight she had lost while she had been in hospital, complaining bitterly about the nastiness of St George's offerings of porridge and shepherd's pie at every other meal. But the sulky look overwhelmed the healthy one and she looked far from good company.

Jessie lifted her brows at Mildred who sat beside her with a glass of mineral water in front of her and said brightly, 'So! It's just the three of us tonight. We got to entertain ourselves. Poor little Robin's got the measles!'

'Trust her to pick her time,' Chloe said crossly and then as she caught Mildred's reproving eye said, 'Oh, I'm sorry! I suppose the poor little wretch can't help it, but honestly! It's so dismal already, a dose of measles is all we need! Can't we just go home, for heaven's sake? It seems silly staying here when the child is ill, and anyway it's no fun at all. I thought this was supposed to help me convalesce, but honestly, the way it is, it's making me feel wretched.'

'You are being somewhat self-centred,' Mildred said and lifted her brows at her. 'Children with measles need to be nursed in quiet dark rooms if they are to avoid nasty complications. I remember well how worrying it was when Poppy herself had it. We nearly lost her – ' And she looked at Jessie who stood there and looked bleakly back at her and for a moment the two women were enclosed in a web of fading memories. And then Mildred roused herself and went on, 'So, she certainly can't travel.'

'I suppose there'd be ructions if I said I wanted to go home on my own then?' Chloe said and sipped her drink, and looked round the bar which was now filling up with people awaiting the dinner gong. 'I mean, honestly, will you *look* at them all? No one under forty, I swear and all as dull as the ditchiest of ditch water.'

And indeed the people who were drifting in were far from exciting, clearly being examples of the French bourgeoisie who had deliberately waited till the end of the high season in Cannes in order to save their money and to avoid the rackettings of the sort of people who did adorn this large hotel when the sun was at its hottest and the beach at its most crowded.

'It is out of the question,' Mildred said firmly. 'It would worry all of us greatly, for neither Jessie nor I would consider leaving Poppy alone here with Robin so ill and we could not consider permitting you to travel alone. You must, I am afraid, make the best of the situation –'

Jessie had been sitting staring down into her lap throughout, and now she lifted her head and looked at Chloe. It was important, she knew, that Poppy be given peace of mind about this child, she told herself. She would worry, surely, if she thought she was so miserable that she was considering just going back to London unsupervised. And not even Goosey in the house in Norland Square! Indeed, Jessie told herself, something would have to be done. And with Poppy herself preoccupied with her child and Mildred far too proper and serious to consider the matter worthy of her attention, who else could do it but Jessie herself?

She leaned forwards and patted Chloe's hand and said, 'Listen dolly, I know just what you mean. It's company you need? Then it's company I'll arrange for you. Listen – ' And she leaned closer and murmured in Chloe's ear and Chloe, listening, slowly began to smile.

'Oh, yes, Jessie,' she said and her smile widened to a beaming grin. 'Oh, yes! That would be lovely.'

23

It was in many ways a good week. At first of course, it was miserable, for Robin's temperature rose steadily and she became very restless and confused, indeed delirious, and that was most alarming. And of course they had to keep the curtains closed to protect Robin's vision – the doctor was very gloomy about the risks of *l'aveuglement*. 'The blindness, you understand. You must keep 'er very dark, to protect – ' And that inevitably made Poppy depressed and tense. But then, once the rash had appeared and Robin lay, cooler if exhausted, her face bluish red against the dim whiteness of the pillows, it all got rather better.

They could open the curtains slightly, for a start; not enough to let in much harmful light but enough to permit the entry of sounds from outside and the warm October breezes from the sea. They could smell the salt and the last of the summer flowers and the dusty road and hear the cheerful French voices chattering and the rattle of taxis and the clopping of hooves from the horse-drawn cabs that plied the Promenade. Poppy devised a game for Robin making use of all that; she would sit there in the armchair beside Robin's bed, holding her hand and murmuring her invented tales of Monsieur and Madame Cocorico and their crew of little ones, *les petits Cocoricos*, who were all dreadfully naughty and chased each other and shouted a lot and teased the cab horses. And Robin would lie and look at her, never taking her eyes from her face, listening and smiling sometimes and once or twice even laughing, and Poppy was deeply content. It was agreeable to spend the long meal times coaxing Robin's capricious appetite with even more stories, fun to sponge her down with cool scented water and then anoint her with special scented skin oil – which Robin adored, spending long minutes with her hands over her nose so that she could snuff up the lily of the valley smell – pleasing to smooth her bed to comfort and to rub her back when it started to ache from lying there so long.

As the week went on and the rash faded and her temperature came down, however, Robin became fractious. When Jessie came and peered round the door to see how she was, she was snappy and unwilling to chatter. When her grandmamma came to see her she wasn't much better behaved and Mildred nodded unsmilingly when Robin lay there against her pillows with her eyes stubbornly closed, refusing to talk at all, and said, 'It is normal for this condition. I remember when you were so ill, you were much the same. Robin of course has not been as ill as you were, and that is fortunate – ' That made Robin very irate indeed and when Mildred had gone she burst out, 'I hate Grandmamma! I was – I was ever so ill, and she's hateful to say I wasn't!'

'Darling, all she said was that it wasn't as bad a go of measles as the one I had when I was small – ' Poppy said soothingly but Robin refused to be comforted and hugged her fury at her grandmother to her for a whole afternoon.

But she was mollified when tea-time came and the special daily treat that Poppy had organized for her came up with her tea tray. There were today little egg sandwiches cut into the shape of ducks, and Robin was enchanted with those and became very sunny indeed. After tea they played Ludo and then Snakes and Ladders and laughed a great deal, and Poppy was deeply content.

This was the part of being Robin's mother she so missed at home. In Norland Square she breakfasted each day with her daughter and saw her on her way to school in Goosey's watchful company, and at the end of the day sometimes managed to have supper with her and talk to her a little before bedtime. But that was all. And sometimes even that was truncated, when the restaurant was extra busy and she couldn't get home till after Robin had gone to bed.

She thought a good deal about that when Robin took her afternoon nap each day, sitting herself at the window by the partly-open curtain, so that she could read her magazines if she wanted to. But she rarely did, being content to sit and watch her sleeping child, sprawled on her rumpled pillows and breathing blessedly quietly and easily. There had been one alarming night when her breathing had become noisy and effortful and the doctor had murmured worriedly, '*Le croup, peut-être – c'est une maladie tres sérieuse –* ' but that had resolved itself and now her lungs were clear and healthy. And Poppy was deeply relieved at that.

Now she would sit and think – what sort of mother am I? She deserves better than to have one who can only be with her and tell her stories and look after her when she is ill. She should have such care all the time, and I am failing to give it to her –

But then she would shake herself, almost literally, and think – I am taking care of her. I'm earning her living and that must surely come first. What good is having a mother who is always there to tell you stories if you haven't enough to eat or clothes to wear or a good school to go to? School fees were a major item in Poppy's budget; indeed a sizeable portion of all her income was earmarked for Robin. As far as Poppy was concerned that was precisely as it should be, and there was a comfort to be found in knowing she was able to provide so successfully for her child. And yet she felt guilt because she could not be with her all the time, and could only manage it now because they were away on holiday. If this attack of measles had happened at home, it would have been Goosey who was doing the nursing while she, Poppy, was at work as usual. And there was nothing Poppy could do to alter the situation.

Ever practical, she eventually decided to give no more thought to the dilemma, accepting it as inevitable and making the most of the time she did have to spend with Robin, and the week went on in tranquillity as the spots finally faded and Robin became ever perkier.

It was clear, the doctor told her earnestly, that she had had a most mild attack of the dreaded *rougeole*; none of the complications of heart, lungs or kidneys and above all of eyes, and a steady recovery was now assured.

'She may emerge from her room in one or two days,' he went on as he put away his stethoscope. 'And then after a few more days you may return to England. You will not need to see me further. I have the honour to present my bill – ' And with suitable gravity he put it in front of Poppy. ' – and will wish you all felicitations for the future. The little one has been most fortunate. Good afternoon!'

'There!' Poppy said when he had gone. 'Isn't that good? You can go downstairs in a couple of days – '

'Now!' Robin crowed, bouncing on the bed. 'Now, now, now! I'm so bored in here! You've told me all the stories and I never want to play Ludo again, not ever – please, Mummy, let me get up!'

'No!' Poppy laughed. 'On no account! He said one or two days, that's all. But I'll tell you what – I'll wrap you in a blanket and you can come and sit by the window and look out at the people. You may even see the Cocoricos – you never know – '

But eventually of course it was impossible to contain the now rapidly recovering Robin any longer. She wanted to be out of the room she now regarded as a prison, and Poppy was not hard to persuade, since she too was feeling very restless after spending eight days in incarceration.

'Tomorrow,' she said at length. 'I promise you tomorrow. We'll arrange for us all to have lunch together down in the restaurant. How will that be?'

'Oh, Mummy, don't make me wait so long,' Robin pleaded. 'Let me go down now this afternoon. Please, Mummy, I don't want to wait. I want to see all the people dancing and hear the music. Oh, please Mummy. Let me put on a dress and go down and sit for a little while where all the people are! I shall be so miserable if I can't – '

Inevitably Poppy gave in. It would be pleasant, after all, to sit and see some of the other visitors to the hotel, even if they were not particularly interesting. And she felt a moment of unease about Chloe, too. She had come once or twice during the first few days of Robin's illness to see her, putting her head round the door and murmuring vaguely about hoping she was getting on all right before vanishing, but had not shown herself at all for the last five days. Poppy had asked Jessie, who was of course a daily visitor and quite indefatigable, how she was, and Jessie had been very offhand about her.

'Oh, she's happy enough,' she had said. 'Sunbathing, you know – and playing some tennis – '

'Who with? Have some young people arrived?'

Jessie had been vague. 'Oh, there are a few people who play. There's a hotel professional as well. Look at that boobalah! Getting better every minute! I found some crayons, Robin darling, and a colouring book – look!' And she had surged over to the bed and sat down and Robin, now quite forgetting her original bad temper, had welcomed her warmly and they sat and played with

Jessie's present, while Poppy had taken the opportunity to take a leisurely bath. She had had little time to call her own this past week, for Robin had been as demanding a patient as she could be, very unwilling to let her mother leave her for very long at a time.

Yes, Poppy thought now, as Robin gazed at her appealingly, it's time I saw Chloe and talked to her. We came here for her after all and I've hardly seen her. Not my fault of course, but all the same – so she nodded at Robin and said, 'All right. You can put on your sailor dress, darling. It's a nice loose one so it won't irritate where the rash was. Come along, a bath first and then we'll take you down – the tea dancing starts at four, so you'll hear the music and see the dancers. Now, don't rush, silly girl. You'll be a bit wobbly after so long in bed –'

Poppy carried her down, without too much protest from an excited Robin who was indeed rather shaky on her legs, and it wasn't difficult to do so, for she had clearly lost some weight while she had been ill, and was not too heavy a burden. Goosey'll soon feed her up, Poppy thought as she made her way down the wide staircase to the broad lobby below. Once we get home. Only another couple of days now, and then we'll be there – and she felt a *frisson* of pleasure at the thought of home and the usual routine again. It had been good to spend time with her daughter, of course it had, despite the measles, but all the same to get back to normal would be very agreeable.

They settled themselves in the far corner of the palm court where the expanse of polished dance floor was empty of gyrating couples, even though the band, a quartet that made rather a tinkling noise as it played its way through some of the more popular dance tunes of the day, were sawing away busily. But Robin was so happy to be downstairs she showed no disappointment at all.

'I expect someone will dance soon,' she said sunnily and smiled at the waiter. 'Was it you who made me the duck-shaped sandwiches? They were very good!'

The waiter smiled cheerfully. 'The leetle girl is better, *hein*?' And then when Poppy answered him in tolerable French chattered away to her busily in his own language.

'I am so sorry the little mademoiselle has been ill. We missed her in the dining-room. Such a friendly little girl! It is good to see she is better now. The measles, yes? She has been fortunate. My sister's husband's cousin's child died of it, a terrible business – egg sandwiches for the little mademoiselle? Of course. And the china tea for madame and the little cakes. Of course – your friends will be here as well perhaps? I bring tea for them?'

'I don't know,' Poppy said. 'I didn't say to them we were coming down. We shouldn't have done till tomorrow but my daughter was impatient – you understand how children can be! – they may all be on the beach. But by all means bring three extra cups, in case they come – '

The waiter nodded and went away and came back with the extra china, and began to set the table, busily chattering, and Poppy watched him and then said, 'You've brought too much, my friend. Just for three more if they come at all – '

The waiter looked arch and shook his head roguishly. 'Oh, no madame, it will be for four if they come at all. It is generally the four now – when it is not the two twos of course, which is also often. But it was ever so, was it not?' And laughing cheerfully at his own totally incomprehensible joke he went away, leaving Poppy puzzled and oddly alarmed without knowing quite why.

Tea came and Robin ate hungrily, which pleased Poppy; the child was definitely in need of extra building up and she sipped her tea and watched her, aware of a vague unease. She didn't know why but she was worried and she thought – is it that now Robin's better I've got

288

time to think of other things? Is it Chloe I'm concerned about? Why should I be? Mamma and Jessie have been here to take care of her – and she tried to shake off her worry. But it would not go so easily.

Robin perked up then. Two couples had taken to the floor and were circling solemnly and she watched them as the band went into a spirited rendition of 'Alexander's Ragtime Band' and made them speed up, and that made her giggle.

'Don't grown-ups look funny when they dance, Mummy?' she said. 'Such silly looks on their faces. Look at that man! He's all sort of tight as though he's got buttons on his mouth.'

Poppy glanced and said reprovingly, 'It's rude to make personal remarks about people, darling, you know that.' But Robin shook her head unrepentantly.

'He does though, doesn't he? And the lady he's with looks as though her feet hurt her. That's how Goosey looks when she wears her black patent boots. She says she's wearing them in but she always looks like that and she's been wearing them in for *ages*! And that lady has patent shoes on. I expect she's wearing them in too.' And she giggled again.

There was a little flurry as the chair beside Poppy scraped back and Jessie's booming voice cried, 'So hello! What's happening here, then? Robin down to tea? It's wonderful! Are you feeling all right, dolly? You look all right – '

Robin beamed at her. 'I'm having a lovely time, Auntie Jessie,' she said. 'Look at that funny man and lady. He's got buttons on his mouth and she's got tight shoes. They're ever so funny – '

Jessie looked and obligingly laughed. 'You're right, you little monkey! You're exactly right. Such a clever one this baby of yours, Poppy. Dolly, how are you? Tired? It's been a nasty week for you.'

'I'm fine, Jessie, thank you. Some tea?' And she began to pour. 'Where are Mamma and Chloe?' she said casually. 'Shall I pour theirs too?'

'Millie's having a little rest,' Jessie said and took her tea and began to sip it. She didn't look at Poppy, keeping her eyes on Robin and the little thread of worry inside Poppy thickened and became a wriggling worm. 'So, Robin, have a little cake, hmm? Those chocolate ones look wonderful. Not so good as I make, I grant you, but good all the same. I'll cut one up for you – '

'I can cut my own cake!' Robin said indignantly as Poppy leaned forwards and said a little sharply, 'And Chloe?'

'Of course you can cut your own cake! I just thought maybe you'd like me to help. But go ahead, cut already – ' And she slid a cake onto Robin's plate.

'Jessie!' Poppy said a little more sharply. 'I asked you, what about Chloe? Is she resting too?'

Jessie looked vague and Poppy, staring at her, thought – she's hiding something from me. She knew Jessie too well not to be able to read every thought that slid across her mind, leaving its traces on her expression and she knew now that Jessie was uncomfortable.

'Jessie, what's going on?' she said now in a low voice, very aware of Robin's sharp ears. But the child was apparently concentrating on her chocolate cake and seemed unaware of her elders' conversation. Jessie still said nothing and Poppy said even more urgently, 'You might as well tell me. I'm not stupid. It's obvious there's something going on. What is it?'

Jessie looked at her then and after a moment let her eyes slide away. 'Nothing that needs cause anyone any worry, for God's sake!' she said with some pugnacity. 'The child was bored and irritable, right? She'd broken her leg, came here to get over it, right? So there was you looking after poor little Robin and Chloe threatening to go back to London and I knew you'd go mad if that happened. So I did the best I could to keep her happy. And she is – she's stayed here, she's under my eye all the time and anyway, you were wrong. There's no harm in them seeing each other, for God's sake! How can there be?'

Poppy felt a chill starting deep in her belly and moving up into her chest. 'Jessie, what have you done?'

'Nothing to make you look at me that way!' Jessie said, still pugnacious. 'You're not the only one with a child to think about, Poppy. You go on about Chloe and about Robin, you'd think no one else ever worried about their children! Me, I'm a mother too, you know.'

Poppy knew then and closed her eyes, taking a deep breath at the same time. The anger that was rising in her was so hot, so very clamorous, that she was at risk of letting it out in a great roar and this was neither the place nor the time for such a display. And anyway, there was Robin –

'Look,' Jessie said then into the darkness and Poppy opened her eyes. 'Look. What's so terrible, hmm? They look lovely together – ' And Poppy turned her head and looked in the direction of Jessie's fond gaze and saw them.

Her first thought was that Jessie was quite right. They did make a handsome pair. She was wearing a dress of floating cream chiffon tied with matching satin ribbons, against which her slender tanned arms glowed richly. Her head was tucked against his chest and her eyes were half closed as he led her in the intricate steps of the tango the band were now playing, swooping and bending langorously as he took her half way across the floor with each trill of the melody. He was wearing elegant white flannel trousers and an impeccably cut blazer over a shirt so white it made Poppy's eyes ache to look at it, and he too had a tan which suited him extremely well.

'Whatever they look like,' she said harshly, 'they shouldn't be together. He's not good for her, Jessie, I told you that. What on earth were you thinking of to bring him here? How could you do such a thing to me?'

And Jessie looked at her with her brows raised and an expression on her face that Poppy had never seen before and certainly not directed at herself: cold and angry and very remote. She said nothing at all, but turned her head as the music stopped and the dancers came drifting over to their tables, their heads together as Chloe murmured dreamily into her partner's ear.

'We're here,' she called and her voice was loud and clear. 'Come and sit down both of you. And Bernie, say hello to your cousin!'

And she turned and looked challengingly at Poppy, daring her to say anything at all.

24

The next three days were very difficult indeed for Poppy. She was angry, deeply so, and much of her anger was directed at Jessie. She had known perfectly well how Poppy felt about any friendship between Bernie and her stepdaughter, and yet she had ignored her expressed anxiety and gone ahead and brought the man here. It was intolerable of her, quite intolerable.

But then she would stop herself from thinking so and would try to be dispassionate, would try above all to see it from Jessie's standpoint. In her eyes her son could do no wrong, even though there had been many times over the years when he had treated her disgracefully. He had robbed her of money, caused her intense anxiety, indeed anguish, had distressed her by his prolonged silences over and over again; yet equally over and over again she had forgiven him and drawn him back into the warm circle of her love.

And such love! Poppy tried hard to understand it. Wasn't she herself a mother, hadn't she too just one precious child, the offspring of a widow? If anyone could understand Jessie's adoration of her son, surely it should be Poppy? Yet she couldn't, because there was an element in Jessie's attachment to Bernie that was quite missing from Poppy's feeling for her Robin. Jessie was frightened of Bernie. Frightened of his temper – which could be considerable – but frightened above all of losing him. That he would if it suited him turn and leave her with never a backwards glance or a moment's concern for her feelings was obvious to everyone, including Jessie. And she would do nothing to risk such a happening.

But that was not the only reason she had brought Bernie here to Cannes to spend time with Chloe against Poppy's own expressed wishes. There was, Poppy suspected, more to it than that, and watching her over the next few days as she chattered and sparkled at Bernie – for Jessie always behaved quite unlike herself when her son was about – Poppy tried to understand so that she could lose her anger. It was horrid being angry with Jessie. It made her feel detached and lonely in a most uncomfortable way. If only she could forgive how much more comfortable she would be.

So, she asked herself over and over, *why*? Could it be, as Jessie had assured Poppy it was, genuine concern for Chloe? Had she realized that Chloe cared for Bernie and chosen to make her happy by bringing them together? But it wasn't that; she would never have done such a thing just for Chloe's sake? Of that Poppy was quite certain. It was Bernie who mattered most to her, Bernie who always came first.

As the days slid past, and Robin became ever stronger and the time to return to London drew blessedly closer, Poppy came to the conclusion that she did know why and her heart sank. It was because Jessie was being at her most muddled and absurd, she told herself, and yet at her most understandable.

She was matchmaking. Chloe was attractive, if spoiled, had some income of her own, and was clearly besotted with Bernie. That much was obvious to everyone who looked at her, for she sparkled and glinted in his company even more than his mother did, as he sat and basked in her regard with such unctuous self-satisfaction that sometimes it was all Poppy could do not to raise her hand and actually strike him. And Jessie clearly thought it time her wayward son was married.

She probably thinks of it as settling down, Poppy told herself sourly as she sat beside the dance floor for yet another evening and watched Chloe and Bernie dancing as indefatigably as ever. As if he ever would! Even if he does marry – and she was determined that no matter what Jessie did or said he would not marry Chloe – he will be as selfish and wicked as ever. And then as well as a frightened and anxious mother he'll have a frightened and anxious wife. He really has to be stopped.

She considered confiding her anxiety to her mother, who sat with her and Jessie for most evenings, at least until nine thirty when she always retired to bed, but decided against that. Mildred had a sardonic look in her eye as she too watched the dancers, but offered no comments, and somehow Poppy was sure that Mildred would refuse to become involved. That was her style; always a quiet and withdrawn person, now she had become almost monosyllabic.

She finally decided, on their last night at the Hôtel des Pins, to talk to Bernie himself. He had been punctilious in his treatment of her ever since they had been brought together there beside the dance floor of the Palm Court, always polite even when her irritation got the better of her and she made the odd barbed comment, but they had not actually talked. And on the last afternoon, while Chloe was unwillingly upstairs packing her case ready for their morning departure, Poppy marched along the corridor to his room, and knocked on the door.

'Oh, hello, Poppy,' he said easily and opened his door wide. 'Come along in. Did you ever see such a mess? Never mind, I'll soon get it sorted out and packed. I dare say you've got all yours finished, hmm? That'd be your way. Everything in order at exactly the right time. You never get anything wrong, do you?'

'Why are you here, Bernie?' she said without any pre-amble. 'You're not wanted, you know.'

He raised his brows at that and went lounging over to his cluttered bed to throw himself on it and to half sit, half lie against the bed head, his hands linked behind his head.

'Really? You surprise me. My mother sent me the ticket to get here and she's paying my hotel bill, so she seems quite keen on the idea of my presence, and young Chloe – well – ' His lips curved contentedly. 'She gave me one hell of a welcome.'

'You know perfectly well what I mean,' Poppy said and the anger began to bubble higher. 'That child is far too young and too innocent for you – '

'Innocent?' he said and laughed pleasantly. 'Young, I grant you – '

She clenched her fists at that, but managed to control her temper. 'Innocent too. She has no idea what a worm you are. She's as beguiled by a pretty face as most people. But I know you. I know what a cheat and a liar you are, and a thief – '

'Easy, coz!' he said then and his voice was a little harder. 'That's the sort of talk that brings people into court, you know that?'

She ignored that. 'A *thief*. I've covered up for you, remember? When you were sixteen, for heaven's sake! And you don't seem to have changed your ways one bit. I don't know how you got hold of Chloe, but since you have, there's been nothing but trouble. She ran off to Paris, for pity's sake! Went without a word to me, without a word to anyone, behaved like a – '

'Listen, Poppy,' he said and sat up and looked at her hard. 'That girl is well able to take care of herself. I met her by accident. She came to my club. I didn't snatch her from her nursery, you know. She was well able to get out and about in any way that suited her. And that's your affair, not mine. She walked into my club one night. I

296

didn't know her from Adam's off ox and found out later that she was your brat. By that time, I was interested. The girl's a looker, she's fun and I like her, okay? It's no affair of yours what I do. If you can't keep your hands on the people you want to control, that's your problem, like I say. Don't come whining to me about her. Talk to her, why don't you?'

'Because you've made her even sillier than she already was,' Poppy said scathingly. 'She's mooning over you like a sheep. I never saw anything so sickening – '

He smiled then slowly. 'Do you know what I think, Cousin Poppy? I think you're a teensy weensy bit jealous. Poor old widow lady getting a bit long in the tooth, not getting any of her share any more since the old man popped his clogs and you see this little bit of deliciousness whooping it up and you're as jealous as hell – '

She stopped trying to control her temper and lashed out at him, her hand spread wide, but he dodged her easily and laughed.

'Much good that'll do you!' he jeered. 'You're out of your depth, Poppy. Admit it and leave me alone, will you? If I want to play games with Chloe, I will. It's her affair and mine and none of yours. You're only a stepmother, anyway. And now if you don't mind, I'd like you to leave me to get on with my packing. Or do I have to call the management and tell 'em there's this rampant woman chasing me around my bedroom?'

She went. She had to. There was clearly nothing she could do to get through to him, nothing she could do to persuade him to leave Chloe alone, and she thought with a sudden scalding self-awareness that she had done it all wrong. She should have gone to him cap in hand asking him as a favour to leave Chloe alone. Instead she had gone to him in a temper and put his back up; and she didn't know who she was most angry with, herself or him.

The last dinner of the holiday was a strained affair. Bernie told them in easy tones that he was taking Chloe out to a special last night dinner at a local restaurant and before Poppy could say a word Jessie beamed and cried, 'Such an idea! Have a lovely time! You got enough money?'

He grinned and tucked Chloe's hand into his elbow and she looked up at him with eyes so bright that they literally glittered. She looked as though she had been bathed in light, she was so alive.

'Bless you for the thought, ducky,' he said easily. 'We'll do. See you in the morning, then!' And he winked at them all and turned to go. Chloe favoured them with a vague smile as she clung to his arm and Poppy watched them go and felt murderous.

Mildred went to bed earlier than ever, murmuring about the need for extra rest before travelling and when she had gone Jessie and Poppy remained at the table, sipping coffee and carefully not looking at each other. As far as Poppy was concerned there was little point in conversation. She was still angry with Jessie, still furious with Bernie, but she was impotent and knew it. What was there to say, therefore?

So it was Jessie who spoke first. 'You're still gefrunzled with me, Poppy?'

'I don't understand you,' she said shortly.

Jessie sighed. 'When it suits you you're willing to understand the bits of Yiddish I throw in. When you're angry like now you wouldn't listen even if I spoke like the man on the wireless. All right, are you still annoyed with me?'

'Very.'

'It's silly,' Jessie said firmly. 'It's not as though it really had much to do with me. All right, I sent the boy a telegram asking him to come here to convalesce. He was hurt too, you know. Had concussion. Is that such a crime?

I wanted to take care of him. Anyway, he stopped your Chloe from running off back to London, didn't he? She could have got into worse mischief there. Here at least I could watch them, be on my guard.'

Poppy lifted her head and looked at her. 'Really? Are you sure?'

'Sure I'm sure! What else have I got to do?'

'You watched them the way you're watching them now,' Poppy said. 'Is that what you mean?'

The expression on Jessie's face was ludicrous. 'How do you mean?'

'Oh, Jessie, Jessie, do be sensible! The fact that you're here, that Mamma is, that the world and his wife and children are here, makes not a penn'orth of difference. They're together, aren't they? She's got a ridiculous crush on him. You've only got to look at her to see that. And that means that she's vulnerable. And I have to tell you that – ' She stopped then and looked again at Jessie, who was looking back at her with her face crumpled with anxiety. What was the point in going on? To spell out in direct words her fears for Chloe wouldn't help. Jessie could not or would not see her son as he was, a man with no scruples who would do exactly as he chose no matter what. A man who had encouraged a silly girl of barely nineteen who had always been protected and looked after to go and work in a sexy nightclub in Paris. How could Jessie be expected to enter into Poppy's feelings on the matter?

She got to her feet heavily. 'Let it be, Jessie. It's done and there's no point in going on about it. We'll just have to sit tight and hope for the best. I'm going to bed. Don't forget – the train for Calais leaves at seven am. Have you arranged a morning call? Fine. We'll take breakfast on the train then. Goodnight.'

And she went, leaving Jessie sitting alone at the wreck of the dinner table. She looked miserable and lonely, but for once Poppy was too angry to care about her aunt's welfare. She'd just have to manage as best she could.

She went back to work, of course. The fact that she and Jessie had had disagreements while they had been away could not be allowed to come between them and the running of their business. Poppy was after all a partner now. But it wasn't the same. The old camaraderie seemed to have gone, and Jessie stopped coming to the new restaurant where Poppy perforce spent most of her time now, and reapplied herself to the demands of the Cable Street kitchens, and did so to such good effect that in a matter of just a few weeks the sell-out orders increased so much that Poppy had an extra burden of office work to do, connected with the buying of supplies and the settling of bills. So, she spent longer and longer days at the office instead of going home at a reasonable hour, and was often too tired to go out in the evening. Anyway she had lost much of her interest in what she was doing. Everything seemed to be such an effort now and she had to work ever harder to get through each day. It was no fun at all, and she told herself sourly on one particularly dull evening that her first holiday in so many years had clearly been a major mistake. She couldn't remember when she had last felt so low.

The same was not true of the rest of her household. Goosey had fallen on Robin with such a clucking and fussing and had set herself to building her up again to such good effect that within a matter of weeks, the child looked just as she had before her illness, and seemed quite to have shaken off any remnant of invalidism. She seemed happy at school, busy with her friends and as content as she had always been, and Poppy was glad of that at least. She had worried that Robin would react unhappily to her mother's extra busyness and late nights, but she need not have been anxious. David Deveen might

300

be unhappy because he seemed to see the over-busy Poppy so little these days; her daughter was not.

As for Chloe, she seemed to glow as much as ever. Her leg was now completely well and she went about the house, when she was there, as sunnily as a girl could, polite and kind to Robin and amazingly so to Goosey, who blossomed under such treatment from her old nursling. So everything should have been, Poppy told herself, wonderful.

But it was not, and Poppy brooded over that. Am I becoming a miserable old creature? she asked herself, sometimes, as she contemplated the change in her mood and in her general feelings about life. I used to be contented enough, but now look at me. Watching Chloe like the proverbial hawk and what could be nastier than that? It's no wonder she finds me a disagreeable stepmother. And there's David phoning me trying to be affectionate and what do I do? Push him away and behave so coolly that he must think me as hateful as Chloe does. And as for Jessie – do I have to be so angry with her because her wretched son behaves so badly? It isn't reasonable of me at all –

October dribbled away to a chilly November and then Christmas began to loom on the horizon as the trees in Hyde Park became more and more naked under the attention of the high winds which assaulted London in the first week in December and Poppy's bedroom windows were laced with frost in the mornings when she woke. She was still feeling low and a good deal sorry for herself, but at least she had been wrong about Bernie, she would tell herself gratefully. Clearly he had done Chloe no harm. She was as content as ever, bustling about her life of shopping and visiting her friends and it seemed spending most of her evenings with Bernie; though Poppy did not know where.

She had managed to find out that Bernie no longer had

any involvement with The Rat Trap and it seemed, from the occasional things that Chloe said, was not working at anything at all. He certainly seemed to have plenty of time to squire Chloe about, much to her delight. So Chloe remained highly content, and even her Uncle George, dropping in oh-so-casually to see Chloe one Sunday afternoon, commented with approval on the change in her and did not lecture her for more than half an hour about her Paris adventure. Which relieved Poppy as much as it did Chloe.

But then in the second week in December, as the shops on Oxford Street sported Christmas trees and glittering streamers and Robin spent her time after school in making paper chains with much laborious effort with curly strips of coloured paper and pots of glue (much to the detriment of her school uniform), the cautious optimism that Poppy had begun to permit herself to feel was blown away.

She had been sitting over her ledgers at the office, trying to untangle an unexpected confusion of figures and had had to ask Barney to come up to explain something to her. He had been running the restaurant and kitchens at Cable Street while she and Jessie had been away in Cannes and perhaps he could sort out her confusion, she told herself. Bookkeeping had never been his strong point, bless the man, but she was sure that a few minutes spent over the books now would sort it all out perfectly well.

But it didn't. Barney came limping up to her cluttered office and sat down beside her to peer through his small wire-rimmed glasses at the columns of figures that Poppy showed him.

'Could you explain what you entered here, Barney?' she said easily. 'I know it was a while ago now, but it's taken me this long to catch up with this ledger. I don't have to do it so often, as it's the casual costs anyway.

But I'm sure you'll remember – see? I can't quite follow it. It's all a bit of a tangle and there seems to be a lot of money on the wrong side of the books. Do you see what I mean? The debit side's gone potty – '

He looked at the figures and then at her, owlish in the dark office, the light from the lamp on Poppy's desk glinting on the lenses of his spectacles.

'That's nothing to do with me, Mrs Bradman,' he said. 'I didn't have nothing to do with that. When you was away, wasn't it? That was the time Mr Bernie came in. I never entered nothing in the books, you see. Thought I'd leave it together with the bills and invoices there was for you to do when you got back – '

He looked down at the figures again and shook his head dolefully. 'See, Mrs Bradman? Look at that. Isn't that Mr Bernie's writing? I remember it from before. He must have done something there. I know I never did. Like I said, I thought I'd leave it till you got back.'

He sighed heavily then and looked at her miserably over his glasses. 'Don't say he's up to his old tricks again, Mrs Bradman! I really do hope he isn't – '

But he was, of course.

25

She didn't finish that evening until well after nine. She sat in the winter dark office with just her desk lamp for illumination, her head down and her shoulders aching with tension as she slowly untangled the figures and discovered just how wily he had been. It was only her familiarity with her own system that had shown her that there was anything wrong at all. Anyone else might well have not noticed, especially as this particular ledger was not one that dealt in weekly matters but unusual casual costs. But casual though the costs might be, Bernie had managed, she discovered, to mulct fully £400 from the credit side. And she leaned back in her chair and stared almost in disbelief when at last she had it all sorted out.

It was a massive sum and he had contrived to make it so by the simple device of appearing to buy a couple of large pieces of kitchen equipment. There were of course no bills or statements of any kind but since they were normally kept in a different file, that was not a matter that would normally excite attention. No doubt the discrepancies would have been noticed at the end of the financial year, when the auditors came and married all the ledgers to central accounts, but by then, who would remember what had happened back in October?

She closed the ledger and sat there for a long time, gently flexing and relaxing her aching shoulders as she tried to think what to do. There hadn't been a swoop like this by Bernie for some time. The last time it had happened she had threatened him with exposure to his mother and had managed to get the money back, just as she had when it had happened the very first time when he had been sixteen. She had never intended to tell Jessie, of course. How could she be so cruel to her? She'd known enough about his minor milking of his mother's funds to be aware that he was misbehaving, but she had always managed to shrug it off as mere boyish peccadillo.

'After all,' she would cry defensively, 'What's a few pounds between a mother and a son, for heaven's sake?'

And Poppy had bitten her tongue and said no more. It was, after all, Jessie's money.

Or it had been then. She sat and stared sightlessly at the wall opposite her desk with its shabby wallpaper and the calendar that was pinned there slightly askew. It had been then. But now it was not quite so simple. Now Poppy was a partner. She and Jessie had entered into an agreement under which she had been given thirty three and a third per cent of the equity in Jessie's Foods Ltd in recognition of her past work for the company and for her future efforts. So this time Bernie had not just robbed his mother. He had robbed Poppy too. Of – she worked it out very swiftly – £133,6s.8d. She thought of the cheque she had written this very morning for Robin's school fees for next term, and of Goosey saying, 'She's outgrown those brown shoes already, Mrs Poppy! Would you believe it? They're not too worn, you understand, but I think they're tight.'

'Then take her for new ones this afternoon after school,' she had said and dug into her purse for the necessary money. 'Make sure they're good quality, Goosey, won't you? We mustn't stint on such things as good shoes – '

And now Bernie had robbed her of how many pairs of good shoes? And she tightened her mouth and thought – what do I do? Cover up again, for Jessie's sake? Wait till the auditors come and let them tell her? Where's the sense in that? It will come out eventually, so why not now? It won't hurt Jessie any the less if it's delayed.

And anyway, she thought again, with increasing anger, it isn't just Jessie's money. It's mine too. I'm hurt as well, if not in the same way Jessie is. Surely I have a right to protect myself against further financial pain? I don't want to be greedy, but there is Goosey as well as Robin to think about. Soon Goosey will no longer be able to do anything much and someone else will be needed to take on the heavy household work, and that will cost money too. It isn't greedy to worry about that, just practical; and she had hoped that as a partner some of her financial problems would be eased –

She got to her feet in a sharp little movement and went across the room to take her coat from the shabby old stand in the corner. Silence was not the answer this time. Jessie had to know and Bernie would have to be dealt with. Even Jessie must see that this could not be allowed. Four hundred pounds? And she rolled the syllables around in her mind as she pulled her hat down over her brows and tugged on her gloves. Four hundred pounds – an enormous sum.

She tucked the ledger into a big envelope and put it under her arm and then hesitated and reached for the phone. Better to warn Goosey that she might be very late and put her mind at rest. The old dear got a bit agitated sometimes when she wasn't there. It would take some time to get her to answer of course; not only did she hate the phone and wait when it rang in the hope that it would stop and leave her in peace; if she did get up to answer it took her a very long time to make her way to the instrument in the hall.

So she was startled when it only rang a couple of times before it was picked up and she heard Chloe's breathless little voice answering.

306

'Hello, Chloe!' she said. 'It's Poppy – how is it you're at home at this time? I thought you were going to Mary's.'

'I – er, well I didn't,' Chloe said and her voice sounded rather small and distant. 'I mean, I went and came home early. What is it you want?'

'Hmm? Oh, it's just that I have to be rather late. I'm still at the office – '

'Oh,' Chloe said with a clear lack of interest. 'Really?'

'And I – I have to make a visit on the way back. I might be very late – tell Goosey, will you, and tell her not to worry? Robin's in bed of course – '

'I imagine so,' Chloe said. 'Is that all?'

'Yes – Chloe, are you all right?'

The distant voice sharpened. 'How do you mean, all right?'

'You sound a bit – I don't know. Odd. Are you off colour? Feeling ill or – '

'Of course not!' Chloe's voice became louder suddenly and Poppy pulled the earpiece away from her head for a moment in surprise. 'Why on earth should I be?'

'I don't know,' Poppy said mildly. 'I just thought the way you sounded – and being at home at so early a time, too.'

'Well, you can stop thinking and stop nagging,' Chloe snapped, quite in the manner of the old Chloe rather than the gentler happier one she had been since their return from Cannes. 'I can't bear such fussing, for heaven's sake – '

'I'm not fussing,' Poppy said sharply. 'Merely showing an interest. I'll remember not to do so again. Give Goosey my message then – '

'If I see her,' Chloe muttered and when Poppy said, 'What did you say?' repeated it at a shout that again made Poppy wince. 'If I see her!'

'Make sure you do,' Poppy said crisply. 'I won't have her worried unnecessarily. Do you hear me?'

'Oh, yes, yes, yes, and yes again,' Chloe shouted. 'Can I go now? I want to go *now*, for heaven's sake! Right now – ' And then she made an odd little sound that made Poppy frown.

'Are you sure you're – ' she began and then shrugged. 'Well, all right, I'll see you tomorrow, no doubt. Good night – ' And Chloe grunted something and the phone clicked and then buzzed as she hung up at the other end in a great rush.

Poppy stood and frowned at the earpiece in her hand for a moment and then cradled it against the trumpet. Clearly something was worrying Chloe and she wondered for one hopeful moment if it could be that Bernie and she had had an argument. That would make Chloe miserable indeed and though Poppy didn't want the girl to be unhappy, there would be nothing she would welcome more than Chloe jilted by him, and her spirits, which had been very low ever since she had realized what Bernie had done with the ledger, took a very small lift. But not much of a one, and as she turned to leave they slumped again. The next hour or so was not going to be at all agreeable. So she pushed Chloe out of her mind and went down the stairs and out into the street to walk swiftly up to Aldgate East station to get the train that would take her over to Stamford Hill to talk to Jessie.

She sat in the cold tram as it clanged its way through the foggy December evening, her chin down into her collar so that she didn't get great lungfuls of chilly smoky air, watching the lights outside glinting past the windows and trying to work out the words she would use. It would have been bad enough had they been on their old comfortable terms, the way they had been before the Cannes episode; now it would be even harder, she told herself. Jessie would be cool and distant and then would try to be sensible but she knew how short her own fuse was and how likely she was to get snappy, especially when she was tired and upset as she now was; and she tried to promise herself she wouldn't be bad tempered in any way, just relaxed and friendly and nice and sympathetic and tried to imagine the conversation they would have, she and Jessie. But it kept going wrong in her head, with Jessie shouting at her and her shouting back, until her thoughts spun out of control and she felt a great anger at herself. This was precisely the sort of silliness she most hated in other people, and here she was doing it herself. And she got to her feet as the tram clanked to a stop at the gates of Finsbury Park and got out, slipping a little on the greasy stones. Across the street she could see the small block of neat flats to which Jessie had moved a couple of years ago and looked up at the third floor. Jessie's lights were on, glowing redly behind her closed crimson curtains and Poppy found herself smiling for a moment. Jessie had such a passion for red; and it was understandable for the room looked as if it would be very welcoming out in this dank evening air.

The room *was* welcoming; and so was Jessie. She came to the door to peer round the edge in some suspicion, and then flung it wide when she saw Poppy and grinned exactly as she had in the good old days before Cannes, and Poppy grinned back gratefully and said, 'Hello Jessie. Is this a bad time?'

'Of course not, how can it be a bad time? I'm finished supper. I'm just sitting listening to the wireless – ' And she cocked her head and Poppy heard the slightly tinny strains of dance music coming from inside the flat. 'From the Savoy,' Jessie said and then bustled Poppy in. 'I'll turn it off– '

'No need,' Poppy said and shrugged out of her coat in the warm hallway, aware of the agreeable smell of coffee and hot yeast cake. She was conscious suddenly of not having had any supper and Jessie with uncanny prescience said, 'I'll make you something to eat? A sandwich, maybe, or I got a piece of fried fish in the larder, lovely piece of halibut. I did it here at home, not at the restaurant at all. I'll fix it, a little horseradish with it, a bit of rye bread maybe, you'll feel better – '

'No, I won't Jessie. Honestly I won't. I – I mustn't be too late. And – well, I had to talk to you – '

They were in the living room now, a big square space, heavily carpeted, with a broad run of windows covering almost a whole wall with Jessie's richly swagged crimson velvet curtains making a brave show over them. There were deep comfortable armchairs, a couple of tables in highly fashionable green and blue chinoiserie and a tall standard lamp to match. Against one wall there was a broad sideboard and on it a most elegantly decorated square wireless set to which Jessie hurried to switch off. Then she reached for the front of the sideboard and pressed a button and the whole side of it lifted to reveal a very lavishly appointed cocktail cabinet much trimmed with gilt and chrome and reflective peach glass panels and full of bottles.

'If you won't eat, you'll have a drink at least – ' she said and cocked her head at Poppy. She was wearing a long deep red dressing gown in soft wool and looked oddly vulnerable, for all her size; as though she could be toppled with a touch; and Poppy bit her lip for a moment and then smiled, a little uneasily.

'You're so determined – well, not a drink, but I'll have a cup of coffee, all right? And a slice of your yeast cake – '

Jessie went happily into the kitchen as Poppy knew she would and she went over to the fireplace in which clear bright flames were leaping and rubbed her hands at the blaze, grateful for the respite. This was going to be even harder than she had thought.

Jessie came back with a tray piled high with coffee things and her yeast cake and chattered busily as she poured a cup and then filled a plate and Poppy made no attempt to stop the tide of words, not really listening and quite unaware of what Jessie was saying. And then jumped a little as some of the sounds penetrated her brown study, and put down her cup with a little clatter.

'What did you say?' she said then. 'I'm sorry – I was so busy eating I didn't hear properly – '

'I said he's gone to New York. Sailed this afternoon, bless him. I'd have gone to see him off, but he said why should I upset myself? Not that I'm upset. Well not exactly. It's a great chance for him – '

She settled herself in the chair opposite Poppy and began to sip her own coffee. 'I told him, "Of course I'll miss you, but it won't be for long. What's a month after all?" Just a month – ' But she looked a little bleak.

And Poppy said carefully, 'Bernie's gone to New York. This afternoon?'

'Didn't I say so? On the *Ascania* out of Southampton – ' She was silent for a moment and then said, 'To tell you the truth I think maybe – well, maybe it's just as well.'

'How do you mean?' Poppy was guarded now.

'He says it's an opportunity for him, like I said, a chance to get the money to set up the London end of Joe Mendoza's business – not quite sure what, but it's a good business – and very nice too. But me, I can't help wondering. He's been that worried lately I thought maybe his ex-partners are after him, you know? People in business can be very nasty, very nasty. We're not all the same after all, not all like us, more's the pity – '

She knows something, Poppy thought, watching her over the rim of her cup. She knows something about Bernie she doesn't like and she's not telling me. She's maybe not even being honest with herself about it, but she's worried. He's in some sort of trouble –

And because she was tired and therefore perhaps a

little less sensitive than she might be, she thought – if she knows he's up to some sort of villainy already then it won't make a lot of difference hearing a bit more. She'll get it all at once and get over it all at once. Better than stretching it out –

And she set her cup down in her saucer with a little clatter and said as carefully as she could, 'It was about Bernie I came to talk to you.'

'Oh?' At once Jessie's openness seemed to change. It was as though her dressing gown was a tortoise's carapace and she had pulled her head inside it to guard herself against a threat. 'Why should you want to talk about Bernie? Not this Chloe business again? I told you, that's – '

'No. Not Chloe,' and she pushed away the memory of Chloe's oddness on the phone. She'd think about that later. 'No, it's strictly business.'

Jessie said nothing, staring at her with bright watchful eyes, and Poppy stopped and took a deep breath.

'This isn't easy,' she said abruptly. 'It's never easy.'

'When you talk to me about my son you're always ready to have a go,' Jessie said shortly. 'So if you're having another go I dare say it ain't easy at that.'

'You make it sound as though – as though I'm prejudiced against Bernie,' Poppy said, almost desperately. 'It isn't that – '

'Isn't it? Always you have a go at him? You criticize, you complain, you niggle. How would you feel if whenever I spoke so to you of your Robin, I badmouthed her, God forbid? I couldn't, I love that child, she's a dolly. And I love you and so how can I be nasty to you about your only baby? It's that I can't understand. I thought you cared for me – '

'I do!' Poppy protested. 'You know I do!'

Jessie ran on, ignoring that. ' – but every time you speak of my only baby you make me feel bad. And then

312

you complain to *me* it ain't easy for you! It ain't easy for me to listen, believe me.'

Poppy took a sharp little breath and steeled herself. 'I believe you. But it has to be done all the same. He's been robbing the books again. Only it's much worse this time. Four hundred pounds.'

There was a long pause and all Poppy could hear was the hissing of the coals in the grate and the flickering of the flames and from outside in the fog-muffled street the clang of the trams and occasional clattering footsteps as people ran to catch them. And then Jessie said in a harsh little voice, 'What did you say?'

'Four hundred pounds,' Poppy said. And then almost without realizing she was doing it, she let her tongue run on. At the back of her mind she was aghast. She should have said no more at this stage; should have let the information sink into Jessie's mind and let her make her own reactions.

But she didn't do that. Instead she burst out into the stupid speech she had been rehearsing in the tram coming here, even though she knew it was the silliest thing she could possibly do, even though it was obvious it would cause the sort of distress to Jessie she wanted most to avoid.

'And it's not just you he's robbed, is it? It was bad enough when it was. I got angry on your behalf then, and I'm still angry for the same reason. But there's a difference now. I'm a partner. I'm supposed to have shares in the business and in the money it makes. And if he's robbed you – well the books – of four hundred pounds it means he's robbed me as well as you. I've worked it out. It's a hundred and thirty three pounds six shillings and eightpence. That's a lot of money – '

As the words came tumbling out she had seen Jessie's face change. The stricken look that had appeared there when she had first been told of Bernie's crime went to be replaced by a huge and glittering anger. Poppy watched her eyes change and darken and could have bitten her own tongue out. But it was too late. Jessie was on her feet and staring at her, and then walking across the room, moving lightly for one of her size, to a little chinoiserie desk in the corner. She sat down and opened it and, without a word reached in and pulled out her cheque-book and then began to scribble in it.

She came back, holding the cheque she had torn from the book in front of her as though it were a dead and disgusting thing she had found lying around, and stood in front of Poppy with it.

'A hundred and thirty three pounds six shillings and eightpence?' she said in a voice Poppy could hardly recognize. 'Here's the cheque. And tomorrow I'll see to it the lawyers organize the cheque for the rest that is due to you. A third of the business I gave you because I loved you, because I was grateful to you, because I wanted to give you a stake in the future, because I wanted to help care for your Robin as well as you. Well, I should have known better. I've always been a soft mug, I know that. I thought better of you, but I was wrong. So here's your lousy money and you'll get the rest as soon as I can fix it. Now get out, out of my flat, out of my business, out of my life, you hear me? I never want to see you ever again. Take your stinkin' money and go – '

26

Poppy had been sitting by the drawing-room fire, mending Robin's school socks. She had stretched the work as long as she could, making exquisitely neat darns in the heels and then reinforcing perfectly sound toes that needed no such attention, but now she was finished, and there was no more she could do. Goosey had always kept up well with all the sort of work that Poppy was now taking off her hands, and with the best will in the world could find nothing else at all that needed any sewing. And even if she could, she thought now, as she rolled the socks into neat bundles ready to be tucked away in Robin's chest of drawers, it wouldn't solve the problem.

She got to her feet and went over to the window to stare out into the Square. The naked trees drooped sadly over the scrubby grass and the dripping tattered shrubs that edged it, and the rain-sodden sky pressed down on it all like a pall, and she took a deep breath and thought with sudden panic – I can't stand this. How can I live without a job to do, something important and useful to fill the days? The fact that most women lived all their lives shut up in just the way she was shut up this morning didn't help. If they could make their domestic duties and mothering tasks sufficient to fill the long days, well and good for them, but she knew she could not. She was out of the way of it, that was the thing; if she had ever been a woman who had sat at home and busied herself solely about domestic affairs it would be different. She would have been trained to it. But she had from her earliest days been a worker. As a girl she had forced her way into a newspaper office to be a typist, much to her mother's regret, and after that there had been the war years and the FANYs followed by the days of her marriage to Bobby when she had to work to keep the household together. And so it had gone on, even when Robin had been born. She had remained at home for a month then to recover (and even that she had found excessive, for the birth had been comfortable and she was, she told everyone, fully recovered within a week) but had been back in the office with Jessie as soon as she could. With Goosey to look after her baby, why not?

But it had not been just the fact that she was accustomed to working; above all she had needed the money she earned. Now she stared with glazed eyes at the dismal square and its few scurrying passers-by with their heads down against the bitter December wind that sent scraps of rubbish and a few dead leaves swirling round their ankles and faced the reality of her dilemma. Again.

Because that was what she had been doing all week. At first she had been kept going by the white heat of her anger. Yes, she had been tactless, yes, she had upset Jessie, but did she have to react quite so violently? To have written that cheque and to have spoken as she had – it was intolerable, and thinking of it now Poppy felt her face redden with the memory of her hurt.

She had of course torn up the cheque, there and then, and dropped the pieces on Jessie's handsome carpet before turning and marching out of the flat to climb with shaky knees and a burning face onto the tram to go home, and had the next day flatly refused to speak to the lawyer who had telephoned her, in a state of mystification, about the 'extraordinary instructions' he had received from Jessie. There was no question of her accepting a penny from Jessie, she had said firmly, even for the work she had already done this month – and her outstanding salary was a considerable sum – and even though her resources were as always under strain. So now she needed to find work that would pay her enough to maintain this house and Goosey and Robin and her costly school and –

She turned away from the window with a sharp little movement. However often she went over it all in her head the end result was the same; a major problem that offered no immediate solution. What sort of work could she get that would provide a salary sufficient for her needs? To go back to being a typist again at a time when the offices of London were swamped with eager young girls with adequate skills was out of the question. No one would want her for a start, not at her age and anyway she had not typed for a great many years. Her job managing Jessie's Foods Ltd had involved a whole number of skills, including the laborious bookkeeping that had led to her present situation and though it was an impressive whole she knew that individually her abilities offered small enticement to a would-be employer. Companies looking for the sort of manager she had been and providing the sort of salary she needed, would not dream of taking on a woman. They would see that as a man's job, and would have no compunction about saying so.

She knew that because she had spent the first week of her enforced idleness telephoning and writing to a large number of such companies, combing the advertisements and generally trying very hard. And it was clear to her now that in the eyes of the commercial world at large she had nothing to offer that was wanted. She might yet have to get work to regain her typing abilities and would have to swallow her pride and go seeking the sort of lowly and low-paid occupation that would be all that was now available to her. It was a thought that rankled – and also alarmed, because there was no guarantee that even if she did make that effort she would achieve any success.

The door opened and Goosey came in, panting a little from the climb up the stairs.

'I thought I'd go for Miss Robin a bit early, Mrs Poppy,' she wheezed. 'I need some extra potatoes for supper. I thought I'd do some fried ones the way Miss Robin likes them. Is there anything else you want from the shops?'

Poppy thought for a moment of insisting that Goosey go and put her feet up while she went to shop and fetch Robin from school; heaven knows even that little outing would make a break in the interminable dullness of the day. But that would upset the old woman too much. She had shown a lively alarm when Poppy had suggested altering her routine that way last week and now Poppy had not the heart to upset her again. Collecting Robin from school was the highlight of her day; Poppy had no right to rob her of it.

The house sank into silence once Goosey had gone, creaking out of the house in her neat grey coat and hat, and Poppy stood in the hall and tried to think of what she could do to make herself feel better.

Inside her mind somewhere deep she knew of course what she ought to do; pick up the telephone and call Jessie, tell her that they were behaving foolishly and ask her to agree to a meeting so that they could sort out their argument and get back to normal. That Jessie was by now aching to do just that Poppy was sure; she knew Jessie well enough for that. Her temper might flare, but her feeling for her niece was just as powerful, if in a different way, as her feeling for the egregious Bernie; but Poppy also knew that there was no possibility that Jessie would climb down first. Show her a way out of the morass, however tortuous, and she would respond with alacrity, but she had a stubborn sort of pride that would not allow her to make the first step towards reconciliation. And as the younger of them it would be up to Poppy to take that first step –

She actually moved towards the telephone as she thought that, but stopped short as she reached it. No, she could not. Bernie had behaved appallingly and that fact had to be faced by Jessie. If Poppy phoned now was there not a risk that Jessie would see this not as an attempt to mend fences but as an apology from Poppy for what she had said about her beloved and thoroughly reprehensible son? Indeed there was, and Poppy had no intention of withdrawing a single word she had uttered about him. So, she remained in her impasse.

She wandered down to the kitchen which lay quiet and comfortable in the dull afternoon, the fire glowing richly behind its bars and Goosey's knitting left on the chair beside it in its usual way, and she stood at the top of the stairs and looked down and found herself remembering with incredible vividness the kitchen she had first known as a very young child. A warm firelit place like this, it had been, with just such a scrubbed wooden table and a dresser with blue and white china on it, and the scent of freshly baked cakes in the air; and then knew that was why she had remembered so suddenly, for there was cooling on a rack on the table a neat round cake and the smell of coconut and eggs and butter and sugar drifted up to her in a great wash of nostalgia. Tears pricked her eyes for a moment, tears of self pity, for she really was so unhappy –

She went on down the stairs to the kitchen briskly, annoyed with herself. This wallowing was really absurd. She must mind herself or she would become positively maudlin and she went about the kitchen with determined movements, setting a tea tray for herself and including on it a plate of the little sugar dredged biscuits that Goosey made so well. There was everything to be said for giving herself a little treat like that.

319

She almost jumped when, as the kettle began at last to hum on its way to the full throated singing that would show it was at boiling point, a bell jangled and she turned her head to look at the panel above the door at the top of the small flight of kitchen stairs. The flapping indicator showed that it was the doorbell of course and she made a face at herself for being so foolish as to think there was someone else in the house who should not be there – her first reaction – and to be scared. It was another index of how anxious she was at present. Clearly something would have to be done about the matter of a job soon –

She went up to the hall and to the door, only vaguely concerned about who it might be. Chloe perhaps, for she had a most amazing tendency to forget her door key and would never put herself out to come down the area steps to the kitchen door, and was so sure it was that she paid little attention to the shadow on the coloured glass which might have identified who stood on the step. So when she did pull the door open and saw who was there she was startled and stared speechlessly for a long moment.

'I know you told me not to come just at present, Poppy,' he said cheerfully, turning his hat between his hands in a way that betrayed his nervousness, in spite of his apparent insouciance. 'But there it is – I never was one for doing as I was told. And I had to see you – '

'Hello, David,' she said after a long pause and managed a smile. 'I – it's kind of you to – but really I – I mean, I don't want to seem unfriendly. But – '

'Then don't be and ask me in.' He moved forwards a little and she had to step back and he bobbed his head cheerfully and walked past her into the house to hang his hat on the stand and to shrug off his big coat.

'What a divine smell,' he said. 'One of Goosey's cakes? Coconut, if my nose is truthful. May I have some? A cup of good English tea would be very welcome too. It's one the best things about being in London, tea – '

'David,' she said. 'David, you really are – '

He grinned at her. 'Persistent. Yes. Dreadful, isn't it? Put it down to my being a pushy American. We don't take no for an answer so easily. I had to know, you see. You said on the phone it was nothing to do with me, that you had things of your own to sort out, but there, I'm as paranoid as the next guy. I think it has to be something to do with me, and I just can't go on any longer wondering what it is. So I've come to find out from you. May I have the tea and cake?'

She took a sharp little breath and then managed to smile again. 'Of course. Come on down then. I was in the kitchen.'

He followed her down the stairs. 'All alone? Oh, of course – Goosey's gone to fetch Robin from school – '

'You know this household as well as I do,' she said with a sudden snappishness and didn't look at him. She had phoned him the day after the argument with Jessie and told him simply that she could not go to dinner with him that night as she had promised and that she had one or two things to sort out and please not to call for a while. She'd be in touch, she had promised him, when she could. Meanwhile please don't take it personally – and she had hung up feeling a little less harassed. She had felt she had to deal with this situation alone. David would want to help whatever happened to her, but this was something she had to sort out alone, she had been sure, though quite why was not clear. But it had to be so. And that had meant she couldn't explain to him what was happening.

And now here he was, as relaxed as ever, making it clear that he had an intimate knowledge of her household and therefore, in a sense, of her and that made her feel – well she wasn't quite sure now. Crowded, perhaps, a little overwhelmed even, and she didn't like it. Or was trying not to like it; it would be all too easy to throw herself and her problems at his feet, and to leave it to him to sort them out. He had been such an incredible help over the business of Chloe in Paris, so very sensible and useful, and that was why, she told herself stubbornly now, she had to manage it alone. Leave it to him as she had before and she would become as helpless and silly as any other woman. If ever there was a time when she needed all her strength it was now. And that meant keeping her distance from this man, charming and comfortable to be with though he was.

She moved quickly to the kettle and made the tea and then brought it to the table and poured it for him, and indicated the cake. 'Help yourself,' she said shortly. 'I expect it's cool enough to cut by now.'

'Hey, hey,' he said softly, staring at her. 'What have I done? You don't have to bite my head off. I'm just trying to be what I thought I was. Your good friend.'

She still would not look at him but moved to the dresser to fetch another cup and saucer for herself and poured her tea and then, deliberately putting space between them, went to sit in Goosey's fireside chair instead of at the table with him.

'I told you, David. I have some problems to sort out and I just don't have the time to –'

'I know about the problems and you do so have the time. Plenty of it. Too much of it. That's one of the problems,' he said and now she did look at him. He was sitting there at the table with his cup between his hands and his elbows planted firmly on the bare scrubbed wood, staring at her over the rim of the cup, and she felt a great rush of warmth for him and an even stronger desire to throw all her worries and fears in front of him to let him pick them up, and relieve and reassure her; and then steeled herself against that urge. It was a dangerous one, not to be allowed, not on any account.

'It's my concern, not yours,' she said.

'It is very much my concern. For heaven's sake, Poppy! I told you I love you. I have ever since the War in France, dammit. That was one of the reasons I went back to the States, frankly. I'd planned to stay in London, maybe get my own news agency going but I couldn't live in the same city as you and Bobby, could I? Of course I had to go back. And then when I couldn't stand it any longer and came back and found you were alone and – wow, Poppy, I told you how I felt. And I thought you told me that you too – ' He left the words hanging in the air; but still she refused to look at him and said nothing.

He sighed then, a long soft little sound in the big room, and went on in a quieter tone. 'I spoke to Jessie. Went to see you at the office, and she said you were gone, but would hardly speak to me. I made her, of course – '

'Of course,' Poppy said with a bitter note in her voice, and he laughed at that.

'Like I said, a pushy Yank. She's very unhappy, Poppy.'

'I'm not exactly singing and dancing myself.'

'I'm sure you're not. Look, I still can't be quite certain what it's all about – mayn't I ask? Now I'm here?'

She shook her head irritably and set down her cup and saucer on the floor beside her so that she could lean back in the chair and lie against Goosey's old cushions with her eyes closed. 'You have asked,' she said, 'Is there any way I can stop you from – '

'No,' he said. 'No way at all. So you might as well – '

'Oh, all right, then! I discovered that Bernie had embezzled four hundred pounds. I was angry enough over the way he'd got himself involved with Chloe. Jessie brought him to Cannes, encouraged him – and now this. And I – well I spoke more impulsively than perhaps I should. And she was angry – '

'And hurt,' he said quietly.

'So am I hurt,' she flashed. 'She offered me a cheque,

323

dammit. Told me to go, said she'd arrange for me to get a third of the money out of the business and to never come back.'

'She didn't mean it, I don't think,' he said. 'When I spoke to her she was very – '

'David, I know you mean kindly, but stop it, do you hear me?' She looked at him very directly. 'I can't cope with your acting as – as a peacemaker. This is between Jessie and me, and no one else. Not even you. That was one of the reasons why I – why I told you I thought it better not to see you for a while. You were marvellous over the Paris business and I'm very grateful, but I have to deal with this one on my own. You understand? On my own.'

'That sounds reasonable enough,' he said after a long moment. 'Okay, not another word about Jessie or – even though I think she'd want me to – no, all right! Don't look at me that way! I swear not another word until you give me permission. So, what are you going to do?'

She slid her eyes away from him to look at the fire, which flickered contentedly behind its polished bars. 'I – find a job.'

'Have you tried yet?'

There was another long pause. 'Yes,' she said.

'And not much joy.' He was sympathetic. 'It's a tough time for workers now. Even though the strike's been settled the coalfields are bad news. There's still bad feeling about and that knocks on to other parts of business. Times are hard and they'll get harder, I'm afraid. I reckon we're heading for one hell of a recession. It's the same in the States. They're making money on Wall Street but where it matters, on the farms and factories, it's like here. There aren't a lot of good jobs lying around, especially for women, hmm?'

'You're a great reassurance,' she said sardonically. 'I'm looking for a job and you preach economics at me.

Have you been writing an article on the subject lately and got some facts to share out?'

'I've been looking, yes,' he said equably. 'And I'm sorry if it sounded like a lecture. Because I don't intend it to be. I just want to talk about what you're going to do.'

'Go on looking for a job,' she said. 'I'll find one. Eventually.'

'And meanwhile?'

'Meanwhile, I'll manage!' she flared. 'David, please don't – don't *nag* me!'

'I'm not nagging,' he said mildly and then smiled at her. 'I'm not nagging at all. I'm just asking you to marry me. As soon as possible.'

She stared at him blankly. 'What do you say?'

'I thought it was clear enough. I said, marry me. That'll solve it all, won't it? Then you can stop worrying and –'

There was a small sound above his head and behind him and Poppy lifted her eyes to look. It wasn't easy to see, for the short winter afternoon was dwindling into evening and she had no lights burning; only the soft flicker of the firelight gave them much illumination in the dim glow from the window.

'Who's that?' she asked sharply and then the light flickered on and she saw Robin standing by the door, her school coat hanging open and her hat dangling down her back, held there by the elastic that was slung round her neck.

'Hello darling!' Poppy said and her voice was warm with gratitude. Now she would have time to catch her breath and think. 'Have you had a good day at school?'

'Quite good,' Robin said gravely after a moment and then turned. 'I'll put my coat and hat away and start my homework upstairs, shall I? Goosey won't be long. She's just taking off her things.' And she went, leaving the kitchen door swinging open behind her.

27

It had been such a good day, too, till now. School had been fun all through with all her most favourite lessons like English and history and of course art, and no maths classes at all. Molly and Cynthia had both been sensible and they had played their best ball games at break-time and that new girl Maryanne who had just come to the class had swopped an annual Robin had never seen before for one of her old ones that she'd read three times already. A really good day. And now this to spoil it all.

She sat on her bed in her room, her satchel dangling between her knees and her head down, trying to think. It wasn't easy because her head felt all cluttered inside. Pictures of the things that had happened at school mixed themselves up with the picture of Mummy and that man – she couldn't bear to think his name – sitting in the dark kitchen and talking about getting married. Soon it would be the way Goosey had said it was when people got married for the second time. She'd be all left out the way Chloe thought she was. She'd be miserable and nasty to everyone just like Chloe and wouldn't be liked by people and Mummy would –

She got to her feet quickly and took her books out of her satchel. Miss Trent had said today she was a clever girl and if she worked hard at her homework she could perhaps get a special scholarship to Godolphin and Latimer School.

'Which would be nice for your mother,' she had added briskly, 'School fees are high there, Robin, and I am sure you will want to make it easier for your poor mother, a widow as she is. If you work hard you could well get an assisted place. The money saving could be considerable. So I shall give you extra work to do at home to ready you for the entrance examination. Make sure you do three pages of the sums tonight will you? And then learn the poem by William Allingham – you see – "Up the airy mountain, down the rushy glen, we daren't go hunting for fear of little men" – It's an easy one to learn, so please work hard at it – '

And she had meant to. She had thought of doing the sums first because they were the hardest and dullest and then learning her poem after supper when it wouldn't matter that she felt a bit sleepy. But now she wouldn't do either. She had to find out first of all what was going to happen in her house. Was that man going to come here and spoil everything? Someone surely should be able to tell her?

But who? She piled her books on the small desk Mummy had fixed up for her when she had gone up into her new class after coming back to school from having measles, because of having extra work to do at home to catch up. She had loved the little desk because it had red leather stuck on the top of it in a fine pattern along which she could run the point of her pencil when she was thinking, but now she found no pleasure in it at all. Her head was too full of questions. Who could she ask? Goosey? Of course not. Goosey would just tell her not to be so silly, Miss Robin, and would make her eat something. And the person she usually talked to most easily was the one person she couldn't ask, because it was about her she wanted to talk. And that was the nastiest feeling of all.

She went and stood by her bedroom window and

looked out into the patch of garden below, where her old swing was tied up for the winter and the herbaceous borders were all draggled and dead-looking, and she felt a deep sense of empty misery. It was like the way she had felt on her birthday, she remembered suddenly, a feeling that nothing nice would ever happen again, and it made her feel sick as well as empty. A horrid sensation and just as bad as it had been that day, all those long months ago when she had been so very much younger than she was now. She worked it out in her head and marvelled a little. Why, she was getting very close to eight now. An old sort of person, someone who ought to be able to sort out things like bad feelings much better than someone who had only just stopped being six, as she had been on her birthday.

Old enough to be sensible, she told herself then, and tried to think about how to do that. The teachers at school talked a lot about being sensible, but didn't tell her how to be so. Who was the most sensible person she knew who could help her? After Mummy, of course – and then she knew exactly who she could talk to, and lifted her head with a little surge of excitement and then went over to her door to look down the stairs to the hall below.

It was quiet everywhere, Goosey was obviously still in her room and clearly Mummy and That Man were still in the kitchen and quietly she went back to close her bedroom door and then went swiftly down the stairs and out of the front door, closing it swiftly behind her.

She felt really incredibly good, considering how bad she had felt before. Now, with her hat still bobbing on her shoulders from its stretched old elastic and her open coat flapping round her cold knees as she went hurrying along the darkening pavements of Norland Square, she was pleased with herself. She had had a very good idea and was doing something about it right away. That was being sensible the way the teachers told her to be, so of course she felt good.

When she got to Holland Park Road she hesitated for a moment before turning left and beginning to walk along the pavement. It had stopped raining now but it was wet everywhere and now and again mud splashed up from the paving stones and landed on her bare legs and she looked down at her shoes and saw how grimy they were and thought – she won't like that. She always notices things like dirty shoes. But when I explain to her it'll be all right. I'm sure it will.

She had never walked all the way to her grandmother's house on her own. Usually when they went, she and Mummy, it was in a bus or sometimes in a taxi. She knew the way of course; it was easy. Just straight along the Bayswater Road, past the shops and the big houses until you came to Leinster Terrace and then turned left. And there was Grndmamma's house. It was easy.

But a very long way, and after a while her legs began to ache. She pushed her hands into her pockets and then stopped walking and pulled out what she had there and looked at it. Her threepenny bit, the one she had been given as change to give Mummy after paying for her school milk. She had forgotten about it, and there it was. A threepenny bit. Enough to ride all the way to Grandmamma's house on the bus, and back again too.

But it wasn't her threepenny bit, and she stood in the street staring down at the small coin, brilliantly illuminated in her palm by the light pouring out of the bookshop beside which she had stopped. Inside there were bright rows of books in red and blue covers and a window full of more books with jackets which had pictures on them, pictures of men with guns and ladies in lovely clothes and lots of lipstick like Chloe's, and she looked at the window for some sort of sign to tell her what she should do. She often did that, when she was worried about things, looking around for a message from – well wherever it was messages came from. And now she found herself staring at a book jacket which had a very bright picture on it in red and green and the very richest of yellows. It showed a picture of a woman looking worried and the writing said, 'Rose Macaulay – *Crewe Train*,' and she found herself relaxing as she looked at it. That was a very good sign. It would have been better if it had said Crewe Bus, or even Bayswater Train, but it was about travelling; and it meant it was all right for Robin to do it and to spend Mummy's threepenny bit.

The next bus stop was quite a long way away but it wasn't so hard to walk now she knew she was going to get on a bus and when she got there she only had to wait a little while before a bus came along, huge and red and lumbering in the dark evening – for now all the daylight had quite vanished – and she climbed on, feeling very brave. It was the first time she had ever got on a bus without having a grown-up with her, and it was a bit strange. But she knew what to do, and sat down in the first seat there was empty until the conductor came along with his rack of tickets, calling, '*Any* more fares please. Fares *if* you please – '

'A penny half,' she said carefully and gave him her threepenny bit and for a moment was terrified as he stood and looked at it; would he stare at her and shout, 'This is a stolen threepenny bit! This is what it is, a stolen one! It belongs to your mother, not to you, Miss Robin Bradman'? But he put it into his leather pouch and pulled a ticket from his rack and pinged it cheerfully on his machine and gave it to her together with two pennies and cried cheerfully, 'I thank you! *Any* more fares *if* you please!' and went swaying down the bus to the other people.

She began to feel very pleased with herself indeed as she sat and stared out of the window looking for the right stop to get out. She would know it, she was sure. A letterbox on the corner, a tall tree just behind it on the side of the road with a bit of tired grass growing round the square of earth at its foot. Oh, she'd know it all right –

But she missed it and suddenly discovered she had not stood up in time to ring the bell and went running to the back of the bus to cry to the conductor, 'Make him stop, oh make him stop, please – '

The conductor peered at her. 'Missed your stop, have you, little girl? Well, not to cry. It ain't that far back to walk – ' And he pinged the bell and at last the bus stopped, but it seemed a very long way back in the dark road to the familiar corner with its letterbox and tree.

But she managed to walk there somehow, even though her legs were aching at the back quite dreadfully now. She had never walked so far, ever, in all her life and she began to wish she had never come. It would be so lovely to be at home now, in her room with her lovely desk with the red leather on it or by the fire with Goosey making supper and talking to herself all the time the way she did, and Mummy sitting by the table and –

She began to cry, the tears sliding down her face in a steady trickly sort of way that made her rub her face hard with her hands. But the more she rubbed the more she cried and now her face began to hurt a bit as the cold air bit into its wetness. But then at last there was the letterbox and tree corner and she turned into Grandmamma's road and somehow managed to run up it to her house and to drag herself up the seven steps that led to the front door. She had arrived and now she could stop crying.

But she couldn't. She stood there with the tears still running down her face and aching all over and waited after ringing the bell, and the longer it took for anyone to come the more the tears ran down and made her face itch. And she rubbed again and reached once more for the bell pull and tugged it hard.

And this time at last someone arrived. The light sprang up behind the dark panes of the door and she stood there and waited as the tears continued to run down and make her nose run, too, hoping it might be Grandmamma who came.

But it was Queenie, of course, who answered the door, old Queenie who was even older than Goosey and much much slower, and she stood there peering short-sightedly into the darkness and said in a thin voice, 'Who is it? What do you want?'

It was more than Robin could bear. She ought to explain and wait till Queenie said, 'Come in.' That would be the polite way to be, and usually Grandmamma was very strict about people being polite. But she couldn't wait another moment and she pushed past Queenie, who let out a sort of yelp and went to the stairs, calling breathlessly over her shoulder. 'I've got to see Grandmamma – it's very important. I've got to see Grandmamma – ' and went running up the stairs.

Mildred had, truth to tell, been dozing in her chair. She hated to admit she did it for it seemed to her such a feeble and silly thing to do, to sleep in the daytime. Her old stepmother had used to do that, constantly snoozing her long dismal days away in snores and flushed cheek emptiness and she had despised her for it. She had less reason to sleep so herself of course. She was not one to take too much sherry in the afternoon as Maud had been. But even that had been no excuse for Maud and her laziness in Mildred's opinion. So she had told herself and still did. To sleep away daytime hours in a high-backed chair was the sort of behaviour she deplored. Especially in herself.

So when she woke with startling suddenness to see a small bedraggled figure with a tearstained face and dirt streaked cheeks standing in her drawing room her first reaction was to be angry. She had been caught out in behaviour of which she disapproved, and she stared sharply at the apparition and barked, 'What do you want?'

It was too much for Robin. She burst into a great wail of misery and stood there knuckling her eyes and weeping as though her heart would break and Mildred stared and then got to her feet a little stiffly and went over to her.

It was not easy to crouch beside her; she had not made such a movement for years, for truth to tell her joints were getting painful now, not that she would dream of admitting it to anyone. But she managed it and after a moment, as Robin went on howling her misery, she put her arms around her.

It felt very odd to Mildred and she remained there crouching beside the heartbroken child, holding her close, feeling her bones light and fragile beneath the thickness of her school coat and the trembling of the small muscles and it was as though the years had melted under her fingers. This was not her· granddaughter standing here but her own daughter, her own small Poppy, whom she had loved so dearly and who had somehow, as the years had gone by, slipped out of her grasp.

After a little while she began to croon at the child, putting her lips close to her ear and murmuring an indeterminate sort of sound, low and burring in her throat and slowly Robin's shoulders began to relax and the sobbing slowed and she reached again to her face to rub it.

'Well,' Mildred said and moving gingerly, straightened up. Her knees shrieked a protest, but she managed to ignore it, and stood with one hand on Robin's shoulder, looking down at her. 'Tell me what's the matter. And how did you get here? Why are you alone?'

Robin gulped and looked up at her and then Mildred, to her own surprise, found herself smiling. It was not some-

333

thing she did easily at any time, and she was at some deep level startled that she should do so now. But the child looked so very woebegone with her dirt-smeared face and red eyes and nose tip and she was so funny in a sweet sort of way that she responded very directly. And Robin, looking up at her, managed to produce a watery smile of her own and moved closer to her, and the two stood there looking at each other and glad to be together. It was a long and special moment, and then they were interrupted by Queenie who had come panting slowly up the stairs at last to see what was going on.

'Fetch a wash cloth for her face and a towel,' Mildred commanded. 'And find something for her feet. Her shoes are drenched and she'll catch her death. And then warm milk or something of the sort to comfort her. As fast as you can, now – ' And Queenie went creaking away as Mildred led Robin to the fireplace.

'Now,' she said and settled herself back in her chair. 'Tell me all about it. Is someone ill?'

'No,' Robin said in a small voice and then stood passively as Mildred reached forwards and started to peel off her coat.

'Well, then, as long as no one is ill, we can take our time,' Mildred said comfortably and indicated to her that she should sit on the hearthrug so that her wet shoes and socks could be taken off. Robin watched as the muddy items were removed to leave her feet pink and a little pathetic under the crusting of mud splashes that adorned her legs all the rest of the way up beyond her knees and bit her lip in mortification.

'I'm sorry my shoes are dirty, Grandmamma,' she said in a small voice. 'They aren't usually.'

'I know they aren't,' Mildred said and again smiled at her. Really, Robin thought, she wasn't being a bit like Grandmamma. Or yes, she was, but better. And she felt a great wave of comfortableness come inside her to replace the empty feeling; she had been exactly right to come here, to choose Grandmamma to explain to about how worried she was. And as Queenie came back then with a bowl of warm water and a flannel and a towel followed closely by an agog little housemaid with a tray bearing a glass of warm milk with butter melting in it and a plate of dry biscuits she beamed at them and then at Mildred and felt better than ever.

When at last the two servants had gone and she was sitting wrapped in a rug which Queenie had insisted on putting around her in spite of the glowing fire, and sipping the milk – which had sugar and nutmeg in it too and was really very delicious – she looked up at her grandmother again and said simply, 'I didn't know who to talk to.'

'So you came to talk to me?' Mildred said and felt again the glow of pleasure she had known when she had crouched beside the child to hold her till her tears abated. 'I am gratified.'

'You know about things, you see,' Robin said. 'And I couldn't talk to Mummy because it's about Mummy.'

Mildred said nothing, just sitting there and looking at her and the light from the fire reflected off the brooch she was wearing at the throat of her cream silk blouse and lighting her grey hair to a glinting silver.

'That Man,' said Robin darkly and stopped. 'Do you know That Man?'

'Possibly,' Mildred said. 'If you will explain a little more – '

Robin took a deep breath and set down her empty glass on the tray on the little table beside Mildred's chair and pushed off the blanket which was becoming far too warm now.

'Well, when I came home from school he was in the kitchen and he was talking about getting married and Goosey said that when people get married it puts noses out of joints and things like that and I don't want to be like Chloe – '

Mildred blinked. 'You will do better if you tell me slowly and only one thing at a time,' she said. 'It is difficult to understand otherwise. Your mother and Goosey and That Man? You mean Mr Deveen, perhaps?'

Robin made a face, her mouth turning downwards. 'That's the one.'

'They were all in the kitchen after school – '

'No!' Robin was getting impatient. 'No, only Mummy and him. But once Goosey said – '

'Never mind Goosey at present,' Mildred said with a return of her usual acerbity and Robin, a little chilled, sat back on her heels, for she had been kneeling up with her hands on Mildred's lap and almost shaking her in her impatience to explain it all. 'Just tell me what happened after school this afternoon.'

So, Robin told her, and with the right prompting from her grandmother managed to explain Goosey's involvement too. And Mildred, understanding at last, looked down into her small imploring face and nodded slowly. She did indeed understand what was upsetting Robin and what had to be done to put it right.

28

They listened as the sound of Robin's footsteps died away upstairs and the other sounds of the kitchen took over; the faint hiss from the kettle on the hob and the crackle of the fire with beyond that the distant hum of the traffic in the main Holland Park Road; and then Poppy very carefully looked away from him and said nothing at all.

He smiled, and now that the light was burning over their heads she could see his face more clearly. He seemed relaxed and easy, but behind that there was an air of tension, a thin vein of anxiety, and she thought, he's acting. This isn't at all what it seems. He's acting. And a spirit of perversity seemed to rise in her and she refused to think about what at a deep level she knew was the real cause of his anxiety: a fear she would reject him. Instead she stared at him and told herself in clear words, writing them inside her mind so that she could almost read them off. He's putting on an act because he's sorry for me. This is all because of pity, and I am not pitable, I will not be pitiable.

'Timing is all,' he said ruefully and grinned at her. 'One of these days I'll get it right, eh? I met you after Bobby died, and now I propose just when young Robin gets home from school. I really couldn't get it more wrong, could I?'

'You have more than your timing wrong,' she said a

little harshly and got to her feet. 'Look, David, let's leave it, shall we? Let's leave it that you said nothing of – of any importance before Robin came in. Finish your tea and then be on your way, do you mind? I've a lot to do – and Goosey will be down soon to make supper and – well, I really think it would be better if you left.'

He sat very still and then said quietly, 'I can't do that.'

'Can't go? That's absurd – ' she said, but he shook his head.

'Can't leave it at that. Can't pretend I said nothing. Nor can you. I asked you to marry me, I should have done so a long time ago, but – well, like I said. Timing was never my big gift. But I've asked you now and we can't pretend I didn't and I would appreciate an answer.'

'Oh, dammit!' she cried then and banged the table. 'Why do you have to do this to me? Haven't I got enough to deal with at the moment? Why do you make it harder for me?'

'Harder – ? But Poppy, my dear beloved Poppy, it's the reverse! I want to make it easier. I want to take all the problems away and – '

'And you think that all you have to do is ask me to marry you and there's an end to it? That's – that's romantic claptrap, David! This is what happens in silly films and books. That isn't real life. In real life when you've – when a person has a fight with someone they love very much and feel bad about it, they don't get miraculously better just because some man comes along and offers to marry them.'

He had gone a little white around the mouth. 'I wasn't suggesting for a moment that I could make you stop caring about Jessie and what has happened with her,' he said in a low voice. 'I wouldn't insult you so. But I might be able to help you bear the – well, the pain of it. If that isn't romantic claptrap too, I want to take as much misery away from you as I can. I want to look after you and protect you and – '

'I can look after myself!' she cried, deliberately fanning her anger.

'And I want to be looked after, to have my pain taken away,' he went on implacably. 'I want to feel needed and important and – that was my side of the equation. If I spell that out, will it make it easier for you to accept me? If I tell you I love you and need you, that my life only has any meaning when you are part of it? Yes, I know. I can see it in your face. Romantic claptrap again. Well, I can't help that. It's the way I am. A soggy sentimentalist, that's me. I love you, I love everything about you and to do with you. I love your daughter and your mother and even old Goosey, because I love you. I want to take care of all of you. So, will you marry me? It's the best care-taking way I can think of.'

She sat very still, unable to speak. Somewhere inside herself she knew that what he was offering was in a sense all she had ever really wanted. It was what she had wanted with Bobby, and the need he expressed for her now was precisely the need she had told Bobby of all those years ago in a small French farmhouse in Revigny. And the irony of it bit into her, for wasn't the basic situation exactly the same? Hadn't she adored Bobby, ached for him, needed him desperately and hadn't he told her that he would always love his first wife? She thought now of Barbara, long dead Barbara whom she had never met but whose daughter she had looked after for so many years and thought – I'm like her now. In a way. I have a man who loves me as she was loved, and as Bobby never loved me. And there he sits and he's willing to do what I did; he will marry me and care for me and do all I want, in the hope that one day I will love him as much as he wants to be loved. As I wanted Bobby to love me, though he never did –

339

Tiredness seemed to fill her and she closed her eyes and rested her head back on her chair. 'I can't think,' she said huskily. 'Or I'm thinking too much. I'm not sure which.'

'Do you love me, Poppy?' he said and she stared into the pink-tinged darkness behind her lids and tried to be honest, more because she needed that honesty for herself than for him.

'Yes,' she said at length. 'I love you. But it's not the way you love me – '

'You can't know that!' His voice sounded louder and stronger now and she had to open her eyes to look at him. He was sitting very straight and staring at her and his whole face seemed to have a light switched on behind it. 'All that matters is that you love me and – '

'And I love Robin and I love Jessie and – loving comes in so many different ways, for heaven's sake,' she said. 'Surely the sort of love people have for each other when they marry ought to match? I don't think ours matches as it should – '

'Did it match with Bobby?' he asked and some of the light seemed to fade from his face. But not all of it.

She flushed. 'I don't know what you mean,' she said, uneasy because he had so unerringly picked on her own line of thought.

'Oh, yes you do,' he said. 'You loved him. I know. I used to see you there at Revigny and in the little café and – I remember how you looked when you were with him. Incandescent. You would look at him and – oh, God, I was so jealous. Especially as I knew – ' He stopped then, seeming embarrassed.

'Knew what?'

'It doesn't matter – '

'Of course it does! It matters more than – especially because you know what?'

'He'd told me about his first wife,' David said after a long pause and leaned back in his chair and bent his head

340

so that his features were in shadow. 'We used to sit in the dug-out waiting for the push to start, or for the men to come back from the forward trenches, and we'd talk a lot. He told me about Barbara – '

'I see,' she said dully. 'I see.' She felt very strange. He had moved into the heart of the dilemma; picking up with uncanny accuracy her own thoughts. She didn't have to explain, didn't have to spell it out without any dishonesty at all. She could relax and let him take over her pain as he had promised, take over her loneliness and her fears. She could be cared for as a child is, as she cared for Robin. It was a deeply seductive prospect and she let her mind play with it, imagined herself as his wife, living a relaxed and easy life, not having to worry about paying school fees for Robin, not fretting over the rent of the house, shopping when she wanted to, being lazy when she wanted to –

'I can't do it,' she said aloud, not realizing she had spoken her thought at first until she saw his face and he looked stricken. 'Don't look like that!'

'Then you don't care for me as you said you did,' he said. 'For God's sake, why did you say it then? To be polite or something stupid like that? To shut me up? To – '

'No, it wasn't like that!' she cried. 'Truly it wasn't. I do care for you. You – ' She reddened but still went on. 'I want to make love with you. You make me feel very – well, aware of the fact that I'm a woman and you're a man and all that sort of thing. And it's been so marvellous knowing you were there. So comforting. But I know now that – I mean, David, if you can choose a time like this to ask me to marry you, how can we ever be right together? You just don't understand me, do you? To offer yourself as some sort of lifeline when everything couldn't be worse – makes me feel dreadful. As though I'm useless and stupid and helpless – and I'm none of those things. Am I?'

'Of course you're not. And I never for one moment meant you to think I thought so – '

'But that's the point! What you want and what happened are two different things. I feel bad enough about not having an income or a source of it any more. Do you think you make me feel any better saying you'll marry me and keep me? It's as though all I've done all these years, all my adult life really, has been nothing. I've worked and looked after people but now, when for the first time I'm looking at a situation where it's difficult, you come along and wave a hand as though none of my problems are really important, you can solve them all with a wedding ring.'

There was a long silence and then he nodded. 'I see,' he said. 'Like I said before, timing – '

'It goes a little deeper than that.'

'It was just that I couldn't bear to see you so – well, bereft. I've wanted to ask you for any time this past – oh, months. As soon as I saw you and heard that you – that Bobby – that it would be okay for me to ask. How I didn't say it that first evening on the doorstep I'll never know. And God knows I've tried often enough since. That night when we had dinner in the garden, you remember? We made a deal that night. You said if I stopped talking romance then you'd let me do so when you got back from Cannes. But when you got back you were so distracted, what with Robin's illness and the egregious Bernie being there I said nothing. I made up my mind I wouldn't leave it a minute longer than I had to, and today I reckoned – well, I was wrong. Clearly very wrong.'

He got to his feet and stood looking down at her. 'I know you say you care about me. I know you say you want me – and I guess I should be grateful for that much. But you don't love me, really, do you? That's the real problem.'

'I don't know!' she cried. 'God, I just don't know!

342

Can't you see that? Here am I trying to find out just how well able I am to cope and you come along in the middle and kick the struts out from under me, offering me all that comfort and – how can I know how I feel? Give me some time, please David – '

'Well, if anything sounds like something out of a romantic movie that does. I can see it all – the Southern *belle* in her frills and furbelows telling the luscious Beauregard that he has to give her time to think while she sits and simpers at him and – '

'That is grossly unfair!'

'It may be,' he said grimly. 'But it's what it sounds like to me. I'd hoped you were someone with more sense than all this, Poppy. It's ridiculous to – '

Once again there was a sound above their heads that interrupted them and Poppy looked up and then got swiftly to her feet.

'Hello, Goosey,' she said as easily as she could. 'Is it time to get supper ready? I thought it must be – I'll help you – Mr Deveen is just going – '

'It's all right with me if he stays, Mrs Poppy,' Goosey said and began waddling heavily down the stairs. 'I got enough for the three of you if you fancy it sir. Will you be stopping? I got some nice potatoes, all new ones, very good, lovely little scrapers, and some – '

'No thank you, Goosey,' he said at the same moment that Poppy said, 'Mr Deveen has another appointment – ' And then they both stopped, not looking at each other.

'I'll see myself out,' he said then in a low voice as Goosey reached the kitchen and went over to the sink to start work on her lovely little scrapers, tumbling them into a basin with a little clatter and turning the tap on to them noisily. 'But I'll be back.'

'Please,' she said, and moved away towards the staircase. 'Please don't go like this. I mean, I do think it's time you went but not – '

343

'Not bad friends,' he murmured and looked over her shoulder to Goosey's back; but clearly she was oblivious of them, industriously scraping her potatoes. 'I could never be that. I was mad, but I'll get over that. And I'll be back. I may have timed this crazily wrong but it takes more than that to put an end to me. I love you, you see – '

And with one more glance at Goosey, he put both hands on her shoulders and before she knew what was happening had bent his head to kiss her. His mouth was hot and his tongue pushed hard against her closed lips and forced them open and she felt the sensation go through her as far as her feet, leaving out no part of her body in between. It was a shockingly exciting sensation that made her burn as though she had been doused in hot water and without realizing what she was doing she arched her back so that she pushed her body against his, clinging to him with both hands at his waist, digging in her fingers to hold on.

He lifted his head at last just when she thought she'd never be able to breathe again and grinned down at her. 'Oh, yes,' he said loudly and with a note of exultancy in his voice. 'Oh, yes,' not seeming to care whether Goosey heard him or not. 'I'll be back.' And then went running up the stairs, his coat flapping open behind him, to vanish through the door into the hall.

She stood staring up absurdly at the place where he had been, amazed and very shaken. She had meant every word she had said. She did love him, but not as she had loved Bobby; she did not want to be offered marriage now, when everything was so disordered in her life; but that kiss had done something very odd indeed to her, and now she drew the back of one hand across her mouth, trying to erase the sensation. Because it made it very hard for her to think clearly.

Goosey turned away from the sink, bearing a saucepan in her hands, to set it on the stove.

'I'll have it all ready in about half an hour, Mrs Poppy,' she said placidly and Poppy turned and looked at her, startled. It was as though nothing had happened at all, as though it was just an ordinary evening and she opened her mouth to remonstrate with Goosey for being so very matter-of-fact at such a moment, and then stopped, amazed at her own silliness. It had only been a matter of seconds after all. Goosey hadn't even noticed, and why should she, half deaf as she was. She, Poppy, was being absurd and really must stop behaving so. There were important things to be thought about, and tomorrow she must set out even more vigorously on job finding. Even if it was an ordinary lowly position. The sooner she was back on some sort of steady keel the sooner she would be able to think sensibly instead of in this stupid way she had been this past few days.

'I'll lay the table,' she said then and began to move around the kitchen quietly, spreading the cloth, putting out knives and forks and plates and napkins and finding it a soothing occupation. Dealing with the minutiae of ordinary domesticity always helped and she thought – we'll have supper and then I'll bath Robin and see her to bed. Goosey can rest and I'll have the time to talk to her and be comfortable with the child. It's been hateful since I left the office; I've been so wrapped up in myself that poor Robin will be feeling awful. And as she finished the table laying she stretched her back and said happily, 'I'll go and call Robin then, Goosey, shall I? Then after supper I'll see to her bath and bed, and you can have an early night – '

Goosey was drying her hands on her apron and already moving across the kitchen to the stairs. 'No, Mrs Poppy. I'll fetch her. I have to put away her ironing and that. I took it up before but didn't stop to put it away. You just keep an eye on those vegetables for me, and if the soup boils up, move it to the back of the hob, will you? We

345

won't be long – ' And she was off, climbing the stairs laboriously before Poppy could stop her.

She sat down in Goosey's chair again, and once more leaned her head back and tried to doze. She didn't want to think about David at all and the only way she could avoid that was by deliberately trying to sleep, even for ten minutes. It was a skill she had learned long ago in her ambulance driving and nursing days and valued it highly. It helped greatly to be able to take a little nap to refresh herself when –

She felt as though she had been deeply asleep for hours rather than for just the few moments she knew it had been and she sat bolt upright and stared up the stairs as Goosey's voice echoed in her ears.

'Mrs Poppy,' she called again from the landing. 'Mrs Poppy. Did Miss Robin say to you she was doing her homework?'

'What? Why, yes, of course she did – ' Poppy blinked and then shook her head to rid herself of the sleepiness that clung to her. 'Why?'

'Well, she's not in her room, you see. I thought perhaps she'd come down when I wasn't looking – I went to my own room to get the ironing I'd took up and left there on account of I'd forgotten, to tell the truth, where I'd put it, and when I went to her room she wasn't there – ' She stopped uncertainly. 'Maybe she's in your bedroom, Mrs Poppy. I mean, she can't be far, can she?'

Poppy frowned. 'Of course not! Did you call her?'

'Well, yes,' Goosey said uneasily. 'But I can't shout like I used to, do I? I mean, maybe she didn't hear me – '

'I'll find her,' Poppy said and went to run up the stairs to the little landing and patted Goosey's fat shoulder reassuringly. 'Little wretch – she's just not paying attention. Lost in a book, I dare say. You know how she is.'

'Yes,' Goosey said, but still sounded very uneasy indeed. 'But all the same – '

But Poppy had gone, running up the stairs and calling cheerfully, 'Robin? Where are you, darling? Time for supper soon. Time to wash your hands. Do come along, now – '

But there was no comfortable answering call and Poppy ran right up to the attics to peer into all the rooms, including the two small empty ones full of the collected detritus of the years, and nowhere was Robin to be seen. In her own room there were just the piles of her school books on her desk, and her satchel on the floor; and then Poppy felt a sudden chill. There was no sign of her coat or hat, both of which she usually tossed onto her toy box in the corner (a habit for which Goosey constantly upbraided her) and she stood there for a long moment and then went running headlong down the stairs.

'Goosey!' she cried as she reached the hall; and then the front door opened, and she whirled, full of sudden hope. Robin never went out on her own, of course, but maybe for some reason or other she – ?

But it was not Robin. Chloe was standing there on the mat, pushing her key into her coat pocket and she looked up at Poppy as she began to pull off her hat and stared at her.

Poppy felt a bitter disappointment at the sight of her; she should have been Robin, of course she should, and she bit back her anger as she saw the girl's pale drawn face. It wasn't her fault she wasn't Robin after all; and she turned to go down to the kitchen to call Goosey and see if together they could find out where Robin was hiding, as it was now clear what the silly and rather naughty child was doing. But Chloe's voice called her back.

'Poppy,' she said. 'There's something I'd like to talk to you about. I mean, I have to talk to you about. I don't know what to do, you see and I thought perhaps you could tell me – '

'What?' Poppy stood there, hovering, aching to go down to the kitchen. 'Is it important, Chloe? I haven't time right now, dear. I really haven't. It's Robin, you see. We can't find her – look, just let me find her, the silly child – I dare say she's playing hide-and-seek – and then of course I can talk. Come down to supper, will you? Goosey has enough for all of us, of course she has, and we can talk then – but forgive me now – '

And she fled down the kitchen stairs calling, 'Goosey, is she hiding do you think? Where does she like to hide if she plays with the other children, Goosey?'

29

Chloe stood on the doormat and listened as Poppy's voice receded down to the kitchen, calling out something disjointed about Robin, and the anger that rose in her made her feel suddenly shaky. It had taken her all this afternoon to make up her mind to speak to Poppy about whether to keep the appointment or not, and now she had behaved like this; and she pulled her hat back on to her tousled head and turned with a sharp little movement and went out again.

It was dark outside now, with the light from the street lamps glowing softly in the wet pavements and she shivered a little and pulled her coat collar up round her ears, but it wasn't the cold that made her so tremulous. It was because she had made up her mind, or had it made up for her, she corrected herself, by Poppy's refusal to talk to her. She *would* go to Knightsbridge; and she went running along the pavement and out to the main road, her heels clicking noisily on the paving stones, letting her anger with Poppy thicken and curdle inside her.

Not that she was being entirely fair, she knew that, but it didn't make things better. She was angry and frightened and shaking inside and someone had to be blamed for all of that. Why not Poppy, who by being so busy over her wretched Robin had let her down so badly?

The internal arguments kept her going all through the taxi ride over to the other side of the park as it took her rattling along Park Lane past the early diners and the top-hatted strollers and then into Knightsbridge before plunging into the network of small streets that lay behind St George's hospital. It wasn't until the cab pulled up in front of a very small house in a mews and the cabbie reached out and rang down his flag that she realized just how far she had come, and for a moment she cowered into the corner of the cab, too scared to get out.

The man looked over his shoulder and said crossly, 'Well, Miss? Ain't this where you asked for? Seventeen Wilmington Mews – just orf Knightsbridge you said. Well this is it. That'll be one an' ninepence if you please. I got an 'ome to go to, you know, even if some other people ain't – '

Somehow she managed to get out of the cab, in spite of shaking knees and paid him, pushing a florin into his hand and turning to stare up at the house. The driver, somewhat mollified by his tip, muttered goodnight and put the cab into motion with a crash of the gears and went noisily away, and she stood there and stared up, holding her bag close to her chest, too scared to move any further.

The house was small and neat and looked thoroughly nondescript. There were several others like it along the tiny street, one or two with boxes of frostbitten geraniums on their window sills, but this one was shuttered and dim and she thought with a sudden surge of hope – maybe it's a mistake. Maybe he's not here and I can just go home and – and what?

And at the impossibility of imagining beyond the point when she got home again in the same state as she had been in when she had left, she found the impetus she needed to take her to the doorway and to pull the bell.

Nothing happened for fully half a minute and again she thought – I can just go home and forget all about it. Maybe it's all a silly mistake, anyway. Maybe it isn't true and I'm all worried over nothing.

But she couldn't keep her belief in that outcome afloat. It sank inside her mind like a rock and she felt the wave of sick terror wash over her yet again, the same wave she had felt so many times ever since the possibility had first crossed her mind that she had a major problem to contend with. She had to lean against the wall beside the door until the sick feeling passed.

The door opened then, silently and with such suddenness that she jumped and again felt the rush of fear, though less urgently this time. A man was standing and he looked at her with eyes that gleamed a little behind his glasses and said, 'Ah, Miss um – Brown, is it? Do come in –'

She managed somehow to make one leg move in front of the other as he stood there with the door held half open, and at last walked in; and he quickly looked over her shoulder to the deserted street outside, and, apparently satisfied, quietly closed the door behind her and stood and stared at her in the hallway as she stared back at him.

He was a small man, not much taller than she was herself, and very neat. He had a round pink face with a fringe of white hair round an equally round pink skull and rather thick glasses behind which blue eyes peered in an apparently amiable manner. But there was a glitter in them that she didn't like and she let her own gaze slide away to take in the rest of the place she was in.

It was, she realized at once, redolent of money; thick white carpet, walls clad in pale green Chinese silk hangings, low lamps with costly coloured glass shades, and everywhere scent, a rather queasy mixture of roses and, she thought, lilies of the valley, and something else. And she took a deep breath and once more fear filled her; for it was antiseptic. It made her suddenly dreadfully aware of why she was here and she moved involuntarily towards the door.

351

'You're alone, my dear? A pity,' the man murmured and took her arm in what seemed a gentle but was in fact a hard and tight grip. 'But no need to be afraid. My nurse and I will take exceptional care of you, *exceptional*. You will come to no harm. And above all it is all quite confidential. There is no need at all for you to have any fears or doubts on that score. Your name – and I am sure the one we have is not your own, of course, for why should it be? – will never be told to anyone else. There will be no connection with you in any way, so you see there is no need for this anxiety on your part – '

Talking all the time in the same soft and rather monotonous voice he half led, half pulled her towards a door at the far end of the small hallway, in the shadow of the staircase that ran up on the left hand side, and he pushed it open with his foot and manoeuvred her in in front of him and then closed it firmly behind them both.

Inside she stood stock-still and tried not to look around. But she had to. There was the same smell in the air, though it was intensified here, but the appearance of the room was quite different. A severe desk stood against one wall, and on another a consulting couch was set so that its head was blocked by the wall but the sides were left unencumbered, and she looked at it in horrible fascination. It was covered in shiny black material of some kind and partly covered with a white sheet, and beside it there was a humped table with a similar sheet thrown over it. She stared at that the hardest of all, trying not to imagine what might lie beneath the shroud that covered it; and then the man beside her spoke softly now.

'Now, Miss – um – Brown, here is my nurse Miss Jennings, and a dear woman, I know you'll agree. Miss Jennings, here is Miss Brown, a little nervous you know, but I am sure you can deal with that. Now, my dear, I will get myself ready – we do all here with great fastidiousness you know, all very clean and nice, none of your

352

nastiness, oh dear me no – while Miss Jennings is arranging matters – ' And he patted her hand and went past her to another door at the far side and disappeared through it, his feet clattering on the linoleum-covered floor. Chloe looked down at it and saw the black and white tiles and felt sick again. It all looked so very clinical and so very terrifying.

Miss Jennings, in full hospital uniform, was brisk to the point of rudeness, with none of her superior's soft emollient charm at all. 'Now, Miss Brown, or whatever it is, first things first. You have the money?'

'Money,' Chloe said a little stupidly and then nodded convulsively. 'Oh, yes, yes. Here it is – '

She reached into her bag with fingers shaking and slippery with sweat inside her leather gloves to scrabble for the little roll of money Bernie had given her. And suddenly she remembered the getting of it.

It seemed so very long ago that he had done it, but it was only two or three weeks – or was it longer? She couldn't remember clearly now – anyway, on the day he had caught the boat train for Southampton.

'Use it,' he'd said peremptorily. 'You hear me, ducky? Use it for what it's for. Because believe you me, if I come back and you haven't, then forget everything. I won't know you. It'd be like you never was. I can't, you see, in my position. It's not possible. But you use this money right – and believe me old Fanshawe's okay. He's seen a lot of my friends all right – then you'll be fine. And when I get back – and it shouldn't be too long – then we can go on where we left off, and all very nice too. But I don't want no nonsense, you understand, ducky. No encumbrances, no nonsense. So you be a good girl – ' And he had kissed her and slapped her bottom lightly and gone and left her standing there at the barrier as he had led his porter down the platform, to the first class end of the train, whistling as he went.

Now she pulled out the money and pushed it at the nurse and she took it and clicked her tongue in irritation because there was a rubber band round it. She pulled it off and with no attempt at discretion smoothed and then counted it loudly, her fingers flicking through the greasy old notes in a blur of experienced long handling.

'Fifty pounds,' she said briskly. 'It's just for this stage, you understand. If you have to come back for anything it will be extra – '

'Come back?' Chloe said and shrunk back. 'I couldn't come back, not ever. I don't know how I got here to-night – '

'It's up to you,' the nurse said indifferently. 'Some of them say they worry over getting pregnant again when they want to. Well, that's what they say. And they want Dr Fanshawe to check them up. For my part it's all – well, as I say, it'll cost you extra if you do. Now, undress. Take off your knickers and your stockings – and shoes of course. The rest doesn't matter. Climb up on the couch.'

She bustled over to the couch and smoothed the sheet on it, arranging it so that the long strip was perfectly aligned to show a line of waterproof blackness on each side and Chloe looked at it and thought – it's like a coffin. And shuddered again.

'Now, really,' the nurse said sharply. 'We don't have all day you know. It's late already and we have another patient in half an hour. So do please get a move on. You don't want to be still getting ready when Dr Fanshawe comes out, do you? I should think not, indeed! I'll help you, then – '

And she came over to Chloe and with firm hands took her hat from her and then began to tug at her coat.

Somehow it was all done and Chloe found herself lying on the strip of white sheet – which felt as cold on her bare buttocks as though it were the surface of the couch itself – with a flimsy matching white sheet over her. The nurse began to bustle about the trolley, pulling off the cover, and Chloe turned her head and looked and then closed her eyes tightly. All she had seen had been the glitter of chrome and the blinding white of an enamel basin, but that had been enough.

'Now, have you emptied your bladder recently? No, I dare say not. Well, the state of nerves you girls get into I wouldn't trust you anyway. I'll just pop in a catheter – '

The next few minutes were ghastly and she lay there with her face flaming as the nurse without any further ado pushed the sheet that covered her legs right up to her belly and then with one sharp movement made her crook her knees and put her heels together. She was painfully aware of her nakedness as the nurse turned back to her trolley for a moment and then came back to her.

'Now,' she commanded. 'Open your knees – yes, that's it – sideways, of course sideways! It's the only way you can! How can I get to you if you don't – now, don't be so silly.' And with one sharp elbow she dug into the soft part of Chloe's thigh so that she winced and let her legs fall apart, exposing herself completely.

It felt as though she had been impaled on a very long hot piece of very hot iron as the nurse slid the red tube she held in one hand into her and she was almost overwhelmed with the urgent need to pass water, and automatically clenched her muscles; at which the nurse tutted furiously and shoved even harder with her tube. Chloe whimpered a little and then felt shame flood over her as she heard the tinkling gush of water hit the enamel dish. She peered up into the nurse's face then, looking for some sort of sympathy, but the woman just stood there, her starched veil framing her face, staring down at the space between Chloe's legs.

She had thought that was bad enough – and when the nurse pulled the catheter out she went on burning there disagreeably for a long time – but then the door opened and the man reappeared. He had put on a white coat and was looking very severe and Chloe thought – this is a show. It's to make me think it's like a hospital. But it isn't. It's a house in a little hidden street and it smells of scent and I hate it and I hate him and I want to go home – and again she tensed her mucles, this time ready to get to her feet to swing herself off the couch. She would announce, 'I've changed my mind. I won't have it done. I've changed my mind – ' And she would go.

Would you? whispered a secret voice inside her head. It won't go away just because you change your mind –

'Now, Miss – um – Brown – ' Dr Fanshawe said. 'Let's get on, shall we? First, we need a little antiseptic. We really must take all care that we do this as it should be done. We want no nasty problems do we? Of course we don't – '

He did not stop this flow of talk for one moment. The nurse stood grimly beside him and handed him the pieces of chrome and said not a word, but he babbled on and on while doing so many unspeakable things to Chloe that she wanted to scream. But she hadn't the ability to do so. All she could do was lie there with her head back in a great curve so that her neck did not touch the pillow but ached dreadfully and with her face twisted in a rictus of pain as she whimpered her misery. Not that either of them paid her the least attention.

The antiseptic stung cruelly and she had barely been able to cope with that before the worst part happened; he seized a chrome instrument that looked to Chloe to be unbelievably huge, with wide lips like a duck's bill, but bigger, and without stopping to warn her, pushed its coldness into her as the nurse held her knees apart with a grip so firm that her fingers seemed to bite into the soft flesh. At that point Chloe did scream. But neither of them seemed to hear and just continued with what they were doing as though she had made no sound at all. And then there was the sound of metal against metal as he wrenched open the beak of the duck, and she felt herself stretched painfully, and again she cried out, with the same reaction from both of them; total unawareness of her distress. The pain increased then as Fanshawe began to scrape and dig at her. And all she could do was lie there sweating and weeping and sometimes crying out. 'No – stop it, oh, please don't.' But it was as though she weren't there at all, not as a whole person. They never looked at her face, never spoke to her, even though the man went bumbling on and on with his stream of words; but it was quite clear that it was for his own and the nurse's benefit and not for her at all.

And then at last it was over. The great piece of chrome was pulled out of her so suddenly that it hurt again, but at least it was blessedly gone and the nurse thrust a large pad against her body, and fastened it in place with a strip of bandage tied round her waist.

'It will be like a heavy period for a few days,' she said brusquely. You'll need maternity pads. I'll give you one for tonight but you'll have to buy your own for tomorrow. Take plenty of fluids and make sure you get some iron to make up. You'll be anaemic if you don't.'

The doctor had gone now, and the nurse stood there looking down at her and the sneer that had been in her voice throughout was visible on her face now.

'And it if happens again you'll need another fifty pounds,' she said. 'But for your sort I daresay that's no problem, is it? Get dressed, and you can go as soon as you like. There's a chair out in the hall if you want to rest. You'll probably get a taxi in the main road – '

Chloe managed to drag herself up and to get her legs over the side of the couch. She felt shivery now with cold, for she was still damp with sweat.

'Please, can't someone get one for me?' she managed. 'I don't feel at all well – '

357

'I dare say you don't,' the nurse said. 'But you should have thought of this when you had your fun, shouldn't you? You bright young things – isn't that what they call you? Well, you don't look so bright now and you won't feel it either. Like I say, a bit more thought and you'd do better. You girls are really – but I dare say my opinion won't matter to you. Your sort don't care about anyone but yourselves, do you? Well, you've nothing left here to care about – ' And she picked up the dish from the trolley and looked down into it. 'This one's good and dead – '

Chloe stared at her, feeling anger rise in her again and shook her head to clear the dizziness that was still there. 'Why do you hate me?' she managed in a husky voice. 'What have I done to you?'

'Done to me?' the nurse said and turned her head away. 'Done to me? You've done for this – ' And she looked in the dish again. 'But you've done nothing to me. Mind you, I trained to look after the ill, not to deal with the likes of you. You make me sick, if you must know. And you can tell whoever sent you here the same – '

'Then why are you here? Why do you work here?' It suddenly mattered to Chloe to know why this woman was so hateful to her. Hadn't she suffered enough? Hadn't she been hurt dreadfully, lying there on that dreadful couch? And shouldn't nurses be kind and caring – and she blinked back the tears and said again, 'Why?'

'I have to work somewhere, don't I?' the nurse said scathingly. 'I've got a living to earn. With my hands, not on my back, like some.'

And she turned and went, leaving Chloe alone in the room to dress as best she could. It was not until she was at last back into her coat and hat and out on the street that she realized what it was the nurse had meant with her parting words, and then she really was sick, standing by a lamp post out in the mews and vomiting into the gutter.

30

Poppy stretched her stiff back very carefully and moving equally gingerly, flexed her arms slightly to try to ease the pins and needles that were burning there. Robin stirred and moved her head heavily against Poppy's chest, but she didn't wake and Poppy looked down at her, and touched her warm cheek with one finger.

On the other side of the drawing-room Mildred sat, looking somewhat incongruous, perched as straight-backed as ever on Poppy's oriental-style sofa, but clearly contented enough. She too was looking at Robin and the expression on her face was a benign one.

'I think, you know, that she will sleep for a long time,' she said quietly. 'The child was exhausted when she reached me.'

Poppy looked up at her and managed a smile. 'Thank you, Mamma. You'll never know how grateful I am. When you appeared on the doorstep with her – I – well, I can't tell you. I was frantic – '

'I know. It doesn't help to get over-anxious, of course, but I can understand. There was an occasion once when – ' She stopped, and then after a moment continued stiffly, 'I don't suppose you remember, but I once had to leave you with someone who – who turned out to be less than reliable. I can remember how I felt then about you. So you tonight – well, I hope it will not happen again.'

'I won't let it,' Poppy said fervently. 'I won't ever let

it. I'll never let her feel that way again, no matter what.'

'I hope you won't send him away,' Mildred said and lifted her brows at Poppy. 'That would be very unwise.'

Poppy frowned sharply. 'What? But of course I must!' In her surprise at Mildred's words she had forgotten to whisper, and Robin once more stirred in her arms and she looked down at her anxiously, and then, as the child slept on, went on in a low voice, 'Of course I must! What else can I do, if the mere thought of the possibility of my remarrying upsets her so? It would be wicked to distress her so again – '

'It would be more wicked, my dear Poppy, to allow her to believe she can run your life for you,' Mildred said. 'That would be too difficult for her altogether. Children require to feel that their parents are in charge, not that they are. I believe that very strongly. It is soon enough that they begin to make their own decisions, after all, and not always in their own best interests. You, for example, refusing university – No, I shall say no more on that. But do understand that a child as young as Robin should not be allowed to feel she has so much power. It is too heavy a burden for her.'

Poppy stared at her and then said a little uncertainly, 'I see what you mean – but what can I do? If I do decide to marry – oh, for heaven's sake!' And again she looked down on Robin. 'I don't know why I'm even talking about it. I told him I didn't want to. I was very angry with him.'

'Angry?' Mildred lifted her brows. 'From what Robin said I understood that she overheard a perfectly proper proposal of marriage.

'Oh, it was. Perfectly proper. You would have approved, Mamma. He wants to look after me, to take my problems from me, to pay my bills – ' And she flushed suddenly at the memory of it. 'It made me very angry indeed.'

Mildred looked at her curiously. 'How strange you are!

360

Why should that make you angry? That is what husbands should do. Take care of their wives.'

'But you never married, Mamma,' Poppy said very deliberately and looked directly at Mildred. 'You chose to take care of me on your own rather than accept my father.' And she lifted her brows interrogatively at her mother who sat silently looking down at her hands clasped on her lap.

This was not a subject they talked about any more, her parent's past history. It had been a bad time, a painful time, long ago when Poppy had first learned of it and discovered the facts about her own birth and the identity of her father, and equally painful when she, Poppy, had found him for herself after years of not knowing of his existence. She and Mildred had avoided the pain ever since those days by simply not speaking of it. But tonight was different; tonight Robin had let loose a great flood of feeling by her action. It was as though she had pulled a cork out of a bottle that had been long sealed and which was now pouring out its contents in an uncontrolled cascade.

There was a long silence and then Mildred lifted her head. 'That is hardly fair,' she said. 'Your – your father was not as Mr Deveen is. I find him a most delightful person, full of good feelings and sense.'

'My father was too,' Poppy said shortly and looked down at Robin again, still sleeping deeply in her web of blankets and curled against her mother's warm body in total abandonment.

Again there was silence and then Mildred sighed softly. 'I must say I am sad to hear you have sent Mr Deveen away,' she said. 'It is clear to me that he cares a great deal for you. I have watched him – at Robin's birthday party, for example. And I was of the opinion that you cared for him.'

Poppy did not look at her, trying not to let her words

get into her mind, but it was not possible to prevent it. Of course she cared for David. She did more than care; she wanted him, physically, in a way she had forgotten was possible for her. And she had not sent him away; she had simply made it clear to him that he had chosen the wrong moment to offer her marriage and had chosen the wrong reasons for doing so. One day, she knew at a deep level, she would change all that. One day she would accept him. How could she say no to him, feeling as she did? .

But equally how could she say yes? Robin had been so alarmed at the prospect she had behaved in what was for her an extraordinary manner. She had gone out alone, had made the really very long journey for a seven year old to her grandmother's house, had told her, of all people, of how unhappy she was. The child to whom she had always felt so close and who she had believed trusted and loved her enough to speak to her at any time of any worry had turned her back on her and gone to Mildred. It hurt dreadfully, and Poppy bent her head and set her cheek against Robin's smooth warm face and wanted to weep.

'I would not make any firm decision on the matter at present,' Mildred said then. 'You are tired and anxious over what happened. Wait till later, when you and Robin can speak comfortably. Then you can decide. But please allow me to advise you – remember not to give her too great a burden of decision.'

'I'll remember,' Poppy said. 'And now I suppose I must try to get her into bed.'

'I would say so,' Mildred said dryly. 'It's almost eleven o'clock, you know?'

'Is it so late?' Poppy said, horrified. 'Oh, Mamma, I am so sorry. You're always in bed long before this.'

'Indeed I am,' Mildred allowed. 'But it is not a usual evening, after all. Perhaps you can ask Goosey to fetch a cab for me so that I can return home – '

Poppy looked anxious. 'But she's gone to bed,

Mamma. Once she knew that Robin was all right, I had to send her there. She was so very upset and quite shaky. She's ageing so fast these days.'

'Ah. Then, Chloe perhaps?'

Poppy's expression hardened. 'She's in bed too. She came in just after you arrived with Robin. I was so anxious and she knew I was, for I'd told her before but she had gone out – and then came back and went straight to her room. She is really becoming more and more selfish with every day that passes.'

'She is a sad girl,' Mildred said unexpectedly. 'You do not really understand her, do you? I have a considerable sympathy for her, tiresome though I know she can be. But we should not speak of her now. So, I cannot get home without walking to Holland Park Avenue and hoping to find a cab passing by – '

'You will do nothing of the sort,' Poppy said decidedly, and moving very slowly got to her feet, humping Robin up to her shoulder more firmly. 'You will stay here. You may telephone home to tell Queenie so that she won't fret and you shall sleep in my bed. I had every intention of sharing with Robin tonight, anyway. She may have one of her terrors after the stress of the day, and I want to be there. So there'll be no problem – '

Mildred looked uncertain. 'I have no toothbrush, no fresh clothes for the morning, no – '

'A toothbrush I can provide. And a wrapper. As for fresh clothes – tell Queenie to send one of the younger maids over in a cab in the morning with whatever you need. I'll certainly not hear of you wandering around Holland Park Avenue looking for a taxi at this time of night, so don't argue with me – '

'I do not intend to,' Mildred said calmly and got up as well. 'Do you need any help putting Robin to bed?'

'No, she'll be fine,' Poppy murmured. 'Just let me settle her and then I'll see to whatever you need – '

'I always have warm milk late at night,' Mildred said. 'I shall fetch it for myself,' and she went off downstairs leaving Poppy to carry her sleeping daughter up to bed.

She settled her easily, sliding her between the sheets and gently taking away the blanket in which they had wrapped her after she had been bathed and put into her nightdress, with Goosey fussing and exclaiming over her in a continuous stream of scolding and loving and scolding again. Poppy stood there looking down on Robin for a long time, at the way her curly hair spread on the pillow and the curve of her arm, flung back over her head, and then bent and tucked her in, pulling the covers snugly around her as a wordless murmur of thanks to Providence, or whatever force it was that had brought her safe home, went threading through her mind. She had never had much interest in religious matters, for Mildred had had her own cogent reasons for avoiding giving her daughter any sense of religious commitment, but tonight she felt a sense of gratitude and wonder that she had lost her child and found her again and needed to show her feelings to something or someone. She knew it had been a minor affair; in most people's eyes it would be nothing to make any fuss over. Her little girl had disappeared for two or three hours and had been found in the care of her grandmother. Hardly an important event. But to Poppy it had been a very major experience that had shaken her to her foundations. It had given her an awareness of her own needs in her child, of her child's needs in her, that startled her in their power.

She left the light burning and then brought sheets and blankets and a pillow from the airing cupboard to make up the sofa against the wall into a bed for herself for the night. She had used it many times before, over the very young years when Robin had needed nursing through the fevers and coughs of infancy, and it would be no hardship to use it again tonight.

364

And it would be agreeable, she thought as she smoothed the sheets into place and plumped up the pillow, to have her mother in the house overnight. She could not remember when she had last felt so warm towards Mildred; for a long time now she had regarded her as a responsibility, a duty, even sometimes, somewhat of a burden. But not tonight. Tonight she had been the proverbial tower of strength and it comforted Poppy greatly to have her near her. And she must carefully, she told herself as she went to her own bedroom to fetch her nightwear and to find the items that Mildred needed, very carefully indeed, about what Mildred had said about David. That thought had to be given to Robin's feelings in the matter was obvious; but she must not be burdened –

She was deep in thought as she went quietly past the staircase to her own bedroom door, and then, as she reached for the knob she stopped. She had heard a sound from above and after a moment of puzzled listening she went back to the foot of the stairs and peered up. Only Goosey and Chloe had their rooms on that floor; could it be that Goosey was ill? She had had a severe shock, poor old dear. It would not be amazing if now she was showing some reaction to the fear she had suffered when Robin had not been in the house and they had worried so about how to find her.

But there was only silence from above and she was about to turn away to return to her bedroom when she stopped again. Perhaps the cry she had heard – and she was sure that it had been a rather thin mewing sort of sound rather like a tired baby – had been Goosey in a weak state? Perhaps she was too worn out to call again? And now the idea had come into her head she had to act on it.

Mildred had appeared now at the top of the staircase from the ground floor and she looked enquiringly at

365

Poppy over the small tray she was bearing with a steaming cup and saucer on it.

'Is she asleep still?' she asked. 'I hope she didn't wake – '

'What? Oh, Robin – no, bless her, she's fast asleep. It wasn't her I was concerned about. I thought I heard someone cry out – '

Mildred lifted her head and listened and after a while shook it. 'I hear nothing.'

'Nor I now. Let me get you to bed and then if all is quiet I'll not worry. But I'll pop up and check on Goosey before I settle for the night. Just to make sure all is well. She had a bad day, poor dear soul – '

'Fiddlesticks,' Mildred said crisply. 'I'll come too. Come along – ' And she set her hot milk down on the table outside Poppy's door and went to the staircase; and after a moment's hesitation, Poppy followed her.

It was silent upstairs too. The top landing was lit by a small bulb in a pink shade and they stood in its rosy light listening and then, moving carefully, Poppy opened Goosey's door.

They could hear her then; the thick burring sound that was the snore of an exhausted sleeper and after a moment, Poppy closed the door again.

'That's all right then,' she said with relief. 'I dare say I was misled. A cat outside, probably. Go on down, Mamma, and I'll follow you.'

Mildred went, and Poppy lingered for another moment or two as she saw her mother reach the landing and walk to her bedroom door, before reaching for the light switch to turn it off and then follow her. And then stopped again.

The sound had come again and now she knew it was from Chloe's room and she stood there for a long moment trying to decide what to do. Chloe had made that odd mewing little cry, but it could have been in her sleep. Or it could have been just a way of drawing attention to herself after an evening in which her half-sister had been the centre of everyone's concern; that would be very like Chloe, Poppy told herself with some bitterness. There was no doubt that the antipathy that existed between them was very strong in Poppy tonight. She had been so frightened over Robin, so very alarmed and so grateful when she had come home bedraggled and tearstained. Chloe had walked into the middle of that just as she had when Robin had first vanished; and had shown no interest at all. And for a moment Poppy had hated her for being so self-centred and so oblivious of everyone else. She had stared at Chloe who was white-faced and bleak, and had thought for a moment – she's miserable about something – but then had begun to tell her what had happened with Robin, so very full of the excitement of having her home, but Chloe had just shaken her head at her and turned and gone upstairs without saying a word. And Poppy had watched her go, full of hurt and anger and to an extent surprise. Even Chloe had never been quite so horrid before.

And now there were little mewing sounds, cries, coming from her room. The proper thing would be to go in and see if she were all right. Crying out was not, after all, her normal behaviour. Yet still Poppy lingered, and stared at the door from behind which now there was just silence.

Mildred appeared again at the foot of the stairs looking upwards.

'Is everything all right?' she called softly.

'What? Oh, yes,' Poppy said after a moment and went hurrying down the stairs. 'I'll find you a toothbrush. I have a couple put away. And you'll need a nightdress. Mine, I know, will fit you though they're not the sort you like. Crêpe de Chine, I'm afraid, instead of winceyette – '

'It's not important for one night,' Mildred said equably and followed Poppy into her room.

It was forty minutes later, when Mildred had said goodnight and retired with her hot milk and Poppy had herself washed and brushed her teeth, that she thought again of Chloe. She was sitting on the edge of her make-shift bed in Robin's room, brushing her hair a little dreamily, staring across at the humped shape in the little bed, and thinking vaguely grateful thoughts when the memory of that odd little cry came back into her mind so vividly it was as though she heard it again. But she knew she hadn't; it was her imagination, and after a moment she pulled off her dressing gown and pushed back the sheets and blankets ready to get into bed.

But somehow she couldn't; and she sighed then and put her dressing gown back on and went padding over to the door. She'd listen once more to Goosey, she told herself, make sure all was well, before she turned in; and with that piece of mendacious thinking to support her, went upstairs.

Goosey was of course still snoring. Poppy had known she would be. And she stopped outside Chloe's door and thought for a while and then with a sharp little noise, almost an impatient one, opened it. She was being absurd of course, but now she was up here, she might as well –

The bedside light was on, which was the first surprise and she stood in the doorway and looked in, past the usual messiness of clothes left on the floor and strewn over the dressing table and the tallboy, to the bed. The covers were rumpled and the pillows all awry and in the middle of them Chloe lay stretched out. The covers were pushed back and Poppy could now see clearly what had happened and went swiftly across the room to the bed and looked down in horror.

There was a broad patch of blood across the sheet, and Chloe's cream silk nightdress was bloody too. She was lying with her hands thrown over her head and sleeping, it seemed, though her eyes were not fully closed, leaving a rim of white clearly seen beneath the line of lashes, and she was breathing much too rapidly for normal sleep.

'Chloe?' Poppy said uncertainly and put her hand out towards her and at once the eyes flew open and Chloe lay there staring at her with wide and at first unseeing eyes. But then she focused and opened her mouth and the same odd mewling little sound came out and Poppy let her knees fold beneath her as she crouched down beside the bed and said urgently, 'Chloe! What is it? What has happened?'

'Please, Poppy – ' she said and now her voice sounded almost its normal self though it was breathless. 'Please, Poppy, I need some pads. I – it's a heavy period. She said it would be like a heavy period – but it's never been like this. Oh, Poppy, please help me. I'm so frightened. Poppy, please do something to help me. I'm so very scared – '

31

'No,' Mildred said firmly. 'No doctor.' She was standing at the side of the bed looking down at Chloe and then slid her eyes sideways to look at Poppy. 'You must see what will happen if you let a doctor see her! It is illegal. He will have to report it to the police. It causes great – problems.' She looked again at Chloe. 'It happened once to one of our maids and I recall the outcome well. The girl was taken to court. All very disagreeable.'

'To court – ' Poppy said. 'My God! I hadn't – but we have to do something – Chloe – tell me exactly what happened. Properly and calmly. You're all right at present, I do promise you, but I have to know what happened to make a decision about what to do next, courts or not.'

Chloe was lying flat on the bed, with no pillows, and looking pale and exhausted but less agitated than she had been. Poppy's first reaction had been one of horror, but her second had been practical and almost automatic. The time she had spent in the ambulance service had come to her aid and moving with despatch she had set to work on Chloe, tipping the foot of her bed up on a pile of books, to help slow the bleeding, and then examining her as best she could as she cleaned her up.

To Poppy's great relief it had been obvious that though the bleeding was heavy it was not uncontrolled. It had looked horrendous at first, but Poppy knew better than most just how little blood was needed to create the appearance of an abattoir. Chloe, she estimated, had lost perhaps two ounces or so, but it had made a dreadful mess and frightened her greatly. But her pulse was steady and she showed no signs of physical shock, only of emotional stress. And that was indeed understandable.

As she had washed her, and put her into a clean night-dress and clean bedding, Poppy had questioned her and at first Chloe had just babbled and made no sense at all, but then slowly, it had all come out. The story of the small house in the mews, the hatefulness of the nurse and the dreadfulness of the neat little doctor's great chrome instruments, all of it. And as she had moved softly around Chloe, doing all that was necessary, Poppy had felt a great wave of pity wash over her. The child had been through a dreadful experience at uncaring hands, and had suffered it alone. No one ever should have to experience such a thing, not ever.

And then Mildred had appeared at the door, and Poppy had cursed softly beneath her breath when she saw her. She had tried to be very quiet but with Chloe's room immediately above the one where Mildred was it had been clearly impossible not to alert her, and now there she stood, looking rather odd in Poppy's blue silk wrapper over a crêpe de Chine nightdress and with her hair in its tight grey plaits hanging over her shoulders.

Chloe had looked at her and then held out both hands in an appealing little gesture and Mildred after a long moment had walked across the room and grasped them and then bent and kissed Chloe's cheek. She seemed to know what had happened without being given an explanation, for she glanced with great composure at the pile of bloodied sheets that Poppy was holding and nodded and said, 'My dear, I am so sorry. I was afraid of something like this.'

'You were – ' Poppy had begun and Mildred had nodded again.

'I had imagined it had occurred to you that there would be tears at the end of it? After all, was not that why you were so angry with Jessie? Didn't you expect something of this nature?'

'I did not – ' Poppy said sharply. 'I was anxious, obviously. I saw him as trouble for Chloe from the word go, of course I did. I've known him too long, he and his dishonesty and his selfishness, to expect otherwise. But I didn't imagine anything as specific as *this*, for heaven's sake – but Mamma, really this is no time to talk. We can worry about him later – right now I'll have to call the doctor – '

Now, looking down at Chloe's weary little face Poppy knew that Mildred had been right to be so definite about not calling him. The family doctor, old Hetherington, was a good enough man, kind and bluff in his treatment of Robin's childish complaints and generally easy to get along with, but trying to imagine him being sensible and discreet about Chloe's dilemma? Poppy could not visualize that at all. He was a dogmatic sort of man, she remembered, with many strong views on many matters which he expressed freely. If he chose to be difficult about this situation he could create great problems for Chloe. Who had clearly had enough already.

'I'll get rid of all this,' she said then. 'And then we'll see how things are. Chloe, if we can avoid getting a doctor we will. Or perhaps I can call the one who did this – '

'No!' Chloe cried and turned beseeching eyes on her. 'Oh, Poppy, please don't. I couldn't bear it – he was very – he wouldn't come anyway, not without a lot of money. It was fifty pounds and the nurse said I'd have to pay again if I had to go back and – '

'Fifty pounds!' Poppy said. 'Good God! You spent fifty pounds on – '

'It wasn't mine,' Chloe said then and turned her head on the pillow fretfully and looked again at Mildred. 'You would have paid it, though, if you'd been me, wouldn't you? Wouldn't you? If you'd been in that state and he'd gone away and told you you had to do it or he'd never talk to you again and – you'd have done it, wouldn't you?'

Poppy sat down on the edge of the bed and reached across and set her hands on each side of Chloe's face and with a firm but gentle movement made her turn and look at her.

'Chloe, you really must explain more clearly, and tell me of *all* that happened. All, you understand? First of all, are you saying that Bernie gave you the money for this? That he *knew* you were pregnant? He's been gone for a long time, after all – '

'Yes,' Chloe muttered and tried not to look at Poppy, but she was still holding her face between her hands and Chloe could not evade her gaze. 'Yes, of course he knew. I told him as soon as I – as soon as I thought perhaps – we'd been so happy then. At Cannes and everything – when Aunt Jessie fetched him to keep me company I was so glad and he was so sweet and after all that happened with my leg and everything – ' And she stopped and swallowed hard, and closed her eyes, unable to look at Poppy any longer and Poppy took her hands away from her face and slid one of Chloe's into their grasp instead.

'So, you told him,' she said. 'And he said?'

'I thought we could get married,' Chloe said miserably, her eyes still closed. 'I said to him, I could get married, no one would stop me, not if I asked enough and fussed enough, and anyway with a baby coming and – and he said it was mad, he couldn't tie himself down with a wife let alone kids, they cost too much and I said I had money, all the money Daddy left me but he said how much and when I told him he said it wouldn't last five minutes. So then I said what shall we do and he – '

Tears squeezed themselves under her lids and began to

373

run down her cheeks and after a moment Poppy lifted a corner of the sheet and mopped them away for her and Chloe opened her eyes and looked at her and whispered, 'Thanks,' and then closed them again.

'I'm so sorry, Chloe,' Poppy said after a little silence. 'I'm so sorry. He treated you badly, and I'm truly sorry — '

'And you knew, didn't you?' Chloe said and now she opened her eyes and looked at both of them, one after the other, Mildred on one side of the bed and Poppy on the other. 'You both knew. That was why you were so — why you had that fight with Jessie, and — you knew it would happen — '

'I was afraid he'd treat you badly,' Poppy said carefully. 'I didn't expect this — perhaps I should have — '

'Well, I did,' Mildred said sharply. 'And I told Jessie so. Not that she would listen, of course — '

'You told her?' Poppy said. 'When?'

'When she sent you away from the office,' Mildred said, still sharply. 'I was very angry about it. She had no right — '

'She had no — Mamma!' Poppy said furiously. '*You* had no right to interfere in my life. How dare you?'

'I dare to for the same reason I brought Robin home tonight. I am your mother, and independent woman though you are, that gives me all the right I need to care for you. And for yours.' She looked then at Chloe. 'And Chloe is one of yours, too. One of ours. We all belong together.'

'Belong together — ' Poppy said, her irritation melting away as fast as it had risen and she looked from one to the other, and then reddened and tightened her grasp on Chloe's hand. 'Of course we do. We're all the same, really, and we all belong together. You're right, Mamma. I'm sorry I snapped at you. You *are* right — there's you and Chloe and Robin and me — all of us. Goosey too. All women, all together! No matter what the men do to some of us – '

The room slid into silence then as Chloe lay there quietly between them and then she sighed, a long soft sound that ended in a muffled sob.

'I've been such a fool,' she whispered. 'I thought you hated me.'

'If I hated you, I wouldn't care what you did, silly girl,' Poppy said as gently as she could. 'You exasperate me and you make life very difficult for me sometimes, but I care a lot about you. How can I not? You're Bobby's daughter, and my step-daughter. Of course I care about you.'

'But not as much as you care about Robin,' Chloe muttered. 'You love her more than me.'

The silence came back and Poppy stared down at her and thought – is this why? Is this the reason for the long years of arguments and misery? For me it was always so, the way she was. I was sure she hated me and that was why she behaved to me as she did. But perhaps it wasn't hate? Perhaps she wanted me? I never thought she cared about me, but perhaps she did? If she didn't, why be jealous of Robin?

'Chloe,' she said abruptly. 'Does it matter to you who I love?'

Chloe's eyes were still tightly shut. 'Don't know what you mean,' she mumbled.

'Yes, you do. You seem distressed that I love Robin. Does that matter to you?'

'Of course it does,' Chloe said crossly and her eyes opened sharply. 'Of course it does! You spoil her. I never get a chance to talk to you – I wanted to tell you Bernie had told me to go to this doctor, that I'd made this appointment and I didn't want to go, and I wanted to tell you and ask you what to do and all you did was go on about Robin – '

375

Poppy took a deep breath. It was as though she was seeing Chloe clearly for the first time, as though the years of irritations and arguments and even shouting matches had vanished to be replaced by a totally different picture. A child growing up affectionate, biddable, willing to hug and kiss her, willing to share with her; that was how it had been meant to be. The fact that it hadn't turned out that way was sad, but it wasn't as bad as thinking, as she always had, that her stepdaughter loathed her and always had. There *was* affection there, even though it showed itself in such a perverse manner; and Poppy leaned over and kissed Chloe's cheek and said firmly, 'Well, I'm sorry if you feel so. You are quite wrong, of course. I love Robin dearly. She is my little girl and it is right and proper that I should. And I love you too, irritating and tiresome child though you have always been. So let's hear no more of this nonsense – and I'm sorrier than I can say that I didn't understand the urgency when you came in earlier tonight. Robin had vanished and – '

'It wasn't your fault,' Chloe said after a moment. 'I suppose it was just bad luck really. Anyway, I'd have had it done all the same. I didn't want it, you know.' She looked at Poppy then with a challenging gleam in her eyes. 'You couldn't have made me keep it, no matter what.'

'I wouldn't have tried,' Poppy said. 'But at least you wouldn't have been alone. Look, let me check you again. All this talk is all very well, but I need to be sure you're not still bleeding. Mamma, will you fetch me some more cotton wool? There's a large roll of it in the bathroom. I may need it – '

She checked carefully to see what was happening and was filled with relief when she saw that the bleeding seemed to have stopped and then, trying to remember what she could of her anatomy lessons, set a hand on Chloe's round little belly and very gently pressed down, watching all the time to see if any extra blood appeared at the surface of her body. But it did not, and moving gently Poppy reapplied the pad and then pulled the sheets up over her again.

'Give me your wrist,' she said. 'I'll see what your pulse is doing – ' and the room slid into silence as she stood and counted the beats. They were steady and a little hurried but strong and far from showing the threadiness that she had learned to recognize as a symptom of dangerous blood loss; and after a full minute of counting she set Chloe's hand back on the covers and looked at Mildred.

'I don't think she's come to any harm,' she said. 'The bleeding appears to have stopped. Perhaps you're right and there's no need at this stage to involve a doctor.'

'I am very glad to hear it,' Mildred said. 'You say the man used all the antiseptics necessary and so forth, Chloe?'

Chloe grimaced. 'He used lots of it. It stung me. And the nurse did too. And they had gloves on – '

'It seems that at least Bernie sent you to a safe doctor, however illegally he may be working,' Poppy said and again Chloe grimaced and Poppy, who had been about to turn away, stopped and looked at her sharply and said, 'Chloe? When will Bernie be back? He is coming back, isn't he?'

'I don't know and I don't care,' Chloe said loudly. 'You hear me? I hope the ship he's on sinks.'

'That is very wicked of you, Chloe,' Mildred said. 'There will be many other people on the ship as well as he, and it is always wicked to wish death on others – '

'I don't care,' Chloe said passionately. 'You hear me? He is hateful, the most hateful and cruel person in the world and I never want to see him again and I hope he – '

'No more, Chloe,' Poppy said then, and came and set her hand on her forehead. 'You'll get yourself even more worked up than you are. Listen, my dear, I'm going to

377

fetch you a sleeping draught and then I'm going to send Mamma to bed and I shall go too. The bleeding has stopped now, though you might well leak a little. But the heavy loss is over – '

'I can feel it's stopped,' Chloe said. 'I was just so frightened on my own. Don't leave me alone – '

'I shall stay with you,' Mildred said. 'No, Poppy, don't look at me so. You go and sleep near Robin and I shall stay here with Chloe. In the morning we can assess what we do next. For my part, I have some ideas, but we will wait till breakfast time. I am sure you'll sleep well, now, Chloe. You've suffered a nasty experience, you silly girl, and much of it is your own fault, but you'll come to no lasting harm, I'm sure. Now we had all better get some sleep, and consider in the morning what is best to do. Poppy, I shall sleep on this sofa here, if you will fetch me the necessary covers and pillows. And tomorrow I hope we can get back to some sort of normal living. Really, all this upset is very unhealthy for all of us.'

32

Chloe was sitting in a long chair by the drawing-room
window looking out onto the Square. She had a pile of
illustrated magazines in her lap but she made no attempt
to read them. She just sat and stared at the scrubby grass
and untidy trees with their naked branches and said
nothing.

Robin more than made up for her silence however.
She was sitting on the floor in front of the fire with a pile
of cut-out paper dolls and a model theatre in which she
was conducting a play with them. She acted each part
with great energy in a series of squeaky voices, all of
which sounded exactly the same, and was making a great
deal of noise as she did so. Poppy, in her usual corner of
the sofa with a book on her lap, watched her covertly,
enjoying the play of expressions across her face and
amused by the turns of phrase she gave her dolls. They
were involved in some sort of complicated mystery story,
which Poppy had long ago stopped trying to follow, and
one or two of them seemed to Poppy to be very lively
characters indeed. There could be no question, she told
herself, but that her daughter had a vivid and busy imagination. An agreeable thought.

She put her book down then, giving up her attempt to
pretend to read, and looked at Chloe. She had been so
very quiet since it had all happened, doing as Poppy said
she should without argument, and being as sweet to
Robin as anyone could hope. Goosey of course had

379

fussed round her a good deal, but she had managed no
to snap at her, even though Poppy had seen clearly tha
often she found the old woman's attentions very irri
tating, and that had warmed Poppy's heart a good deal
Perhaps she had been changed by the experience she had
suffered? Perhaps she would stop being the impossible
creature she had always been? Or was Poppy being, a
ever, too hopeful?

Mildred had made it clear, however, that she though
Chloe had been greatly sobered by what had happened to
her.

'My dear Poppy,' she had said the morning after tha
dramatic and difficult evening when they had breakfasted
in the kitchen while Robin still slept, and Goosey took a
tray up to Chloe. 'This will be the making of her. No, do
not look so sceptical. She has been in love, she has been
betrayed by the wretched man, and has suffered the
consequences of her own foolishness. This will make her
grow up in a way that should have happened long ago
had she not been so spoiled. That was partly your fault,
though not entirely I know. The work had been well
started by your husband and his sister, and of course by
Goosey. But all this will change matters, you will see. As
long as you are firm with her.'

And Goosey had said, to Poppy's amazement, much
the same. She had been anxious about what she would tell
the old woman about her beloved girl, and had hoped she
would be able to be protectively devious without being
precisely dishonest with her, but her worries had been
needless.

Goosey had worked out shrewdly enough what had
happened and said as much when she reappeared in the
kitchen with Chloe's tray after she had breakfasted.

'I knew it would end in something like this,' she
muttered as she came creaking down the stairs. 'Stood to
reason it would. I told her she should watch her step with

those boys she was always racketing round with, but would she be told? Not her, poor little lamb, and looking so sorry for herself as she is this morning. But there, no sense in breaking your heart over what can't be cured, is there? Well, she's over the worst of it, and she'll pick up again, as long as we all see to it she does as she's bid and doesn't run wild no more. We've all let her have it too easy, that we have, and it's time she changed her silly ways. She'll have to, won't she? Silly girl, wouldn't listen to her old Goosey, and I told her, over and over again I told her – '

Still muttering, she had taken the dirty dishes to the sink and then had begun to clear the table and Poppy had got to her feet to help her. But Goosey had wanted no help.

'Now, Mrs Poppy, you be on your way. I don't want you under my feet and there's the truth of it. Here's Miss Robin's breakfast still to make before she wakes up. I looked in on her, blessed little lamb, and she's still asleep. Good thing it's no school today, one way and another – so you go and get yourself sorted out, Mrs Poppy, and leave me be – '

'Indeed we will, Goosey,' Mildred had said firmly. 'For I must go home. I am glad that Queenie sent the cab with my things so early – perhaps you will fetch me another cab now, Poppy, for I really cannot stay any longer. There is no need for me, I think – '

Poppy had taken her up to the hall and gone to find her a cab and helped her into it, and then had stopped her as she was about to close the door on herself.

'Mamma,' she had said. 'I haven't thanked you properly for all your help. I – it was very good of you to be so – '

Mildred had lifted her brows at her, sitting straight-backed and neat on the edge of the leather seat of the cab and staring out of the dimness at her.

'What else should I do? You are my daughter and of course I am available for your help. Even if you do not always want it.'

Poppy had grinned at that. 'Well, I can't deny I was upset that Robin should have run to you as she did. But not because of you, you understand – because she couldn't tell me. Well, it won't happen again. I'll see to that.'

'But remember,' Mildred had said austerely. 'Don't send him away. It would not be right for her. Nor for you. He is an excellent man in many ways and – '

'Now, Mamma,' Poppy had said firmly and put her hand on the cab door ready to close it. 'I said thank you and I meant it, but that is enough. I really must make my own decisions about what I will do – or won't do – and I do hope you won't meddle.'

'Hmmph,' Mildred had said and smoothed her gloves over her fingers. 'That's as may be. I too have a mind of my own, remember. Goodbye, Poppy. I will expect to see you on Wednesday evening as usual. Drive on, cabbie!' And she had pulled the door closed on herself and the cabbie had set the vehicle into noisy motion and taken her away as Poppy watched her go, trying not to think of David. That was a problem she still had to face but at present, with both Robin and Chloe to occupy her mind, she could set him aside. Or at least try. And she had run up the steps back into the house definitely not thinking of David.

Now, on Sunday afternoon, sitting in the drawing-room with them both as the day began to crumble away into evening she could not avoid her private thoughts any longer. She had three people dependent upon her, and no employment to provide an income for them. Her alternatives were starkly simple. She could go on seeking a new post and hope to find one that would provide enough to pay her way and to shore up her rapidly dwindling

382

savings; she could go cap in hand to her mother and accept her hospitality at Leinster Terrace for her household – for Mildred's offer to take them all had been reiterated often enough for Poppy to know it was always open – or she could marry David and let him take her burdens away from her.

She stared bleakly at the dull sky that pressed against the drawing-room windows and tried to decide which of the three was the least disagreeable, for there was no doubt that none of them made her feel right. Least of all marrying David in order to be safe and secure. That she wanted him was undoubted, but not, definitely not, in that way. It would destroy any hope of happiness they had to come together for such a reason, she told herself miserably. I'm caught between the rocks and the sea, it seems, and whatever I do, I'll be buffeted.

'Shall I make some tea for us, Poppy?' Chloe said suddenly and swung her legs to the ground. She was wearing a day frock in a deep green which gave her a rather subdued air. She had none of her usual dash and was wearing no cosmetics, which was yet another indication of the new Chloe, and Poppy looked at her and thought – she's so depressed, poor girl. So very depressed –

'That would be very kind, Chloe,' she said. 'Goosey likes to take a rather long nap in the afternoons these days, and especially on Sundays. Do you feel up to it?'

'Oh, of course,' Chloe sounded impatient for a moment, almost like the old Chloe and paradoxically that made Poppy feel a little better about her. This new air of quiet virtue was almost too good to be true and rather too much to be comfortable. 'I'm – ' She threw a glance at Robin still murmuring over her dolls and theatre and then went on in a low voice. 'It's all right now. I mean, it hasn't been bad again, you know? It's stopped mostly. Still a bit, but not a lot.'

'Good,' Poppy said. 'Have you taken the iron medicine we got for you yesterday?'

Chloe made a face. 'It's horrible.'

'I dare say. But you need it. Take some now. And again tonight.'

'I don't – ' Chloe began and then caught Poppy's raised eyebrows and said, 'Sorry, I'll take it. Some tea then?'

'Lovely. But don't bring it up. We'll come down. Robin! Come and have tea, now, will you? It's almost time – '

'In a minute, Mummy, let me come in a minute.' Robin cried. 'I've just got to the best bit – let me get to the end of this bit when the curtains comes down and then I'll come – I won't be hungry till then, honestly. It'll be soon – I'll make it the interval and I can have tea in the interval, can't I?'

'Muffins,' Chloe said. 'You like muffins, Robin. I'll see if there are any. Don't be too long – ' And she went downstairs and after a moment Poppy got to her feet and went over to the window to look out. She'd wait for the end of Robin's play and then they'd go down together, and perhaps call Goosey on the way. She'd be ready for some tea; she usually was.

She gazed out into the quiet Square and tried again to think of what she would do tomorrow. Perhaps it was not enough to look at advertisements for employment. She would have to start going to the agencies. And she felt a pang as she thought that. For so long she had found employees for Jessie's from various agencies, had been so secure in her position as an employer, arrogant even, as one who stood in a superior position. Now she would have to be the supplicant, the one who asked for a job please, and that was a horrid thought. She had never yet had to do it; always it had been there. First the FANYs and then Jessie's, but now she was just one of the faceless thousands who had to scrape their way through as best they could –

A cab came rattling round the corner of the Square and she watched it with half-glazed eyes, still buried deep in her own musings, but then it swung over to her side of the road and stopped outside and she craned a little, trying to see who was in it. Someone got out, but the overhang of the little balcony outside the drawing-room window made it impossible to see clearly. All she could see was the cabbie's arm outstretched to take money but not his hand, and therefore not the person who was paying him. She stood there as the cabbie touched his hat and then set the vehicle moving again, and waited. Perhaps it wasn't her house to which the cab had come? It had stopped almost directly under her drawing-room window, which meant it was a little to one side. It could be going to the house next door – but then the front door bell pealed and she took a deep breath.

David, she thought. He's come back and I'm so glad. No, I'm not. I don't want to see him, I can't. I need time and space and – I can't.

The bell pealed again and Robin shouted, 'Curtain!' and then scrambled to her feet.

'Shall I go, Mummy? There's someone at the door and Goosey's having a nap and – '

'No,' Poppy said hastily. 'No, darling. I will.' It would never do for Robin to see him on the doorstep. She had got over her distress of Friday pretty well, it seemed, showing all a child's resilience, but it was too soon for her to have to face David. She needed more time, more opportunity to talk to Poppy about it all, needed reassurance – 'You go down to the kitchen, and I'll see who it is.' And she held the door open invitingly and Robin obediently went skipping down the stairs.

There was a shadow blocking the coloured panes of the front door, and Poppy kept her eyes away from it. She

385

still needed time to school her face and to show the sort of calm response that was needed. If she let herself look at that familiar reassuring outline against the glass her pulses would start speeding up and she would become flustered. She knew that as surely as she knew she breathed. So she watched as Robin went down to the kitchen and then took another deep breath to compose herself and went to the door.

The bell rang again imperiously as she got there and she was suddenly hugely irritated. To ring three times for an answer? What was he thinking of? He must know that Goosey needed time to get to the door, because of her aching joints. He had always known that, and she fanned her anger at his impatience as a way to make it easier to confront him with a stony face, and flung the door open and stood there blocking the doorway to make sure he couldn't do what he usually did, and just march in, pulling his coat and hat off as he came.

And then she stood there, amazed, and stared.

'Hello, Poppy,' Jessie said in a rather hoarse voice. 'I'm so glad you're in – I was worried maybe you wasn't and – please, Poppy, can I come in? I got to talk to you – '

She had taken her to the little study on the first floor, alongside the drawing room, for it had been obvious at once that she was in no state to face Chloe or Robin. Her face was ravaged under the make-up and her eyes red-rimmed and puffy. And though Poppy's first feeling had been of outrage that Jessie should come to her house when they had parted on such appalling terms last time they had been together, once she had seen the way she looked, all that melted away.

'Wait here,' she said and pushed her into Bobby's old armchair. 'I'll fetch you some tea and see the children are all right – take a little rest. You look – ' And then she had patted Jessie's shoulder awkwardly and gone to tell Chloe and Robin, not looking at them, that it was just someone calling about local politics and please to get on with their tea. She'd be down herself as soon as possible –

She had carried the tray of tea upstairs with dragging feet. Facing Jessie was painful enough; facing Jessie in a state of obvious misery for whatever reason was even worse. And she lingered outside the study door for a moment before strengthening her resolve, lifting her chin, and walking in.

Jessie was sitting slumped in the chair and Poppy glanced at her as she set the tray down on the desk and was startled at the pang that went through her. Jessie looked dreadful. She was sagging and old, looking as though all the stuffing in her great bouncing body had gone adrift. She seemed lumpy and awkward and her face was pouched and grey in the soft lamplight.

She lifted her head as Poppy handed her the cup of tea and said huskily, 'Ta. I need it – ' and began to sip. And Poppy pulled another chair towards her and sat down beside the desk too to drink her own tea.

Neither of them spoke until the cups were empty and Poppy had refilled them and then Jessie said in a voice that still sounded husky, as though it had been rusted by her onslaught of tears, 'I need you, Poppy. I don't know who to turn to.'

'Oh?' Poppy was guarded. She could still see in her all too vivid memory the way Jessie had looked that evening in her flat, her eyes glittering with anger and – was it hatred? – it had seemed so to Poppy, as she thrust her cheque at her, could still hear the contempt in her voice as she told her to take it. That the Jessie now sitting in front of her was in a very different state of mind was obvious, but if her misery was based entirely on what happened between them that night Poppy knew she could not be beguiled. It had been unforgivable. How could she now forgive it?

And then Jessie lifted her head and said, as though she had been inside Poppy's own mind, 'I was – I behaved unforgivably, Poppy. I treated you bad. You was right and I was wrong and I treated you bad. I – he – I – oh, Poppy, what shall I do?' And she burst into a flood of tears that was so intense that Poppy was filled with a sudden shock of cold fear. She had never seen anyone so abandoned in grief and for a moment she sat frozen, staring at Jessie who was rocking backwards and forwards as the tears ran down a face so twisted with distress that it was unrecognizable.

But then she moved, and slid to her knees beside Jessie and put her arms round her and held her tightly, and slowly the flood subsided until she was sitting hiccuping softly and holding tightly to Poppy with one hot hand.

'I'm sorry,' she said at last, still very hoarsely, and reached into her coat pocket for a handkerchief. Poppy looked at the scrap of fine cambric with its embroidery of pink roses cascading all over one corner and felt a great wave of affection for this large woman dressed in red who sat there in such a state of misery. She was infinitely unhappy and infinitely touching and Poppy hugged her warmly and said impulsively, 'Oh, Jessie, dear Jessie. You don't have to apologize to me. I should apologize to you. It's been horrid not seeing you – '

'Yes,' Jessie said and leaned forwards and set her hot wet cheek against Poppy's and for a long moment they clung to each other and it was for Poppy as though all the pain and worry of the past weeks was washed away in Jessie's misery, never to come back. They belonged together, she and Jessie, just as Mildred had said last night that they all belonged together; the loss of her had been the real cause of Poppy's unhappiness, more than anything else, and having her back was the best thing that could have happened. No matter what they did in the future, no matter what arguments they had, they would never let themselves be parted again. So Poppy promised herself as she hugged her aunt as close as she could.

After a little while Jessie straightened her back and then scrubbed at her face with her handkerchief, sniffed hard and shoved the sodden rag into her pocket again.

'So I'll tell you. I'll try not to cry again, but I got to tell you and whenever I think of it – it's – listen, look at this. It's easier you read it yourself. Then you'll understand – '

She opened her handbag and scrabbled in it and then pulled out a sheet of folded newspaper and grimly pushed it at Poppy.

Poppy, puzzled, took it and unfolded it and smoothed it on Bobby's desk. It was a full sheet from an American newspaper. Across the top ran the heading, *The Baltimore Sun*, and below it was the usual mixture of columns of type, photographs and advertisements and she scanned the page looking for whatever it was that would matter to Jessie and couldn't see a thing; and looked up at her enquiringly.

Jessie thrust one large finger forwards and stabbed at the bottom right hand corner of the paper, and Poppy looked at the headline, and frowned, still puzzled.

'Dope Runner Nabbed in Attempted Getaway at State Border,' it read. And then below it the story began in a breathless rush.

'Last night it was reported by our correspondent from Hagerstown that Mr Bernard Braham, carrying a British passport as well as an American one, was arrested as he attempted to board the Interstate bus for Chambersburg, Pa., and arraigned on drug smuggling charges. He was searched by Hagerstown Sheriff Dan Mackersley and relieved of seventeen packs of cocaine each containing half a pound of the lethal crystals. He gave the names of accomplices in Pennsylvania as well as other Eastern sea-board States and asked to turn State's witness but District Attorney Vittorio Rigati refused this, maintaining Braham had a known record of drug dealing, and that he alone brought the consignment he was carrying into the USA from Great Britain via New York. His holding of an American passport makes him liable to stand his trial before a US court, and the date has been set for next Friday at noon – '

She read to the end of the report and then very slowly folded the piece of paper and pushed it towards Jessie. She said nothing. There were no words she could find.

'You saw what it said at the end?' Jessie said. 'They think seven years in the penitentiary – seven years, Poppy. What shall I do?'

Poppy sat still for a long time and then lifted her eyes and looked at Jessie very directly.

'Nothing,' she said as gently as she could. 'There is nothing you can do, Jessie. He's been caught and taken to trial. He'll probably go to prison, as they said. Reading that, there doesn't seem any defence. He tried to get out of it by pushing it onto the other people but they wouldn't let him. I think you'll have to face it, darling. He's going to jail for a long time and there's nothing at all you can do.'

She had thought Jessie would weep again, but she didn't. She sat and stared at Poppy with those hot red eyes and then after a long pause nodded, her head seeming almost too heavy for her to move it.

'I know,' she said. 'I think I knew as soon as that arrived. I don't even know who sent it. It just come in an envelope, an American stamp. I thought, a letter from my Bernie! I was really excited, he's never been much of a letter writer. But that was all there was and I thought – that's it. He won't be coming home to me. Not for a long

390

time. Maybe not ever. And I sent Poppy away when she warned me and – oh, Poppy. It hurts so!'

'I know,' Poppy said. 'It hurts dreadfully. And no one can stop it hurting. I'm sorry, dear, darling Jessie. I'm so sorry.'

'You'll come back to me, won't you?' Jessie said then and smiled at her, a thin watery smile that almost broke Poppy's heart with its bravery. 'You shouldn't have gone. I shouldn't have behaved so, for God's sake, come back to me – '

'Of course,' Poppy said, and then managed a smile, albeit a little crookedly. 'I need you more than you need me, my love. I've been frantic with worry – '

'I know. I'm sorry. I swear to you, I'm sorry – '

'Hush, now hush. It's over. Please. Forget it – ' She hesitated then and let her eyes slide away from Jessie's. She had heard somewhere outside the door the sounds of Robin's voice calling and then Chloe's answering her and memory had come rushing back. Bernie and Chloe; and she closed her eyes, trying to work out what she should do about Jessie. Tell her? Try to keep it a secret? What on earth was she to do?

Jessie leaned forwards and set one hand on her arm and it felt very heavy there. Poppy opened her eyes.

'What is it, Poppela?' Jessie said. 'What else has he done? No, don't look like that! I'm not stupid. He's done something else – Oh, God. Chloe – has she gone with him? Don't tell me she's gone with him – '

Poppy looked at her and made an odd little face. 'Oh, no. Nothing like that. I suppose it could have been that. She – yes, it could have been worse, at that. But not a lot. Look, Jessie, this has to be between us. It's not my story to tell but I think you have to know. Get it all over with at once. If I don't tell you now maybe you'll find out one day, later on, when it will hurt even more all over again. This way, we get it all over at once – '

'Tell me,' Jessie commanded. 'What is it, for God's sake? Tell me. I have to know. Then maybe I can start again, with you and our Robin and – tell me!'

So she told her.

33

The buffet table looked as though it had been attacked by a herd of stampeding elephants. What had been a magnificent centrepiece of four massive salmon, set in aspic and decorated with olives, cucumbers and radish roses was now just a tangle of bones and scraps and sad pink juice. The bowls piled high with potato salad and mayonnaise and fish salads that had flanked it were scraped almost clean and there were empty dishes everywhere. But the noise at the tables was as high-pitched as ever as people sat eating cheesecake, of which every table had a massive supply, and drinking champagne which was offered in equally lavish amounts, laughing loudly and generally making it clear they were having a splendid time.

From her vantage point behind Minnie's desk, Poppy could see them all and she glowed as she looked at them. At first there had been no intention of having a birthday party for the new restaurant at all, but Poppy had been very determined about it. It would be good for the restaurant, good for future trade, but above all, good for Jessie and so she had told her, week after week, as Jessie wriggled and dodged, trying to put her off. But at last she had been worn down. Jessie had lifted herself from the depression that was never far away from her and agreed they should; and as Poppy had hoped it would, it had cheered her greatly when virtually everyone they had invited had accepted with alacrity.

In fact the response had been so eager and the number of people who regarded themselves as regular customers entitled to an invitation was so large that they had to have two such parties. This one though was the second of them and, splendid though the first had been, there was no doubt in Poppy's mind that this one was the best. She had never seen so many happy replete people in one place at one time.

There was a great burst of laughter that drowned out even the general noise that was filling the place and Poppy turned her head to see, and there in a corner was a table of seven men, all looking prosperous and contented and rather flushed. She sighed. It had seemed a good idea to take Chloe on as an assistant here when she had said she wanted to do some sort of job and quite liked the idea of being in a restaurant, and it helped Poppy a great deal to be able to keep an eye on her, but she did wonder sometimes. There she was, perched on the edge of the table, looking very pert and pleased with herself in pink georgette which showed a considerable expanse of slender leg, and clearly making the seven diners very happy indeed. But there seemed no harm in the banter that was going on even though clearly she was saying things that were making them all feel very pleased with themselves. Poppy, catching Chloe's eyes, lifted her brows slightly. But she made no attempt to send her any warning message, and Chloe beamed back at her and went on with her chatter.

The big swing doors from the kitchen opened and Horace came out backwards, pulling on a trolley and turned his sweating face towards her, and guiltily Poppy straightened up and came hurrying out of her cubbyhole. She was meant to prepare for this moment and she had somehow managed to forget it. So she pushed her way over to the light switchboard as swiftly as she could and threw the switches so that the room was plunged into dimness.

At once Horace completed his entry from the kitchen with the chef, resplendent in his whites, on the other side of the trolley and it appeared, ablaze with candles: Jessie's restaurant's birthday cake.

Someone started to clap with slow deliberate blows and at once everyone at the tables took it up and then someone else started to chant, 'We want Jessie! We want Jessie!' And Poppy, standing with her hand on the lights, ready to switch them on again, felt a wash of happiness. She did not know who had started the cry but it was exactly what Jessie would need, a little warm appreciation, a little attention. She had been incredibly brave this past six months, battling against her own misery and the continuing silence from America – for no matter how many letters Jessie sent to the State Penitentiary where she had been told Bernie had been incarcerated since the trial which sent him there for nine years, he never answered – and she deserved a reward. And she started to chant as well, 'We want Jessie. We want Jessie!'

She appeared at last, coming out of the kitchen with her head up, and Poppy smiled at her over the heads of the loudly applauding diners and lifted her hands above her head in a salute of her own; and Jessie looked across and saw her and then broke into a simple joyous grin. For one glorious moment there was no strain there, no pretence of happiness covering misery. Just simple pleasure, and Poppy felt her eyes sting as she looked at her.

Behind her a voice said softly, 'I'm glad you were able to persuade her to do this. It was just what she needed.'

'Yes,' she said but didn't turn her head. She knew he was there; she always did. He just had to come into a room and she felt that sense of completeness that was becoming ever more important to her. One day soon, perhaps, she'd be able to make up her mind. Not quite yet, but soon. There was still the matter of Robin to deal with. No matter what Mildred said, Robin had to be consulted. It was not just Poppy's own life that would be changed if she did as David wanted her to. It was Robin's too, and she was well able to express her views.

But it was getting easier. Robin was growing fast and was a very sensible eight year old, though she still showed some suspicion of David. It had been three months before she had been willing to have him come to tea at Norland Square, looking as anxious as a horse at a high fence when Poppy mentioned it; but they had talked – long and often rather late into the evening, somewhat to Goosey's disapproval – and slowly Robin had relaxed about him. Now she was getting ever more comfortable about his involvement in their lives. To rush her wouldn't be wise –

And anyway she didn't need to be rushed. Poppy looked over her shoulder at David now and smiled and he smiled back and patted her in the way he always did, touching her shoulder with a proprietorial air that amused her and comforted her too. It was good to have him around, even though Robin was not sure of him yet. But maybe, one day soon –

There was another burst of applause then, as Jessie blew out the candles on the cake, and Poppy threw the switches and again the room sprang into full light, as the little band in the far corner, which had been having its own dinner until now, burst into a sprightly jazz version of 'Happy Birthday'. And Jessie held up her hands and waited for silence when they reached their triumphant finish.

When at last her guests had managed to obey her – and even then some went on chattering, in a flush of champagne-soaked contentment – she cried, 'Listen, I don't make no speeches. But I just wanted to tell you how glad I am you like our East End restaurant here in the West End. We come from Cable Street where things aren't so fancy as here, but where we understand good food. Not everyone was sure you lot here'd like it the same way, but you do, and I'm glad. You've made Jessie's a big success. And not just you – the people who work here. It's not only me of course. It's old Joe, and the other chefs and it's Horace and the waiters and Minnie, but most of all it's Poppy, my niece and my best friend – '

Poppy reddened and wanted to crawl into the floor as the diners turned and looked for her and then shouted their approval and she shook her head and made a face at Jessie – who grinned back and then lifted her hands again.

'And listen – I want to say it's been lovely having you as customers this past year. Please God you'll all come next year an' all, and all the years after. And I thought you'd like to know, if you get over the other side of town sometimes, we got our eyes on another place. I ain't told Poppy yet, but she'll do it. She's good at working hard, my Poppy. And I'll tell you about it right here and now, dolly.' And she looked appealingly at Poppy over the heads of the crowds. 'It's over at Knightsbridge – I found a lovely place – and we'll call it Poppy's restaurant. What do you say to that?'

The applause was louder than ever now and Poppy stood there and looked at Jessie and then over her shoulders at David and shook her head with a rueful air that was much more real than it was to impress the customers.

'Oh dear,' she said. 'Here we go again!'

THE BLACKBIRD'S TALE

Emma Blair

From Glasgow on the brink of the Great War to the cut-throat world of London publishing – the spellbinding saga of three remarkable generations:

Cathy: A Glasgow factory-girl who experiences love, its loss and a kind of victory in the space of two turbulent wartime years . . .

Hannah: The daughter whose marriage enjoys the fruits of undreamt prosperity. But her love must learn to endure the turmoil of a very personal hurt . . .

Robyn: The product of her generation. Modern, extrovert and vivacious, her heart is broken by the only man she'll ever love. Yet she finally comes to control her destiny – and that of the lover she never really lost . . .

This is the unforgettable story of three women united in their love for books, for life, and for their men. A story which began with the little bookshop that Cathy fell in love with thirty years before: The Blackbird . . .

0 7474 0224 2
GENERAL FICTION

SUMMER SECRETS

Susan Goodman

Twenty-three-year-old Tessa Selway's greatest passion is
her thriving Chelsea flower business – until her wayward
grandmother introduces her to Marcus Reardon. A
worldly journalist with a lived-in past, he sweeps Tessa
headlong into a tempestuous, all-eclipsing love affair.

Through the hot summer of her sexual awakening, Tessa
reaches a new understanding of herself and her family.
Living the London fast life with Reardon, she is haunted
by bitter-sweet memories of the rural childhood that was
so abruptly shattered by her mother's desertion. And in
the background there is Oliver Bingham. A friend since
childhood, he is now displaying a more ardent,
demanding affection. Still powerfully attracted to
Reardon, Tessa is nevertheless faced with temptation –
and a choice which holds her future happiness in the
balance . . .

All Sphere Books are available at your bookshop or newsagent, or can be ordered from the following address: Sphere Books, Cash Sales Department, P.O. Box 11, Falmouth, Cornwall TR10 9EN

Please send cheque or postal order (no currency), and allow 60p for postage and packing for the first book plus 25p for the second book and 15p for each additional book ordered up to a maximum charge of £1.90 in U.K.

B.F.P.O. customers allow 60p for the first book, 25p for the second book plus 15p per copy for the next 7 books thereafter 9p per book.

Overseas customers, including Eire, please allow £1.25 for postage and packing for the first book, 75p for the second book and 28p for each subsequent title ordered.